VICTORIA ALEXANDER
THE Perfect Mistress

"For love, laughter, and lots of fun, read Victoria Alexander."
—Stephanie Laurens

My Wicked Little Lies

"For love, laughter, and lots of fun, read Victoria Alexander."
—Stephanie Laurens

A NEW YORK TIMES BESTSELLING AUTHOR

VICTORIA ALEXANDER

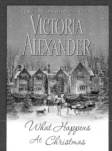

VICTORIA ALEXANDER

What Happens At Christmas

HIS MISTRESS BY CHRISTMAS

"I have no desire to marry again."

"Nonsense." He scoffed. "All women wish to marry."

"I did marry. Once, and once was quite enough."

He stared in stunned disbelief. Was she really turning him down?

"I have, oh . . ." She thought for a moment. "A counter-offer, if you will."

"This is not a negotiation," he said sharply. "It's a proposal."

"Then I have a proposal of my own." She studied him carefully. "I don't wish to be your wife, but I would like to be your mistress."

"My what?" Surely she hadn't said that.

"You needn't look so outraged. People enter into this sort of arrangement all the time."

"Not me. What will people say?"

"I had planned on being discreet. Keeping this between the two of us."

"Nonetheless, there will be gossip."

"Some, I suppose." She considered him closely. "I didn't think you cared about gossip."

"I do when it involves the woman I want to marry! I don't want a mistress! I want a wife!"

She squared her shoulders. "Then I suggest you look elsewhere. . . ."

Books by Victoria Alexander

THE PERFECT MISTRESS

HIS MISTRESS BY CHRISTMAS

MY WICKED LITTLE LIES

WHAT HAPPENS AT CHRISTMAS

THE IMPORTANCE OF BEING WICKED

Published by Kensington Publishing Corporation

His
Mistress
By Christmas

VICTORIA
ALEXANDER

ZEBRA BOOKS
KENSINGTON PUBLISHING CORP.
http://www.kensingtonbooks.com

ISBN-13: 978-1-4201-3451-3
ISBN-10: 1-4201-3451-5

First Zebra Books Mass-Market Paperback Printing: October 2012
First Kensington Books Trade Hardcover Printing: October 2011

10 9 8 7 6 5 4 3

Printed in the United States of America

Chapter 1

November 30, 1885

"He's the one," Veronica, Lady Smithson, said softly, more to herself than to the woman beside her. She smiled with satisfaction. She did so love it when all went according to plan.

"Shhh." Portia, Lady Redwell, hushed her and gazed with pride at the speaker behind the podium on the stage at the far end of the room.

". . . and admittedly, while it was somewhat more adventure than we had bargained for, in hindsight it was not merely exciting but quite remarkable." Sir Sebastian Hadley-Attwater paused in the polished manner of an expert speaker and gazed out at the audience seated before him in the Explorers Club lecture hall.

A knowing smile carved deep dimples in a face that would be altogether too handsome were it not a bit browner than was fashionable. An intriguing scar slanted across his forehead above his right brow. His blue eyes, under hair so dark a blond it was nearly brown, gleamed with humor and intelligence. He scanned the room slowly, and only a woman long in her grave would fail to wonder what it would be like to have those eyes gaze at her and her alone.

Veronica noted the moment he caught sight of his cousin, sitting beside her toward the back of the hall. His eyes lit in recognition, and Portia beamed. Portia's parents had died when she was very young, and her aunt and uncle had taken her in. She'd grown up with Sebastian and six other cousins. He nodded slightly in acknowledgment of her presence, then continued his perusal of the audience. His gaze settled on Veronica briefly, although he was no doubt staring at her hat, one of her most impressive, then continued on.

"In conclusion, allow me to say there is only one thing in life that stirs the senses more than stepping foot upon an unknown land or seeing with your own eyes sights only a handful of your fellow men have ever seen."

His gaze returned to Veronica, this time meeting hers. She raised her chin slightly and cast him a slow smile. A smile of acknowledgment and encouragement, although from what she had heard of the famous adventurer, little encouragement was needed. His exploits with women were as extensive as his adventures in foreign lands, at least according to gossip and Portia.

"And that"—his smile widened and his dimples deepened, if possible—"is at last returning home."

The most delightful sense of anticipation shivered through her. Oh yes, he would do.

Applause erupted from the crowd that had gathered to spend the evening in the illustrious adventurer's presence and listen to his stories of uncivilized lands and unknown peoples. It had been an evening filled with the excitement of daring tales told by a master storyteller. Sir Sebastian had held the crowd in his hands.

Veronica leaned close to her friend and spoke low into her ear. "He's the one."

"I heard you the first time," Portia said absently, clapping with an unusual display of enthusiasm. A proud smile curved her lips. "The one what?"

"The one I want."

"The one you want for what?" Portia's attention remained on Sir Sebastian, who was now accepting the accolades of the crowd in a modest and unassuming manner. While Veronica suspected there was nothing modest and unassuming about the adventurer, his demeanor added to his appeal. He would do nicely.

"And now, as anyone who has heard me speak before will attest, I have been rather more efficient than usual tonight."

An amused chuckle washed through the crowd.

"Therefore we have time for a few questions." Again his gaze sought hers. A challenge sparked in his eyes, as if daring her to do more than meet his gaze. Veronica did indeed have a question, but not one she was prepared to ask. At least, not yet. Immediately a dozen hands shot up. Sir Sebastian pointed to a gentleman toward the front.

"Sir," the man began. "In your third book, you relate an encounter with a tribe during your expedition down the Amazon, and I was curious as to whether . . ."

"Oh yes, he's perfect," Veronica murmured.

Portia snorted in a most unladylike manner. "Nonsense. I was raised with the man. I can tell you any number of ways in which he's not the least bit perfect. Why, I can recall . . ." Portia glanced at Veronica. "The one you want for what? What are you talking about?" Her eyes narrowed. "What are you planning?"

"Sir Sebastian." On Veronica's other side, her aunt Lotte rose to her feet. "I should like to know, given your renown as an explorer and adventurer and as I have been told you are most forward thinking . . ."

"Stop her." Portia clutched Veronica's arm.

"Would that I could." Veronica patted her friend's hand in a comforting manner and bit back a grin. She should have expected this. Miss Charlotte Bramhall had her own campaign to wage.

"Thank you, ma'am. I do try to be progressive." Sir Sebastian favored Aunt Lotte with his compelling smile. A smile that surely made every other gentleman in the hall wish to be him and every lady wish to be with him. Veronica wondered if the older woman was at all affected.

Apparently not. Aunt Lotte's expression remained firm.

"Excellent." Aunt Lotte nodded. "Then I should like to know your opinion as to the acceptance of women as members of the Explorers Club."

A groan passed through the crowd, and Portia's hand tightened.

Sir Sebastian's brows drew together. "I'm afraid I don't quite understand the question."

"It's very simple, young man. Do you or do you not support full membership for women?"

Sir Sebastian chose his words with obvious care. "It seems to me, as you are here tonight and the lectures of the society are open to all, there is no need to grant full membership to the fairer sex as it would only be a . . ." He thought for a moment. "An undue burden, as it were." Again he smiled an altogether pleasant smile, although Aunt Lotte might well interpret it as condescending. Poor man. He might have come face-to-face with uncivilized natives in the far jungles of the globe, but he had never done battle with Miss Charlotte Bramhall. Sir Sebastian continued with innocent disregard for his imminent danger. "It's my understanding that full members residing in London are required to participate fully in all matters regarding governing of the organization."

Veronica winced.

"And you think that a burden?" Aunt Lotte squared her shoulders. "Rubbish. As progressive as you may be, Sir Sebastian, perhaps you are not aware of the significant advancements made in the last twenty years by women through independent travel and sheer determination. Women who can explore the reaches of the Nile can certainly handle the dubious burden of administration of a mere organization."

"I have no doubt of that." He chuckled. "But, my dear lady, there is also tradition to be considered. Progress cannot be allowed to simply sweep aside traditions that have been nourished through the years."

"Tradition, sir, is simply a male excuse—"

"Miss Bramhall!" Sir Hugo Tolliver, director of the Explorers Club, leaped to his feet, fairly pushed Sir Sebastian away from the podium, and glared at Lotte. "This is neither the time nor the place for a debate as to the merits of membership."

"Do tell me, then . . ." Lotte glared right back. "When would you suggest—"

"Now, ladies and gentlemen," Sir Hugo pointedly addressed the crowd. "Refreshments are being served in the foyer, and as is our *tradition,* Sir Sebastian will be joining us." With that, Sir Hugo escorted Sir Sebastian off the stage and toward the door.

People stood and headed toward the foyer, toward what was more than likely tepid lemonade and the chance to make the personal acquaintance of the adventurous Sir Sebastian.

Lotte stared after them. "What an annoying beast that man is."

Veronica rose to her feet. "I assume you are speaking of Sir Hugo. Sir Sebastian struck me as most cordial and quite charming."

Lotte scoffed. "Cut from the same cloth, no doubt."

"He is a man, dear." Veronica smiled. "We must make allowances."

"Ha." Lotte's brows drew together. "Women have allowed men to get away with this kind of nonsense for centuries. It's past time we took our proper place in society." She glanced at Portia, still seated and trying very hard to look as if she had never met Lotte, or Veronica, either, for that matter. "Are you coming?"

"Of course we are." Portia reluctantly got to her feet. "He is my cousin, after all."

"Then you should take him in hand."

"Go on, Aunt Lotte. We shall meet you there," Veronica said quickly.

"Very well." Lotte started off, determination in the set of her shoulders and the spring in her step.

"Whatever possessed you to bring her with us tonight?" Portia glared at her friend.

"I didn't bring her with us. It was simply a coincidence that she had already planned to attend. A *pleasant* coincidence."

"Not the word that immediately comes to my mind." Portia huffed. "I was afraid this sort of thing would happen."

"What sort of thing?"

"I knew she would make a spectacle of herself."

"Scarcely that, darling. She simply asked a question." Veronica took Portia's arm, and they started after the crowd streaming toward the exit.

"But what a question! Women as members of the Explorers Club indeed."

"She was entirely right and I quite agree with her, as you well know," Veronica said smoothly. "And if she hadn't asked, I very well might have."

Portia heaved a long-suffering sigh. "I don't know why the women of your family have to be so . . . so . . ."

"Independent in our thinking? Intelligent and not afraid to show it?"

"Yes," Portia snapped. "It's not at all becoming."

"Pity."

"You'll never find another husband if you don't learn to be more circumspect." A warning sounded in Portia's voice. "Men do not want women who are overly intelligent."

"And I do not want a man who would expect me to be someone I'm not," Veronica said in a lofty manner. "Besides, I have no intention of marrying again."

Portia stopped in mid-step and stared. "Good Lord, Veronica, don't be absurd. Of course you will. I know I will. Although I would prefer to choose a husband myself," Portia added under her breath. In recent months, her well-meaning family had begun a concerted, and not especially subtle, campaign to find Portia a new husband, placing one eligible bachelor after another in her path. "We're women. It's what's expected of us."

Veronica cast her a pleasant smile. "I prefer not to do what's expected of me."

"Yes, I know." Portia rolled her gaze heavenward.

"Furthermore, I don't see why women in our position should be expected to marry."

"And what position is that?"

"Marriage gives women financial security. Even in this day and age women have few ways to provide for themselves." Veronica shrugged. "You and I have independent wealth. Our financial futures are assured. Therefore there is no need to marry."

"No need to marry?" Portia's eyes widened at the blasphemy.

"None at all." She hooked her arm through Portia's and again herded her toward the door.

"But surely you don't intend to spend the rest of your life alone?"

"No, I don't." Veronica shook her head. "It's only been a little more than three years since Charles died, and I am already tired of being alone. And I am not the type of woman to whom the idea of flitting from one man's bed to the next is especially appealing."

"Thank God." Relief sounded in Portia's voice.

Veronica smiled. She hadn't yet decided if she would tell Portia exactly what she planned. Still, she might need the other woman's assistance, even though Portia's proper nature might well be too shocked to permit her to render any true aid.

Veronica scanned the crowd in front of them. An indomitable Aunt Lotte was making her way toward the foyer. Through the open doors she could see Sir Sebastian, surrounded by admirers, most of them female. He spoke to everyone who approached him in what, even from this distance, struck Veronica as a charming and gracious manner. It was most admirable.

"Tell me more about your cousin."

"I don't know what more there is to tell." Portia thought for a moment. "You've read one of his books."

"Two actually."

"Then you know of his foolish pursuit of adventure in the guise of expanding man's knowledge of the unknown.

I can't bear to read them myself. They're rather heart-stopping, you know."

"But he does know how to tell a story," Veronica murmured. Indeed, she had found his prose to be evocative and even sensual.

"The family hoped he would go into business or study the law. Instead he has spent the last dozen or so years traveling to those places on this earth few civilized men have ventured. It's most distressing."

"Well, it's not law." Veronica bit back a grin.

"He always was something of a rebel as a child. Always doing things he shouldn't. Never following anyone's rules but his own. Still . . ." Portia heaved a resigned sigh. "He has always been my favorite."

"Somewhere deep inside you, Portia, you long for adventure."

"My life is rather dull," Portia said under her breath, then realized what she'd said. "Not dull. How absurd. I don't know why I said that."

"Those least likely to bend . . ."

"Are most likely to snap. Yes, yes, you've said it before, but it's utter nonsense." Portia scoffed. "I have no intention of bending or snapping."

"Of course not," Veronica said. "You're quite content with your uneventful life."

Portia nodded. "Indeed I am."

Veronica knew better. It struck her on occasion as both odd and remarkable that she and Portia, along with Julia, Lady Winterset, knew one another as well as they did given they hadn't known each other at all until a few years ago. It was chance that they had happened to meet at Fenwick and Sons, Booksellers, but no doubt fate that they had become fast friends. They had each lost their husbands some three years ago to accident or illness or mishap and had met at a time when each needed a friend who was not tied to her loss. While not one given to overt displays of piety, Veronica often thanked God she had found these friends, in truth, these *sisters* she'd never had nor ever missed. Now she could not envision her life without them.

"Aside from Sebastian, we are quite a proper, well-behaved family," Portia said firmly, although Veronica did wonder how a proper, well-behaved family could produce a man who wandered the far reaches of the earth. Or perhaps it was only a proper, well-behaved family that could.

"He certainly doesn't look the least bit well behaved." In truth, with his rugged good looks, Sir Sebastian looked like a hero from a novel. "He looks like a man who plunges headfirst into adventure."

"It's the scar." Portia studied her cousin. "It makes him look like, well, exactly what he is."

"No doubt a souvenir from one of his expeditions."

"I suspect he likes people to think that." Portia chuckled. "The truth is he fell out of a tree when he was a boy." The closer they got to Sir Sebastian, the slower the crowd moved. They were scarcely walking at all now. Portia tapped her foot in impatience.

"I gather it's been some time since you've seen him."

"He's been back in England for several months, according to the rest of the family. But he's yet to make an appearance at any one of the gatherings they have subjected me to of late. Although with Christmas less than a month away, those gatherings will become even more frequent and Sebastian is certain to attend." Portia craned her neck to see around the crowd. "I understand he's purchased a house in the country."

"Oh?" A casual note sounded in Veronica's voice. "Do you think he intends to stay in one place for a while, then?"

"I have no idea what he intends, but I will certainly ask him if we ever get close enough. Why are you asking questions about Sebastian?" Her eyes narrowed. "And you never answered me. What did you mean by he's the one you want? The one you want for what?"

"I haven't decided yet."

A break appeared in the crowd in front of them, and Veronica urged Portia forward.

Portia stood her ground. "Veronica Smithson, I don't believe you have ever lied to me before."

"Nonsense, Portia." Veronica shrugged. "I have lied to you on any number of occasions."

"And I have never known you to be undecided about anything."

"Ah, well, there's always a first time."

"What are you planning?"

Veronica peered around her. "There's a path opening behind you."

"I don't care!" Portia's eyes widened. "If you are interested in pursuing Sebastian, I should warn you, he is not interested in marriage."

"Nor am I, as I believe we have already established." Veronica took her arm, turned her, and started steering her toward Sebastian.

"Then what do you want?" Portia pulled up short and refused to budge.

"You won't like it."

"No doubt."

"It really isn't any of your concern."

"He is my cousin and you are my friend, so it most certainly is my concern."

"You may rest easy, then. I have no desire to become your cousin's wife." Veronica focused her gaze on Sebastian and smiled. "I intend to be his mistress."

Chapter 2

Portia stared in disbelief. "You what?"

"You heard me."

"I hoped I was mistaken. Or I'd gone deaf. That is the sort of thing that would strike any decent person deaf. There are warnings about things like that, you know." Portia's brows drew together. "You can't possibly be serious."

"I've never been more serious," Veronica said, her gaze lingering on Sir Sebastian. He was a fine figure of a man.

"Well, I won't have it! And I cannot believe you would suggest such a thing. I know you pay no heed to matters of this nature, but this is . . . ," Portia sputtered. "It's immoral. That's what it is. Beyond that." Portia squared her shoulders and met Veronica's gaze directly. "It's scandalous! And I will not permit it!" Several heads turned in their direction.

"Darling, you have nothing to say about it. However . . ." Veronica leaned closer. "It would be considerably less scandalous if you refrained from announcing it to the entire world."

"I don't care!" Regardless, Portia cared more than anyone Veronica knew about scandal, and she lowered her voice. "I know you always do precisely as you please, but this is entirely too much, even for you. It's wrong, Veronica. And it's . . ." Portia searched for the right word. "It's selfish. That's what it is. Selfish."

Veronica raised an amused brow. "How on earth is it selfish?"

"You're thinking only of yourself. Think of the scandal. How it will affect your friends and your family. Your father and your grandmother and your aunt." Portia cast a reproving look at Lotte, still making her way toward Sebastian. "Perhaps not your aunt but . . . Harrison." Portia sucked in a sharp breath at the thought of the overly proper brother of Veronica's late husband. "Harrison would be appalled."

"Harrison is far less concerned about scandal than he once was. Besides, he's now married to Julia and scandal is what brought them together. I daresay my dear brother-in-law now understands the benefits of a certain amount of scandal."

"Well, I don't!" Portia snapped.

"I shall make you a promise, Portia dear. I shall be wonderfully discreet in all matters pertaining to any"— she cleared her throat—"*arrangement* I may come to with your cousin. Which was my intention all along. If you will do me one small, insignificant favor."

"Humph." Portia glared. "And what favor would that be?"

"Introduce me to him, of course."

"That's right." Portia brightened. "You haven't even met him. Why, there's every possibility he won't be the least bit interested in you."

"I can't imagine such a thing." Veronica drew her brows together. "Nor, do I think, can you."

"Admittedly, you're not unattractive." Portia cast an assessing eye over her friend. "Although not as pretty as Julia."

"Yes, well, then I shall simply have to try harder," Veronica said in a firm manner. She knew better than to let anything Portia said annoy her. Although she was never deliberately unkind, Portia did have an alarming tendency to speak without either hesitation or thought.

Portia had made no secret of the fact that, among the three friends, she thought Julia was the pretty one, Veronica was the clever one, and she herself was the most proper of the group. It was absurd. It would be most immodest to admit it aloud, but Veronica considered herself every bit as pretty as Julia, perhaps even more so.

While Julia was the epitome of blond English beauty, one could tell just by looking at Veronica that she was no ordinary creature. If she did not have men falling at her feet, it was not a result of her appearance but rather her nature. She had always been independent and outspoken and had never hidden the fact of her intelligence, qualities she had long ago accepted as not being especially appealing to men. And didn't her mirror confirm that, with her dark red hair and tall stature, her deep brown eyes that flashed more often than not with amusement as well as intelligence, she was striking and very nearly unforgettable? Julia was the pretty one, indeed.

"Why are you frowning at me like that?" Suspicion sounded in Portia's voice.

"Was I?" Veronica favored her friend with her sweetest smile. "My apologies. A random thought captured my attention for a moment. It was nothing of significance."

"I have a random thought of my own." Portia's voice

was cool. "I cannot condone anything as depraved as you attempting to seduce—"

Veronica laughed.

Portia ignored her. "—my cousin, even if Sebastian himself would no doubt be amenable to the idea. He has a certain reputation, you know."

"One of many reasons why I have selected him."

"However—"

"I don't believe I mentioned seduction."

Portia glared. "You wish to become his mistress. I assume there will be a certain element of seduction involved."

"I hadn't thought of it quite like that, but you're right." Veronica bit back a grin. "I daresay there are any number of other concerns I have not yet thought of."

"Perhaps you have not given this proposal of yours due consideration."

"I thought I had, but I may well be mistaken. If you have any other, oh, suggestions or recommendations, or notice any impediments that I have not thought of— aside from the question of scandal or propriety—I should be delighted to hear them. Do go on."

Portia studied her for a moment. "As I was saying, while seduction does not have my approval—"

Veronica choked back another laugh.

"I could certainly approve of any and all attempts to embroil Sebastian in marriage."

"Marriage?" Veronica's brows rose, although she shouldn't be at all surprised at Portia's offer. "Dear, dear Portia, what a wonderfully charming and thoughtful offer, although I suspect your cousin wouldn't agree."

"Goodness no. Sebastian is not at all interested in marriage." Portia cast a resigned glance at her cousin, who was still surrounded by admirers. Most of them female.

"He is entirely too busy with his travels and his books and his lectures to be interested in marriage. But if anyone can lure him to the altar, I would wager it would be you."

"That may well be the nicest thing you've ever said to me. And don't think your confidence in me is not appreciated, as is your offer of assistance, but"—she laid her hand on Portia's arm—"do try not to be shocked. I want a man, darling, not a husband. I've had a husband, and while I have no regrets on that score, I have no desire to have another. I want adventure, not routine. I think I have already made that clear."

"But—"

"However, I do want a man in my life for longer than the usual length of an *affaire de coeur.* I am not interested in a casual encounter."

Portia winced.

"I would be an excellent mistress. I am unfailingly loyal, you know."

Portia stared.

"I do plan to be faithful and would expect faithfulness in return."

Portia's mouth opened in stunned silence.

"I am an accomplished hostess, well spoken, and would certainly be a benefit to any man of ambition." Veronica's gaze strayed back to Sebastian.

Shock glazed Portia's eyes.

"I am something of a catch, Portia. I can't imagine any intelligent gentleman not realizing that. I should add that when it comes to more *intimate* concerns, well, I do not shock easily. Charles could be most . . . creative."

Portia emitted a sort of strangled sound.

"And I don't mind confessing that I find the idea of becoming a man's mistress most, well . . ." Veronica adopted an innocent tone. "Seductive."

Portia's eyes widened. "What you want, Veronica Smithson, is all the trappings of marriage without the restrictions."

Veronica considered her friend for a moment. "Why, yes, I suppose in many ways I do. What an excellent idea."

"It's not the least bit excellent. It's deplorable. It's depraved. It's—"

"Brilliant. Absolutely brilliant." Veronica beamed at her friend. "And so clever of you to think of it."

"I didn't think of it! I would never think of such a thing."

"You deserve all the credit."

"I don't want it!" She narrowed her eyes. "You're teasing me."

Veronica grinned. "Only because it's so much fun to do so."

"I'm glad you're enjoying it," Portia snapped, then drew a steadying breath. "Is there nothing I can do to dissuade you?"

"Goodness, Portia, you needn't look so distraught. It's not as if your cousin has placed an advertisement for a mistress and I am applying for the position."

Portia scoffed. "That would be absurd."

"I'm simply saying this is my intention. Why, nothing might happen between us at all. One never really knows. And we haven't even met yet."

"True." Portia nodded. "And he might not like you."

"I do wish you would stop saying that." Veronica sighed. "More to the point, *I* might not like *him*."

The likelihood of that was minimal. She had chosen Sir Sebastian carefully. Not only had Veronica read his books, but she'd had discreet inquiries made as to his financial stability and character. She might well sound flippant with Portia, but she was quite serious.

This was the man she wanted. This was the man she intended to have. If all went well.

"One more thing."

Portia shook her head in a stubborn manner. "I have agreed to introduce you, but I refuse to lend any further assistance."

"Oh, but you will." She met the other woman's gaze firmly. "I want your word that you won't tell Sebastian, or anyone, for that matter, what we have discussed. Furthermore, should Sebastian and I, well . . ."

Portia raised a brow. "Yes?"

"Enter into any sort of an arrangement, I would prefer to keep it confidential."

"A secret, you mean?"

Veronica shrugged. "It seems wise."

"Why, Veronica Smithson, you are concerned with scandal, after all."

"I would be selfish if I were not," she said in a dry tone.

"I have never been good at secrets."

"Then you shall have to work at it, dear."

"However, as I would prefer no one know of this plan of yours, no matter how it develops, you have my word." Portia thought for a moment. "And as you said, one never knows. Why, nothing might come of this at all."

"You may say a prayer to that effect if it eases your distress. Now then." Veronica again took Portia's arm and started toward the foyer. "It's time to meet my adventurer."

Chapter 3

" . . . and then, on the very next page, when you were surrounded by natives . . ." The young, dark-haired woman gazed up at Sebastian with a worshipful look. He'd seen that look before. "Why, my heart was quite in my throat. I felt I was there beside you."

"There is no greater compliment than that for a writer," Sebastian said. "I'm delighted you enjoyed my account of the incident."

Sebastian favored her with his best Sir Sebastian Hadley-Attwater smile. The very one he had practiced for moments exactly like this. The smile that told young women that, while he was grateful for their admiration and flattered by their adoration, there was no possibility of anything between them beyond a pleasant conversation. And while this one was quite lovely, she was also entirely too young. Young women were as dangerous as anything that might be encountered in the wilds of an uncharted jungle.

"If I didn't know you had survived, I would have

feared for your life. If you had died . . ." She heaved a heartfelt sigh. "It would have been dreadful. Simply dreadful."

"I agree." He chuckled. "I would have considered my death dreadful at the very least. I am quite glad I avoided it."

"As are we all, Sir Sebastian." She fluttered her lashes. "I would have been devastated."

It was at once a benefit and a curse of fame that women, particularly young women, who had read his accounts of travel and adventure thought of him as a heroic figure. And often as their own hero. He'd learned through the years to walk the fine line between encouragement and rejection; he did want them to continue to buy his books and attend his lectures, after all. What he didn't want was their assuming a personal connection that existed only in their own minds. That path led to nothing but the kind of trouble he had thus far managed to avoid. Of course, older, experienced women were a different matter altogether.

"Sir Sebastian." A gentleman stepped forward.

Sebastian cast the young woman a smile that carried just enough regret to allow her to believe he was not both relieved and grateful to turn his attention elsewhere. "Yes?"

"When one traverses the far reaches of the Nile," the gentleman began, "it was my understanding that . . ."

Sebastian adopted an attitude of complete attention, but his mind wandered. This was a question he had answered any number of times and could answer in his sleep.

Where on earth was Portia? And more to the point, where was the woman she'd been sitting beside? There had been something most intriguing about the way she

had met his gaze directly, even boldly. He'd met bold
women before, but he didn't expect such boldness from a
friend of Portia's. A woman who would wear a hat like the
one she wore—tall, feathered, flowered, beribboned, and
no doubt fashionable even in its extremity—was a woman
who knew her own mind. Certainly such women were
often annoying, but they were also more interesting and
less likely to see his fame rather than himself. This was a
lady he looked forward to meeting.

"You must realize that the Nile, and its environs," he
began, "present unique difficulties. . . ."

Not that he wasn't happy to see his cousin, or any of
his family, for that matter. Indeed, it had been far too
long. His fault entirely, as he freely acknowledged, and as
his brothers had mentioned when he had dined with them
at their club. And as his mother had pointed out when he
had visited her shortly after his return to England and on
every obligatory visit since then. His older sister, too, had
chastised him in person when he had called on her,
prompted by a chance encounter with her husband. Chas-
tisement that continued in writing every time he turned
down an invitation to one of her soirees. Even his two
younger sisters, who had always held him in high regard,
had had a few well-chosen words when he had encountered them quite by accident. London was considerably
smaller than most people realized. He had had every intention of calling on all of them, as well as Portia, but
somehow hadn't yet managed it. He'd only been back in
England for a few months, and between his writing, his
lectures and other public appearances, and purchasing a
house, he'd had very little time to spare.

"But as man has inhabited that area of the world for
centuries, it is not as difficult . . ."

It was a feeble excuse, which, he argued to himself,

was better than no excuse at all and was preferable to accepting that he avoided his family whenever possible. In truth, even though the rest of the world viewed him as a success, his family had never been quite able to see him as anything but the irresponsible scamp he had been in his youth. To his public he was Sir Sebastian, adventurer, world traveler, and man of significant accomplishment. To his family he was, and always had been, the son who had never quite lived up to expectations.

"And indeed," he continued, "the machinations of government and bureaucracy in that region do tend to . . ."

That, however, he was determined to change. Indeed, he had changed, matured, if you will. His thirty-third birthday was two days after Christmas, at which time he would come into the inheritance his father had left to him. If and only if his older brothers decreed him worthy and responsible. It wasn't merely the inheritance he wanted: it was the family acceptance it represented. His first step to acquiring a veneer of responsibility had been to purchase a house, a permanent, respectable place of residence. He had decided as well to stay in England for longer periods and curtail his travels.

Truth be told, he had grown tired of never staying in one place past a season or two. Tired of calling his traveling trunks home. Tired of admittedly delightful women who had come and gone through his life and parted with him as easily as he parted with them. Whereas once he had cured his restless nature with travel and adventure and women, he had wondered more and more in recent years if the restlessness in his soul could be eased only with permanence and family and home. Perhaps it was time for a new type of adventure.

"I see," his questioner said thoughtfully. "That does explain—"

"Sir Sebastian." Miss Bramhall bore down on him with the unrelenting momentum of a ship under full sail, Sir Hugo in hot pursuit.

He winced to himself, then adopted a pleasant smile. "Miss Bramhall. I assume you wish to continue our discussion."

"Indeed I do." She glared at him. Perhaps someone should tell her the old adage about catching more flies with honey.

"But might I say, before you continue, that I think you have an excellent point."

"I do?" Suspicion sounded in her voice. "Of course I do."

This might be easier than he thought. "Women are indeed making great strides."

She nodded vigorously. "Yes, we are."

"The issue of membership is one well worth discussion."

The older woman studied him. "Then I may count on your support?"

"Absolutely not!" Sir Hugo's voice thundered behind her.

Miss Bramhall huffed in frustration and turned to face the director. "I don't believe you were part of this conversation."

"I am part of every conversation that has to do with the workings of this organization."

Sebastian noted the crowd around him had dissipated. Obviously, no one wished to be part of this confrontation. Nor did he. He wisely took a step back.

"Sir Sebastian has nothing to do with this debate," Sir Hugo snapped. "Why, he's not even a member of the board."

"Nor does he wish to be," Sebastian said under his breath.

Miss Bramhall drew herself up like a warrior preparing to do battle. "Is he or is he not a member in good standing of this organization?"

Sir Hugo snorted. "You know full well he is."

"And is he not one of your most well-respected and best-known members?"

"We have other members far more accomplished."

"Always nice to hear," Sebastian murmured and took another discreet step back. With any luck he could slip away unnoticed in another minute.

"Regardless, his opinion, as well as the opinions of all the members, should be taken into account." Miss Bramhall's eyes narrowed in a menacing manner. "Do you not agree?"

"Every member's opinion is valued," Sir Hugo said in a lofty manner. "Every member, regardless of their accomplishments, is given a say in the governing of this organization. And were I to put this issue up for a vote . . ." His gaze locked with Miss Bramhall's. "You would lose."

"Aha!" She aimed an accusing finger at him. "Because it's an organization made up entirely of cowards! Narrow-minded, self-absorbed men who dwell in the muck and mire and safety of the traditions of half a century ago!"

Sir Hugo sucked in a hard breath. "Not at all! We are most progressive! We are known for our progressive views on any number of issues!"

"Ha!" She snorted. "You, Hugo Tolliver, have not been progressive since the moment you learned to walk upright!"

He gasped. "You go entirely too far, Charlotte Bramhall! But then you always have."

"And you have never gone far enough!" She lowered her voice and leaned closer to Sir Hugo. Fire flashed in her eyes. Her voice was too low for Sebastian to make out her words, much to his relief, but the look on Sir Hugo's face was more than enough to tell him this was a conversation that had moved far from its original topic. Obviously, there was more to the enmity between Miss Bramhall and Sir Hugo than club membership for women.

He'd been in difficult situations before, and this was an opportunity to flee if ever he'd seen one. Sebastian quickly took another step back, turned on his heel, and came face-to-face with the woman in the hat. Or rather his face to her hat.

She smiled up at him. "Looking for escape, Sir Sebastian?"

He stared down into dark brown eyes lit with amusement and grinned. "Not very courageous of me, I'm afraid."

Beneath the hat, mahogany red curls framed her face. She raised a brow. "You? The fearless Sir Sebastian Hadley-Attwater? Whatever will we tell your admirers?"

He shifted his glance from side to side. "Perhaps we could keep this between the two of us, then. I should hate to shatter anyone's illusions."

"Mine are certainly shattered." She shook her head mournfully. "From your books I thought nothing frightened you. I believe you were once cornered by a rampaging tiger in the jungles of India."

"That was not nearly as terrifying." He glanced at Miss Bramhall and Sir Hugo, who were still arguing, although they had moved out of the flow of traffic in a futile effort to be discreet. He shuddered. "And was far less dangerous."

She laughed, a delightful unrestrained laugh that made the feathers on her hat quiver in a most delightful way.

Perhaps there was something to be said for outrageous hats, after all.

"I fear you have me at a disadvantage."

"Oh, I do hope so." Laughter continued to dance in her eyes.

"You know my name, but I have no idea who you are." He shook his head. "It doesn't seem the least bit fair."

"It's not, I suppose." Her gaze met his as directly as it had from across the room. But now he could see something of a challenge in her brown eyes. Or an invitation. "I am scarcely ever concerned with fair."

He laughed. "But how can I call on you if I don't have your name?"

"And do you intend to call on me?"

He leaned close and lowered his voice. "I suspect you intend me to."

She turned her head slightly to stare into his eyes, her face just inches from his, her mouth no more than a kiss away. "And if I don't?"

His gaze slipped to her lips, then back to her eyes. "Then I shall be devastated. My heart will be crushed as thoroughly as dust beneath your feet."

"Oh, we can't have that." Her eyes widened in an innocent manner he didn't believe for a moment. "I quite detest dust."

"Her name is Lady Veronica Smithson," an indignant voice sounded off to one side. "And I am Lady Redwell. Portia? Your cousin? Although apparently you have forgotten."

He straightened, stepped away from Lady Smithson, and turned to his cousin. "Portia!" He took her hands and kissed her cheek. "I was just coming to look for you."

"Humph." Portia sniffed. "I doubt that."

"Come now, Portia, you shouldn't and you know it. I

was quite pleased to see you in the audience this evening." He favored her with an affectionate smile. "How are you, little cousin? You look as lovely as ever."

"Don't try that with me, Sebastian," Portia said, but a charming blush washed up her cheeks. He'd always been able to make her blush. "I am quite annoyed with you."

He ignored her. "No, I was wrong. I think you are lovelier than ever."

"It won't work," Portia warned.

He considered her thoughtfully. "Dare I hope the blush in your cheek and the sparkle in your eyes are due to a new gentleman in your life?"

"Sebastian!"

Lady Smithson choked back a laugh. He inclined his head toward her and lowered his voice in a confidential manner. "My mother says the entire family thinks it's time."

Lady Smithson's voice matched his. "It's my understanding they are doing everything they can to encourage her in that direction."

"I am still standing here, you know." Portia huffed and straightened her shoulders. "Yes, Sebastian, I may well be lovelier than ever, for whatever it's worth. However, all the compliments in the world do not make up for the fact that you have been in London for some time now and have not called on me."

"My apologies, Portia. I meant to. Indeed, I still mean to. But what with one thing and another . . . Say." He drew his brows together. "Why haven't you called on me?"

"Me?" Portia's eyes widened. "Why, I couldn't possibly. I—"

"Don't tell me it wouldn't be proper." He slanted Lady Smithson a knowing look. "Portia has always been overly concerned with propriety, you know."

"Has she? I hadn't noticed." Lady Smithson's wry smile belied her words.

"You're my cousin and as close to me as one of my sisters." He cast Portia a chastising look. "Surely you knew I was back in London? I've made no secret of my presence."

"Well, yes, I was aware—"

"You know whenever I am in the city, I stay at Mr. Sinclair's residence."

"He is no better than you," Portia said. "I suspect he has not called on his relations, either."

"As most of them are in America, I daresay that is the case. I admit I have been remiss by not calling on you, but that's to be expected of me." He glanced at Lady Smithson. "I am well known for shirking my familial responsibilities in favor of fun and frolic. Portia can confirm that."

Portia's jaw clenched.

Lady Smithson looked like it was all she could do to keep from laughing.

"But we do expect better from Portia." He heaved a dramatic sigh. "I never imagined such treatment at her hands. I am her favorite cousin."

"You most certainly are no—" Portia rolled her gaze at the ceiling and sighed in surrender. "You always have been, although I have no idea why."

"We balance each other." He turned his attention to Lady Smithson. "Portia always keeps propriety in mind, whereas I do not."

"You two have a great deal in common," Portia said under her breath.

"Do we, Lady Smithson?" He met her gaze and grinned wickedly. "How delightful."

"The delight of it remains to be seen, Sir Sebastian." Lady Smithson's voice was cool, but her eyes twinkled.

"Perhaps we could further discuss our mutual lack of concern for propriety." He glanced at Miss Bramhall and Sir Hugo, who showed no signs of coming to agreement. If anything, their discussion appeared even more heated than before. "Now that I have made my escape."

Lady Smithson glanced at Miss Bramhall and Sir Hugo, then studied Sebastian thoughtfully. "Tell me, Sir Sebastian, do you really think she has an excellent point?"

"I do," he said firmly. "The value of any organization that prides itself on being at the forefront of progress is being able to debate and discuss new ideas, no matter how outrageous they would seem."

"And you think full membership for women is an outrageous idea?"

Portia groaned softly.

"One must consider all aspects of the proposal." He chose his words with care. "The Explorers Club is locked in an eternal struggle with the Royal Geographic Society for recognition and prestige. Regardless of the merits of the argument, until the society accepts female members, we would be at a disadvantage to open our own membership."

"So until one monkey jumps off a cliff, none of the others will do so?"

He frowned. "It's a very steep cliff and a long way to the bottom. One hates to jump alone."

Portia's gaze slid from Sebastian to Lady Smithson. "Perhaps this is not something—"

"Then all that about being at the forefront of progress"—Lady Smithson waved in a blithe gesture—"is nothing more than an idle claim? Simply a slogan that looks nice at the top of the club stationery?"

"Not at all." He bristled. "We have always taken a leadership position."

"But you'd rather be the monkey that follows than the monkey that leads?"

"At least that monkey has something to cushion the fall," he said sharply. Good Lord, he was right. She was annoying. He drew a deep breath. "We have made great strides forward in any number of areas."

"But not in this particular area."

"The weather is exceptionally cool for this time of year, don't you agree?" Portia said, a note of panic in her voice. They ignored her.

"This particular area," he said firmly, "is somewhat contentious."

Lady Smithson shrugged in an offhand manner. "No doubt because most of the members of the Explorers Club also have membership in the Geographic Society. Therefore it is not surprising both organizations would see this issue in precisely the same way."

"Then we agree on that?"

"We do." She nodded. "But you have not answered my question."

Portia scoffed. "Nonsense. Of course he—"

"And which question was that, Lady Smithson?"

"I asked you if you thought membership for women was an outrageous idea. Well?" Her voice was cool. "Do you?"

"Lady Smithson." He paused. As much as he wanted to know this woman, he had no intention of deceiving her. Still, there was no need to be completely candid. "I walk a narrow path between these two organizations. They have both sponsored and provided support for my expeditions and travels and other endeavors."

"And you don't want to alienate either of them."

He breathed a sigh of relief. "Absolutely not."

"Speaking out in favor of female membership would not endear you to either group."

"Then you understand."

"Completely." She smiled slowly. "But as I am obviously a member of neither organization, your answer—your secret—would be safe with me." She leaned closer and stared into his eyes. "Tell me, Sir Sebastian, do you think women should be members of this club or, for that matter, the Geographic Society?"

He stared into her eyes, deep and endless and altogether mesmerizing. Damnation. He blew a long breath. "No, I do not."

She straightened. "I see."

"Do you?" he said.

"Unusual weather, really," Portia said quickly. "It's surprisingly cold and rather—"

"It comes as no surprise. Your opinion is very much the same as most men and, I would think, most members of the Explorers Club. You think women have their place. I think women should do whatever they wish if they have the ability to do so," Lady Smithson said smoothly. "Be that belong to an organization or explore undiscovered lands or manage their own finances."

He drew his brows together. "Then I fear we shall have to agree to disagree."

She cast him a brilliant smile. "I don't find that a particular problem."

He stared at her for a moment. "You are the type of woman who enjoys a rousing debate, aren't you?"

"Good Lord," Portia muttered.

Lady Smithson laughed. "It was great fun, wasn't it? There is nothing like a good debate to make the blood race."

"Then you don't think women should be members," he said slowly.

"Nonsense. Of course I do." She shrugged. "This particular cause simply isn't one of my passions."

"What are your passions, Lady Smithson?"

"Hats," Portia said a bit more vehemently than was necessary. "She likes hats. Hats are her passion. A grand passion."

"Indeed. Hats are certainly among my many . . ." She met his gaze directly, and his breath caught. "Passions. As is debate."

"Then will you try to change my mind on this subject?" He smiled slowly. "Bend my way of thinking to yours?"

"Absolutely, as I am right and you are wrong. However." She smiled pleasantly. "I do not expect you to change simply because I wish it. You are who you are and should be accepted for who you are. As should I."

He chuckled. "Perhaps if you were leading this charge, rather than a shrew like Miss Bramhall, this cause would have a modicum of success."

Portia winced.

Lady Smithson raised a brow. "Do you think so?"

"I do."

"Why?"

"Because I can't imagine any man resisting you, or rather your argument, for long." Again, his gaze met hers.

"Even you?"

"Especially me."

"Because it's an excellent argument?"

"Because you make it so beautifully."

"I beg your pardon," Portia said indignantly. "I am still here, you know. Not that either of you has noticed."

"My apologies, dear. We are well aware of your presence." Lady Smithson cast Portia an affectionate smile. "No one would ever forget you."

"Forgive me as well, Portia." Sebastian smiled at his cousin. "We were carried away by the"—he cleared his throat—"passions of our convictions."

"And it's past time I rescued Sir Hugo from the passionate convictions of the *shrew*." Lady Smithson glanced at the couple who were still arguing, and chuckled. "Sir Hugo's face is a rather distressing shade of red, but it does look like she is having a grand time. To be expected, I suppose." She glanced at Sir Sebastian and smiled. "She is my aunt, after all."

"Of course, she would be," he said weakly.

"All becomes clear now, doesn't it?" Portia said under her breath.

"I must say I enjoyed our encounter, Sir Sebastian. And your lecture was fascinating." Lady Smithson nodded. "Portia. Good evening." She started toward her aunt.

"Lady Smithson." He stepped toward her.

She stopped and looked back. "Yes?"

"Should you ever wish to debate just for the sheer pleasure of it . . ." He smiled. "I suspect there are any number of topics on which we most heartily disagree."

"Indeed, the list could well be endless." She considered him for a moment. "I intend to drive in the park the day after tomorrow. In the afternoon."

He gasped. "I intended to drive in the park the day after tomorrow, in the afternoon."

"What a coincidence," Portia muttered.

"Then perhaps our paths will cross?"

"I shall be devastated if they don't." He chuckled. "And amazed."

"As will I." Lady Smithson nodded, turned, and headed to rescue Sir Hugo.

Sir Sebastian's gaze lingered as she crossed to the dueling couple. Her hips swayed enticingly, emphasized by her bustle. High above her head, that feather continued to quiver, matching a tremulous feeling somewhere deep inside him. Odd and decidedly familiar. Not unlike the feeling he always had whenever he began a new adventure.

"Well," Portia began. "That was certainly—"

"Tell me about her," he said abruptly. "I want to know everything about her."

"That does seem to be my lot tonight." Portia huffed. "You inquiring about her. Veronica asking . . ."

"Oh?" He shifted his gaze to his cousin. "Was she asking about me?"

"You are a public figure, Sebastian. Everyone knows everything about you."

"Not everything." He couldn't resist a smug smile. "So she was curious?"

"If I tell you, it will simply go to your head." She heaved a long-suffering sigh. "What do you want to know about her?"

"Is she married?"

"Her husband died some three years ago, around the same time I lost David. We met that next year."

"I see." His gaze strayed back to Lady Smithson, who was now trying to separate the combatants. "Is she still mourning him?"

"One never stops mourning in some manner," Portia said sharply. "However . . ." She sighed. "If you are asking if she has left the past behind, I suppose in most ways she has."

"In most ways?"

"Veronica has her own way of looking at the world. While she has become a very close friend, in that respect we couldn't be more different."

He turned his attention back to Portia and frowned. "I have no idea what you are trying to say."

Portia thought for a moment. "Veronica has never hesitated to do or say exactly as she pleases. I suspect that was her nature before her marriage, and it certainly hasn't changed." She paused. "Her husband was considerably older than she and had never been married before. I have always wondered if it wasn't her unique spirit—for lack of a better word—that attracted him in the first place. She is very strong-willed and has no sense of tradition."

He nodded. "You mean about a woman's place."

"About everything. It's most annoying, and there have been any number of times that I would like nothing better than to box her ears. Regardless"—she shrugged—"she is one of my dearest friends."

"Why, Portia." He stared in surprise. "I never would have imagined you to have a friend that was the least bit unconventional."

"She's not the least bit unconventional." Portia shook her head. "She's *extremely* unconventional and far more progressive in her thinking than any decent woman should be." She leaned close and lowered her voice in a confidential manner. "Why, she thinks women should vote."

He gasped in mock horror. "Not that."

She ignored his sarcasm. "I find some of her ideas most shocking and others truly scandalous. And yet, I wouldn't change her for the world." She pinned him with a firm gaze. "Nor would I permit anyone else to change her."

Sebastian raised a brow. "It seems you have changed, little cousin."

"Not in the least. I," she added firmly, "never change. Nor do I ever intend to. Now, about Veronica. You should know she's very clever. Quite the most intelligent woman I have ever met."

"Good." He grinned. "I like intelligent women."

"Probably more intelligent than even you."

"Not likely." He scoffed. "What else?"

"She is always right and rarely admits when she is wrong."

"Interesting, as I am always right."

"She is entirely too independent."

He nodded. "As am I."

"Yes, but she is a woman. It's unseemly."

He bit back a smile. "Go on."

She hesitated. "While she is the strongest woman I know, I think she is more vulnerable than she appears."

"A brave face on it, then?"

"Don't mistake my words. I simply think there is much she doesn't reveal." She narrowed her eyes. "I would hate to see anyone toy with her affections."

"I have no intention of toying with her affections."

She snorted. "Then you, too, have changed, Sebastian Hadley-Attwater." A warning sounded in her voice. "Veronica is not the sort of woman one toys with."

"I think you're absolutely right." His gaze returned to Lady Smithson. "She's not the sort one toys with." Lady Smithson had taken her aunt's arm and was firmly steering her toward the door. He smiled slowly. "She's the sort one marries."

Chapter 4

Good Lord, she was an idiot.

Veronica settled deeper into the well-padded back of her open landau and pulled her cloak tighter around herself. Whatever had possessed her to tell Sir Sebastian she would be driving in the park today? Certainly she'd been distracted by the need to separate her aunt from Sir Hugo before one of them did the other bodily harm. She had realized as well that, given the time of year, there would be very few people in the park, which suited her purposes. As much as Veronica did enjoy flouting convention, she preferred not to be stupid about it. One was completely public here, no one could be accused of anything untoward, yet without people about there was a certain privacy. During the season one could scarcely move at anything other than a snail's pace, but then, during the season, a drive through the park was for no other reason than to see and be seen. And while she did like driving in crisp weather, this year crisp had quickly turned to cold.

Why, it had already snowed in October and again in November. Who knew what December would hold?

Her servants, no doubt, thought her quite mad when she'd insisted on having the top down. Her driver had tried to dissuade her, as had her butler and her maid, although they should have known better. Veronica very rarely changed her mind. Why hadn't they just said, "But, my lady, it's bloody cold outside?" She ignored the thought that perhaps, in their own way, they had. Still, it wasn't all that bad. She had a lap blanket and a warm brick at her feet. It was really quite invigorating, once one stopped shivering.

Surely a little thing like the weather wouldn't keep an adventurer like Sir Sebastian away. Although one did wonder where he was. She sat up and scanned the park, then settled back with a sigh. Perhaps she had been too subtle. Or too forward. Perhaps she had scared him away with her penchant for heated discussion and her progressive thinking. Still, one would think it would take more than an outspoken manner to scare away a man of courage and fortitude, as Sir Sebastian's exploits had proven him to be, unless that, too, was an illusion. It was possible that he was as apprehensive about this meeting as she.

Veronica wasn't at all used to being apprehensive or uncertain. But then she had never set her sights on a man before. Truth be told, she wasn't entirely certain what she was doing or how to go about accomplishing it. She grimaced. She had been teasing Portia when she'd said it wasn't as if Sebastian had advertised for a mistress. But it was a pity, really. It would have made this much easier and completely straightforward to be able to apply for a position without having to justify her reasoning.

How lovely it would be to simply say to him she had decided on this course for any number of reasons that were really none of his business. And to further say she had selected him for reasons that again were not his concern, although those she would be willing to share.

She straightened again and noted a lone familiar figure on foot heading toward her across the snow-covered grass. Relief washed through her. His strides were long, determination apparent in the very lines of his body, as if he had a purpose far more pressing than a mere drive in the park. She bit back a satisfied smile. And indeed this was no mere drive.

She'd been aware—even if not overly interested—of his books and adventures long before she'd ever met his cousin. He was, after all, extremely well-known. Her late husband had been something of an admirer and had Sir Sebastian's books in his library. But it wasn't until recent months that Veronica had read them. She wasn't at all sure if the idea of becoming Sir Sebastian's mistress was a result of having read his words or if it was just a happy coincidence that she had become intrigued with the man behind the books at very nearly the same time she had decided she would much prefer to be a mistress rather than a wife. Not that it made any difference in the scheme of things. And how convenient that he was related to one of her dearest friends.

He drew closer and her heart fluttered. Nerves, of course, and apprehension. To be expected, really. While Veronica was outspoken on very nearly every topic, and had her own particular set of morals and rules of behavior that might well offend those governed by strict propriety, she had never been with a man other than her husband. She'd never been seduced by anyone other than Charles, and indeed, she had not been averse to his seduction. She had, on occasion, wondered if any woman would or had. Charles had been quite a disreputable rogue when she'd met him, at least where women were concerned. Not that she had fallen into his bed without due consideration. She had too much pride to value herself lightly. She had, admittedly, wanted him with the sort of ache she'd never experienced before. It was as much lust as love. And she'd not been disappointed. Veronica thought it exceptionally odd that so many wives considered intimate relations a duty rather than a pleasure. But then Charles had been unique. And so was she.

"Henry," she called to her driver. "Do stop the carriage."

"But, Lady Smithson," Henry began, then caught sight of Sir Sebastian. Realization dawned on his face, and he cast her an assessing look. "Do you intend to walk, my lady?"

"Not in these shoes." Her gaze settled on Sir Sebastian. A broad grin spread across his face. He waved and picked up his pace. "I suspect Sir Sebastian will be joining me."

"As you wish, my lady," Henry said in a noncommittal manner, but there was a distinct hint of approval in his tone.

Portia's relations weren't the only ones who thought three years was long enough to mourn for a woman of her age. Still, if Henry knew exactly what she had in mind, his disapproval would show on his face. The benefit of having servants who had been with you for years was unquestioned loyalty. They were nearly as much a part of her family as her blood relations. On the other hand, while Henry and the others were too well trained to say anything aloud, they were not at all reluctant to let their opinions of her behavior show. She often wondered how difficult it was to be a properly trained servant with a mistress who preferred her own rules to those of society's.

"Good day, Lady Smithson." Enthusiasm rang in Sir Sebastian's voice. She did hope it was for her.

"Good day, Sir Sebastian." She nodded. "I'm surprised to find you on foot. I thought you intended to drive today."

"On a day like this? Never." He drew a deep breath and glanced around. Apparently his enthusiasm was for the weather. "What a fine day this is."

"Is it?" She raised a brow. "One might think it rather cold."

"I find it refreshing." He drew another breath deep into his lungs. "And most stimulating. Makes the blood rush through your veins."

"In a futile effort to keep warm, no doubt," she said under her breath.

He laughed. "Come now, Lady Smithson. Admittedly, it is a little colder than usual for this time of year, but there is something about the sharp tang of cold air that makes one feel alive."

"I should think someone who has frequented the tropical climes as you have would be averse to the cold."

"Just the opposite." He shook his head. "When one has felt sun so intense it blisters the skin, one appreciates the more varied climate one has lived in most of one's life. At least I do."

"Perhaps your next adventure, then, should be as a member of a polar expedition."

He scoffed. "I daresay that is too cold even for me. But this is a perfect day to walk. Will you join me?"

She smiled. "I would be delighted. Henry," she called to her driver. "I believe I will walk, after all."

Henry choked, then coughed. "As you wish, my lady."

"If you would be so good as to follow us."

Sir Sebastian opened the carriage door and helped her out. His hand on her arm was warm and firm. Once more, a lovely sense of anticipation shivered through her. He offered his arm, and they started off at a sedate pace. He was half a head taller than she, but matched his longer strides to hers.

"Tell me, Sir Sebastian, do you intend to stay in England long, or are you already planning another venture?"

"My plans are never entirely certain." He chuckled. "But, at the moment, I shall stay in England for the foreseeable future. I would rather like to concentrate on my writing for a time. Most people will never see the places I've been, and I must say I find a great deal of satisfaction in sharing my adventures. I am toying as well with using my own experiences as the basis for fictional works."

"Like Mr. Haggard and his Allan Quatermain?"

"Something like that."

"*King Solomon's Mines* has been most successful, you know. It was advertised as the most amazing book ever written."

He glanced at her. "Have you read it?"

"Not yet. I must confess my reading of late has been confined to the true adventures of Sir Sebastian Hadley-Attwater."

"And?"

She raised a brow. "Hoping for a compliment?"

He grinned. "Absolutely."

"Very well." She thought for a moment. "I found your books most intriguing. I like, as well, the way you set words to paper, the style of your writing, as it were. In truth, though, I can't imagine the adventures of a fictional hero to be any more compelling than what you have actually experienced. Is that compliment enough?"

"It will do." He nodded. "Aside from pursuing my writing, this is home, and I must confess, I have missed it."

Surprise widened her eyes. "Have you really?"

"Shocking, isn't it?" He chuckled. "One doesn't think of men like myself as being especially sentimental about things like home and family." He glanced at her. "I have a rather extensive family, you know."

"Portia has mentioned that." She nodded. "Three sisters, I believe, in addition to your cousin, as well as two older brothers."

"In truth, I am the youngest of four brothers, but my eldest brother, Richard, died several years ago."

Sympathy washed through her. "My condolences, Sir Sebastian."

He shrugged as if it didn't matter, but the shadow that passed over his eyes told her otherwise. "He was never quite as robust as the rest of us." His good humor returned and he grinned. "We are a hardy lot. Even Portia, although I daresay she would prefer not to be considered as such."

"No, hardy is not a quality Portia aspires to." Veronica chuckled. "However, she has mentioned the need for resilience when one is raised with seven other children."

"Make no mistake, the stubborn nature of my siblings in no way negates the stodginess of the family as a whole." He shook his head in a mournful manner. "Portia is not alone in her admiration for propriety. We are a remarkably proper family, eminently respectable and not at all prone to scandal."

"Except for you?"

"I've always enjoyed a good scandal, much to my family's dismay." He leaned closer in a confidential manner. "I am the black sheep of the group, you see."

"You do have a certain reputation."

He chuckled. "I assure you, while it is not unearned, it is somewhat exaggerated."

"It would have to be, wouldn't it?" She cast him a pleasant smile.

"One of the more annoying costs of notoriety."

"Annoying? I find that difficult to believe."

He shook his head. "I much prefer to be credited with those things I actually do, good and not as good, rather than those I am simply assumed to have done."

"Then you have not been with legions of women?"

He choked. "Good Lord, Lady Smithson." He shook his head in amusement. "You are direct."

She raised a shoulder in a casual shrug. "Didn't Portia warn you?"

"She did say you were most outspoken. She finds it shocking."

"Might I confide something to you, Sir Sebastian?"

His eyes widened slightly. "Please do."

"From the moment I met her, there is nothing I find quite so enjoyable as shocking Portia."

He grinned in a wicked manner. "It is fun, isn't it?"

"And irresistible." She laughed. "Tell me, do you enjoy shocking the rest of your family as well?"

"My family is easily shocked." He blew a long breath. "Everyone would have been much happier if I had studied law or served in the military or even gone into some sort of reputable business. Or the church." He raised a brow. "Can you see me as a member of the clergy?"

"I daresay your sermons would be most interesting."

"I would be defrocked after the very first, I fear." He laughed. "Even then there are those in the family who would prefer an inept parson to an adventurer, traveler, author, lecturer—"

"Don't forget explorer."

"Explorer is a relative title and loosely given to anyone who ventures outside of the normal boundaries of experience. I think it should be earned." He shook his head. "I have never been the first civilized man to step foot upon an unknown land. I have never discovered a lost civilization or the heretofore unknown headwaters of a significant river. Nor have I ever made an important discovery of any kind, although I have had a grand time of it."

"I see." She studied him for a moment. "Do you regret that?"

"Having a grand time?" He flashed her a grin. "Not for a moment."

"I meant not discovering anything of importance."

"I should, shouldn't I? It would have been nice, I suppose." They walked on in a companionable silence for a few moments. "It was not my intention to discover undiscovered worlds when I first set out on my life of travel. Although it was what one might call an instrument of discovery that set me on my course through life."

"Oh?"

He stopped, reached into his waistcoat pocket, and pulled out a small pocket compass. "I found this in an old trunk when I was a boy. No one in the family seemed to know who it belonged to, but it is quite old. I've kept it with me ever since. It is my most prized possession, I suppose." He held it out to her, and she took it curiously. It was still warm from the heat of his body. "There's an inscription on the back."

She flipped it over and studied the faint engraving. "*In Ambitu, Gloria.*" She glanced at him. "I was never good at Latin. What does it mean?"

"In the quest, glory."

"Is that a family motto?" She handed the compass back to him.

"No, simply mine now." He replaced the item in his pocket. "It suits me. The journey being more important than the destination, that is."

"How profound." She thought for a moment. "If you did not intend to discover the undiscovered, was your only intention in your choice of profession to shock your family?"

He stared at her, amusement in his blue eyes. "Lady Smithson, if I didn't know better, I would think you were a journalist for one of those periodicals that never seem to have their facts correct." His brows drew together in mock suspicion. "Are you?"

"Of course not." She laughed. "But what a splendid idea."

"You do ask a lot of questions."

"And you manage not to answer many of them."

He winced. "My apologies. I don't mean to be evasive. I simply don't have the answers." He thought for a moment. "When I began what has admittedly been a most interesting life thus far, I had no particular goal except, perhaps, as you have noted, not to do what was expected of me by my family." He fixed her with a firm look. "It is not an admirable goal upon which to base one's life."

"And yet you seem to have succeeded at it admirably."

"Believe me, no one is more shocked by that than I am."

She laughed. He offered his arm, and they started off again.

"The paths in life I was expected to take all seemed dreadfully dull. The idea of spending my days in any sort of profession that had no appeal was, to me, a fate worse than death. Existence rather than living. If that makes any sense."

She nodded. "At least you had a choice."

"What do you mean?"

"As a man you could do whatever you wished, whether your family approved or not. Women have no such options."

"And yet, as I understand, *you* do precisely as you please."

"I am not typical of my gender." She smiled. "I am fortunate in that I have a very progressively minded family. In addition, I have never had to be dependent upon others for my welfare. There is nothing more freeing from the strictures of society than having the financial resources to do as one wishes. Most women are not that lucky."

"Luck should never be underestimated." He chuckled. "I have learned that it is usually better to have luck on one's side than skill. Luck is often what places you in the right place at the right time. Luck is what makes you bend to dislodge a pebble from your shoe and thus avoid an arrow whizzing by your head."

"You wrote about that incident." She clung tighter to his arm, merely in an effort to share his warmth. Nothing more than that. "I would say luck is something of an understatement."

"And luck, Lady Smithson . . ." He met her gaze firmly. "Luck is what makes your favorite cousin become fast friends with the lady who is going to change your life."

Her heart leapt, which made no sense at all. This was not to be an affair of the heart. There would be affection, certainly, but nothing more. Apparently, her heart wasn't aware of her plans. Odd, she'd never known it to be rebellious before.

She sniffed. "What utter nonsense."

"I'm very good at utter nonsense," he said in a sober manner. "As well as infernal nonsense, splendid nonsense, and that's quite enough nonsense, if you please."

"Then that's quite enough nonsense, Sir Sebastian, if you please." She tried and failed to hide a grin. The man was most amusing.

"Would you do me the honor of calling me Sebastian?"

"That would be most improper," she said in a lofty manner.

"Ah, but neither you nor I am especially enamored of propriety."

"Still . . ."

He leaned close in a conspiratorial manner. "It would scandalize Portia, you know."

"Then there is no choice. Sebastian it is." She paused. "And in turn, we shall dispense with Lady Smithson. I am simply Veronica."

"There is nothing simple about you, Veronica." His tone was casual. "I suspect I will discover you are the most complicated woman I have ever met. And that . . ." He covered her hand on his arm with his. "Is an exploration I fully intend to be successful."

Again her treacherous heart fluttered. She ignored it and adopted a flippant tone. "Well, I am the lady who is going to change your life, after all."

He smiled an altogether too satisfied smile.

She studied him curiously. "What exactly did you mean by that?"

"I should think it's self-explanatory."

"Apparently not." She drew her brows together. This was not going entirely as she had planned. First, he had her agreeing, or at least not disagreeing about the weather, and she couldn't recall the last time she had acquiesced to anyone else's opinion on the weather or anything else. Then he had her walking, which she'd had no desire to do, as it was indeed bloody cold and her shoes, while quite fetching, were not conducive to long walks. She'd had no intention of walking and yet here she was. Admittedly, he was amusing and candid and undeniably charming. She had no idea how it happened, but somehow he had the upper hand with no more than the utterance of one enigmatic comment about her changing his life. What utter non—how absurd.

She stopped, unhooked her arm from his, and drew a deep breath. "Sebastian, I—" Without warning she sneezed.

"Good Lord, you're cold, aren't you?" Concern showed in his eyes. "My apologies, Veronica. How thoughtless of me." He took her gloved hands in his and rubbed them briskly. "I should have realized. You're really not dressed for a walk." He tucked her hand back in the crook of his arm and walked her back to her carriage. "Can you ever forgive me?"

She stared at him. "It's really not—"

"Allow me to make amends." They reached her carriage, and he turned toward her. "I have tickets for the play at the Prince's Theater three nights from tonight, and three nights after that is a banquet at the Explorers Club in honor of something or other. I would be delighted if you would join me on both those evenings."

She shook her head. "I'm not at all sure—"

"And your delightful aunt as well," he added. "To observe all those rules of propriety, of course."

"I thought we were of one mind on our view of propriety?"

"Indeed we are." He took her hand and raised it to his

lips, his gaze locked with hers. "I have every intention of flouting propriety with you, Veronica, but not quite yet."

"No?"

"No," he said firmly, helped her into the carriage, and turned to her driver. "Henry."

"Yes, sir?" Henry said.

"Henry, please take Lady Smithson directly home and see to it she is properly warmed." Sebastian leaned close and lowered his voice. "I regret I cannot see to it myself."

Heat washed up her face and she ignored it, lowering her voice to match his. "What do you mean by 'not yet'? What are your intentions?"

"Come now, Veronica, you really don't want to know. It would spoil all your fun." A wicked light flashed in his eyes. "And mine." He signaled to Henry and the carriage started off.

"I haven't agreed to the theater or the banquet," she called after him. "I may well have previous plans!"

He grinned that same satisfied smile she'd seen before, touched the brim of his hat in farewell, and nodded. "Good day, Lady Smithson."

He turned and strode off. She stared after him. No, this was not at all as she thought this first encounter would go. Admittedly, she wasn't sure how she had expected this meeting to be. She certainly hadn't planned to ask him of his intentions. It scarcely mattered. She had intentions of her own. And she intended to become his mistress. Why, one could easily say she was in pursuit of him, not the other way around. Apparently, the blasted man didn't understand that.

Somehow, she'd lost control of the situation. He had her . . . flustered. That was what it was. Flustered. Veronica Smithson was never flustered, and she didn't like it one bit. Then there were those moments when an odd sort of yearning had fluttered within her. What on earth was the matter with her? Well, things would be different when she met him at the theater. If she met him at the theater, that is.

That was as much utter nonsense as anything he had said. Of course she would attend. As for bringing her aunt, that would defeat the purpose of being alone with him. Still, it was not a bad idea, at least in the beginning. It would be proper and, more important, safe.

She gasped at the thought. Good Lord! She'd never been concerned with *safe* before. Women who planned to become mistresses were certainly not worried about *safe*. Even so, there was something about that man that struck her as dangerous somewhere deep inside her. To that treacherous heart of hers, no doubt. It had no business leaping or fluttering. There would be no yearning or aching or any of that nonsense.

That obviously explained why he had flustered her. She had never pursued a man before, and her heart was confused as to her intentions. While there would be affection, there would be no question of love. It was her observation that love mucked up everything and prodded women to make foolish choices. She was not looking for love. She'd had it once, and it was quite wonderful. Besides, the chances that any man could love her for who she was, not who he thought she should be, were infinitesimal and not worth pursuing.

Those were her terms, and from this moment on, this— whatever *this* was to be with Sebastian—would be on her terms, not his.

"I do hope your intentions are not the least bit honorable," she said under her breath and settled back in her seat. "Mine certainly aren't."

Chapter 5

"And where are we off to tonight?" Fordham Sinclair leaned against the jamb of the open parlor door at the foot of the stairs, a glass of brandy in his hand, his casual manner belying the formality of his clothes. His gaze swept over Sebastian. "And so formally attired."

"No more so than you. Although I daresay it suits me better." Sebastian adjusted the cuffs at his wrists.

"You're English." Sinclair sipped his brandy. "You were born to be stiff and stodgy and wear uncomfortable clothes." He glanced around the foyer. "And live in drafty houses."

"Might I point out this is your house, not mine."

He shrugged. "Not by choice."

Sinclair's residence, which he graciously shared with Sebastian whenever one or both of them were in London, belonged to his family but was at his disposal. The product of an American railroad magnate father and the youngest daughter of the Earl of Marsham, Sinclair nonetheless considered himself fully American. He was no better at obligatory visits to his English relations than Sebastian. That, plus their similar natures and passion for exotic locales, was among the factors that had made them partners in adventure and travel, as well as fast friends, through the six years of their acquaintance.

"Per the telegram from my father that arrived today, I am being forced to represent my family at what will, no doubt, be a dreadfully dull evening at the American embassy."

"Forced?"

"It was a request that left little doubt as to my attendance." He raised his glass. "I am preparing myself."

Though the heir to enormous fortunes on both sides of his family, Sinclair was no more enamored of his family's expectations for him than Sebastian had been with his own. Yet another thing the friends had in common.

"You might enjoy it."

"Oh, I fully intend to enjoy it. One way or another." His expression brightened. "Say, you're already dressed for the occasion. Why don't you come with me? Moral support, as it were, for your closest friend."

"Sorry, old man. I am attending the theater." Sebastian stepped to the mirror that hung in the foyer and assessed his image. "There is nothing like a night at the theater. You should try it."

"I have tried it." Sinclair swirled the brandy in his glass and studied him suspiciously. "While I am not especially averse to it, and God knows tonight I would rather attend the most boring of plays than the most sparkling embassy party—"

Sebastian choked.

"It is not my first choice of how to spend my evening. Nor has it ever been yours."

Sebastian ignored him, studying his image in the mirror. "Is my tie straight?"

"No." Sinclair's eyes narrowed. "Is this part of your plan to prove to your family that you have changed?"

"It's the theater, Sinclair," Sebastian said coolly. Both men were more accustomed to casual clothing than the stiff collars and white ties required for formal occasions, although Sinclair appeared far more at ease than Sebastian felt. No doubt the brandy had something to do with that. He adjusted the tie. "It's scarcely a watermark of respectability."

"I suppose that depends. What are you going to see?"

"An opera, I think." Sebastian paused. "Or maybe Shakespeare. I don't remember."

"Ah, well, that explains it."

"*The School for Scandal,*" Sebastian said. "That's it. That's the name of the play." Sebastian met his friend's gaze in the mirror. "Explains what?"

"I asked the wrong question. The question isn't so much what you are going to see but rather who."

Sebastian smiled. "Is the tie straight now?"

"No. Try again." Sinclair returned his grin. "Who is she?"

"*She* is Lady Smithson." Sebastian huffed in frustration and yanked the tie free. He blew a long breath and started over. This blasted noose would not get the best of him.

"Lady Smithson? A new acquaintance?"

"She was at my lecture," he said absently, concentrating on the stubborn silk around his neck. "She has the most amazing dark red hair and deep brown eyes that flash when she is amused."

Sinclair smirked. "Now I understand."

"It's not like that," Sebastian said in a sharper tone than he had intended.

"Like what?"

"She is not another mere admirer. Veronica is a friend of my cousin."

Sinclair's brow furrowed. "The very proper cousin?"

"Portia, yes." Sebastian studied the newly tied neck-cloth. Perhaps a jaunty angle was best, after all. He did have a certain reputation to maintain.

"At last the fog lifts." Sinclair nodded knowingly.

"And all has become clear?"

"As crystal, my friend."

Sebastian turned to his friend. "Then do tell me. What profound revelation has struck you?"

"You want your family to see you as respectable and responsible. Therefore you cultivate certain symbols." Sinclair nodded sagely. "The symbols of responsibility."

"Oh?" Sebastian considered his friend with amusement. "I had no idea you were so wise." He crossed his arms over his chest. "Tell me more about these symbols."

Sinclair circled him in the foyer like a great cat stalking his prey. "What else would you call an estate complete with a grand house in the country? What was the name of it?"

"Greyville Hall, and admittedly it's large, but it's not grand," Sebastian said quickly. "It was once and hopefully will be again. It needs a great deal of work, which will cost a great deal of money."

"You got it for a good price, did you not?"

"Practically stole it."

Sinclair winced. "There is nothing more responsible than a man who pursues a bargain. Symbolically, that is."

Sebastian laughed. "That's absurd, but most amusing. Do go on."

"Next, you intend to curtail your travels for the immediate future." Sinclair shook his head in a mournful manner. "To write not merely of your own adventures but adventurous fiction for those people too cowardly to chance adventures of their own."

"Surely you would not deny those who do not have your fortitude, or fortune, I might add, the chance to experience the thrill of adventures, fictitious or otherwise."

"Oh, then this is a charitable enterprise?"

"Not at all," Sebastian said. "I expect it to be even more profitable than my previous works."

"So that you may pour money into your crumbling manor in the country?"

"Exactly."

"That"—Sinclair paused and aimed his glass at his friend—"is the very definition of responsible."

Sebastian grinned. "Then my plan is working."

"Add the friend of your proper cousin on your arm and your brothers can't help but approve your inheritance."

Sebastian shook his head. "My inheritance has nothing to do with Veronica."

"Come now, you can't tell me that after the respectable house and responsible profession, the idea of a proper"—the American winced—"wife hasn't crossed your mind."

"Admittedly, it has occurred to me—"

Sinclair groaned.

"But," Sebastian added quickly, "I have no intention of marrying anyone simply to get an inheritance or the respect of my brothers. And from what I know thus far, Veronica is not what anyone would call proper. At least not entirely. And I have no idea if I wish to marry her or not."

"Veronica?" Sinclair's brow rose.

"That would be her name, yes."

Sinclair studied him for a long moment. He chose his words with care. "I am going to tell you something I never thought I would say to you."

The tone of the conversation was at once serious. Sebastian stared at his friend. "What is it?"

"When we are engaged in a game of cards and you are bluffing, in fact whenever you say anything that isn't the complete truth, a muscle on the side of your jaw twitches. I noticed it years ago."

"Why didn't you ever tell me?"

Sinclair scoffed. "Why would I?"

Sebastian narrowed his gaze. "I suspect you owe me some of the winnings you have taken from me through the years."

"You should be grateful I never shared my discovery. As for *my* winnings, they are a burden of guilt I am willing to bear. I'm only telling you now because that muscle is twitching."

"Nonsense."

"Which means either you are not being entirely truthful about using this woman to get your family's approval or you have already decided to marry her." Sinclair sipped his brandy thoughtfully. "I'm just not sure if you're lying to me or yourself."

"As I said, marriage is not a step I would take simply to get an inheritance. As for marrying Veronica . . ." He chose his words with care. "There have been any number of incidents through the years—you and I have discussed them at length—when we have been forced to rely on nothing more than instinct. A sixth sense, if you will, that has yet to fail either of us."

Sinclair's eyes narrowed. "And?"

"And now that same instinct is telling me that if I do not make this woman part of my life for the rest of my days, I will regret it. So it's possible I have decided. It sounds mad, doesn't it?"

"At the very least. You scarcely know her."

"I suspect marriage will afford me the opportunity to know her much, much better."

Sinclair stared. "That sounds like a decision to me."

"Yes, I suppose it is."

"Are you in love with her?"

"Perhaps. Almost. I don't know. I do know I haven't been able to think of much else but her since we first met." He shook his head. "I've never experienced that before."

"Never?"

"Not that I can recall."

"Not even with the French ambassador's daughter in Cairo?"

"No."

"Or that lovely widow in Algiers?"

Sebastian shuddered. "Heavens no."

"Or with the—"

"No," Sebastian snapped. "Not once, not ever."

"That is interesting." Sinclair studied him for a long moment, then smiled and raised his glass. "Good luck to you, then."

"I shall probably need it. Veronica Smithson may well pose the greatest challenge I have ever faced." He cast his friend a confident smile. "But then I suspect she will be the grandest adventure as well."

Still, there would be no adventure at all if the blasted woman refused to make an appearance.

Sebastian resisted the urge to get to his feet and check the corridor outside the private box he had reserved for tonight. Again. He forced himself to stay seated, serenely gazing out at the theater seats filling on the floor beneath this level of boxes. Veronica hadn't actually said she'd join him. But she hadn't returned the tickets he'd had delivered to her house yesterday, either. Two tickets, of course. He grimaced. While having her aunt accompany them was not his idea of the perfect evening, it would be best to avoid undue speculation and gossip.

Odd, he'd never been concerned with the appearance of propriety before. But then he'd never considered marriage before. Sinclair was right—he hadn't been entirely truthful. While he wasn't sure if this was love or not, he did feel he stood at the edge of a very deep precipice. It was absurd, really, the speed with which these feelings had struck. He'd always thought love would grow, not pounce with the stealth and speed of a hungry tiger. If indeed love was what this was. But he hadn't been able to get her out of his head. He'd never admit it to Sinclair or anyone, but he kept seeing the two of them together in his mind's eye. Not today or tomorrow but twenty years from now. Thirty years from now. At the very end of their days.

Every rational part of him screamed this was entirely too soon. But every instinct he'd ever had, every sense he'd ever trusted or relied on told him this was right. Mad, certainly, but perhaps that was inevitable. He'd never known love or anything like this before. Who could say if this was wrong or very, very right?

And if this was right, there was a proper way to go about it. After all, one did not take excessive liberties with the woman one planned to marry.

"Did you think I wasn't coming?" A voice sounded behind him.

He bit back a satisfied grin, stood, and turned toward her. "Not for a moment."

She raised a skeptical brow.

"Very well, then, in the interest of honesty, I confess." He laughed. "There was a moment, possibly two, when I had my doubts."

"I'm not sure if I'm gratified or disappointed."

"Oh?"

"You strike me as the kind of man who is supremely confident about everything."

"I am." He took her hand and raised it to his lips, his gaze never leaving hers. "Except, perhaps, about you."

"My, that is gratifying and quite delightful." She smiled. "You do that exceptionally well, you know."

He could feel the heat of her gloved hand in his. Her scent wafted around him. A vague mix of enticing spice and exotic flowers that suggested not so much the markets of the mysterious East that he had stepped foot in but those places he'd never been. The hidden harems of that concealed world—secret and erotic and unexplored. His stomach tightened. He cleared his throat. "Do what?"

"Kiss my hand while staring into my eyes." Her tone was light, but her eyes simmered. "It's quite effective, you know."

"Thank you?"

"However"—she removed her hand from his—"it is entirely too practiced."

"But it is effective?"

"Oh my, yes."

He stifled a satisfied smile. "Even on you?"

"Goodness, Sebastian." She tilted her head and studied him. "I am female and subject to the same desires as any woman. Even if I am far too intelligent to be taken in by them."

He grinned. "Pity."

"Indeed it is," she said under her breath and moved to

a chair, one of two he had positioned far back from the box's railing.

He peered around her. "And your charming aunt? Will she be joining us this evening?"

Veronica's brow furrowed. "I do wish you would refrain from using *charming* in quite that manner."

"What manner?"

"As if it were a curse rather than a compliment."

He chuckled. "I meant it in the best possible way."

"Most people do when it comes to Aunt Lotte." She shook her head. "We encountered friends of hers in the lobby, and she decided to join them for a bit."

"To my eternal regret." He wondered if that annoying muscle in his jaw was twitching.

"But she will, no doubt, be here soon. She takes her position as chaperone very seriously."

"Does she?" Surprise raised his brows. "I wouldn't have thought she would be concerned with such matters."

She considered him thoughtfully, then sighed. "She isn't really, not usually. However, as you specifically invited her and provided her ticket, she feels under some sort of obligation to actually make an appearance." She met his gaze directly. "I tried to tell her she needn't come at all, but she insisted it would be rude as you have been so thoughtful."

Sebastian stared. "Then it was not necessary to invite her?"

"Do I strike you as the type of woman who insists on a chaperone?"

"Not exactly." Still, it was the proper thing to do.

"You should keep that in mind," she said primly. She settled in a chair and arranged her skirts around her.

"Then we are alone for now?" He took the chair beside her.

"Scarcely." She glanced around. "We are in the midst of hundreds of people."

He refrained from mentioning the obvious: With the curtains on either side of the private box, and the chairs placed well back from the railing, they were very much alone. "Yet another pity. I do like being alone with you."

"We were alone in the park," she pointed out. "Aside from Henry, of course."

"Ah, but there's an enormous difference between being alone in a park in the light of day and being here, in the dim recesses of a theater box. Why, who knows what scandalous behavior might occur?"

"Who knows indeed?" Her gaze met his, an assessing look in her eyes. "Are you intent upon scandalous behavior, then, Sebastian?"

He nodded. "Absolutely."

She smiled pleasantly. "Good."

"Good?"

"Why on earth would I be here otherwise if not to indulge in scandalous behavior? After all . . ." She leaned forward and scanned the other boxes. "I have seen this play."

"You should have told me."

"Why?"

"We could have seen something else." In truth he had picked the theater more than the play. He had been to the Prince before and was well aware of the potential for privacy in the boxes.

"But neither of us is really here for the play." She cast him a quizzical glance. "Are we?"

He stared in confusion. "Well, I did think—"

"Come now, Sebastian, in the interest of honesty, did you really wish to see *The School for Scandal*?"

"I do appreciate the theater," he said staunchly, "and—"

She laughed.

"Very well." He leaned closer to her. "The theater was simply a ploy to spend time with you, to know you better, in an altogether acceptable manner."

Her gaze slipped to his lips, then back to his eyes. "Do you intend to kiss me?"

"Indeed I do."

Her lips parted. "Now?"

"Not now." He settled back in his chair. "I do think the lights should dim before indulging in scandalous behavior."

"Then I am disappointed." She shook her head in a mournful manner. "I thought you had no concern for proper behavior."

"I don't know what's come over me."

"I should have expected it, I suppose." She sighed. "You are a well-known figure, and, no doubt, your being here has been noticed. With your reputation, just being in your presence is enough to thrust me into the center of gossip. Given your family, however . . . Well, as I said, I should have expected it. And inviting my aunt along as a chaperone confirms it. You, Sebastian Hadley-Attwater, are apparently a gentleman."

"Am I shattering yet another illusion?"

"Actually, I am pleased." She studied him for a moment. "I much prefer to share scandal with a gentleman, a man of honor. All ends so much better that way."

"I will warn you right now, I am not at all interested in endings, only beginnings. Ours." He paused and forced a casual note to his voice. "So, have you shared scandal with many gentlemen?"

Amusement curved her lips. "And you accused me of being direct."

"We are an excellent match."

"I rather thought Portia would have told you everything there is to know about me. Especially when the topic is scandal."

"Portia is remarkably discreet." While he had certainly quizzed his cousin, she revealed no more information about Veronica than what was common knowledge.

"Nonsense." Veronica scoffed. "Portia has never met a secret she could keep."

"Perhaps she thought you should tell me of your past."

"There is very little past to speak of. I have always been far more concerned with today than yesterday. However . . ." She smiled pleasantly, as if they were about to discuss something of no consequence. "It did strike me after our last meeting that, while I learned a great deal about you, we scarcely talked about me at all."

"My apologies." He winced. "How very thoughtless of me."

"Not at all." She waved off his comment. "It wasn't your fault in the least. I gave you no opportunity to ask me anything of significance or anything at all, if I recall. You did compare me to a journalist." She flashed an amused smile. "I still like that, you know."

"Regardless, I should have at least asked you if you'd seen the play."

"That's neither here nor there at the moment. But, in the interest of honesty, there are some things about me you would be wise to know." She pulled out a small folded paper from her glove. "I have made a list."

"Have you?" He chuckled. "How very efficient of you."

"I hate to waste time." She glanced at the note. "First of all, I have never minded being the subject of gossip as long as it is relatively accurate."

He nodded. "Excellent. Go on."

"I have the resources to do precisely as I please, and for the most part, I do. While I am not overly concerned with propriety, I do not go out of my way to flout it, either."

"Very clever."

"Yes, it is. I am clever, and I see no need to hide my intelligence."

"Nor should you."

"I enjoy nothing so much as a good argument."

He grinned. "That I have noticed."

"Unless, of course, it's a grand hat."

"I have noticed that as well."

"I expect my opinions to be respected." Her eyes narrowed. "Even when they disagree with yours."

"I see."

She pinned him with a firm look. "I do not believe in regrets."

"Nor do I."

"I cherish my independence and my freedom."

"Understandable."

"At the end of my life, I want my epitaph to be 'She was never dull.' "

He chuckled. "I shall remember that." He glanced at the note. "Is that all?"

"For now." She refolded the paper. "Unless there is something else you wish to know."

"There is a great deal I wish to know. But none of it is written there." He plucked the note from her hand, crumpled it, then tossed it aside. "Indeed, I have a list of my own."

She laughed. "Oh, then please, do tell me."

"I know how your eyes flash when you are amused." He leaned closer. "I want to see them glaze in the heat of desire."

"Do you?" Her lovely brown eyes widened, but she did not lean back. *How interesting.*

"I want to know how your lips feel pressed against my lips." He lowered his voice. "How it feels to have your breath mingled with mine."

"Really?" Amusement sparked in her dark eyes.

"Really." He leaned closer. "I want to know if your skin is as silken as it looks when your naked leg is wrapped around mine."

"My . . ." The word was little more than a sigh curving her lips in a slight smile.

"I want to know how the beat of your heart feels pressed against my chest."

"Goodness . . ." A breathless note sounded in her voice.

"I want to know the fullness of your breast under my hand, the curve of your hip beneath my fingers."

She leaned toward him. "Sebastian . . ."

"I want to know if your hair spread across my pillow glows like red gold in the morning light."

"The morning?" She stared into his eyes. "I have always loved mornings."

His gaze locked with hers, his lips scarcely a breath away from hers. "I want to know how it sounds when you scream out my name. How it feels when you cling to me in the throes of passion."

"Oh . . . my . . ."

"I want to know"—his lips whispered against hers—"how you look when—"

The door to the corridor swung open, and Sebastian jumped to his feet. *Bloody hell.* Veronica drew a deep breath.

"Here you are." Miss Bramhall swept into the box. "I feared I would miss the beginning. One should never miss the opening lines, you know, even if one has seen the play before. The opening lines set the premise for the entire production."

"Miss Bramhall." Sebastian stepped to the older woman and took her hand. "How delightful to see you again."

"I must say I was surprised by your invitation, Sir Sebastian." Miss Bramhall cast a speculative look at her niece. "Although I was pleased."

"I am delighted you could join me," he said in his most gallant manner.

"I thought you intended to stay with your friends, Aunt Lotte." Veronica cast the older woman a serene smile. Admiration swept through him. He knew full well she had been as affected as he by his list, yet now she didn't appear the least bit flustered. It had taken all he had just to keep his hands from shaking.

Miss Bramhall took the chair he had vacated. "Now then, Sir Sebastian, tell me about this banquet at the Explorers Club. It's not just for their male members?"

"As I understand it, many of the gentlemen will be attending with their wives." The moment the words were out of his mouth, he realized his mistake.

"Humph," Miss Bramhall huffed. "The only way women get into that sanctuary is to attend public lectures or to marry one of those old fools who run the place."

"You really shouldn't refer to Sir Hugo as an old fool," Veronica said firmly.

"Why not?" Miss Bramhall's brows pulled together. "He is."

"Nonetheless, it does your cause no good whatsoever to antagonize him." Veronica looked up at Sebastian. "Don't you agree?"

"Yes and no." He chose his words with care. Veronica's aunt could well be an ally if he needed one at some point. "On one hand, I agree with Lady Smithson that never-ending provocation of Sir Hugo does not endear your case to him."

Miss Bramhall's eyes narrowed.

"However, there is also the question of whether or not Sir Hugo is indeed an old fool." He chuckled. "I admit I have heard him called far worse."

Miss Bramhall's expression eased.

"Furthermore, as he is not present to hear himself being called an old fool, I see no reason why Miss Bramhall should keep her opinions to herself." He smiled at the older lady. "And you have my word, he will not hear of your comments from my lips."

"It scarcely matters." Miss Bramhall shrugged but was clearly placated by Sebastian's words. "He knows exactly what I think of him."

"Well played, Sir Sebastian," Veronica said with a smile. "Well played indeed."

Miss Bramhall glanced at her niece. "It was at that." She turned her attention back to Sebastian. "You do realize that inviting us, specifically me, might not be especially wise."

"He needn't have invited you at all. I have no need of a chaperone."

"I was told I could invite whomever I wished as I am among those being recognized at the event," he said staunchly.

"It may be somewhat awkward," Miss Bramhall warned.

"On the contrary." Sebastian grinned. "I anticipate a most stimulating evening."

Veronica choked back a laugh.

"Yes, well, we shall see." Miss Bramhall chuckled. "Thank you, Sir Sebastian. I am quite looking forward to it."

"As are we all," Veronica said.

The lights in the theater dimmed.

"This chair is entirely too far back." The older lady stood. "Sir Sebastian, if you would be so good." He obediently moved it closer to the railing. She looked at Veronica. "Aren't you going to move forward? You can barely see the stage from there."

"I am quite comfortable here," Veronica said smoothly. "My view is more than adequate."

"As you wish." Miss Bramhall took her seat, then gestured at Sebastian to join her. This was not what he'd had in mind. He glanced from one woman to the other, then surrendered and moved a chair into place beside Veronica's aunt. "But don't expect Sir Sebastian or me to explain anything you might miss."

"Of course not." Veronica covered her mouth to hide what was obviously a grin.

Sebastian cast her a pleading look. Her gaze met his and laughter danced in her eyes.

"Perhaps you're right." Veronica stood and, before he could assist her, moved her chair into place on the other side of her aunt and then sat. "Oh my, yes, this is much better. Don't you agree, Sir Sebastian?"

He smiled weakly. "Yes, it's an excellent view."

"Hush, both of you," Miss Bramhall said. "The play is about to begin. Oh, I do so love farce."

"Don't we all, Aunt Lotte?" Veronica grinned. "Don't we all?"

Chapter 6

It was perhaps the longest play Sebastian had ever had the misfortune of sitting through. Not that it wasn't amusing, even if its humor was lost on him. He was in the midst of a farce of his own.

He had known privacy with Veronica would be next to impossible with her aunt present. But the occasional stolen glance shared with her when Miss Bramhall leaned forward to get a closer view was not what he'd hoped for when he'd reserved this private box. He had planned to sit beside her and much farther back than Miss Bramhall preferred. But then Veronica's aunt was interested in the play.

He had hoped for the occasional accidental brush of her hand with his. The intermittent mutual observance whispered in her ear, commentary on the play or the crowd in display of his cleverness. Even, with luck, a kiss shared in the dark recesses of the box when her aunt's attention was elsewhere.

It was both annoying and frustrating. It was all he could do to keep from drumming his fingers impatiently on the arm of his chair. Or leaping from his seat and sweeping her into his arms in front of her aunt and the entire theater and God himself. As a grand romantic gesture, it had definite appeal. It would certainly be more dramatic than anything happening onstage and would have been worth considering if he wasn't trying to behave in a proper manner.

One did not embroil the lady one intended to marry in undue scandal. But, damnation, it was proving more difficult than he had imagined.

Still, it could have been worse. Miss Bramhall could have been with them right from the beginning. At least he'd had the opportunity to discuss his *list* with Veronica. And that had gone well. He smiled to himself. Very, very well. There was little doubt the woman was as taken with him as he was with her.

At last the houselights came on for intermission. Hopefully, Miss Bramhall could be encouraged to rejoin her friends. Or, at the very least, the chairs could be rearranged.

"Sir Sebastian," Miss Bramhall said in a cordial manner. Perhaps her obvious enjoyment of the play had eased her earlier pique. "I find I am exceptionally parched. Would you fetch us some refreshment?"

"It would be my pleasure." He groaned to himself and stood. Apparently, she planned to remain with them.

Veronica smiled wryly, as if she knew exactly what he was thinking.

"On second thought, I shall accompany you." Miss Bramhall rose to her feet. "I saw Lady Lovett earlier, and I should like to have a word with her before the play resumes."

"Do take as long as you wish," Veronica said. "I dare-say we shall bravely carry on without you."

"I've no doubt of that, my dear." Miss Bramhall nod-ded to Sebastian to open the door and then passed in front of him.

"Sebastian," Veronica said in a low voice. He turned back to her. "That last bit of utter nonsense about your list."

"Yes?"

"It didn't seem the least bit practiced." She cast him a provocative smile, and his heart caught. Odd that a mere smile could do that. "And it was most effective."

He grinned. "Was it?"

"Oh, it was indeed." She rose, stepped to him and, be-fore he could say a word, framed his face with her hands, then pressed her lips to his.

Her lips were warm and full against his. And intoxicat-ing, like a fine wine that had gone directly to his head. A faint ache squeezed his heart.

"Most effective."

He slid his hands around her waist, but she stepped back. "Aunt Lotte is waiting."

"Yes, right, of course." He drew a deep breath. "And this is not the place. . . ."

"But do hurry back."

He nodded and followed her aunt, his step lighter than it would have been a moment ago.

The corridor was crowded with theater patrons, and he had to dodge one person after another to keep up with her. They reached the vestibule, and she stepped to one side, then turned to him.

"I would like a word with you, Sir Sebastian," Miss Bramhall said in a no-nonsense manner.

At once he felt as if he were ten years old again and

had been caught doing something he shouldn't. How absurd. He was an adult, a man of accomplishment. He had faced far greater dangers than this short, determined termagant.

He adopted his most charming manner. "Anything for you, Miss Bramhall."

"First of all, I was quite impressed that you included me in your invitations for tonight and the banquet."

"It seemed the proper thing to do." He had nothing to fear at all.

She studied him for a moment, then laughed. "Goodness, young man, the last thing Veronica is concerned with is propriety."

"Then one of us should be," he said and winced to himself. Good Lord, he sounded like one of his older brothers. "What I mean is that I would not wish to subject Lady Smithson to undue gossip."

"Excellent answer." She nodded thoughtfully. "Veronica's mother died when she was very young. My mother and I helped her father, my brother, raise her. My brother is often something of an idiot, but a good man nonetheless. My mother and I are both . . . Oh, what is the word?"

Any number of words sprang to Sebastian's mind. He ignored them.

"Independent, I would say, is most appropriate. Veronica has been strongly influenced by our opinions." She pinned him with a firm look. "You should keep that in mind."

"I will. Thank you."

"You're not at all as I expected, you know."

He raised a brow. "Is that good?"

"I haven't decided. You are a man, and generally I have found men not to be trusted." She paused for a moment. "I should ask you if your intentions are honorable."

He opened his mouth to respond, but she held up her hand to stop him. "No, I don't wish to know. It's none of my concern. We value privacy in my family as much as we do independence. Veronica is not a child and is intelligent enough to make her own decisions about such things."

"I really do think—"

"No, no." She thrust her hand out in front of her. "My opinion of you at the moment is most favorable. If you tell me your intentions are honorable, I shall feel compelled to intercede on your behalf, and that wouldn't do at all. Or I won't believe you, which is worse. If you say they are not honorable, I shall think you quite stupid to admit such a thing, even if I will give you credit for honesty. I shall also feel it necessary to convey your intentions to Veronica, and I don't know what her response might be."

"Wouldn't most women be pleased if a man's intentions were honorable?" he said slowly.

"Veronica is not *most women*." She sniffed. "Nor are any of the women in her family. You would be wise to remember that as well."

"I will."

"Now"—she scanned the crowd—"there is still time for a quick chat with Lady Lovett before the play resumes." A wicked light shone in her eye. "I suspect if you hurry, you might be able to return to the box before I do."

He chuckled. "Then I shall hurry."

"One more thing, Sir Sebastian." She studied him intently. "The heart of even the strongest woman can be exceptionally fragile. Veronica is the daughter I never had." A warning sounded in her voice. "And I have a very long memory, as Sir Hugo will attest."

"I don't doubt it for a moment."

"And, dear boy." She leaned close and lowered her

voice. "Do try not to be quite so obsequious. While I appreciate the effort, it's not at all attractive." Her gaze flicked over him. "And you are most attractive."

". . . and he returned to the box moments before the intermission ended, with Aunt Lotte right on his heels." Veronica tapped her fingers impatiently on the table in the ladies' reading room of Fenwick and Sons, Booksellers. "As I had already seen the play—"

"And who hasn't?" Portia said. "It's a very old play."

"And yet always enjoyable." Julia nodded. "I never fail to be amused by it."

"It depends on who is playing the role of Lady Sneerwell, I think." Portia nodded. "As she is the villainess of the—"

"Would you two stop discussing the theatrical merits of a silly play and turn your attention to my dilemma?" Veronica glared at her friends.

"We're not entirely sure what your dilemma is, dear." Julia sipped her tea.

"Aside from the fact that you wish to become Sebastian's mistress and he does not appear to be cooperating." Portia smiled in an altogether too smug manner. "I know I, for one, am shocked."

"His cooperation has yet to be determined." Veronica's tone was sharper than she'd intended, and she drew a calming breath.

"You expected him to leap into your bed or immediately sweep you away to his," Portia said.

"He does have that reputation."

Julia nodded. "Which is why you selected him."

"Not entirely. I also selected him because I enjoy his

books. There's something quite compelling about his writing, even, dare I say, seductive."

Portia snorted. "I've read his books. I didn't find them the least bit seductive. The very idea," she added under her breath.

"Then, when I met him . . ." Veronica blew a long breath. "I suppose I should confess all now." She paused to pull her thoughts together. "The entire idea of becoming a mistress was only a vague sort of tickle in the back of my mind. I knew I didn't want marriage and I am tired of being alone and I also knew only the right man would do. It wasn't until I actually met Sebastian that I decided on this course. And on him."

"Right there?" Portia's eyes widened. "You decided to become his mistress right there in the lecture hall? In the Explorers Club lecture hall?"

"It's not as if it's sacred ground, Portia," Julia said.

"No doubt this sort of thing is why they don't allow women to be members," Portia muttered.

Veronica ignored her. "It sounds odd, but I knew, I just knew, he was the right man for me. I was most taken with him. He's undeniably handsome, and that little scar on his forehead makes him seem mysterious."

"The scar is—"

"Yes, Portia, I know, but it doesn't matter. The way he held the crowd in his hands and how very gracious and kind he was to all his admirers, and then he was even pleasant to Aunt Lotte, well . . ."

And she couldn't stop thinking about him. Even in her sleep, he was there with his wicked smile and his endless blue eyes and his laugh. She could still feel the heat of his body beside her when they'd walked in the park. And when she'd kissed him . . . something inside her had fluttered and ached. She'd felt something similar long ago, when she'd fallen in love with Charles. But this was lust, nothing more. Nor would she allow it to be more.

Julia studied her. "Well?"

She drew a deep breath. "I found him most remarkable."

"And?" Julia said.

"And desirable."

"And?" Portia prompted.

"And, I want the man." Veronica's gaze slid from one friend to the next. "There you have it. I want him. He's the perfect Christmas gift to myself. And I am determined to have him."

"I still don't understand your dilemma," Julia said calmly.

"I don't know what I'm doing." Veronica's voice rose.

"My, that is a dilemma," Julia murmured.

"I knew it." Portia blew a relieved breath. "I knew you'd come to your senses."

"I haven't come to my senses," Veronica snapped. "I haven't lost my senses. I simply don't know how to go about this."

"About . . ." Confusion sounded in Julia's voice. "About what?"

"Seduction!"

The heads of the ladies at the next table swiveled toward them. Veronica winced. This was perhaps not the best place to have this discussion. The ladies' reading room was always full and had been since Veronica had encouraged Fenwick to offer refreshments. Or perhaps *bribe* was a better word, as her encouragement had carried with it financial incentive. Veronica was now a silent partner in Fenwick and Sons. Usually it was most gratifying to see the establishment busy, but today she would have preferred a few less patrons.

She lowered her voice and leaned closer to her friends. "I don't know how to go about seducing a man."

"You did kiss him," Julia pointed out.

Veronica waved away her comment. "A stolen moment and scarcely significant."

Portia's brow furrowed. "I wouldn't have thought this would be a problem with Sebastian."

"Nor did I, given his reputation." Veronica sighed. "But the man is being a proper gentleman. For the most part." Certainly there was his list of what he wished to know about her, which wasn't the least bit proper, but that discussion had been brief and interrupted entirely too soon. "And I don't know what to do to encourage him to be less of a gentleman. I don't want him to think—"

"That you're a tart?" Portia said sweetly.

"Yes. I suppose." Veronica huffed. "I don't want him to think that I do this sort of thing all the time. I've never seduced a man before, and I've only ever been seduced once."

Julia nodded. "By your husband."

"Yes, of course."

Portia stared. "Only by your husband?"

"Yes." Veronica narrowed her gaze. "Did you think otherwise?"

"Not at all," Julia said quickly.

"I did," Portia said. "I most certainly did."

"How could you think such a thing?" Veronica glared.

"I'm sure she didn't mean—"

"How could I not?" Portia snapped. "You're so free-thinking and independent and full of confidence and assurance. You go on and on about how women should vote and be members of men's clubs and handle their own finances and how we are every bit as competent as men to run our own lives. And how you'd rather be a mistress than a wife. You've always gotten everything you wanted because you never hesitated to take it. I assumed that, in this particular area, you would have been quite as . . . as *accomplished* as any man!"

Veronica stared in disbelief. She wasn't sure if she should be furious or . . . "Thank you."

"You're quite welcome!" Portia sniffed. "And furthermore I have always admired that about you. You do precisely as you please, regardless of what other people think. I don't agree with you about anything, but I think you're extremely courageous. And, of the two of us, I would rather be you than me!"

"Good Lord," Julia murmured.

"I do hope I haven't disappointed you," Veronica said slowly.

"Because you're not a tart?" Portia waved in an offhand gesture. "One learns to live with disappointment."

Julia snorted.

"I shall try to do better in the future." Veronica bit back a grin. "Or worse, as it were."

"See that you do," Portia said in a prim manner.

Julia looked from one friend to another. "This is the most absurd conversation we have ever had." She shook her head. "I can scarcely believe my ears. Always proper Portia is encouraging Veronica, who has never needed any encouragement whatsoever, to be improper."

"It does sound absurd when you say it that way," Portia muttered.

At once the answer struck her and Veronica stared at Portia. "But you're right." She turned toward Julia. "She's absolutely right."

Julia's brows drew together. "She is?"

"I am?" Suspicion sounded in Portia's voice.

"Completely. I have always followed my own path. I

have never doubted myself. And I have never been the least bit flustered by anyone, let alone a mere man."

Julia raised a brow. "*He* flusters *you?*"

Portia scoffed. "Surely not."

"Darling, I am sorry if I am disappointing you again, but yes. The man makes me feel . . . well . . . somewhat confused and completely . . ." She thought for a moment. "Not at all myself. That's it. I've become this tentative, hesitant creature who concerns herself with things like safety."

"Oh, no, not that," Julia said with barely concealed amusement.

Veronica ignored her. "Although I don't think he's noticed."

"No one has," Portia said under her breath.

"Why, I allowed him to do as he pleased in the park. I let him take the reins, so to speak. He wanted to walk and we walked."

"In *your* shoes?" Portia asked. "I can't imagine such a thing."

"And then he invited Aunt Lotte to accompany us as a chaperone for the theater last night and again to a banquet at the Explorers Club. We all know I have never seen the necessity of chaperones, but I never even protested."

"My, that is odd," Julia said.

"A man with his reputation does not become a proper gentleman overnight. He's up to something." Veronica drummed her fingers on the table. "I don't know what—apparently, it's not overt seduction—but I intend to find out. No man is that perfect."

"Veronica, dear." Julia laid her hand over Veronica's. "*You* are the one who is up to something. You really can't—"

"No." Portia shook her head. "She's right. This doesn't

sound at all like the Sebastian I know. I would have expected him to appear unannounced on your doorstep when he could be confident you were alone and seduce you."

Veronica huffed. "One would have thought."

"Instead he's biding his time." Portia's brows furrowed in thought. "If I didn't know better . . ." Her eyes widened. "He's courting you! That's what he's doing. As absurd as it sounds, my cousin's intentions might be completely honorable."

A heavy knot settled in Veronica's stomach, and she shook her head. "That's not at all what I have in mind."

"Well then, there's only one thing you can do." Portia leaned close and met Veronica's gaze firmly.

"Portia." A warning sounded in Julia's voice.

"Seduce him, Veronica." Portia's eyes were lit with the fire of the newly reformed. "Don't allow him to be the one to seduce you."

Julia gasped. "Portia."

"Don't give him time to plan or plot." Determination rang in Portia's voice. "Seduce him at once."

"Yes, of course." Why hadn't Veronica thought of it herself? "Unfortunately, I don't have a plan as to how I shall accomplish that now and never did. I just assumed all would fall into place."

"Oh, you definitely need a plan." Portia nodded. "I said right at the beginning that you had not given this due consideration."

"And you were absolutely right. I should have listened to you."

"Perhaps next time you will," Portia said in a lofty manner.

Veronica drew her brows together and thought for a moment. "I don't suppose either of you has a plan in mind?"

Julia and Portia traded glances.

"Veronica, dear," Julia said slowly. "In spite of Portia's moment of enthusiasm, do keep in mind that, while we might well condone this desire of yours to become Sir Sebastian's mistress, we are in no way encouraging it."

"No, indeed," Portia said quickly. "I still think it's morally reprehensible."

"Seduction was your idea," Veronica pointed out.

"Obviously, I am the one who has taken leave of her senses," Portia said, as if she were confessing a great crime. "I can only say I was swept away by the desire to help one of my gender best the opposition. The very fact that I am thinking of men, specifically my own cousin, as an opposing enemy indicates how far I have sunk." Portia heaved a heartfelt sigh. "Apparently, in spite of my best intentions and to my eternal horror, I have fallen under the influence of Veronica."

"Goodness, Portia." A wry note sounded in Julia's voice. "It's not as if she has taken you by the hand and led you astray."

"Not thus far." Veronica grinned at her friend. "But there is hope for you yet, darling."

"Yes, yes, those least likely to bend . . ." Portia rolled her gaze toward the heavens. "I know."

"A plan." Veronica thought for a moment. "I shall have to think of something clever."

Julia shrugged. "Or you could be completely honest and tell him that he is what you want for Christmas."

"I could never . . ." *Why not?* Veronica stared at Julia. "That does sound like a plan."

Portia groaned. "I am at least grateful I will not be here to see it."

Julia frowned. "Where will you be?"

"Italy," Portia said with a blithe wave of her hand. "My

aunt and I have let a villa for several weeks. I have no desire to stay here and be forced to attend one event after another in which my family will offer up eligible gentlemen like Christmas sweets."

Veronica's brow rose. "So you're running away?"

"I wouldn't put it exactly in that manner, but yes." Portia squared her shoulders. "Julia has recently married. You refuse to marry for no real reason that I can see. And, while I wish to marry again, I much prefer to find my own husband rather than have one served to me on a platter."

"Like a goose served for Christmas?" Julia grinned.

"Why, Portia." Veronica cast the other woman an affectionate smile. "How very courageous and independent of you."

"This, too, is probably a direct result of your influence." Portia shook her head in a mournful manner. "God help me."

Julia's gaze passed from one friend to the other. "I wouldn't count on God, dear. He's going to be very busy."

Chapter 7

Sinclair snapped the library doors closed behind him, then flattened his back against them as if he were barring the invasion of the barbarian hordes.

Sebastian looked up from the pages before him on the desk and stared. "What in the name of all that's holy are you doing?"

"You have guests."

"Then . . . ," Sebastian said slowly, "shouldn't you show them in?"

"I'm your friend. Your partner." Sinclair shook his head. "And I don't think showing them in is a good idea. In fact . . ." He nodded toward the window. "I think escape is a much better idea. There's a vine right outside that window, and even if it doesn't hold, it's a short drop to the ground."

"What?" Sebastian stared.

"Out the window with you. Go now. Quickly." Again Sinclair indicated the window. "I'll try to hold them off."

"I appreciate the offer but . . ." Sebastian choked back a laugh. "You've gone mad, haven't you?"

"Me? Ha." Sinclair narrowed his eyes and approached the desk. "I thought we had an arrangement, you and I."

"An arrangement?"

"About women coming here." Sinclair crossed his arms over his chest. "Women are permitted only if they are in our company. It was expressly agreed that neither one of us wanted unexpected female visitors popping in without a moment's notice. Something like that could be extremely awkward, even dangerous."

"I—"

"Especially if said female visitors are"—he shuddered—"single-minded, determined, obstinate, and unyielding."

Sebastian stared in confusion. "I don't . . . oh." He chuckled and got to his feet. "You've met Veronica."

"Good God, for your sake, I hope not." Sinclair huffed. "Besides, neither of these women has red hair."

"How many are there?" Sebastian said cautiously.

"Two." Sinclair winced. "Frightening, terrifying termagants. But admittedly, not unattractive. Quite pretty, really. Especially the shorter, fair-haired one. Although she also appears to be the most irate."

"Did these terrifying creatures give you a name?"

"I didn't have the chance—"

The library doors flew open, and two young women stormed into the room in a flurry of cloaks and furs and indignation.

"There you are!"

"How long did you think you could hide?"

Sebastian stared at the women, then chuckled. "I have no idea what you are talking about, although I can't imagine the need to be quite so adamant."

"I told you." Sinclair glared at the women.

Both women cast the American looks that would have made even the most stalwart gentleman cringe. To his credit, Sinclair didn't so much as flinch.

"I don't believe you've met my sisters," Sebastian said smoothly. "Miranda, Bianca, this is my very good friend Mr. Fordham Sinclair. Sinclair, may I present Miranda, Lady Garret, and Mrs. Bianca Roberts."

"We are his *younger* sisters," Miranda said pointedly. "He has an older sister, Diana, as well."

"How fortunate for him. It's a pleasure to meet you both," Sinclair said with a distinct lack of enthusiasm.

"We've heard a great deal about you." Bianca's gaze slid over Sinclair in a suspicious manner. Sebastian suspected his friend no longer found the shorter Bianca as pretty as he had. "Most of it quite disgraceful."

"Then you have me at a disadvantage," Sinclair said smoothly. "As I have heard nothing whatsoever about you."

His sisters aimed outraged glares at Sebastian.

He chuckled. "That's not entirely true."

"If you will excuse me." Sinclair edged toward the door. "I shall leave you to your happy family reunion."

"Impudent American," Bianca said under her breath.

"English witch," Sinclair murmured as he stalked past her.

Bianca sucked in a sharp breath and looked as if she had every intention of following Sinclair out the door to thrash him thoroughly with her bag. She took a step, but Miranda caught her arm.

"We have other matters to attend to," Miranda said firmly. Miranda was the younger of the two, but by only a year. She and Bianca were as close as if they were twins.

"Indeed we do." Bianca turned her attention to her brother. "What do you have to say for yourself?"

"I'm not sure." He propped his hip on the corner of his desk and studied his sisters. "What have I done?"

"We saw you," Bianca said.

"Dear Lord, not that!" He gasped in mock horror.

"Now is not the time for sarcasm, Sebastian." Miranda sniffed. "We saw you last night at the theater."

"And we want to know what you were doing with Lady Smithson," Bianca added. "She is not one of your trollops."

He raised a brow. "How did you know her name? Do you know her?"

"No, but we asked," Bianca said. "We know a great deal about her, and she is not at all the type of woman you usually pursue."

He frowned. "What do you mean, you know a great deal about her? You only saw her last night."

"Goodness, Sebastian." Miranda cast him a disparaging look. "It's already mid-afternoon."

"We know she is a widow and eminently respectable," Bianca began. "She has a sizable fortune at her disposal—"

"From her late husband and her own family, as we understand it," Miranda added.

"—a grand house here in town and an estate in the country as well," Bianca finished.

"My." Sebastian looked from one sister to the next. "You have been busy."

Bianca ignored him and continued. "While she has never been involved in any notable scandal, as far as we can determine, she is known to be outspoken and supportive of any number of women's causes."

"Which we quite admire, by the way," Miranda said quickly. "But we want to know why someone like her was with someone like you."

"How very flattering of you to be so shocked," he said mildly.

"Don't put words in our mouths," Miranda said sharply. Then her tone softened. "We were quite pleased to see you with a lady who isn't . . ."

"An actress or a dancer or someone not at all suitable." Bianca's eyes narrowed. "Lady Smithson is most suitable."

He chuckled. "I think so."

The sisters traded glances.

"Sebastian." A conciliatory note sounded in Bianca's voice. "Do tell us what your intentions are toward Lady Smithson."

"Are you sure you want to know?"

Bianca scoffed. "Why else would we be here?"

"Very well, then." He paused, relishing in the drama of the moment. "I intend to make Lady Smithson my wife. By Christmas."

Miranda's eyes widened. "Christmas is a scant few weeks away."

"I am well aware of that."

"Surely you haven't known this lady very long," Bianca said.

"When I see something I want, I see no need to waste time." He paused. "When I know something is right, I do not hesitate."

"How . . . how . . . ," Bianca began.

"How utterly romantic," Miranda said with a sigh.

"And terribly exciting." Bianca cast him a reluctant smile.

"I'm glad you think so."

"Oh, we do, Sebastian, we do. Some of us thought you would never marry." Bianca turned to her sister. "Wait until the family hears."

Miranda nodded. "Mother will be ecstatic. She had hoped, of course, but she thought you'd never marry. She has very nearly given up on Hugh marrying again. Wait until we tell her."

"Oh no." Sebastian shook his head. "I don't want a word of this to Mother or anyone else. I will tell everyone when the time is right."

Miranda stared. "And when is that?"

"After Veronica and I are married," he said firmly.

His sisters stared.

"In sheer numbers alone, we are a most imposing lot. I do not wish to scare her off."

Miranda scoffed. "That's absurd. We are not the least bit frightening."

"Perhaps." He narrowed his gaze. "But this is the way I wish it."

"It would be a lovely Christmas gift, you know," Bianca said. "And, if you recall, as you are usually absent, we always gather for Christmas together in the country."

"Not this year." Miranda shook her head. "It's to be a smaller group at Waterston Abbey than usual."

Bianca's brows pulled together. "Why?"

"Mother has decided to accompany Portia to Italy for Christmas, although why Portia wishes to go to Italy is beyond me. She'll miss any number of parties and gatherings."

"Perhaps she wants to avoid any more of the matchmaking I hear she has been subjected to of late." Sebastian smiled innocently.

Both sisters looked at him as if he were mad.

"As I was saying," Miranda continued, "Diana's mother-in-law is insisting they spend Christmas with her. You know how demanding she can be. Adrian and Evelyn will be there, of course."

"As it is their house," Sebastian said wryly. His older brother, Adrian, was the current Earl of Waterston and took his position as head of the family very seriously.

"Hugh will come, as will you and I." A slight wistful note sounded in Miranda's voice. No doubt she was thinking of past, more joyous, family gatherings with everyone present. She had lost her husband nearly two years ago. Hugh's wife had died some five years ago. Bianca's husband no longer shared a house with his wife. His brothers had filled him in on that situation, although neither Adrian nor Hugh knew what had caused the rift between husband and wife. For once, Bianca hadn't said a word, although he suspected Miranda knew the truth of the matter. Miranda met her brother's gaze directly. "It would be lovely if you and your new wife could join us as it has been a very long time."

"Not this year, I'm afraid," he said gently. "Perhaps I am being selfish, but I plan to spend Christmas in my new country house with my wife. Alone."

"It's not selfish at all," Bianca said staunchly. "I think it's quite romantic. We shall bravely carry on without you." She paused. "And do you plan to spend your birthday alone with your wife as well?"

"Oh, do join us, at least for your birthday." Miranda smiled at her brother. "That would be wonderful."

"I promise to give it a great deal of thought. But, this is not the only Christmas I will be in England, merely the first. You know I have bought a house. What you don't know is that I plan to curtail my travels and concentrate on my lectures and writing."

"How very . . ." Bianca chose her words with care. "Adult of you. And quite like a responsible Hadley-Attwater. It's somewhat frightening, and I'm not sure I believe it."

"We all change, Bianca, with the passage of time. What we want and how we wish to live." He smiled. "Now then, if you would care to take off your wraps, I would be happy to call for tea and we can have a nice chat."

Miranda laughed. "You've never been one for a nice chat."

Bianca studied him curiously. "If all this is the result of Lady Smithson's influence, you have our wholehearted support."

"And best wishes," Miranda said quickly. "We only want you to be happy, you know."

He grinned. "I fully intend to be."

"You should probably know, if you had chosen an actress or dancer or someone completely unsuitable"— Bianca blew a resigned breath—"we would have accepted it. All of us. Even Mother."

"I know."

"But it is much easier this way," Miranda said with a grin.

"Then it is fortunate that I had the good sense to fall in love with a suitable lady."

"Most fortunate," Bianca said firmly. "And as much as we would love to stay for tea, as, God knows, such invitations from you are unknown, we have a great deal to do. Christmas is fast approaching, and there are parties to prepare for and dinners to arrange—"

"And presents to decide upon for nieces and nephews and everyone else." Miranda paused. "I have a short list of what I might like, should you be so inclined."

"We both have lists." Bianca's eyes sparkled. "Should you be so inclined."

He chuckled. "I shall keep that in mind."

They chatted for a few moments more; then his sisters

took their leave amid hugs and promises on both sides. He did hope they would stay silent, although no one in his family had ever been good at keeping secrets. In truth, it scarcely mattered, although he would like to be the one to tell his family, if only to see the looks on their faces.

The idea of spending Christmas with Veronica at his new house had popped into his head at very nearly the moment he had said the words. And why not? His first Christmas back in England in years spent in his new house with his delectable new bride sounded very nearly perfect. Alone, with no one to bother them, save the small staff he had hired when he bought the house. And perhaps, after Christmas they would travel to Waterston Abbey, where he would introduce his wife to the rest of the family. And claim his inheritance, of course. It would be a Christmas to remember.

He brushed aside the thought that perhaps Veronica would not wish to marry a man she scarcely knew. They knew each other far better than many couples he could name did when they'd wed. And she couldn't deny that there was something unique and intense and quite wonderful simmering between them. He had no doubt the woman wanted him as much as he wanted her. Why, she'd kissed him and with her aunt scarcely out of sight.

As brief as it was, that kiss lingered in his mind. The feel of her lips against his, the warmth of her body pressed close to him, the erotic scent of her perfume conjured up all sorts of wicked images of her lying naked in his bed. The kiss was no more than a taste, really, a hint of the delight yet to come. Delight he intended to savor for the rest of his life. Desire shivered through him, and he drew a deep breath. He wasn't entirely sure how long he could continue to be on his best behavior when all he really wanted was to take her in his arms and have his way with her. He chuckled at the thought. Or let her have her way with him. After all, *she* had kissed *him*.

Oh yes, Veronica would soon be his wife. He loved her, even if he hadn't realized it himself until he'd told his sisters. He should have told Veronica first, but that was an omission easily corrected. He loved her, he wanted her, and he would have her.

Yes, indeed, this would be a Christmas to remember.

Chapter 8

"I think it's all going remarkably well, don't you?" Veronica leaned closer, her voice low and innocently seductive. "It was very brave of you to invite my aunt."

Sebastian stared into her sultry brown eyes and marveled that he wasn't drowning. Although, perhaps, he was. Or he already had. In the two days since he'd seen her, he could do little but think of her. And his determination to make this woman his wife had only grown stronger. "There is a fine line between bravery and foolishness. I'm not sure what this is yet."

Veronica glanced down the banquet table to where her aunt was seated, and his gaze followed hers. "She seems to be on her best behavior."

"As are we all," he said under his breath.

Miss Bramhall did appear less combative than she had been when last at the Explorers Club. Indeed, every time Sebastian had glanced at her thus far this evening, she had been engaged in lively, yet not confrontational, conversation with the gentlemen around her. When he'd invited Veronica and her aunt, he'd had to give the club the names of his guests. Whoever had arranged the seating had done a splendid job. The gentlemen on either side of Miss Bramhall looked like they were not merely enjoying themselves but were quite taken with the lady as well.

And why not? She was probably a year or two younger than Sir Hugo, who was in his midfifties. He hadn't noticed before, but she was a handsome woman, when her determined expression eased, and must have been quite lovely in her youth.

"Did you threaten her?"

Veronica gasped in mock dismay. "Goodness, Sebastian, I would never have done such a thing. Besides"— she smiled—"it would have been pointless."

Miss Bramhall laughed in response to something said by one of her companions.

"Correct me if I'm wrong, but is she flirting?"

Veronica chuckled. "So it would appear." She studied her aunt thoughtfully. "I'm rather surprised she remembers how."

"She does look to be enjoying herself," Sebastian said. Sir Hugo was seated farther down the table, not close enough to Miss Bramhall to engage in battle. Odd, though, whenever Sebastian glanced in the older man's direction, his gaze was on Veronica's aunt. "I believe Sir Hugo has noticed. He can't keep his eyes off of her."

Veronica chuckled. "He is probably being cautious."

"When I informed the club of my guests for tonight, I rather expected him to object. To my surprise, and relief, I didn't hear a word from him."

"That is surprising." Veronica's gaze shifted from her aunt to Sir Hugo. "And most intriguing. I don't think I've ever seen them in the same room together without doing battle. They've been adversaries for years. But, as I said, she is on her best behavior. To your credit, I think."

He raised a brow. "Mine?"

"She was most impressed that you were willing to invite her. I don't think she wants to embarrass you."

"And for that she has my everlasting gratitude." The gentleman beside Miss Bramhall leaned close and whispered something in her ear. She gasped, but her eyes lit with amusement. "Why has she never married?"

"She was engaged once."

"And?"

"And the marriage did not occur. It was before I was born, but I understand it was an irreconcilable difference of opinion between my aunt and her fiancé."

"Pity."

"Why? A woman doesn't need to be married to be content," Veronica said mildly.

He turned toward her. "But is content all one wishes out of life?"

"*Content* may well be the wrong word." Veronica thought for a moment. "Perhaps *satisfied* is a better word."

"Is it?"

"She seems happy enough with her lot, a life that was not thrust upon her, but one she chose. There is a great deal to be said for being able to decide the path of one's life. She is independent and answers to no one but herself."

"And yet . . ." His gaze turned back to Miss Bramhall. "I think it's sad."

Veronica studied him curiously. "Why on earth would you think it sad?"

"She has no one to share her life with. No children, no family to speak of—"

Veronica bristled. "She has me and her mother and brother."

"It's not the same. She has no one to grow old beside. No one to hold her hand as her days grow shorter. No one to look back on shared laughter and tragedy with." He shook his head. "My apologies if my opinion dismays you, but, yes, I do think it's a shame."

She stared at him. "Good Lord, Sebastian."

He chuckled. "Have I shocked you?"

"Yes. I had no idea." She considered him with amusement. "You have the soul of a poet."

He smiled. "Is that what I have?"

"So it appears." She nodded. "I must say, I'm . . ."

He leaned toward her. "Yes?" Her gaze met his, and something undefined passed between them, a question perhaps. Asked and answered. Or never asked at all. His heart quickened. "You are?"

"Surprised, I suppose. I had rather thought from your writing that you were an extremely practical sort of man and not given to the sentimentality of those with a poetic nature."

"Can't I be both?"

"Apparently."

"When all is said and done, we are the sum total of all we have experienced. All we have observed." He thought for a moment. "I watched my parents grow old together, although my mother would protest my use of the word *old*."

"Women are not at all fond of that word," she said with a smile.

He returned her smile and continued. "My father was not given to overt displays of affection. Nonetheless, it was obvious how deeply they cared for each other. From the moment they first laid eyes upon one another until the

day he died. They'd barely met when they decided to marry."
He met her gaze. "We are like that in my family."

"Impulsive?"

"Not at all." He grinned. "We simply know what we
want when we see it."

"What a remarkable coincidence," she said lightly. "So
do I." Her tone sobered. "How long has your father been
gone?"

"Nearly a dozen years now." He paused to pull his
thoughts together. "I think the strength of what they
shared in their long years together is what gave my
mother the courage to go on without him." He chuckled.
"That and still having three of eight children—including
Portia—underfoot.

"My parents set an example of what life and love
should be. It hasn't always worked as well as their lives
did." He shrugged. "My brother Hugh was married only
briefly when his wife died. My youngest sister, Miranda,
also lost her husband, almost two years ago now. My
other younger sister is estranged from her husband. But
my brother, Adrian, is quite happily married and my older
sister, Diana, is happy as well with, oh, I don't know,
thirty or forty children."

She laughed. "Surely not."

"It might only be four, but it feels like dozens when
they are underfoot."

"And are you a doting uncle?"

"Hugh is better at that sort of thing than I am. I am
usually the absent uncle." He smiled, then sobered. "I
envy them, though. Adrian and Diana for what they have
found and even Hugh and Miranda and Portia for what
they once had, even if it is now lost."

"Now you've done it." She stared. "I'm not merely surprised but impressed."

"Then my plan is working." Again his gaze met hers.

"She has no regrets," Veronica said abruptly, efficiently changing the subject. "My aunt, that is."

"As far as you know."

"She has said as much to me."

"Ah, but what one says is not always what one feels."

"She has had a most interesting life thus far." A firm note sounded in Veronica's voice. He wasn't sure if she was trying to convince him or herself. "She has traveled, and she has any number of causes she believes in and works for." Or was she looking into her own future? "She's quite passionate about those, you know."

"So I have seen." He studied her closely.

"I know what you are thinking."

"Do you?" She had no idea yet, but he would not let her aunt's fate be her own.

"You're thinking her passion has been wasted."

"Not at all." He shook his head. "I simply pity the poor fool who let her go."

Her brow rose. "And a romantic poet at that."

"Now you have ferreted out my secret." He chuckled.

"Oh, I suspect you have any number of secrets."

"I am a man of mystery." He grinned.

"Do tell me one."

"It seems to me I have already revealed very nearly all of my secrets to you." He drew his brows together. "You already know of my poetic soul and my heretofore unknown gentlemanly nature. You know how my family views me and how I view them. And you know what my plans are for the immediate future." He shook his head in a sorrowful manner. "Yet I know none of your secrets."

She laughed. "I have very few secrets."

"What are your secrets, Veronica?"

"Let me think." She picked up her glass and sipped her

wine. "To be honest, I can't think of one. I am very much an open book. Not nearly as adventurous as one of your books, however."

"I doubt that. You may well be the greatest adventure of my life."

Her eyes widened. "What an absurd and charming thing to say. Surely you aren't serious."

"Ah, if I tell you, it would spoil your fun. And mine." He grinned.

"You've said that to me before. About your intentions, I believe."

"And I was right, wasn't I?" He resisted the urge to lean forward and kiss the tip of her charming nose. "Tell me, Veronica, what do you want for Christmas?"

She laughed. "My secret desire, as it were?"

"If you wish."

"Very well, then." She met his gaze firmly. "I wish for adventure."

"There are many kinds of adventure." He smiled. "One can find adventure in travel—"

"I have traveled a bit. Nothing like you, of course. I do wish to travel extensively someday. I would love to see the places you have seen."

"One can find adventure without leaving home. In the pages of a fictitious tale, for example."

She grinned. "For that I shall have to wait for your next book."

He smiled. "And are you willing to wait?"

"I am most impatient." She leaned closer. "You must promise to tell me your story of adventure as you write it."

"I should like nothing better." He considered her thoughtfully. "There is also the adventure to be found in unlocking secrets."

Delight lit her eyes. "Are you speaking of my secrets?"

He nodded. "I am."

"But I can't think of even one." She heaved an overly dramatic sigh.

"Which does not mean you don't have them." He stared into her seductive dark eyes. "Perhaps we shall have to discover them together."

"Oh, I would like that." She paused, then drew a deep breath. "I do have something I wish to ask you."

"Anything."

"Do you—"

"Sir Sebastian," Lord Chutley, a portly older gentleman seated across from him, cut in. "I beg your pardon. I don't mean to interrupt." He directed Veronica an apologetic look. "But I was hoping you could settle an argument for us."

Sebastian pushed aside his annoyance and adopted a gracious expression. "How may I help?"

"We seem to be at an impasse—"

"I beg your pardon, Lord Chutley," Veronica said pleasantly, "but as you did indeed interrupt, I assume you will forgive me. Sir Sebastian and I were engaged in a discussion I should dearly like to finish. So if you would be so good as to allow one more moment . . ." Veronica cast him the kind of look that would make any man with breath left in his body acquiesce to anything she might ask.

"Most certainly." The older man stared, a look that was part adoration, part animal lust in his eyes. "My apologies. Most inconsiderate of me. Please, take as long as you need."

"I am most appreciative." She favored him with a blinding smile, and at that moment, Sebastian would have wagered the man would walk through fire for her. And, in truth, who wouldn't? The copper-colored gown she wore added flecks of flame to her eyes. The woman was a vision. And she was his.

He chuckled and turned to her. "Thank you."

"I have only saved you for the moment." Her brown eyes twinkled with amusement.

"You were about to ask me something."

"Yes, I was." She leaned closer in a confidential manner. "I was wondering if you planned to seduce me tonight."

He choked.

Her eyes widened. "Are you all right?"

"Quite. Thank you."

"Well?"

He chose his words with care. "I thought I would kiss you first."

"But I kissed you." She shrugged. "That should suffice."

"And yet it doesn't." In spite of their hushed tones, indignation sounded in his voice. "*I* wish to kiss *you*. Quite thoroughly and for a very long time."

"Excellent." She beamed. "As kissing often goes hand in hand with seduction, might I suggest both?"

He stared.

"Well?"

He drew his brows together. "Have you taken leave of your senses?"

"Not at all." Her gaze slipped to his lips, then back to his eyes. "Tell me, Sebastian, do you intend to seduce me tonight or not?"

"Good Lord, Veronica, this is the Explorers Club!" The words came without thought, and he groaned to himself. He had become his older brother. Or his father.

"Do keep your voice down. My God, how stuffy you sound." She grinned. "It's most endearing. And oddly exciting. And I didn't mean here. How absurd. Although"—a wicked light flashed in her eye—"that would be something of an adventure."

"Veronica!"

"Do you want to know why I think it's endearing?"

He had no idea how to respond. "Probably not but go on."

"Because you're trying so very hard." What was surely at least affection shone in her eyes and curved the corners of her mouth. "Because you've been entirely too proper for a man of your reputation."

Because one behaves properly with the woman one wishes to marry! "I—"

"Therefore it is not far-fetched to consider, and Portia agrees, that you might well have some sort of plan."

"Oh, well, if Portia agrees—"

"Although one does wonder to what end, but it scarcely matters." Veronica raised a shoulder in a casual shrug. "As I have a plan of my own."

He swallowed hard. "A plan?"

"Yes, a plan." She nodded. "Do you wish to hear it?"

"I'm rather afraid to hear it."

"Nonsense." She laughed. "Most of the speeches before dinner attested to your courage."

"I suspect I shall need it." He narrowed his gaze. "Tell me of your plan."

"It's brilliant in its simplicity." She grinned. "I imagine, when we are finished dinner, the men will retire into whatever gentlemen's smoking lounge is provided here and the ladies will be banished to a poorly decorated ladies' parlor. Aunt Lotte and I shall make our excuses. I believe I will plead an aching head. That usually works nicely. Gentlemen are sympathetic, and ladies wish they had thought of it first. We shall take our leave, and when you are done here, join me for brandy at my house."

"This is your plan?" he said cautiously. She hadn't mentioned seduction, but perhaps that omission was part of the plan.

"Part of it. I said it was simple." She cast him a brilliant smile, then directed her attention to Lord Chutley. "Thank you, my lord, for your patience. Now then, you had a question for Sir Sebastian?"

Lord Chutley stared for a moment, then shook his head as if to clear it. "Yes, of course, Lady Smithson. And might I say you look lovely tonight."

"You are a dear man." She smiled. "I don't see Lady Chutley about. Do give her my best."

"Yes, of course." Lord Chutley turned to Sebastian with obvious regret. "Sir Sebastian, we were debating the relative merits of a trek with . . ."

Sebastian tried to concentrate on the gentleman's query and was fairly confident anyone watching him would think he had nothing on his mind but settling Lord Chutley's dispute. No one watching him would suspect the way his muscles clenched each time Veronica's skirts brushed against his leg when she turned in her chair to speak to someone. No one watching would have known his stomach tightened when he heard her laugh and seduction immediately came to mind. And no one would have been more surprised than he by his shock at her question.

He did not shock easily, especially when it came to matters like this. He was no stranger to seduction. Indeed, he had seduced and, on occasion, been seduced. And never less than willingly.

But one did not seduce the woman one intended to

marry. He wasn't sure why he was so inflexible on this point, but he was. It wasn't at all like him. He'd never had any qualms whatsoever about seduction before. But then he'd never planned to marry before, either. Obviously, the decision to marry carried with it all sorts of respectable behavior. Good Lord, what had happened to him?

Veronica, that was what had happened.

He glanced at her. She spoke to the gentleman beside her and he watched her for a moment. The way her eyes sparkled, the animation in her speech, the graceful gestures of her hand that emphasized her words. His heart thudded. He had to marry her as soon as possible. He'd go mad if he didn't. Besides, he wasn't sure how long he could hang on to these newfound principles. The thought had already occurred to him that perhaps the seduction of the woman one planned to marry might be a gray area as long as one's intentions were ultimately honorable.

No. He gathered his failing resolve. He had to do this right. It might well be wise to forgo a visit to her house tonight, especially given her plan. Whatever it was. Still, she had invited him, and it would be rude not to make an appearance. Besides, her aunt would be there. What could possibly happen?

He wasn't at all sure if he was afraid to find out or very, very eager.

Chapter 9

From the looks her servants had given her when she'd dismissed all but her butler for the night, one would think she did this sort of thing all the time.

Veronica paced the length of her sitting room, a glass of brandy in her hand. There was nothing better for courage than brandy. Who knew the intention to seduce a man would be quite so nerve-racking? Something not nearly as charming as butterflies fluttered in her stomach. Besides, it was entirely possible he wouldn't come at all. Sebastian had been oddly shocked when she'd asked him if he intended to seduce her. Only an idiot would have failed to realize her question, coupled with her invitation, meant she was ripe for seduction. Good Lord, if she were any more ripe, she'd burst.

What was wrong with the man, anyway? Or perhaps the problem was with her. No. She dismissed the thought with a wave of her hand. She might have allowed herself to be seduced only by one man, but that didn't mean other men hadn't tried through the years. And, aside from Sebastian, they still did. She turned on her heel and crossed the room, stopping in front of one of the two ornate gilded Italian mirrors that flanked the open doors to her bedchamber. She considered her image carefully.

She had changed into an amber-colored dressing gown, French with yards of lace and silk. Completely impractical for sleeping, which scarcely mattered as sleep was not her intention. With her hair down and curling around her shoulders and the heightened color in her cheeks—no doubt due to her nervous state and the brandy—she was definitely desirable. Even bloody well irresistible. Lord Chutley had obviously thought so. She raised her chin, nodded to the image, then turned and resumed pacing.

Where was the man? Surely he had had his fill of cigars and listening to the older members of the club reminisce. Veronica had had more than enough time to deliver Aunt Lotte to the house she shared with Veronica's father and grandmother, return to her own home, and change into this ruffled instrument of temptation. He should be here by now. If he didn't come soon, she might well change her mind.

What if he had decided not to come? The thought pulled her up short, and she took a small sip of the brandy. It was her first glass, and she had no intention of overindulging. She needed her wits about her tonight. But if he didn't come . . .

She sank down onto her chaise. It could be that he simply didn't want her the same way she wanted him, although she doubted it. She could see desire in his eyes when he gazed into hers. Feel it in the brush of his hand against hers. And when she'd kissed him—no, there was no mistaking desire. His as well as hers. So surely there was another reason why he still wasn't here.

She listed the possibilities in her mind. Number one:

Sebastian might be concerned about the propriety of an evening call, which made no sense at all. The man might not have been with legions of women, but one did not get a reputation like his by being reluctant to be alone with a lady. Number two: Sebastian might still be embroiled in whatever manly pursuits the members of the Explorers Club engaged in late into the night. Number three: He could have been run over by a carriage and his dismembered body parts carried off by rats to gnaw on at their leisure deep in the sewers.

She sipped the brandy. If he was lucky, it was number three.

Sebastian nodded at the butler, ignoring a twinge of guilt triggered by the suspicious look in the servant's eyes. He had nothing to feel guilty about. His intentions were completely honorable. The butler proceeded up the stairs in front of him, then around an open gallery that overlooked a ballroom below. His sisters were right. Only a woman with a sizable fortune could support a house this imposing. He wasn't sure how he felt about marrying a woman whose wealth was greater than his. He brushed aside the question. He wouldn't care if she had no money at all. Why should he care if she had a great deal?

The butler led him to a set of doors, knocked, then opened the doors and waved him in. Sebastian stepped into a large sitting room filled with the opulent furnishings of at least a century ago. French probably, but he wasn't sure. The room spoke of quality and luxury but was not overly feminine. Veronica reclined on a chaise with one of his books in her hand and a half-empty glass on a table beside her.

She didn't look up when he entered.

Her copper-colored gown had been replaced by a sort of frilly silk concoction that caressed the curves of her body like the hand of a lover. There wasn't an improper inch of creamy flesh revealed; indeed, what she wore now was less revealing than the gown she'd had on earlier. And yet, it was the most provocative thing he'd ever seen. His mouth was abruptly dry.

She turned a page.

He cleared his throat.

"I wasn't sure you were going to come," she said coolly.

He chuckled. "Neither was I."

She looked up and met his gaze. "Why not?"

"It didn't seem especially . . ." He struggled for the right word.

"Goodness, Sebastian, if you are about to say 'proper,' I shall throw your book at you." Her eyes narrowed. "And I have excellent aim."

"I've no doubt of it." He chuckled.

"I'm beginning to believe you lied to me." She sat up, swinging her legs over the side of the chaise to plant her feet on the floor, and he caught a glimpse of a gracefully turned ankle.

He swallowed hard and stepped toward her. "Never."

"When we met, you said you were not concerned with propriety." She snapped the book closed. "Yet, it seems to me, you have been overly concerned with propriety."

"I don't think I should apologize for that."

"I do not expect an apology." Her tone softened. "But I would like an explanation."

"An explanation? I'm not sure I have one." He pulled a chair close to the chaise and sat down. "You, Veronica Smithson, are the most intriguing and remarkable woman I have ever met."

"Am I?" She cast him a reluctant smile.

"And you are, well, special."

"Special?"

He nodded. "And you deserve better."

"Better than what?" she said slowly.

"Better than my usual behavior." The firm note in his voice bolstered his resolve. This was far more difficult than he had imagined, given where they were and what she wore and the fact that he had wanted her since very nearly the moment he'd met her.

She stared in stunned silence.

"Veronica?"

She stood and he got to his feet. She crossed the room, poured a glass of brandy, and returned to hand it to him. "What do you mean by 'special'?"

"I mean . . ." He shook his head helplessly. "I mean special."

"Do you mean special in the sense of being especially clever or especially pretty or especially well spoken?" Her brow furrowed. "Or do you mean special in the sense of being odd and even somewhat mad?"

"Oh, I don't—"

"My grandmother has a friend who cannot seem to remember, on any given day, exactly where she has left her hat or her gloves or her house. Grandmother says she has always been *special*."

He laughed.

"It's not amusing." Nonetheless, her lips quirked upward. "The poor dear grows more *special* every day. My grandmother has *special* moments as well, although I have always suspected her age is a convenient excuse for saying and doing exactly as she pleases. Not that she has ever hesitated to do just that, regardless of age. And you haven't answered me, you know."

"I meant all of it. Not special like your grandmother or her friend," he added quickly. "But the rest of it."

"I see." She picked up her brandy and took a sip. "That might well be the nicest thing anyone has ever said to me."

"Then I'm glad I was the one who said it." This was going well.

"Are you being charming because you took so long to get here that I didn't think you would come at all? And you are now trying to get back in my good graces?"

"Absolutely, if it's working." He flashed her a grin, then sobered. "But I meant everything I said."

"I know you did. That's precisely what is so charming." She took another sip of her drink and replaced the glass on the table. "I think you're rather remarkable, too." She stepped toward him.

He resisted the urge to step back. "Don't forget endearing. You called me endearing earlier tonight."

"Endearing and charming and remarkable. Practically perfect." She reached out and ran her finger along the edge of his lapel. "How do you bear up under the pressure?"

"It's a burden," he said with a weak smile. What was she doing? He took a deep swallow of his brandy. Not easy, as she was so very close.

She plucked the glass out of his hand and set it on the table.

He stared into her eyes. Good Lord, he was an idiot. This was her plan! *She* was going to seduce *him!* Unless . . .

"Is your aunt planning on joining us?"

"Goodness, Sebastian." She untied his tie. "You are adventurous. But neither my aunt nor I would ever consider—"

"Veronica!" He gasped. "I would never suggest such a thing!"

"I know, darling." She pulled his tie free and gazed into his eyes. "It's most endearing."

"Stop saying that," he said sharply. "Aren't you concerned that your aunt will come in at any minute?"

"I'm not an eighteen-year-old virgin, Sebastian. I certainly don't need a chaperone. Besides"—she tossed aside his tie—"Aunt Lotte isn't here."

"Where is she?" Caution edged his voice.

"I assume she is where she lives." She unfastened his collar. "At my father's."

"She doesn't live here?"

"No." She pulled his collar free.

He stepped back. "What are you doing?"

She cast him an exasperated look. "I should think it's fairly obvious."

"Yes, well . . ."

"Sebastian." She huffed. "Look me directly in the eye and tell me you don't want this every bit as much as I do. And if you don't, why, I shall even pick up your tie for you before I have you bodily thrown out."

He groaned. "Bloody hell, Veronica."

"I shall take that as an affirmative answer." She stepped close, reached up, and pressed her lips to his.

He wasn't sure how long he could battle her and himself. Every second her lips were on his, his resolve weakened. As did his knees. She pushed his coat over his shoulders, and he shrugged it off.

Only a saint could keep this up, and he had never been anything close to a saint.

She pushed him backward, and they tumbled onto the chaise together. Veronica lay slightly on top of him. She stared into his eyes.

"You should know," she said in a matter-of-fact manner that belied the breathless note in her voice, "I have never done this before."

"What do you mean, you've never done this before?" Not that they were going to do anything now. No, indeed. He was not that weak. "You have been married."

"Dear me, Sebastian, you are confusing seduction, which is what I am attempting, with lovemaking. One is not the same as the other."

Confusion furrowed his brow. "It's not?"

"Of course not. One leads to the other. Seduction is the prelude, as it were. The prologue. Perhaps even chapter one." She thought for a moment. "Or possibly it's more of an invitation. You know, one of those invitations that carry with it some sort of promise of an exceptionally good time. That's it." She nuzzled the side of his neck. "It's a persuasive invitation."

"But you never seduced your husband?"

"When one is married, at least in my experience, little persuasion is involved."

"That is good to know," he said under his breath, struggling to maintain his defenses against the feel of her luscious body on his and her lips against his skin.

"Although I suppose it depends on the wife." She raised her head and smiled into his eyes. "I was never particularly averse to marital relations."

He stared. "You weren't?"

"Not at all. I quite enjoyed it."

"You did?" He shivered with suppressed desire.

She chuckled. "Have I shocked you again?"

"I'm not sure you could." He grinned. "I rather suspected as much." And—damnation—ultimately his intentions were honorable. He would not be less than honorable now. "So are you trying to seduce me?"

"I am trying."

He slid his arms around her, rolled her onto her back, and gazed into her eyes. "One doesn't seduce the woman one intends to marry. Nor does one allow that woman to seduce him. So right now I am going to kiss you quite thoroughly, then summon all my resolve and strength of purpose, which—God knows—are very nearly at their limits right now, and then I am going to say good night."

"That's completely absurd. One can certainly seduce . . ." Her eyes widened. "Sebastian—"

"Veronica Smithson, will you marry me?"

"What?"

"Marry me. Marry me tomorrow."

She stared wide-eyed. "Why?"

"Why?" Hardly the answer he expected. "Because I asked."

"Surely you don't ask every woman before you—"

"No, of course not," he said staunchly. "I have never asked anyone to marry before now."

"I am flattered." She smiled in a weak sort of way. "But why do you want to marry me?"

"Because there is no one more perfect for you than me. We are right for each other, meant for each other." Yes, that was good. Women generally loved the whole idea of fate. "Because I want you more than I've ever wanted any woman."

"Oh my." She sat up and stared. "How very—"

"Don't say 'endearing.' "

"But it is. Very much so. I'm not sure what to say."

" 'Yes' is the usual answer."

"And an excellent answer it is, too," she said slowly. "It's simply not, well, mine."

He drew his brows together. "What do you mean, it's not yours?"

"Exactly what I said." She edged away on the chaise and shook her head. "I have no desire to marry again."

"Nonsense." He scoffed. "All women wish to marry."

"And I did marry. Once, and once was quite enough."

"But—"

"Sebastian, I like my life. I like my independence, my freedom. I like not having to be accountable to a husband for what I say and what I do. I like being able to make my own decisions."

"That needn't change." Was she actually saying no? To him?

"It needn't but it will." She shook her head. "Once I marry, my independence is gone. My fortune becomes yours. I become little more than chattel."

"I would never think of you as chattel!"

"Perhaps not, but the rest of the world will."

"Veronica." He chose his words with care. "You were married once before. Were you happy?"

"Yes."

"And independent?"

"Within reason."

"How is this any different?"

"You are different. And I am not the same as I once was." She sighed, stood up, and stepped to the table. She picked up his glass and handed it to him. "I am who I am now, and I have no intention of changing."

"I am not asking you to change. I like you precisely as you are."

"You do now, but you have certain expectations in a wife." She picked up her glass. "Do you not?"

"I suppose. I really haven't given it any thought."

"Tell me, what do you want in a wife?"

"I want you," he said firmly.

"Yet another excellent answer. Perhaps I should have asked what your expectations are in a wife."

"The same as any man, I would think," he said slowly.

"You want a wife who can manage a household, entertain properly, provide children?"

He nodded. "Well, yes."

"I have managed my own household, as well as my finances, for years. I am an accomplished hostess, and as for children, I have always thought I would like children one day."

"Then I don't understand."

"While I accept the need for a certain amount of compromise, I am not willing to let someone else control my life." She sipped her brandy. "You say you don't want me to change, and I believe you mean that today. You are a very successful man, and you know your own mind. But there will come a time when you won't want a wife who does as she pleases. Who supports causes with which you don't agree. Who handles her own finances. Who thinks for herself and makes her own decisions."

"I want you," he said again.

"I want you too." She shrugged. "But I do not wish to marry."

He stared in stunned disbelief. Was she really turning him down?

"However, I have, oh . . ." She thought for a moment. "A counteroffer, if you will."

"This is not a negotiation," he said sharply. "It's a proposal."

"Then I have a proposal of my own." She studied him carefully. "I don't wish to be your wife, but I would quite like to be your mistress."

"My what?" Surely she hadn't said that.

"You needn't look so outraged." She smiled pleasantly. "People enter into this sort of arrangement all the time."

"Not me."

She raised a brow.

"Certainly, I have been with other women, but I have never . . . *kept* a woman."

"Then it's simply a definition we disagree on, or the word itself. But *lover* is too frivolous. And *paramour* too pretentious. No, *mistress* is definitely the right term." She nodded. "However, I am not suggesting financial support. That would be absurd. Here's what I propose." Her brow furrowed in thought. "We shall be together in all manner except living arrangement. I shall continue to live in my house, and you shall continue to live wherever it is you live now. But when it comes to social events and intimate relations, we shall be exclusive to one another."

He gasped. "That's scandalous. What will people say?" What would his family say?

"I wouldn't think we would announce our arrangement to the world. I had planned on being discreet. Keeping this between the two of us."

"Nonetheless, there will be gossip."

"Some, I suppose." She considered him closely. "I didn't think you cared about gossip."

"I do when it involves the woman I want to marry!"

"You needn't raise your voice, and there's no need to be so indignant." Her jaw tightened. "And, as I do not wish to marry, that woman is not me."

"I don't want a mistress!"

"And I don't want a husband."

"I won't be another one of your lovers. To be discarded when you have tired of me."

Her mouth dropped open. "Another lover? You think I have had lovers?"

"Judging by your behavior this evening, and your *counteroffer,* it is not a far-fetched conclusion." He narrowed his gaze. "Have you?"

"I believe you just lost the right to ask me that!" She glared.

He didn't care. "Have you?"

"That is none of your concern!"

"Of course it's my concern. I asked you to marry me!"

"And I said no!"

"I don't want a mistress, Veronica. I want a wife!"

She squared her shoulders. "Then I suggest you look elsewhere."

"Perhaps I will." He tossed back the rest of his drink, slammed the glass down on the table, and started toward the door, scooping up his tie and collar from the floor on the way.

"Good luck to you!"

"I don't need luck!" He reached the door, then turned back to her. "Do you have any idea how many women would jump at the chance to marry me?"

"Spineless, insipid creatures with no minds of their own? Willing to trade freedom for security?" Sparks flashed in her eyes. "No doubt there are dozens of them."

He gritted his teeth. "If you come to your senses—"

"I won't," she snapped. "Because I haven't lost my senses!"

"—Portia knows where I can be reached." He nodded and yanked open the door and stepped through.

"If you change your mind," she called after him, "don't bother coming back!"

He slammed the door behind him and didn't break stride until he was down the stairs and out the front door. He hailed a passing cab and was halfway to Sinclair's house before his anger eased and rational thought returned. Shock, however, still lingered.

He had never in a thousand years imagined she would turn him down. There was an awful, dull ache somewhere in the vicinity of his heart. How could she? Didn't she realize that, aside from the fact that they wanted each other in a strictly carnal sense, they suited each other? Why, he could easily envision them debating and arguing and laughing together for the rest of their days. It would never be boring or tedious or dull. Not with Veronica. He had no desire to change her, and he resented her accusing him of such a thing.

Oh, certainly life with a wife who did as she pleased and spoke out on ridiculous causes like female membership in the Explorers Club would not be easy. Admittedly, he had not considered that. But it scarcely mattered. Life with her would be a challenge each and every day. And it would definitely be an adventure. What man of his nature could ask for more?

She turned him down? He shook his head in disbelief. Even if one disregarded the fact that they were obviously made for each other—soul mates, as it were—he was Sir Sebastian Hadley-Attwater, adventurer, world traveler, author, and he was bloody well famous. Women fell at his feet. Or into his bed.

Not that Veronica wasn't willing to do that, as per her outrageous counteroffer. Be his mistress indeed. It was shocking. Scandalous. Granted he'd never been concerned with scandal before, but this was different. This was important. This was the rest of his blasted life! And hers. He didn't want the woman he loved hurt by scandal. As strong as she thought she was, she enjoyed her position in life too much not to be affected by gossip.

He should have mentioned that he loved her. It was

certainly a point in his favor. He winced. And he probably shouldn't have accused her of having had lovers. Even if she had, it didn't matter. Not to him. She'd had a life before they'd met, just as he had. As for her outrageous counteroffer . . . He shook his head. He couldn't believe any woman would prefer scandal to propriety—even Veronica. He had no intention of treating her like chattel. Or like anything less than what she was. As for allowing her to make her own decisions, he could accept that, within reason.

Perhaps he was going about this all wrong. Perhaps the first step to convincing her to be his wife was accepting her as his mistress. No. His jaw tightened. He was not going to begin their lives together with her dictating all the rules. Absolutely not. Veronica Smithson had no idea who she was dealing with.

Sir Sebastian Hadley-Attwater had always gotten what he'd wanted. He'd wanted to climb the Himalayas, and he had. He'd wanted to follow in Dr. Livingstone's footsteps and feel the spray on his face from Victoria Falls, and he had. He'd wanted to journey up the Rio Negro, and he had.

And what he wanted now was this annoying, stubborn, *independent* woman for his wife, and he would have her. But on his terms, not hers.

He crossed his arms over his chest and settled back against the seat cushion.

He just had to figure out how.

Veronica resisted the urge to throw her glass at the closed door. Instead, she crossed the room to the brandy decanter, refilled her glass, and took a long drink. No need to keep her wits about her now. For all the good it had done her. It might well have been better if she'd been inebriated. At least then she wouldn't have been quite so shocked by his proposal of marriage.

Proposal of marriage? She groaned and stepped into her bedroom. Whatever had gotten into the man? Sebastian Hadley-Attwater was not the type of man to want marriage. Hadn't Portia said that the night of the lecture? Why did he have to want marriage now? It changed everything. And Portia was right—he had been ever so proper because his eye was on marriage.

She downed the rest of her brandy, set the glass on her nightstand, and fell onto her bed. Maybe she was *special,* after all. Or seriously insane. Or at the very least a tart. What kind of woman would rather be a mistress than a wife? But the very idea of marrying again clenched her stomach.

She rolled over on her back, sighed, and stared up at the ceiling. It had been different with Charles. She'd been twenty-two and, even then, strong-willed and independent. And Charles had been, well, not unlike Sebastian, although Charles apparently really had been with legions of women before her. He'd lived an outrageous, roguish sort of life before they'd met, and his family had never imagined he'd marry at all. He was also some twenty years older than she, far wiser, and a man who understood exactly what he was getting in a wife. He had once told her, he wouldn't have married at all if not for her. He hadn't wanted a wife who was perfect, as the world viewed wives. He had cherished her spirit and determination and all those qualities society as a whole deemed unsuitable. He had found it amusing to have a wife who knew her own mind and didn't conceal her intelligence. He had accepted her for exactly who she was. Even so, he had made the decisions regarding their finances and their life. But Charles had died three years ago, and she was now accustomed to making her own decisions. She couldn't give that up.

She'd been lucky once. How could she possibly expect another man to accept her unconventional nature? In spite of his words, Sebastian would hate marriage to her. He would want things his way. She would want to do as she wished and thought best. There would come a time when he would expect her to be conventional, to acquiesce to his desires. To behave in a respectable and proper sort of way. To keep her opinions to herself. There wasn't a doubt in her mind about that. Hadn't his recent respectable manner proved it?

But, oh, she did so want to be with the man. Wanted to be in his bed and in his life.

Portia was right on one other point, too. Veronica hadn't given this mistress idea due consideration. She hadn't really thought about scandal or gossip, although she'd never particularly cared about such things. It was her observation that when one had a great deal of money, society forgave almost anything. Not that it wasn't a moot point at the moment, since she had yet to do anything that needed forgiveness. Thus far, she couldn't even manage to seduce the man. She was obviously as inept a mistress as she was improper a wife. But it had sounded like such a good idea in the beginning. And still had a great deal of merit.

What if she never saw him again? Her heart ached at the thought, treacherous organ that it was. She couldn't let him walk out of her life. Or stalk, as the case may be, slamming the door behind him. No. She propped herself up on her elbows. She *wouldn't* let him walk out of her life. She'd never given up on something she'd wanted. She had to do something. Something short of marriage, that is. A new plan was definitely needed. She snorted in disdain. After all, the plan to seduce him had worked out *so* well.

She wanted him and she would have him. There was no question of that. The only question was how to go about it. She absolutely refused to consider that she might well have lost him completely. The thought occurred to her that perhaps he was thinking the same thing. Surely one didn't propose marriage and then go on with one's life without a second thought. It was entirely possible that his night would be as sleepless as hers. Her spirits lifted. Good. Even better, several sleepless nights should convince him of the need to keep her in his life. Under her conditions. One way or another, she would be in his bed—she would be his mistress—by Christmas.

And this would be a Christmas to remember.

Chapter 10

"Are you mad?" Sinclair stared at him as if he were indeed quite insane.

"I don't think *my* sanity is in question here." Sebastian huffed.

"Let me make certain I haven't overlooked something." Sinclair lounged on the sofa in the parlor and gestured with the cigar in his hand. "You proposed marriage?"

"I did." Sebastian sat on a nearby wing chair, his feet propped up on a table beside their glasses of whisky. There was much to be said for living in a household without women. A wife would never permit such behavior. He ignored the thought.

"And she said no?"

Sebastian's jaw clenched. "She did."

The American chuckled. "The nerve of the woman."

"I thought so."

"But she is willing to be your mistress?"

Sebastian blew a long plume of blue smoke. "She is."

"And you turned her down?"

"Well, yes."

Stunned disbelief colored his friend's face. "What a complete idiot you are."

"I have no desire to have a mistress. I want a wife."

"Correct me if I'm wrong," Sinclair said slowly. "You were not interested in marriage until you met Lady Smithson."

"The idea had occurred to me, but admittedly, I was not especially looking for a wife."

Sinclair studied him closely. "Then it isn't a wife you want as much as it is her."

"Possibly."

"There's no possibly about it." Sinclair shook his head.

"Very well, then, I admit it. I want her." He aimed his cigar at his friend. "But I want her as my wife."

Sinclair's brow furrowed. "Why?"

"I have no idea." He sighed. "I love her?"

"You needn't sound so convincing."

"I know I love her. I don't have any doubts about that." He thought for a moment. "It seems to me when you find the right woman, the woman you love, you wish to be with her for the rest of your days. Which inevitably means marriage."

"I have loved many women." Sinclair puffed his cigar. "And it's never made me want marriage."

"I don't think we're using the same definition of *love*."

"Let me ask you this." Sinclair thought for a moment. "Would you love her any more if she were your wife?"

"I expect to love her more tomorrow than I do today," Sebastian said firmly.

"That's very good, but don't waste it on me." Sinclair laughed.

"My apologies," Sebastian muttered. "I was carried away."

"Once again, would you love her more if she were your wife?"

"My love is not contingent on her position," he said loftily.

Sinclair groaned. "Good Lord."

"The answer is no, of course not. I wouldn't love her more if she was my wife. I already love her to the depth and breadth and height my soul can reach."

"Poetry now?" Sinclair snorted. "Or rehearsal?"

"Admittedly, I have been thinking of what I should have said." Sebastian puffed his cigar. There were all sorts of things he should have said. He should have mentioned love. He should have told her that he couldn't imagine living the rest of his life without her. And he shouldn't have lost his temper.

"One generally rehearses before the play."

"I am unique."

"I repeat, you are an idiot. As most men in love are." Sinclair shook his head. "And you used to be so clever."

"I am still clever." Sebastian blew a perfect smoke ring, then grinned. "As will be evidenced by my plan."

Interest gleamed in Sinclair's eyes. "You have a plan?"

"Not yet." Sebastian nodded in a sage manner. "But I will."

"You went into this without a plan?"

He shrugged. "I didn't see the necessity for one."

"Ah, because no woman in her right mind would turn down Sir Sebastian Hadley-Attwater?"

"No. Not entirely." He winced. "Something like that." *And because I know she loves me.* He knew it the same way he knew his compass always pointed north. He couldn't possibly be wrong about that even if she hadn't said it. Or was too stubborn to admit it. Or hadn't yet realized it herself.

"It seems to me you have played this game by someone else's rules thus far."

Sebastian narrowed his eyes. "Whose rules?"

"Society's or perhaps your family's. You've been trying to be a proper gentleman."

"One does not seduce the woman one intends to marry."

Sinclair scoffed. "Why not?"

"I don't know." Sebastian glared. "It just seems wrong."

"I see." Sinclair placed his cigar in the saucer and picked up his glass. "Well, it's all clear to me, if not to you."

"Then perhaps you would be so good as to explain it to me."

"You want your brothers' respect. You want them to see that you've become a responsible, proper sort exactly like them."

"This has nothing to do with my inheritance," Sebastian said sharply.

"No, it's far beyond that." Sinclair took a sip of his whisky and studied his friend. "In spite of her unusual views, Lady Smithson is a suitable, respectable match for you. And you want to be accepted. To take your place, I think, among your family."

Sebastian puffed his cigar. "That makes a certain amount of sense, I suppose."

"So tell me this." Sinclair leaned close and met his friend's gaze. "You're living every man's dream. To have a woman you adore who doesn't wish to marry but is still willing to provide all the benefits of marriage. If not for your family, would you still want to marry her?"

"It's an interesting question." Sebastian stared at the other man, a dozen thoughts running through his mind. "My marriage would please my family. The prospect of my marrying Veronica certainly excited my sisters."

Sinclair snorted.

"However . . ." He drew a deep breath. "I don't want to continue the life I've led so far. I have no regrets on that score, mind you," he added quickly. "It's been great fun."

Sinclair raised his glass. "For us all."

"But even before my return home, I had begun to think what I want in life now isn't the adventure of new places and foreign lands but the gentler adventure, for lack of a better term, of home and hearth and family. And, yes, eventually, marriage." He met his friend's gaze firmly. "Veronica is that adventure, my adventure."

"So she is why you are no longer opposed to marrying?"

"I was not really interested in marriage, at least, not yet. I was not looking for a wife. Until I met her. She makes all the difference." He paused. "If I had met her a decade ago, in the middle of the Sahara, when all I wanted was to wander the world, she would have been my adventure. I would have married her then." He smiled. "And now I would still want to marry her if she were completely unsuitable. If I had to choose between my family and Veronica, I would choose her."

The American stared.

"I want her as my wife because I want her in my life forever. I will settle for nothing less." He shook his head. "I am under no illusions that it will be easy, but I look forward as much to debate and disagreement with her as I do joy and laughter." He shrugged. "I want her hand in mine on the day I die."

"Good God." Sinclair shook his head. "You are in love."

He chuckled. "I'm as shocked as you are."

"All right, then." Sinclair uncurled his lanky frame and got to his feet.

Sebastian's brow rose. "What are you doing?"

"I always think better on my feet." He picked up his cigar and took a puff. "I am your closest friend, am I not?"

"Absolutely."

"And you would do whatever necessary to help me, should I need your help, correct?"

"Without question."

"Then the least I can do is help you win the hand of the woman you love."

"Should I pace, too?"

Sinclair shook his head. "Not enough room. Besides"—he nodded at Sebastian's glass on the table—"you've always come up with your best plans with whisky in one hand and a cigar in the other."

"True enough." Sebastian picked up his glass.

"You know evenings like this will be at end once you're married?"

"I'm afraid so." He cast his friend an apologetic look. "And I suspect Veronica will be my traveling companion in the future, even on my more adventurous treks."

"From what you've said, I doubt she will allow otherwise," Sinclair said wryly. "But first, you have to put a ring on her finger." He blew a long breath. "You do understand that plotting marriage, as opposed to plotting the avoidance of marriage, goes against everything I believe in?"

"And you have my heartfelt gratitude."

"For what it's worth."

Sebastian raised his glass to his friend. "Someday I shall do the same thing for you."

"That day, old friend, will never come," Sinclair said firmly. "Now, back to the matter at hand."

The American resumed pacing. Sebastian downed the

rest of his whisky, then puffed thoughtfully on his cigar. He did need a plan or, at the very least, an idea, but nothing brilliant came to mind. Perhaps more whisky was needed.

At last Sinclair paused and cast him a triumphant look. "I have it."

"Well?"

"You do realize it's not unheard of for men to marry their mistresses."

"Something like that had occurred to me."

"It's been my observation that the best way to get a woman to do what you want her to do is to let her think she's getting exactly what she wants."

Sebastian stared. "That's brilliant."

"I know." Sinclair blew a victorious smoke ring. "She wants to be your mistress. I say, for now let her."

"I am sorry, Veronica," Julia said mildly, "but I really don't understand your problem."

"My problem is that he wants to marry me." Veronica's voice rose, and she got to her feet to pace Julia's parlor. She was entirely too restless to sit and sip tea.

"So you said." Julia, however, was more than content to sit there on her sofa with her teacup in hand. And why not? Her life was proceeding exactly as she wished. "I think it's wonderful."

"It's not wonderful!" Veronica stopped and stared. "I don't wish to marry."

"So you say." Julia's words belied her tone.

Veronica widened her eyes. "You don't believe me!"

"Of course I believe you, dear." Julia chose her words with care. "I'm just not certain if you believe you."

"I have said for some time that I'd rather be a mistress than a wife."

"Yes, but that was, oh, academic, I would think." Julia smiled pleasantly. "It's one thing to say you would prefer to be a mistress when no one has asked to marry you. Now that someone has, it's a different story entirely."

Veronica drew her brows together. "I don't see why."

"You had no choice. It's all very well to say you prefer apples to oranges when all you have is apples."

"Nonsense." Veronica sniffed.

"But if, without warning, someone offers you an orange . . ." A wicked light shone in Julia's eyes. "Someone peels it for you and holds it out to you."

"Julia."

"And you get a whiff of that lovely scent, somewhere between sunshine and honey—"

"Stop that!"

"And it's so ripe, it fairly begs to be peeled."

"I am warning you."

Julia leaned forward. "And the juice runs through your fingers and you have to lick them because you can't not. And it would be a dreadful shame to waste that heavenly flavor."

Veronica stared. A few weeks of marriage had certainly had an interesting effect on Julia.

"Now, Veronica," she said in a matter-of-fact manner, "what do you want?"

"I want an orange," Veronica said without thinking.

"I thought so." Julia settled back on her sofa with a smug smile.

"It's a metaphor, Julia, I know that." Veronica huffed. "And I much prefer apples."

"Then you should find yourself an apple."

"I did! Indeed, I thought I had picked a rather impressive apple. He looked like an apple. He had a wicked sort of apple smile complete with dimples. He definitely had the reputation of an apple. In each and every respect, the man was an apple." Veronica folded her arms over her chest. "Who would have imagined he'd turn out to be an orange?"

"Julia, I was wondering—" Harrison strolled into the room and pulled up short when he saw his late half brother's wife. "Veronica." A genuine smile curved his lips. "I didn't know you were here. How delightful."

"Good day, Harrison." Veronica smiled weakly. She and Harrison had forged a new relationship in recent months, thanks, in part, to his turning to Veronica for help in his pursuit of Julia. Whereas once he was merely Charles's overly proper and stuffy half brother and she was his dead brother's annoying widow, now they thought of one another as the sister and brother neither of them had ever had. But as much as Harrison's attitude about propriety had eased, Veronica had no desire to put him to the test by involving him in this particular discussion.

His gaze slid from Veronica to his wife. His eyes narrowed in suspicion. "What is going on here?"

"A simple difference of opinion," Veronica said in an offhand manner.

"We were discussing fruit, darling." Julia smiled at her husband, and the oddest sense of envy twisted inside Veronica.

"Fruit?" He raised a brow.

"Oranges mostly." Julia bit back a grin. "Your sister simply adores a good orange."

"I do not," Veronica snapped. "I much prefer apples. I have always preferred apples. And apples are what I want."

"Unless, of course, the orange is extremely juicy and quite sweet." Julia glanced at Veronica. "And easy to peel."

Veronica narrowed her gaze. "Apples."

"I've always been fond of pears myself, but I suspect I do not wish to know what you are really discussing." He met his wife's gaze. "Do I?"

Julia shook her head. "No, dear. It would only annoy you."

"I thought as much." He stepped to his wife's side, bent low, and whispered something in her ear. A charming blush washed up Julia's face. Again, a twinge of envy stabbed Veronica. Harrison straightened, cast a look at his wife that could only be described as hungry, and turned to his sister. "I shall take my leave, then, and allow the two of you to sort out whatever it is you are sorting out."

"I think it's best." Julia's gaze followed her husband out of the room. A secret sort of smile curved her lips.

"My God, Julia." Veronica rolled her eyes toward the ceiling. "You and Harrison are not easy to be around these days."

"Really?" Julia grinned wickedly. "How delightful."

"*Delightful* is not the word I would use," Veronica said sharply, then sighed. "My apologies. I am very glad to see the two of you so happy."

"I never thought I'd be this happy," Julia said in a matter-of-fact manner. "I didn't know it was possible." She met her friend's gaze firmly. "You could be this happy."

"I would like to be. Indeed, I had thought I would." Veronica narrowed her gaze. "But he is not being cooperative, the blasted creature."

"Yes, indeed." Julia nodded. "What a vile man. He wants to make an honest woman of you. The beast."

"There is no need for sarcasm."

"No, sarcasm is your weapon."

"And I use it well. But it won't help me now." Veronica sighed. "I don't know what to do."

"You could always marry him."

Veronica cast her a withering glance.

"I think it's absurd that you won't." Julia heaved a long-suffering sigh. "I know any number of women, as do you, who continue to do precisely as they please in spite of their marital state."

"Ah, but are they happy? Or are they merely content?"

"One never knows what occurs within a marriage, but those of my acquaintance seem to be happy."

"Still . . ."

"Good Lord, Veronica Smithson." Julia stared. "I never thought I would see such a thing, but you are scared."

"That's absurd." Veronica scoffed. "I'm not the least bit afraid."

Julia raised a brow. "Aren't you?"

"No, I most certainly am not." She thought for a moment. "I could be somewhat apprehensive, I suppose."

Julia studied her.

"Very well, then. I admit it. I might be a bit fearful." Veronica huffed. "As much as Sebastian says he likes me exactly as I am, what if a year from now, five years from now, or ten years, he no longer finds it acceptable that I am independent and freethinking and outspoken? What if he discovers the woman he likes today is not the woman he can spend a lifetime with?" She turned and paced. "What if our life together becomes one argument after another, with neither of us giving an inch? What if he grows to hate me? Or I grow to resent him?"

She twisted her hands together. "It's not that I won't change, Julia. I can't. With Charles, it was different." She glanced at her friend. "I was not quite as independent then as I am now."

"Imagine that," Julia said under her breath.

"I know it's difficult to believe, but it's true. Keep in mind, I went straight from my father's house to my husband's. Until Charles died, I had never managed my own affairs or made a serious decision for myself." She shook her head. "I don't think I can go back."

"There is such a thing as compromise."

Veronica snorted. "I have never been good at compromise."

"I suspect it would take some effort." Julia paused, then drew a deep breath. "Do you love him?"

"Yes. No. I don't know. Perhaps." Was this love? It wasn't what she had felt for Charles. That had been rather definite and without question. Whatever it was she felt for Sebastian was vague and elusive, as if something lingered just out of reach. Something quite remarkable. "Possibly."

"Yet another thing I never thought I'd see." Julia chuckled. "You uncertain about anything."

"I'm glad you're enjoying this."

"Oh, dear friend, but I'm not. Not really. Seeing you afraid and uncertain is most distressing." Julia's eyes twinkled. "It's as if a hero has fallen."

"That's ridiculous." Veronica smiled reluctantly.

"And I am most concerned about you."

"Thank you," she said, somewhat mollified.

"Now then." Julia patted the spot beside her on the sofa. "Let's play one of your little games, shall we?"

"I don't want to play a game." Veronica sighed but sat down nonetheless. "Let alone one of mine."

"You made me play when I was trying to decide what to do about Harrison. It's your turn now. It's only fair."

"I've never been enamored with fair."

"Yes, I know. We all know." Julia narrowed her eyes. "As for the game." She paused. "Answer me this. If Sebastian took you at your word last night and did not bother coming back, how would you feel?"

"That's a silly thing to ask." Veronica waved away the surprisingly disconcerting question. "I'd have to think about—"

"Oh no," Julia said firmly. "There's no rational thought permitted in this game. You're to give me the first answer that pops into your head."

Veronica drew her brows together. "Those aren't the rules."

"They are now," Julia said firmly. "Besides, it's my house, and since it's now my game, you must play by my rules. And as you dismissed the last question, answer this one."

"Very well. Go on."

"How would you feel if, again, he took you at your word?" Julia leaned forward. "And he found someone else to marry?"

"Well, I'd . . ." An awful weight settled in Veronica's stomach. "I . . ."

"Yes?"

"I'd hate it. And I'd hate him. No, I'd hate myself." She shook her head. "I'd be devastated. And it would be entirely my own fault." She met her friend's gaze. "I can't allow that."

"No, you can't."

"I have to do something!"

"Indeed you do."

Veronica jumped to her feet and paced, her feet barely keeping up with her racing thoughts. "Something . . . something . . . definitive."

"Yes, yes!"

"I can't lose him!" But how did one keep a man who wanted to marry when one didn't wish to wed?

"No, no, you can't! Don't let him get away!" Excitement rang in Julia's voice and brought her to her feet. "Marry him, Veronica!"

"Don't be absurd." Veronica waved in a dismissive gesture. "I'm not going to marry him."

"Oh." Julia sank back down on the sofa like a deflated balloon.

"But you said it yourself, just a few minutes ago." The idea sprang into her mind fully formed and utterly perfect. "You're brilliant, Julia! Just brilliant."

"I said to marry him," Julia said cautiously.

"Julia, darling, you are a dear, sweet, wonderful woman. I am lucky to have you as my friend and eternally grateful that you married my brother." Veronica dropped down on the sofa, took her friend's hands, and stared into her eyes. "You also said compromise."

Julia nodded. "I did."

"So that's what I shall do!"

Julia's brow furrowed. "Compromise?"

"Exactly." Veronica nodded. "Sebastian wants a wife, not a mistress. I have no desire to be his wife but wish to become his mistress. What is somewhere between a wife and a mistress?"

"Disaster?"

"Not at all." Veronica laughed. "Oh, it's splendid. Perhaps my most splendid idea ever. I shall become . . ." She paused in the dramatic manner befitting of such a splendid idea. "Sebastian's fiancée."

Julia stared. "Correct me if I'm wrong, but doesn't betrothal imply marriage at some point?"

"At some point perhaps in the far, far distant future." Veronica shrugged off the question. "I can name, without any effort at all, at least three couples who have been engaged for years."

"Don't you think Sebastian will insist on marriage eventually?"

"I have no doubt I can distract him," Veronica said with a wicked grin. "I can be very distracting. Once Sebastian thinks I have acquiesced to his wishes, seduction will be much easier. He shall have a fiancée in public and a mistress in private. Certainly I would rather do things my way, but this is the perfect solution and compromise at its very best."

"Veronica." Julia shook her head. "You can't have your cake and eat it, too."

"Oh, but I can, darling, and I shall." Veronica grinned. "And I very much suspect that cake is apple flavored with an irresistible orange icing."

Chapter 11

Veronica paused at the door to her parlor and drew a deep breath. It had been five days since Sebastian had stormed out of her house. *Five!* What was wrong with the man? After all, wasn't she the woman he wanted to marry?

Admittedly, she had planned to give him a full week before taking matters into her own hands and seeking him out. Discreetly, of course. There was no need for him to know how eager she was to see him. How she had missed him. How she'd scarcely slept as she couldn't get him out of her thoughts. She'd refused to consider that he might not come back at all, yet the idea did insist on creeping into her head. An accidental meeting that had been precisely planned seemed best. On the other hand, just arriving on his doorstep and demanding entry had a certain amount of appeal as well.

She had been determined to wait the entire week, even though each day proved more difficult than the last. Veronica freely admitted a lack of patience was one of her greatest flaws. She'd spent her time reading and rereading all three of Sebastian's books. They were even better now that she knew the author personally. She could hear his voice in his words. It was as if Sebastian was in the room with her, telling her his stories of travel and adventure. One would think she would then dream of his adventures. Instead, in those brief moments when she had slept, she dreamt of what hadn't happened between them. Of his lips on her throat, of his hands skimming over her body, the heat of his skin next to hers, her legs entwined with his. She shivered and pushed the persistent images aside.

She'd rehearsed what she would say to him as well, although nothing seemed right. Should she be pleased to see him or merely polite? Should she pretend nothing had happened between them at all, or should she continue the discussion they'd started? Should she wait for him to bring up the topic of marriage, or should she? His accusation about her having had lovers still rankled, although, given her proposal, she really couldn't blame the man. An apology was definitely in order. And once he apologized, she would do the same, even if she had nothing to apologize for save losing her temper.

In spite of hours spent debating what to say and what not to say, now that he was in the parlor, waiting for her, she had absolutely no idea how to begin. And no idea what to expect. How did one propose an engagement without agreeing to marry? She did so hate to lie unnecessarily. Still, nothing would be accomplished at all with her on one side of the door and him on the other. Something would come to her. She squared her shoulders. Uncertain and afraid, indeed.

Veronica pulled open the door, adopted a pleasant yet noncommittal smile, and moved into the parlor. Sebastian paced the room, his back momentarily to her. Her spirits lifted. This was not the attitude of a man completely confident in his position. She had the nearly irresistible desire to step close to him, run her hands over his broad shoulders, and kiss the back of his neck.

Instead she adopted her cheeriest voice. "Good day, Sebastian."

He turned toward her and nodded, a smile just as pleasant as hers on his face. "Good day, Veronica."

"Good Lord." Her gaze skimmed over him. "You look dreadful."

He winced. "As bad as that?"

"Well . . ." He looked tired, weary, and slightly rumpled around his blue eyes. "Yes. As bad as that." Her heart caught. "Dear God, don't tell me you're ill! It's not malaria, is it? Or some other horrible tropical disease? One of those parasitic illnesses where worms burrow out through your skin?"

His brow furrowed. "Worms?"

"Yes, you know. In the Amazon there are those insects that lay eggs that get under your skin and then . . ." She shuddered and waved away the disgusting image. "Worms."

"Oh, those worms." He chuckled. "You've been reading my books."

"Just something to pass the time. They happened to be handy, that's all." She studied him. "Then you're not fatally ill?"

"If I told you I was, would you throw yourself into my arms and declare your undying love?" His eyes twinkled with laughter.

Yes! "No." Relief washed through her. "But I would send you a polite note wishing a speedy recovery or, should you take a turn for the worse, a well-attended funeral."

"One always hopes for a well-attended funeral if a funeral is unavoidable."

"You may certainly count on my attending."

"Ah, well, that will ease the pain of my demise."

"Something to look forward to," she said pleasantly.

"But not yet." He smiled. "As I am not ill, simply tired." He ran his hand through his hair. "I have not been sleeping well as of late."

"Oh?" An innocent note sounded in her voice.

"Your fault entirely."

"How very odd, as I would have blamed you."

His eyes narrowed. "How have you been sleeping?"

"Like a baby in his mother's arms," she lied. "Why, my head scarcely touches the pillow before I am fast asleep."

"No doubt."

"Shall I call for tea? Of course not. You would probably prefer brandy." She started across the room, then paused and studied him. "Or perhaps an abundance of brandy, or other spirits, is what has interfered with your slumber?"

"Entirely possible," he murmured.

She bit back a satisfied smile and stepped to the side table bearing the brandy decanter. Even if she was about to—she winced—compromise, it was good to know that their days apart had been as unpleasant for him as they had been for her. She poured him a glass.

"I wasn't sure I'd see you again," she said as if she didn't care.

"You told me not to bother coming back."

"You told me there were dozens of women more than willing to marry you." She turned toward him and started back across the room.

His brows drew together. "I did not."

She shrugged. "It was implied." She handed him the glass. "Why did you come back?"

"Did you really think you could get rid of me simply by turning down my proposal?" He took a sip.

"I had no desire to get rid of you. If you recall, I offered a proposal of my own."

"Oh, I recall very nearly every word." He paused. "I have been giving a great deal of thought to our last conversation."

"Really? I haven't given it a second thought."

He snorted in disbelief.

"Well, perhaps one thought. Possibly two." She should probably come right out with it. Still, the time didn't seem quite right. Better to wait and see what he had to say. "And have you come to any conclusions?"

"Several."

"And?"

"First of all, you have my apologies." He shook his head. "I should not have lost my temper."

"No, you shouldn't have." She paused. "Perhaps I should apologize for that as well."

"Nor should I have asked you about previous"—he cleared his throat—"lovers."

"If you are waiting for me to volunteer information, you shall have to wait a very long time." She was not about to tell him there had been no previous lovers aside from her late husband. She smiled pleasantly.

"I'm not." He studied her intently. "As you said, it's none of my concern."

"No, it isn't."

"Nothing of . . . of that nature that occurred before I met you is my concern. And I shall not again ask you about . . . about—"

"Lovers?" This wouldn't be nearly as much fun if indeed she'd had a large number of lovers or any. As she hadn't, this was most amusing.

"Yes." He nodded. "Your past is your past. As is mine."

She raised a brow. "Then I am not to ask you any questions about your amorous adventures?"

"Absolutely not," he said staunchly.

"You needn't sound so indignant."

"I am indignant." His brow furrowed. "I would never discuss one woman with another."

"I daresay I probably wouldn't ask for names. But I can't imagine in all those exotic places you've been, you haven't had equally exotic adventures of an amorous nature that you don't relate in your books. With Chinese princesses or Arabian dancing girls or the daughters of tribal chieftains."

"Wives," he said under his breath.

"What?"

His eyes widened, as if he hadn't realized he had said that aloud. "Oh, um, just a thought."

"Do share, Sebastian."

He hesitated for a long moment, obviously debating the wisdom of sharing, then blew a resigned breath. "There are tribes, in various parts of the world, in which chieftains offer one of their wives to their guests. It's a gesture of hospitality," he added quickly, as if that made it acceptable.

"How very *generous* of them." She smiled innocently.

"It's an accepted—no, expected—practice in those societies," he said firmly.

"Of course."

"It is considered extremely offensive to reject such an offer."

"No doubt."

"I know that look." His eyes narrowed. "What are you thinking?"

"I'm thinking it's a pity you didn't put that in one of your books." She lowered her voice in a confidential manner. "It would surely increase sales, you know."

He smiled weakly.

"And I'm thinking it's fortunate we do not have such customs in this country." She shook her head reluctantly. "I cannot see you graciously accepting the company of, oh, say, Lady Chutley for the evening—who is every bit as portly as her husband, although so pleasant a woman one scarcely notices the mustache."

He chuckled and sipped his brandy. "Not willingly."

"And I am also thinking, I would very much like to hear more of the amorous adventures of Sir Sebastian Hadley-Attwater. I wager I would find them fascinating."

"You are an unusual woman, Veronica."

"Yes, I am. Besides, one never knows . . ." She met his gaze directly, plucked his glass from his hand, took a long sip of his brandy, and returned his glass. Her gaze never left his. "I might learn something quite instructive."

"Yes, well . . ." He downed the rest of his brandy and stepped back. "That would be most inappropriate."

"You telling me of your amorous exploits or my learning from them?"

"Both."

"There you are, being so endearingly stuffy again."

"I know." He shook his head. "You seem to bring it out in me."

"How delightful." She cast him a wicked grin.

"Regardless," he said firmly, "I have no intention of sharing my more intimate encounters with you."

"Why not?" She moved closer. "I have always thought

that one should never pass up the opportunity to learn something of interest."

"I doubt there is anything you can learn from . . ." He turned on his heel, crossed the room, and refilled his glass. "And you have changed the subject."

"Have I?"

"You know you have. As I was saying, I have given our discussion a great deal of thought." He came toward her.

"Yes, you did say that."

"And I have come to a decision." His manner was casual, as if his decision was of no importance.

She drew a deep breath. "As have I."

He studied her closely. "It seems to me that a certain amount of compromise may be in order."

"Compromise? How very interesting." She shook her head. "I have never been fond of compromise."

"No, I didn't think you were." He smiled. "Nor am I."

"However . . ." At once she was grateful she hadn't blurted out her own version of compromise. "I do think, in this particular instance, compromise may be something to consider."

"Now that I have found you, Veronica, I do not intend to lose you." Determination sounded in his tone and echoed in his eyes. The oddest thrill ran through her.

"Well then." An annoying breathless note sounded in her voice, and she cleared her throat. "What sort of compromise do you have in mind?"

"I have a house I recently purchased in the country. I had planned to spend Christmas alone there with my new wife." He aimed her a meaningful look. "However, as my plans did not take into account your unwillingness to marry, obviously I need to reconsider them."

"My, life does seem to be filled with all sorts of compromise, doesn't it?"

"Apparently," he said. "As I cannot have my wife with me for Christmas, I should very much like to have my"—he heaved a reluctant sigh—"my mistress."

Surprise widened her eyes. "Your what?"

"You, Veronica. I want you to spend Christmas with me in the country."

"Christmas?"

"And stay through Twelfth Night, of course."

"How lovely." She paused. "As your mistress?"

"Unless you have reconsidered and would prefer to marry me."

"I haven't." She narrowed her eyes. "This doesn't sound like a compromise to me, as you are yielding to my wishes. What are you not saying?"

"This arrangement is not permanent," he said firmly. "More of a trial, something of an experiment, if you will."

"I'm not sure I like being an experiment," she said thoughtfully. "I've never been one before."

"I might not like having a mistress—"

"Legions of women, of course." She nodded. "Hard to give up. Quite understandable."

He ignored her. "And you might not like being one."

"As it was my idea, I doubt that." Although, there did seem to be a growing number of concerns she had not considered.

"While I have always attempted patience, although it has never been easy, I am apparently quite impatient in regards to you." He shook his head. "I do not relish the idea of being without you. And I had my, well, my heart quite set on Christmas with you. Therefore, in the spirit of compromise . . ." His gaze met hers. "Will you join me for Christmas?"

"Why, Sebastian." Her heart fluttered and she smiled. "This is so—"

"Please don't say 'endearing.' "

"I wasn't." She shook her head. "I was going to say 'wonderful.' Quite, quite wonderful."

"You do understand this is not a victory for you. It is a compromise."

"I understand completely." She beamed. "And I should be delighted to join you for Christmas."

"Excellent," he said gruffly.

"It's still nearly two weeks until Christmas. When shall we leave?"

"The house is only a few hours from London. It was in a state of some disrepair when I purchased it, soon after my return to England. However, I did hire a staff and I arranged for considerable work to be done. If I had a wife . . . ," he said pointedly.

"She could arrange such details?"

"She could make certain the house is as she wants it."

"Well, there are hundreds of other women willing to fill that position. . . ."

He rolled his gaze toward the ceiling. "As I have not seen the house for several months, I should like to assess the progress and speed it along, if necessary, before you join me." He paused. "I plan to leave tomorrow. I would ask that you join me in a week."

"An entire week?" she said without thinking.

He grinned. "Will you miss me?"

Yes! "I have a great deal to do if I am to leave town." She sniffed. "Why, I still have presents to decide on. And Christmas cards to address. And charitable contributions—"

He stepped toward her, wrapped his arm around her waist, and pulled her close against him. He stared into her eyes. "Will you miss me?"

She gazed up at him. Her heart thudded in her chest. "You're a very hard man not to—"

His eyes narrowed. "Will you miss me?"

"Yes, yes, I will miss you. I shall think of you night and day. And I promise to count the minutes until I see you again." She huffed. "There now, are you happy?"

"Blissful." He grinned.

"Are you going to release me now?"

"I haven't decided." His gaze slipped to her lips and back to her eyes.

"If you're not going to release me, you should probably do something."

"Should I?" He slid his other arm around her. She slipped her hands up to rest on his chest. "What would you suggest?"

"What would I suggest?" Exasperation washed through her. "Goodness, Sebastian, if I have to be the one who—"

Without warning, his lips crushed hers, hard and demanding. Her mouth opened to his, and he tasted of brandy and adventure and a hunger she shared. Her hands fisted in the fabric of his coat. Passion, unrelenting and long denied, weakened her bones, and she wondered that she could stand at all. She melted against him, into him, his body hot and hard against hers. And she wanted, she ached, she longed for more. For him.

At last, he raised his head. "The one who what?"

"What?" Dear Lord, she couldn't seem to form a coherent thought. Nor did she think her knees would support her.

He chuckled.

"You needn't look so smug." She drew a deep breath. "It's not at all endearing."

"Oh, but I am smug." His kissed her again, softly this time. His lips warm and caressing against hers. An exploration of desire and more. Whereas his first kiss had been driven by passion, this one was driven by something deeper, something wonderful. Finally, he drew back and smiled. "Very smug."

He released her and stepped away. "One week, Veronica."

"One week," she murmured.

He nodded and strode from the room, leaving her to stare after him. She sank down onto the sofa, a sweet, tremulous feeling somewhere deep inside her. Dear Lord. She pressed shaking fingers to her lips. She could still feel the warmth of his lips against hers. That was not at all like the brief kiss she had given him at the theater. This was a kiss that would linger in a woman's memory or perhaps her heart. A kiss to cling to for a lifetime. The man certainly knew what he was doing. Still, it didn't strike her as the kind of kiss that came from practice or lust but rather from affection, even, dare she say, love?

Was it possible? Could he be in love with her? And, more to the point, was she in love with him?

The question alone struck her as extremely odd. She was never indecisive about anything. With Charles she had never doubted love, although, admittedly, she had never experienced it before, but desire was a bit more tentative. With Sebastian, love was elusive and teasing and, as of yet, uncertain, but passion and longing were unmistakable. She wanted this man without question or hesitation. Perhaps it was because she was now older and more experienced.

Odd as well that even though Sebastian did not call this her victory, in truth, it was. Why, she didn't even have to offer engagement as a compromise, although that still might be useful at some point. He was willing to accept her as his mistress, at least, for Christmas. Sebastian was not the type of man to surrender what he wanted this easily. But she had gotten exactly what she wanted, and he had, well, lost.

Of course. She should have realized it at once. The man was not giving up his quest for marriage. He was simply changing his field of battle. What better way to convince her to marry him than by placing her in a domestic setting—at Christmas, no less—with a house in need of being set to rights and a new staff to be trained? After all, what man could truly run a household? And what woman could resist such a challenge?

She gasped with the realization. The man planned to seduce her into marriage, but not the kind of seduction she wanted. Indeed—she narrowed her eyes—with that nonsense he spouted about not seducing the woman one intended to marry, she suspected he had no intention of sharing her bed until there was a ring on her finger. Oh, he was a crafty, clever devil.

It was obvious that, in a carnal sense, he wanted her as much as she wanted him. She drummed her fingers on the arm of the sofa. Perhaps she had been going about this all wrong. She'd been trying, however unsuccessfully, to seduce him in her best mistress-to-be manner. Aside from today's kisses, he had been restrained and proper. And hadn't it made her want him even more?

Perhaps she should abandon attempting to seduce him altogether? Perhaps she should behave every bit as properly as he did? Given the manner in which he had kissed her today, it wouldn't be long before his resolve shattered. Perhaps the key to making this plan work was not to be seduced too easily, to encourage but not surrender. To resist her own desire until he couldn't resist his. After all, men always wanted what they couldn't have. And once Sebastian had broken his own rule about not seducing the woman he intended to marry, he would abandon the idea of marriage altogether. And he would accept her as his mistress. Exactly as she had initially proposed. She would have her independence and Sebastian as well. Exactly as she wanted. One could indeed have one's cake and eat it, too.

Even if one might well be losing one's appetite for cake.

Chapter 12

"Charming little cottage you have bought yourself, Sebastian," Veronica said wryly, gazing up at the towering facade of Greyville Hall. "I must confess, a three-story Jacobean edifice is something of a surprise."

"It looks much better now, surrounded by snow, than it did when I first saw it. One can't see how much work is needed on the grounds." Sebastian's gaze wandered over the manor. "What did you expect?"

"Oh, I don't know." She considered the question. "Something less civilized, more rustic, I think. With antiquated plumbing and insufficient heat."

"Then you shall not be disappointed." He chuckled. "What kind of house did you think I would purchase?"

"A castle perhaps."

"A man's house is his castle." Pride sounded in his voice.

"An ancient castle, with parapets and a drawbridge and pennants flying, emblazoned with a . . . a . . ."

He cast her a suspicious look. "A what?"

"A compass. Your compass." She smiled. "Yes, that would be perfect. And your motto—*In Ambitu, Gloria*—embroidered beneath it."

"That is a splendid idea," he said with a grin. "I should have pennants sewn to fly from each corner of the house."

"Although this house may well be grand enough without them." The house did indeed remind her of a distinguished elderly lady surveying the world she had once dominated. With its red brick punctuated by white stone quoins, and its square corner towers topped with graceful lead cupolas and stone finials, it was imposing yet somehow welcoming. "I quite like it, and the more I look at it, the more I think it suits you."

"I'm delighted that you like it." He cast a skeptical eye at his servants filing past him, carrying her luggage. It was a surprisingly long line. She hadn't realized she had brought that much. "I see you intend to fill every empty corner."

"Goodness, Sebastian." Veronica hugged her furs tighter around her and called to a footman carrying a precarious stack of boxes. "Do be careful with those, if you please."

"And what is in the boxes?"

"Glass ornaments from Germany." She cast him a firm look. "I suspect you have not given much thought to the decoration of a tree."

He winced. "I might have overlooked that."

"So I brought ornaments. Extremely fashionable ones, I might add. Consider them a gift for your new house. As for the rest, well, I shall be here for more than two weeks at least."

"At least."

"And one never knows what kind of social event one might be called upon to attend, even in the country."

"You are as practical as you are lovely." He took her

hand and raised it to his lips. "And you are exceptionally lovely."

"And you are incorrigible." She laughed. "You needn't expend so much effort, you know. I am here."

"And here is where I intend to keep you for as long as possible. I have missed you, Veronica. It's been a very long week. Have you missed me?" he added in an overly casual manner.

"How could any woman fail to miss the famous Sir Sebastian Hadley-Attwater?" she teased.

"I am not concerned with any woman. Only you." He tucked her hand into the crook of his arm and led her up the few steps to the open door and into the entry hall, dominated by a massive carved stairway.

"Have you accomplished much since your arrival?"

"There was far more progress made before I arrived than I had expected." He glanced around with obvious appreciation. "Would you like the grand tour?"

"I fear without it, I should easily get lost." She removed her hat and cloak and handed them to a footman. She wasn't sure what she had expected, but the house did appear well staffed. Apparently, Sebastian didn't need a wife to manage his household, after all. She ignored the annoying thought. "I see you have not yet decorated for Christmas."

They started up the stairs. "I thought we would do it together."

"How charmingly domestic of you."

He leaned close and lowered his voice. "Endearing, isn't it?"

She laughed. "Most."

"I daresay, she'll smell better with the scent of freshly cut pine boughs in the air rather than paint. Although, given the state of the house when I bought her, I find I appreciate paint. Still, as it turns out—"

Veronica paused on the stairs and stared. "She?"

"Oh." He nodded. "She, yes, Lady Greyville. She's the house." He took her elbow and urged her upward. "She's a grand old lady, so it seemed a shame to refer to her as *it*. After all, they refer to ships as she. Why not a house?"

"Why not indeed?" she said under her breath.

He bit back a grin. "I know. It's uncharacteristically whimsical of me, but endearing, nonetheless."

"Or mad," she said pleasantly.

They reached the top of the stairs, and he turned toward her. "Do you mind spending Christmas with an endearing madman?"

"Darling, you've met my aunt. Her outspoken nature is eclipsed only by my grandmother's, who believes her age gives her license to say anything she wants. My father is a dear, sweet man who does precisely as he pleases by completely ignoring his mother and his sister. They live in the family house in Mayfair, which is large enough to keep them out of one another's way. Christmas was scarcely different from any other day, with the exception of plum pudding. Indeed, Christmas often found us abroad. My mother died when I was quite young. I barely remember her at all. Unfortunate in so many ways but I have always wondered if she hadn't died, if my odd group of relations might not be less odd. They are very dear to me," she said quickly, "but even they would admit that we are *unique*." She smiled. "An endearing madman is something of an improvement as Christmas companions go."

"What of your late husband's family?"

"Charles really had no family save his half brother, who is now married to one of my dearest friends. He and

I spent our Christmases in Switzerland. I continued to do so until this year."

"I do hope you won't find Christmas alone with me too dull."

"I cannot imagine ever finding being alone with you dull. Besides, there is a vast difference between dull and peace."

"Then peace it is." He smiled and started down the wide corridor. "The house is coming along nicely. While the exterior is apparently original, a good portion of the interior has been remodeled any number of times in the last three centuries, according to the whims and needs of the current owner and due to at least one fire that I know of."

"Sebastian." Veronica drew her brows together. "You have an enormous family. Shouldn't you be with them at Christmas?"

"Yet another way in which I have often shirked my familial responsibilities, I am scarcely ever in England for Christmas."

"But this year—"

"This year I am spending it with you," he said firmly, then grinned. "And Lady Greyville."

"Should I be jealous?"

"Yes." He looked around. Carved wood panels covered the walls, rising up to meet a strap-work plaster ceiling. "I have quite fallen in love with her. I liked the house when I first bought it, but I thought it needed far more immediate work than it did."

He continued along the corridor, and she trailed behind him, noting the various features of the hall. The detail of the carved wood was exquisite, with a hunting scene that continued from panel to panel.

"The previous owner was in trade, with a desire to play

country squire. He bought the place some twenty years ago and then decided the country life was not for him. So the house sat empty for more than eighteen years, I believe. Although, to give the man his due, he did make certain the place was minimally maintained. Damned hard to make a profit on a property if the roof has fallen in. There's a great deal left to be done, and it should be completely refurbished. Most of the furnishings are somewhat shabby. But now that it's been thoroughly cleaned and all the bedrooms painted, it's really quite habitable."

"How many bedrooms are there?"

He thought for a moment. "Ten or so." He shrugged. "I'm not sure." He pushed open a door and stepped back to let her enter. "This is the library. Probably my favorite room. The furnishings came with the house, as did the books. I haven't yet had the chance to see exactly what's here, but most of them are extremely old." His gaze swept the room. "I suspect there are volumes—great treasures, really—hidden here."

"And valuable, no doubt."

"No doubt. But . . ." He shook his head. "I've never been able to let go of a book that has come into my possession. I may need more shelves. . . ."

Floor-to-ceiling shelves, filled to overflowing, rose up between tall bayed windows on the outside wall. More shelves crowded with books flanked a massive stone fireplace. The freshly polished dark wood glowed with warmth.

"Will you do your writing in this room?"

"It does seem the perfect place." He looked around the room, pride of ownership in his eyes and his voice. "With all those writers who have gone before as inspiration."

"It's quite remarkable." She nodded. "I can see why you love it."

"Fortunately, most of the public rooms have retained

much of their original features. I like that. That sense of . . ." He thought for a moment. "Continuity, if you will. Permanence perhaps. That no matter what else has changed in the rest of the world, here life is calm and serene and continues undisturbed."

"Why, Sebastian." She stared at him in surprise. The more she came to know this man, the less she really knew him. "You didn't want a house. You wanted a sanctuary. A fortress."

"In some ways, I suppose I did." He chuckled. "But there is much more to my sanctuary than you have yet seen. There's the great hall and drawing rooms and parlors and a huge kitchen and, well . . ." He shrugged in a sheepish sort of way. "My apologies, Veronica. I don't mean to ramble on like this. I have never . . . Well, this is the most significant purchase I have ever made. I've never bought a house before. Never wanted to, really. And now that I have . . ." He grimaced. "Now you really will think you are spending Christmas with a madman."

"I have always liked a little madness in my men. Besides . . ." She heaved an overly dramatic sigh. "A touch of insanity is to be expected. As you just said, you are a man in love."

"Yes, I am." His gaze met hers, and for a long moment neither said a word. Her heart caught. "I should warn you, Lady Greyville is a demanding mistress."

"As are we all, dear man." Without thinking, she leaned close and brushed her lips across his. So much for avoiding seduction. "As are we all."

He reached for her, but she stepped back.

"Beg pardon, Sir Sebastian," the butler said from the doorway. "The estate manager would like a word with you."

Sebastian cast her a delighted grin, looking very much

like a small boy with a new pony. "I have an estate manager."

She bit back a grin of her own. "So I hear."

"Thank you, Stokes. Tell him I'll be with him in a minute," Sebastian said. "And see if Mrs. Bigelow is available to continue showing the house to Lady Smithson."

"At once, sir." The butler nodded and took his leave.

"Mrs. Bigelow is the housekeeper. She was a maid here years ago and was delighted to return."

"That's not necessary, Sebastian." Veronica shook her head. "I can wait to see the rest of the house until you're finished."

"But I can't. I am anxious to hear your opinions. Besides, Mrs. Bigelow probably knows the house better than I do. One other thing." He studied her for a moment. "You have a country estate, don't you?"

She nodded. "It was my late husband's. I've managed it since his death."

"I would appreciate any advice or suggestions you might have on the management of a property like this."

"Would you?" She raised a brow. "But I am a mere woman."

"There is nothing mere about you." He chuckled. "And I would value your thoughts and suggestions."

"I see," she said slowly. "You would accept the advice of a woman, but you would not allow her into your club?"

"I am a complicated and confusing sort," he said in a somber manner but his eyes twinkled. "I think there are places where women do belong and places where they do not, positions they may fill and positions they should not. I will not apologize for that. But make no mistake, Veronica. I do not think intelligence is based on one's gender. You are a remarkable woman, and I value your counsel."

She stared. "You are indeed a most confusing man."

"Just one of my many—dare I say—endearing characteristics," he said with a wicked grin. "I shall join you later for tea. I was fortunate enough to hire an excellent cook. Her biscuits and cakes are known throughout the area. You are in for a treat."

"I do love sweets. I look forward to it."

He turned to leave, then turned back. "Oh, and Veronica."

"Yes?"

Sebastian pulled her into his arms. "Confusing you is not merely one of the things I do well. It's one of my greatest pleasures." He kissed her firmly, then released her. "It's going to be a splendid Christmas."

He grinned and left the library, his step confident, even jaunty. And, good Lord, was he whistling in the corridor?

And wasn't she smiling after him?

Who would have imagined Sir Sebastian Hadley-Attwater would be the kind of man who would name his house? Or keep every book he'd ever had? Or want a house to be a haven? Or welcome the advice of a woman?

She had indeed missed him. More than she had expected, more than she'd thought possible. She'd thought of him every day, dreamed of him every night.

"Lady Smithson?" A woman Veronica assumed was Mrs. Bigelow stood in the doorway, a pleasant smile on her round face. "Sir Sebastian asked me to show you around the house."

"Yes, of course. Thank you." Veronica smiled and followed the older woman out of the library. "I understand you were in service here as a girl."

"I was indeed." Mrs. Bigelow nodded. "And I don't mind saying I am pleased to be back. We all are."

"All?"

"Oh my, yes." She nodded and led the way down the corridor. "Sir Sebastian has made it a point to locate those who used to work here for the last owner or Lady Wellsby before him. Nearly everyone he has hired was either employed here years ago or has a relation who was."

"I see," Veronica said thoughtfully.

"He's a clever man, Sir Sebastian." Mrs. Bigelow pushed open a door. "This is the yellow drawing room."

Veronica made appropriate appreciative comments, easy to do as the room was lovely, if in dire need of refurbishing, but her mind was on the house's newest owner.

"Why do you say that? About Sir Sebastian being clever, I mean," Veronica asked when Mrs. Bigelow led her out of the yellow drawing room and continued her tour.

The housekeeper's eyes widened in surprise. "Because he is." She lowered her voice confidentially. "He writes books, you know."

Veronica smiled. "Yes, I was aware of that. Very good books as well."

Mrs. Bigelow nodded with pride.

"Is that why you say he's clever?"

"Not entirely." Mrs. Bigelow paused. "When you work in a house like this, you become a family of sorts. Sir Sebastian has brought this family back together."

Veronica nodded. "Very kind of him."

"Not at all. Well, yes, he does seem to be a very kind man but . . ." Mrs. Bigelow sighed. "I'm not saying this right." She thought for a moment. "Owners come and go in the life of a house. Oh, Lady Wellsby was born here and lived here until the day she died in her eighty-fourth year. A very nice lady, if a bit dotty at the end." She lowered her voice in a confidential manner. "Some of us think she never left."

"A ghost?" Delight sounded in Veronica's voice.

"We think so, although it might not be Lady Wellsby. Or Lady Wellsby alone. It's a very old house, you know, and hard to leave." She shrugged. "At any rate, as I was saying, when Mr. Edgars bought the house, he retained much of the staff." She sniffed. "Not that it mattered. He didn't live here much more than a year and everyone was let go. For those of us who work here, our loyalties are not only to our employer but to the house itself. It's a clever man who recognizes that."

"Yes, I suppose it is," Veronica murmured.

"Now, then." Mrs. Bigelow nodded briskly and continued down the corridor. "Next, we are coming to . . ."

It took the better part of an hour for the housekeeper to show Veronica the rest of the manor before depositing her in a bedroom that adjoined Sebastian's. A small bedroom off hers was provided for her maid. Mrs. Bigelow didn't so much as bat an eye at the sleeping arrangements. Obviously, the new owner had already earned the unquestioned loyalty of his staff.

"Mrs. Bigelow," Veronica said when the servant turned to leave. "I have an idea for a gift for Sir Sebastian. It's somewhat silly, but I think he might like it. Unfortunately, it involves skills that are beyond my limited abilities. And I was hoping you might be able to help me."

A broad smile spread across the woman's face. "Anything, my lady."

Veronica explained her idea. Mrs. Bigelow made a few suggestions and then took her leave, with a promise to have their project started by morning. The smile never left her face. Sebastian wasn't the only one who knew how to engender loyalty.

In so many ways, Sebastian was more than she had expected. And while calling his various quirks endearing had become something of a joke between them, everything she discovered about him was indeed endearing. More and more with every passing day, the man was quite simply working his way firmly into her heart.

Was this love? It would certainly make everything much more complicated. It was one thing to feel affection for the man whose mistress she wished to be, quite another to love him.

Chapter 13

Sebastian headed toward the red drawing room to join Veronica for tea, caught himself whistling a long-forgotten tune, and grinned. He hadn't whistled like this since he'd been a boy. If anyone had pressed him in recent years, he probably would have said he couldn't remember how. But here and now, in this house—in *his* house—especially since Veronica had arrived, all was right with the world. And whistling or humming or even dancing down the corridor was irresistible. One couldn't feel this good without expressing it.

It had been an endless week. He'd missed her with an intensity he had never imagined. And she'd missed him as much as he'd missed her. Oh, she hadn't said it, but he could see it in her eyes. And in the way she had evaded answering his question and hadn't protested when he'd said he planned to keep her here as long as possible. And especially in the way she'd kissed him casually, as if it were natural to do so. It was a good sign, a very good sign.

But then everything was good at the moment. The estate manager struck him as a decent sort and had come highly recommended. In fact, everyone he had hired thus far had proved to be competent and reliable. Yes, indeed. The woman he loved was under his roof, the roof was relatively sound, and Christmas was only a week away.

He had loved Christmas as a boy, had always thought it was the most perfect time of the year. He wasn't sure when that love had faded. Once he had left home, it had been harder and harder to return. Twelve years ago, he had had the opportunity to join his first expedition to the Amazon and had jumped at the chance, in spite of his father's disapproval. Wandering the globe in search of adventure was not a fit life for a Hadley-Attwater. It could scarcely be called a profession and was both irresponsible and juvenile. Hadley-Attwaters were expected to take their proper place in the world with an appropriate, respectable position, not waste their lives in pointless pursuits. Still, his father had not disowned him, nor had he prevented him from acquiring the trust each of his siblings received when they came of age. Funds Sebastian had relied upon until he had begun writing and lecturing about his adventures and had built his own fortune. But his father had died soon after Sebastian joined that first expedition, and there had never been the chance for reconciliation. In spite of their estrangement, Sebastian had never doubted his father's affection, but he'd had no idea when he had last seen his father, it would indeed be the final time. He knew logically that his absence had nothing to do with his father's death—the earl had taken a bad fall from a horse. Regardless, a vague sense of responsibility, and even guilt, had haunted Sebastian for years.

Since then, Christmas always seemed to find him in a foreign land. It had been impractical to hurry home simply for the holiday, or so he had told himself. It wasn't that he didn't care for his mother and the rest of his family. But at Christmas, much more so than during the rest of the year, he did not wish to be reminded what a disappointment he was.

Now, however, he was a property owner. He was staying in one place and was forgoing travel for the immediate future. His previous books continued to sell well, and he had no doubt his future fictitious work would prove equally successful. Demand for his lectures continued to increase. By any measure, he was not merely accomplished but responsible, even respectable. Surely it was enough for his brothers to give their blessing and allow him to come into his inheritance.

And, aside from all else, he had Veronica. Oh, she wasn't his wife yet, but she would be. There wasn't a doubt in his mind. While this year they would spend Christmas alone, perhaps next year they would join his family. It was past time really to lay the ghosts of the past to rest. Ghosts that, admittedly, might only be in his own mind. Yes, next year would be soon enough. Next year he would be ready. Next year he and his wife would join his family for Christmas. Even better, next year he would invite his family here for Christmas.

But this year, right now, this very moment, he was not merely content but happy. This would be the first Christmas of many yet to come and the only one when Veronica would be his mistress instead of his wife. And once she agreed to be by his side for the rest of their days, his life would be, well, perfect.

"Sir," Stokes called from behind him.

Sebastian turned to see the butler hurrying toward him.

"Sir Sebastian, Lady Smithson is waiting for you in the red drawing room."

Sebastian tried not to grin, but it wasn't easy. He had a red drawing room, as well as yellow and blue drawing rooms, plus a billiards room and stables and at least one ghost. How very respectable. "Yes, Stokes, I am on my way there now."

"I know, sir, but . . ." Stokes lowered his voice. "You have visitors who insist on seeing you at once. I put them in the morning room, which, I might note, is the farthest sitting room from the red drawing room."

"Very well." Sebastian turned and started toward the morning room. "Is there a reason why you put them in the morning room, or was it simply convenient?"

"Lady Smithson is in the red drawing room, sir."

"I am aware of that."

"Your visitors are female, sir, and quite demanding. And they refused to give their names." He sniffed. "They wish to surprise you."

"I have no idea who these women might be." Sebastian drew his brows together. "But that doesn't sound good."

"My thoughts exactly, sir. Which is why I thought it best to keep them as far away from Lady Smithson as possible." They reached the morning room door, and Stokes paused. "Some years ago, between my service here and my return to Greyville Hall, I was employed for a time as a valet to a young lord in London. Discretion forbids me from mentioning his name."

"Of course," Sebastian murmured.

"Suffice it to say, he was a most eligible bachelor with a penchant for fast living. In his employ, I learned the necessity of keeping one female *guest* away from another and the dire consequences of not doing so." Stokes glanced from side to side, as if concerned that he might be overheard. "Never fear, sir. I am most adept in situations like this."

"You have my gratitude, Stokes, but we don't know what the situation is until I speak to these ladies."

"Yes, sir." Only the faintest hint of skepticism flickered in the butler's eyes. He was entirely too well trained. "I shall remain here in the corridor, should you need me for anything." He nodded and pulled open the door.

Sebastian stepped into the drawing room. Two familiar figures stood near the fireplace.

"Sebastian!" Bianca turned toward him, a delighted smile on her face. "What a marvelous house this is! We can't wait to see the rest of it."

Miranda beamed. "We never expected anything like this. It's so grand and imposing."

He stared in stunned horror.

"We never thought you'd buy anything, well, nice." Bianca shook her head. "So impressive and most distinguished."

"We thought you'd get something . . . oh, a token, really," Miranda said. "A cottage perhaps or a house in town. Just something so that you could say you were staying in one place. Something respectable, but not, well, not this."

"This"—Bianca eyed him firmly—"is the house of a country gentleman who intends to stay put for a while."

"We can't tell you how pleased we are," Miranda added. "Mother and everyone will be thrilled."

"What are you doing here?" He could barely choke out the words.

"We've come for Christmas, of course." Miranda rolled her eyes toward the ceiling, as if the answer was obvious.

"And to meet your new wife." Bianca nodded. "We know you planned to spend Christmas alone with her—"

"Which we still think is terribly romantic." Miranda nodded.

"But you haven't been with us for Christmas since before Father died." Bianca shook her head in a chastising manner. "Surely you didn't think we'd allow you to spend your first Christmas back in England without us? Or that we'd wait to meet your wife?"

Miranda scoffed. "After all, Christmas is a time of new beginnings. And what better time for your wife to meet her new family than this?"

He stared at his sisters. "But you weren't invited."

"Goodness, Sebastian." Bianca shrugged. "We're family. We don't need an invitation."

Miranda frowned. "But you're obviously not pleased to see us."

He gritted his teeth. "You noticed that, did you?"

Bianca's eyes narrowed. "You're not being very hospitable."

"My apologies," he snapped. "You two appear unexpected and uninvited and you expect me to be pleased?"

The sisters traded glances.

"Well," Miranda said slowly. "Yes. We rather thought you would be delighted."

"We wanted to surprise you." Bianca sniffed in indignation.

"You have certainly done that. Now . . ." He jerked his head toward the door. "Get back in your carriage and return to London. Or go to Waterston Abbey. Anywhere but here."

"Don't be ridiculous." Bianca settled on a sofa and met his gaze defiantly. "We have no intention of leaving."

"No, indeed." Miranda sat down beside her sister. "We have come for Christmas, and we shall stay for Christmas."

"No." He glared. "You won't."

"I think we should take this to a higher power," Bianca said in a lofty manner.

"As do I." Miranda crossed her arms over her chest. "We demand to see *Lady Hadley-Attwater*. I can't imagine she would be so ungracious as to throw us—*your sisters*—out into the streets."

"We're in the country," he said sharply. "There are no streets."

"Into the cold, then." Bianca glared. "I'm sure she will be appalled that you would even consider such a thing."

"And at Christmas!" Miranda shook her head mournfully. "Oh, Sebastian, how could you?"

"It's remarkably easy." He narrowed his eyes. "You were not invited. Therefore you are not welcome."

"We're not leaving." Miranda settled firmly back on the sofa, a well-remembered stubborn look on her face.

Bianca's expression matched her sister's. "You shall have to throw us out bodily."

"Don't tempt me!"

"We insist on speaking to your wife," Bianca demanded.

"Either send for her or we shall search for her ourselves," Miranda warned. "We don't intend to leave until—"

"Bloody hell! There is no wife!"

Miranda stared. "What do you mean, there is no wife?"

"What have you done with her?" Suspicion sounded in Bianca's voice.

"I have murdered her and hidden her body in a trunk in the attic!"

Miranda gasped.

"Don't be absurd, Miranda. He's teasing us." Bianca glared at her brother. "You are teasing us, aren't you?"

Sebastian's jaw clenched. "If I were to murder someone and hide her body, right now I can think of no better candidates than the two of you!"

"Surely not at Christmas?" Miranda's eyes widened.

"Of course not, dear." Bianca patted her sister's arm.

"Lady Smithson does have a great deal of money," Miranda murmured.

"All of which would be mine if she were my wife," Sebastian said sharply. "Not that I have need of it. I have my own fortune, so there would be no necessity to murder her. However, the need to dispatch the two of you—"

"Nonsense." Bianca waved an impatient hand. "Her money might not be yours at all. There are various marriage arrangements that can be made regarding a woman's fortune that keep her funds under her control. Oh, it requires agreement on both sides and signing a great number of papers." She glanced at her sister. "Don't you remember when I married, Adrian insisted on that?"

Miranda nodded. "Wisely, as it turned out."

"Veronica is not dead, nor is she my wife."

"Why not?" Miranda asked.

"You said you'd be married by Christmas," Bianca said pointedly. "Christmas is less than a week away."

"Unless you plan on being married here?" Miranda brightened. "What a wonderful idea! A Christmas wedding in the country. And with the whole family present! Oh, you are a clever devil, Sebastian."

"He's not that clever." Bianca studied him. "What is going on here, brother dear?"

He drew his brows together. "What do you mean, the whole family?"

Bianca shifted uneasily. "You first."

He stared for a moment, then sucked in a hard breath. "You told them! I specifically asked you not to say a word, and you told them!"

"Not all of them." Miranda winced. "Mother and Portia had already left for Italy."

"Come now, Sebastian, did you honestly think we could keep a secret of this magnitude? Besides, you said you would be married by Christmas. You were quite definite about it." Bianca's brow furrowed. "Why aren't you?"

"She said no, that's why." He sank into a chair. "I asked her to marry me, and she turned me down."

Miranda stared. "I don't believe it."

"How could she possibly turn you down?" Bianca scoffed. "You are something of a catch. You're famous and dashing and not at all unattractive. Why, I can name any number of women who would snatch you up in a minute."

"As much as I am heartened by your defense, apparently Veronica is not among that number." He blew a long breath. "She doesn't wish to be married."

Confusion colored Miranda's face. "Why on earth not? I've never heard of a woman who did not wish to be married."

"Veronica is unique. One of many reasons why I love her." He paused. "She quite values her independence, and she has no desire to turn over control of her life to a husband. Even me."

Bianca nodded thoughtfully. "I can understand that."

"But she is here, isn't she?" Miranda said slowly.

"Yes, she is here." He nodded.

"If she doesn't wish to marry you, why is she here?" Bianca studied her brother.

"It's somewhat complicated," he said under his breath.

"We're surprisingly intelligent. I daresay we can understand even something complicated," Bianca said wryly. "Go on."

"If I confide in you . . ." His gaze shifted from one sister to the next. "I need your word of honor that you will not share this with anyone else."

"Goodness, Sebastian." Miranda huffed. "We know how to keep a secret."

He raised a skeptical brow.

"You asked us not to tell the family." Bianca sighed. "You didn't make us promise or give our word or anything of that nature. Indeed, it was something of a casual request."

"I didn't think it was the least bit casual."

"We didn't think you truly meant it," Miranda said. "But if you mean it now—"

"And I do!"

"Very well, then." Miranda shrugged. "You have our word. We shall keep this secret until our dying day."

He pinned Bianca with a hard look. "I need your word as well."

She shrugged. "You have it."

He considered them for a long moment. He couldn't let his sisters come face-to-face with Veronica without them knowing exactly what the circumstances were. God only knows what they might say to her. Or she might say to them. As his sisters obviously had no intention of leaving, he didn't really have a choice as to whether or not to take them into his confidence.

"Veronica sees no need to marry. She has no desire to be a wife." He drew a deep breath. "She would prefer to be my mistress."

"Dear Lord!" Miranda gasped. "That's scandalous!"

"Isn't it, though?" Bianca studied her brother thoughtfully. "Forgive my confusion, but in order to have a mistress, isn't a man supposed to have a wife as well? Can one be a mistress to a man who doesn't have a wife? Otherwise, I'm afraid I don't see the point."

"The point is it's immoral. Perhaps less so if there is no wife involved," Miranda said. "Regardless, it's still . . . improper at the very least to be . . . to be *intimate* with this woman!"

"Not that it's any of your concern, but I am not." He paused. "Not as of yet."

Miranda gasped.

Bianca raised a brow. "I see. Then—"

"It's a question of terms and definitions, I suppose." Sebastian met Bianca's gaze. "The real point is she refuses to marry me."

"How very interesting," Bianca murmured.

"It's not interesting. It's disgraceful." Miranda turned toward her sister. "Aren't you shocked? Outraged?"

"I am surprised," Bianca said slowly. "But, oddly enough, I'm not outraged. I should be, I suppose, but it makes a certain amount of sense for a woman who wishes to keep what she has. In an unconventional sort of way, of course, but then she is unconventional, isn't she?"

Sebastian snorted.

"Unconventional or not, what she wants is wrong." Miranda's gaze shifted from her sister to her brother and back. "The fact that the two of you don't realize that is shocking as well." She directed a firm look at her brother. "You should send her on her way, Sebastian. Throw her out. This very minute."

He sighed. "I have no intention of throwing her out."

Bianca raised a brow. "You're accepting her as your mistress, then?"

"Only for the moment. I want her to be my wife," he said firmly.

"Let me make certain I understand this." Bianca paused to gather her thoughts. Her brow furrowed. "For reasons that apparently I alone can understand, maintaining her independence and managing her own affairs, Lady Smithson does not wish to marry. However, she does seem to want you." She looked at her brother. "Does she love you?"

"She hasn't said it," he admitted grudgingly, "but I am confident that she does."

Bianca nodded. "Whereas you, Sebastian Hadley-Attwater, who has a sizable and most disreputable reputation when it come to women—"

Miranda groaned.

"—you, who has never shown any interest in marriage whatsoever, you, who has run from the very suggestion of marriage in the past, you are determined to marry this woman who does not wish to marry?"

"That is the sum of it, yes."

Bianca stared at him, then stifled a laugh.

He glared. "This is not amusing."

"Oh, but it is." Bianca laughed.

"Bianca!" Miranda stared. "This isn't the least bit funny."

"On the contrary, this may well be the funniest thing I have ever heard," Bianca choked out. She sniffed back a laugh. "The tables have turned on you, dear brother. It's most amusing, and more than a little ironic and well deserved."

"Thank you for your sisterly support," he said dryly.

Bianca grinned. "I haven't even met the woman and I like her."

"You certainly have our support in your pursuit of marriage." Miranda smiled weakly.

"We can see why you don't want the rest of the family to know of this." Bianca met his gaze. "It might well sway Adrian and Hugh's decision regarding your inheritance."

"That had occurred to me." He ran his hand through his hair.

"They are both rather stuffy," Miranda said under her breath.

"Do you understand why I need to spend time alone with her? I can't possibly convince her to marry me in the midst of a crowd of Hadley-Attwaters." He rose to his feet. "With that in mind, you need to be on your way. At once."

"Sit down, Sebastian," Bianca said firmly. "We are the least of your problems. Or we soon will be."

"I'm afraid to ask what you mean by that." At once the answer dawned on him. He sat and prayed he was wrong. "When you thought there might be a wedding, you said something about the whole family being here."

"Oh dear." Miranda winced.

"There is something else. . . ." Reluctance sounded in Bianca's voice.

He stared at his sisters. "Well?"

Bianca and Miranda exchanged guilty looks.

"If we had known . . . ," Miranda began.

Bianca grimaced. "If you hadn't lied to us . . ."

"I never lied to you!"

"You said you'd be married by Christmas," Bianca snapped. "And are you?"

"No, you are not." Miranda huffed. "Therefore, in very many ways, this is all your fault."

He drew his brows together. "What is all my fault?"

"The fact that you don't have a wife," Miranda said.

"A wife that everyone is expecting to meet." Bianca's words rushed out. "When they arrive later today."

"When who arrives later today?" Sebastian's voice rose.

"It could be tomorrow morning," Miranda said quickly. "Plans were a bit uncertain."

"When who arrives?" Sebastian's voice thundered in the room.

"You needn't raise your voice." Bianca pulled an invisible thread off her sleeve and flicked it away. "We've agreed this is your fault, after all."

"We've agreed nothing of the sort." He stared in disbelief. "When who arrives?"

"The rest of the family." Bianca smiled pleasantly. "Oh, not Mother and Portia, as they have already left for Italy—"

"We did mention that," Miranda pointed out.

"But Adrian and Evelyn and Hugh are coming."

"And Diana insisted on changing her plans," Miranda added. "She was most eager to do so."

"Along with Diana, her husband, of course, and the children."

Shock widened his eyes. "Is there anyone in the family who isn't coming?"

"You're being inhospitable again, Sebastian." Miranda sniffed. "It's not as if we invited any of the aunts or uncles or cousins."

"And Mother isn't—"

"Yes, yes, I know." He jumped to his feet and paced the room. "That's something at any rate. Not much but something. Aside from that, this is a disaster."

"Don't be absurd." Bianca waved away his comment. "It's simply the family together for Christmas."

"Simply? *Simply?*" He stared at her. "It's *simply* the stiff and stuffy Earl of Waterston and his equally proper wife. It's *simply* the eminently respectable barrister Hugh Hadley-Attwater, who has never so much as wandered anywhere close to anything improper. The two men who will *simply* decide if I am yet worthy of receiving the inheritance my father left for me. And it's simply Diana and her husband, Lord and Lady Stick-in-the-Mud, and their dozens of children."

"Only four, I think," Miranda murmured. "Children, that is. Not dozens. Four dozen children would be excessive."

"You have to stop them." Panic sounded in Sebastian's voice.

Bianca raised a brow. "And how would you suggest doing that?"

"They are probably already on their way," Miranda said. "And even if they aren't, by the time we returned to town, it would be too late."

"It's never too late." He shook his head. "Even if you arrived in the middle of the night, you could stop them."

"Sebastian—" Miranda began.

"I could dispatch someone with a note," Sebastian said quickly, his mind racing. "A footman perhaps. Yes, that would work."

"And what would this note say?" Bianca asked.

"I don't know," he snapped. "I'll think of something." He cast her a menacing look. "You should think of something as you are the ones who set this all in motion."

Miranda shook her head. "You said you'd be married—"

"Blast it all, I know what I said!" He resumed pacing, trying to think of something—anything. "I know." Desperation sounded in his voice. "There's a bridge a few miles from here on the road to London. We could . . . tear it down. Yes, that's good. Or, better yet, blow it up."

Miranda stared. "Do you have something with which to blow up a bridge?"

"I don't know," he said sharply. "But at the moment I could certainly tear it down with my bare hands. Of course . . ." He gritted his teeth. "Then the two of you would be trapped here."

"Do calm down, brother dear," Bianca said. "It's not as bad as all that."

"It's not?" He narrowed his eyes.

Miranda stared at her sister. "It's not?"

"Goodness no." Bianca shrugged. "At least not as far as Hadley-Attwater Christmases are concerned."

"Tell me then." Sebastian struggled to keep his voice under control. "How the imminent arrival of my very proper family, a family that expects to meet a wife when all I have is a mistress, is not a disaster of unmitigated proportions?"

Bianca shrugged. "It's certainly not as bad as the year the tree caught on fire and nearly burned down the entire east wing of the abbey. Or the year Father was to give Mother emerald ear bobs and one of the dogs ate one."

Miranda winced. "I remember that. It was dreadful."

"We had to follow that dog around for two days before we finally recovered the ear bob," Sebastian muttered.

"Or the year Great-Aunt Mariah died during dinner and no one noticed until we realized she wasn't joining us in the parlor."

Miranda sighed. "She was always nodding off during dinner. Bless her soul."

"Or the year you and Richard and Adrian and Hugh

decided to reenact the twelve days of Christmas as a special surprise for Mother." Bianca eyed her brother. "Surely you remember that?"

"Perhaps, I might—"

"I remember," Miranda said. "The four of you decided to collect all the gifts from the song, starting with the things that were easiest to find. Swans and geese, I believe."

"And hens," he said under his breath.

"Who would have imagined swans and geese and hens, who had always seemed so well behaved, wouldn't appreciate being indoors?" Bianca smiled sweetly. "I still recall all of us chasing them from room to room."

Miranda nodded. "And finding feathers in the oddest places for years. Father was furious."

"Even so . . ." Sebastian pushed the vivid memory of the dire consequences of that particular Christmas surprise aside. "All of that pales in comparison to this."

"Great-Aunt Mariah wouldn't think so," Miranda murmured.

"You are a clever man, Sebastian." Bianca studied him for a long moment. "It would seem to me the solution is right under your nose."

"You're right." He blew a resigned breath. "There's no way out of it. Only one thing to do, of course. I shall have to confess to Veronica that I led you to believe we would be married by now, never imagining she would turn me down."

"I knew it was his fault," Miranda said to her sister.

"And then I shall admit to the rest of the family that I am not as respectable as I am trying to appear, as I have a mistress instead of a wife."

Miranda cast him a sympathetic smile. "Honesty is always best."

"Don't be absurd." Bianca scoffed. "Honesty in a situation like this is to be avoided at all costs."

Sebastian narrowed his eyes. "What are you thinking?"

"First of all, there's no need to tell Veronica anything at all," Bianca said firmly.

"Won't she notice if someone calls her Lady Hadley-Attwater?" Miranda asked.

"No one in the family will use a title," Bianca said. "We don't call Sebastian *Sir Sebastian,* and we certainly don't call Adrian *Lord Waterston.*" She met her brother's gaze with confidence. "If we all cooperate, keep her away from the others when possible, never allow her be alone with anyone else in the family, oh, and think of lots of things to keep all of us busy, she won't have any idea everyone thinks you're married. Nor will the rest of the family suspect you're not."

"Bianca!" Miranda gasped. "I can't believe you would suggest anything so deceitful."

"Come now, Miranda, of course you can. Besides . . ." She cast her brother an apologetic look. "As one might possibly think, some of the responsibility for this falls on us, so it is up to us to help him."

Sebastian considered his sister. "You do realize, deceiving one's family could be considered wrong."

Bianca shrugged.

"This could well blow up in our faces—"

"Like the bridge." Miranda nodded.

"—my face, really," he continued. "No doubt the two of you would feign ignorance—"

"We have always feigned well." Miranda smiled in an innocent manner.

"—still . . . I . . . well . . ." He nodded slowly. "I like

it." He stared at Bianca. "I had no idea you were so diabolical."

"Diabolical and brilliant." Bianca smirked. "But all I am suggesting is that as the family expects to meet a wife, we do everything that we can to make certain they are not disappointed." She cast him a smug and deeply terrifying grin. "I do so hate to disappoint at Christmas."

Chapter 14

"Well, I think it's a delightful idea." Bianca walked beside Veronica on the road back from the village.

"It's also whimsical and a bit silly, perhaps, but that's what I like about it." Veronica smiled and gathered her cloak tighter around her.

Snow covered the ground on either side of the road, and the late morning air was colder than she had expected. She would have preferred to take her carriage to the village, but apparently the Hadley-Attwaters were indeed a sturdy lot with a penchant for long walks.

Mrs. Bigelow had begged off helping Veronica with the gift she had thought of for Sebastian, pleading a house full of unexpected guests. Two scarcely seemed a houseful, but then the housekeeper was not used to having anyone here at all. She'd sent Veronica to her sister in the village for assistance. Veronica wasn't at all sure how it had happened, but the next thing she knew, Bianca was accompanying her, on foot.

"I think it's perfect for him," Bianca said firmly. "A pennant to fly from one of his towers, with that battered old compass embroidered on it. I wish I had thought of it."

Veronica grinned. Silly or not, it did seem perfect.

The two women continued on in a companionable silence. Veronica had liked her when they had met yesterday evening, and Miranda, too, of course. They had all dined together last night and had had a most cordial time, even if Miranda had appeared subdued and a bit nervous, although that might be her usual nature. Any lull in the conversation was filled by Bianca, who was most charming and didn't seem to find the presence of Sebastian's mistress at all awkward. Sebastian, however, had been preoccupied. Odd, but then his sisters' unexpected company might well account for that.

"He has always fancied himself a knight riding to the rescue of fair ladies, you know." Bianca slanted a quick look at Veronica. "But he has never shown any inclination to remain in the company of the lady in question."

Veronica shook her head. "I have no need of rescue."

"And isn't that interesting?" Bianca murmured.

"Is it? Why?"

"Because you're not the type of woman Sebastian has been known to pursue in the past."

"And what type am I?" Veronica said slowly.

"For one thing, I suspect you are every bit as intelligent as he is. In that respect you are well matched." Bianca paused for a moment. "You are as independent as he as well."

Veronica raised a brow. "I gather my independence has been a topic of discussion."

Sebastian and his sisters had stayed talking until long after Veronica had retired last night, which might be why he had not once knocked on the door that separated his room from hers.

Despite her newfound resolve to avoid seduction, his failure to appear was annoying. At one point, during a long, restless night, she had risen from her bed to turn the key firmly in the lock of the door between their rooms. It was a message, if nothing else.

"Sebastian said that's why you don't wish to marry," Bianca said. "I can well understand your reasoning."

Veronica nodded. Portia had mentioned Bianca's estrangement from her husband but hadn't known much more than that.

Bianca glanced at her. "You know of my situation?"

"Portia is one of my dearest friends," Veronica said simply. No further explanation was needed.

"Then I daresay you know everything about everyone in the family." Bianca laughed. "It was inevitable, I suppose, marital difficulties, that is, when one is named after a character from *The Taming of the Shrew,* even if not the shrew herself. Did you know that everyone in the family is named after a Shakespearean character?"

"Then Sebastian is . . ." Veronica thought for a moment. "From *Twelfth Night*?"

Bianca nodded. "Now it seems quite charming of Mother, but as a child it was rather odd to be named for a fictional character." She leaned toward Veronica in a confidential manner. "I suspect it was an excuse to choose names she found more interesting than Mary or Anne or Jane."

Veronica laughed.

"I am eternally grateful I am not a Juliet." Bianca shook her head in a mock serious manner. "She did not end well."

"You think the name would carry a curse along with it?"

"There are certain expectations, I would think, although even Shakespeare himself asked what's in a name." Bianca smiled. "Sebastian has never quite felt that he has lived up to expectations."

Veronica frowned. "Because of his name?"

"No, because of his choices. At least not Father's expectations. Hadley-Attwaters are expected to make their mark on the world in far more conventional ways than Sebastian has chosen." She shrugged. "In spite of his considerable success, I fear my youngest brother considers himself a disappointment in the eyes of the rest of the family. Especially when it comes to Adrian and Hugh. We don't feel that way. At least, I don't."

"I see."

"But Sebastian has changed, in some respects at least. With his new house and his intention to stay in one place. It's all very responsible. And then there's you, of course."

"Me?"

"Yes." Bianca nodded. "You're a most respectable match for him, in spite of your outspoken nature or perhaps because of it." She slanted Veronica an amused glance. "It's well known, you know."

"I should hope so. It would be pointless otherwise." Veronica chuckled. "But you do realize I do not plan to marry him?"

"And why should you? You have no need of his fortune or his fame. You're the master of your own life. Why, marriage would be like a noose around your neck."

"Oh, I don't think—"

"Oh, no, I think you're wise to choose this course. To flaunt propriety and do precisely as you please. I think it's quite admirable, in spite of the scandalous nature of it all, and most courageous."

"You do?" Caution edged Veronica's voice.

"Oh my, yes." Bianca nodded. "You're the captain of your own ship, Veronica, sailing the seas of your life. Alone and independent. Making your own decisions. Responsible to no one but yourself. Speaking your mind. Doing as you please. Not trapped with one man for the rest of your days should all not work out as you expect. Facing the world on your own terms with no one to disappoint you or fail you. I am not nearly that brave. Why, it's almost perfect. I do so envy you."

"Thank you," Veronica said weakly.

In spite of Bianca's admiration, Veronica's life didn't sound the least bit perfect. It sounded somewhat selfish and rather lonely. Everything Bianca had said was true enough. But Veronica had never heard it expressed in that manner before. She had never equated independent with alone. As much as she valued independence, did she really want to spend the rest of her life alone?

"Speaking of outspoken opinions," Bianca began. "Last night we briefly discussed the admission of women to that silly club of Sebastian's." Bianca chuckled. "I do so enjoy the look on his face when he debates with you. And I would very much like to meet your aunt. But I was wondering what your thoughts are regarding . . ."

Bianca kept up a steady stream of chatter for the rest of their walk. Veronica made appropriate responses, but her mind was far from her political opinions or her thoughts on the latest Paris fashions. The arrival of his sisters had cast her position in a different light that bore consideration. A light she wasn't at all sure she liked.

It was past noon when they arrived back at the hall. From the end of the drive, they could see carriages being unloaded, several adults, and four small, boisterous children. Even from a distance the scene was that of barely controlled chaos.

"It appears you and Miranda are not the only unexpected guests," Veronica said wryly.

"Now, who could that be?" Bianca peered at the scene, then brightened. "Why, it's Diana and her family. And from the amount of luggage, I would say they plan on staying for Christmas. How delightful."

"Delightful," Veronica said under her breath. So much for peace in the country.

"I do hope you don't mind. I know you and Sebastian planned to be alone but . . ." She shrugged in a helpless manner. "We haven't had Sebastian here for Christmas since he began his travels. I fear we are all too excited to have him back to keep our distance. We did bring ornaments, by the way, for a tree. You are going to have a tree, aren't you?"

"It wouldn't be Christmas without one." In truth, in Veronica's family, the tree had always been more fashionable than festive. Without warning, she found herself looking forward to something a bit more spirited.

"And, well, a house like this fairly begs to be filled at Christmas."

Veronica studied the imposing redbrick structure and the crowd being herded into the house and smiled. "She does, doesn't she?"

"You shall like Diana, I think." Bianca took her arm and led her up the drive. "She's very much like you in that she never hesitates to speak her mind. Oh, but I should warn you . . ."

"What?"

"In spite of what Portia might have told you about this being a fairly proper family, we are most casual when we are all together, especially at Christmastime. It's something of a . . ." She thought for a moment. "A tradition, I would say, to call even guests by their given names. Because it's Christmas, of course. So please do not be offended when you're not called Lady Smithson."

Veronica smiled. "Well, it is Christmas, after all."

Bianca smiled in an oddly satisfied way, and they continued toward the house.

The moment they entered the door, the bedlam they had glimpsed from the drive engulfed them. Three little boys and a slightly younger girl seemed to be going in a dozen directions at once, trailed by nannies or governesses or probably one of each. Miranda stood in the middle of it all, looking as if she wasn't sure in which direction to go first. A woman a few years older than Veronica, obviously Diana, stood halfway up the stairs and directed the servants carrying in their bags while issuing instructions to the nannies and admonishing her children to behave. It was impressive and distinctly reminiscent of a circus juggler.

"Diana!" Bianca called.

"Bianca!" Diana waved and gracefully descended the stairs, sidestepping servants with baggage and at least one scrambling child.

"You must be Veronica." Diana took her hands and beamed at her. "I cannot tell you how thrilled I am to meet you. Why, the very idea that Sebastian has at last—"

"Diana!" Bianca flung her arms around her sister. "I am so glad to see you here!"

"You needn't sound so surprised." Diana raised a brow. "We had dis—"

"And all of us here for Christmas!" Miranda said with a smile. "How delightful!"

"Delightful," Veronica murmured. Indeed, it couldn't possibly get any more delightful without another dozen or so people. "Has anyone seen Sebastian?"

"He and my husband have gone off somewhere." Diana waved in an offhand manner. "They would have been less than worthless here, anyway. You there," she called to a footman, then neatly stepped around another servant juggling several bags. "There is a box of ornaments here somewhere that should be put . . ."

Miranda pulled Veronica aside. "We are best in small doses. It can be somewhat overwhelming if one isn't used to it."

"I hadn't noticed," Veronica said with a smile.

Miranda studied her for a moment. "A morning with Bianca can be overwhelming as well, and exhausting, if one isn't used to her. If you wish to retire to your room for a while to rest and"—she glanced around the entry hall— "rescue your sanity, no one would think ill of you."

"I was thinking the same thing myself." Veronica breathed a sigh of relief. "I thought I would wait until there was a distraction, then slip away."

"I daresay you won't have to wait—"

As if on cue, a crash sounded from another room. Miranda grinned and waved her off. "I'll have a luncheon tray sent up."

Veronica didn't so much as hesitate. It wasn't that she didn't like children; she did. And it wasn't that there were more of Sebastian's relations in this one house than she had in her entire family. That wasn't the least bit unnerving. They were very nice, after all. It had simply been a long, tiring day already on the heels of a fairly sleepless night filled with all sorts of questions she hadn't expected. She hadn't realized how tired she was until she lay down.

And tried to ignore the voice in her head that kept repeating Bianca's words like an insistent melody: *alone and independent.*

* * *

Their numbers had increased by three by the time Veronica came down for dinner. Lord and Lady Waterston, Sebastian's oldest brother, Adrian, and his wife, Evelyn, along with his brother Hugh, had also decided to join them for Christmas. They were as welcoming as Diana had been.

The adults gathered in a drawing room in anticipation of dinner, and again, everyone was most genial and behaved toward her as if she were a member of the family. It was at once gratifying and confusing.

"One can only be grateful it is not the season for frogs," Evelyn, Lady Waterston, said under her breath. Veronica sat beside her on the sofa in the drawing room and tried not to laugh.

In the corridor the squeals of Sebastian's nephews, who had been allowed to come downstairs to bid their parents a good night before being herded back to their beds by long-suffering nannies, still lingered in the air. Their mother gave the servants last-minute instructions, her voice fading as she apparently followed them up the stairs. His lone niece, and the youngest of the children, was already safely in bed.

Veronica drew her brows together. "Frogs?"

Evelyn nodded. "Diana's boys have a passion for frogs, but unfortunately, they also have a tendency to misplace them. When they visited Waterston Abbey last summer, one never knew where one might encounter an errant frog." In spite of her words, an amused smile curved her lips. "It was unnerving, to say the least."

"I can imagine." The scene in the entry today with the addition of frogs flashed through Veronica's mind.

Evelyn laughed. "Diana's children are, the boys, that is . . ."

Portia had always said her family was extremely proper. For them to treat Sebastian's mistress so cordially was surprisingly open-minded and modern of them. Veronica hadn't expected that, but then, she hadn't expected to meet Sebastian's family so soon, if ever. What was the etiquette regarding the introduction of one's mistress to one's family, if indeed there were rules regarding this sort of thing at all? This wasn't the type of situation typically covered in finishing school. Indeed, Veronica herself would be hard-pressed to gracefully cope with a social quandary of this nature. Beyond that, she hadn't expected it, had never even considered it, but here, in the midst of this family, she was vaguely ill at ease. Veronica Smithson had always known her place, her position, *who* she was. Yet now she had the oddest sensation of being undefined. It was most disquieting.

Why hadn't she considered this? Certainly, she had planned to be discreet in her relationship with Sebastian. She had no intention of announcing to the world that she was his mistress. Although, in truth, as of yet they had shared nothing more than a few kisses. One could honestly argue she wasn't his mistress at all but simply a . . . a friend. A friend he wished to marry. A friend who preferred not to wed but wanted him nonetheless. She did wonder how Sebastian had explained her.

"Don't you think so?"

"My apologies." Veronica shook her head. "I'm afraid my mind wandered for a moment."

"I'm not surprised." Evelyn's gaze drifted over the room.

Diana's husband sat chatting with Miranda, while Sebastian and his older brothers stood conversing near the fireplace. They were a handsome lot, tall and broad shouldered. They did seem to be enjoying themselves, although every time Veronica glanced in Sebastian's direction, his uneasy gaze met hers. Odd, as whenever she glanced at either Miranda or Bianca, they, too, seemed to be watching her. Sebastian and his younger sisters were definitely concerned about something, although, thus far, it was a most convivial gathering.

"This can be a rather intimidating group for one who isn't used to them," Evelyn said with a sigh. "Especially if one's family is significantly smaller."

Veronica smiled. "There do seem to be quite a few of them."

"And we are missing Adrian's mother, as well as Portia," Evelyn said. "Pity, they decided to go to Italy. Lady Waterston will not be at all pleased to have missed this gathering."

"Nor will Portia." Veronica paused. "Have you been married long?"

"A bit over two years, actually." Evelyn cast an affectionate look at her husband. "I never thought I would marry at all. For years I had no desire to do so."

"One gets used to one's independence."

"Yes, I suppose." She studied Veronica for a moment. "But you have been married before."

Veronica nodded.

"Forgive me if I am being forward, but I couldn't help but notice—"

"Emma wishes you to come upstairs so that she may say good evening to her favorite aunt," Bianca interrupted, startling them both. "Emma is Diana's daughter," she said to Veronica.

Evelyn raised a brow. "I am her favorite aunt?"

"Absolutely," Bianca said staunchly.

"How interesting. And she wishes me to come upstairs?"

Bianca nodded. "You should hurry before she falls asleep."

Evelyn's brow furrowed. "How do you know?"

"One of the maids was sent to fetch you and confused the two of us." She glanced at Veronica. "We can be most confusing."

Evelyn studied Bianca. "I didn't see a maid."

"You must have missed her," Bianca said blithely. "It scarcely matters, as you would hate to disappoint a child."

Evelyn rose to her feet and looked at Veronica. "Would you care to join me? I may be the favorite aunt today, but Emma will no doubt choose someone else tomorrow."

Veronica laughed and stood. "I would love to."

"As would I," Bianca said quickly. "Besides, I had always thought I was the favorite aunt."

Stokes entered the room and announced dinner.

"On the other hand," Bianca said quickly, "as dinner is ready, Emma can certainly wait." She shook her head in a mournful manner. "It would be most inconsiderate of us to be tardy."

"Nonsense. Being a favorite carries some responsibility," Evelyn said firmly. "I shall be back before the first course is served." She cast Veronica a supportive smile and left the room.

"Shall we go into dinner, then?" Bianca said brightly.

"Yes, shall we?" Sebastian said behind Veronica.

She turned and considered him curiously. "Is something wrong?"

He scoffed. "What could possibly be wrong?"

Bianca cautiously edged away. Veronica lowered her voice. "Oh, I don't know. A houseful of unexpected guests, perhaps?"

"Ah yes, that." He offered his arm. "It shall be a splendid Christmas." A determined note rang in his voice, as if he were trying to convince himself as much as her.

"Admittedly, as it is Christmas, it does seem somewhat biblical."

"No room at the inn?"

"Rather more like the return of the prodigal son, I would say." She paused. "Why didn't you tell me how long it has been since you were last here for Christmas?"

"It didn't occur to me to tell you. As for your prodigal son analogy—appropriate, perhaps, but I was thinking more in terms of proportion," he said under his breath and led her into the dining room. "Biblical, that is."

He escorted her to her chair, and she met his gaze. "Tell me, are you embarrassed by my being here?"

"Embarrassed?" He frowned. "By you?"

"Yes."

"Never. I would never be embarrassed by you." He drew a deep breath and forced a smile. "I only hope you can always say the same."

As firm as his tone was, she didn't quite believe him. Or perhaps it was her own guilt making her imagine things that did not exist.

Guilt? Veronica sucked in a quick breath. Where had that come from? She had absolutely nothing to feel guilty about. At least, not yet. Still, there was the whole matter of intent, and her intent was certainly improper. Even sinful. Not that such concerns had bothered her before. Why they appeared to be bothering her now made no sense unless it had something to do with Christmas and family and . . . Oh, she had no idea. It was all most confusing.

She couldn't possibly be wrong, could she? About Sebastian and what she wanted and what she didn't. The very fact that doubt had arisen at all was unsettling and bore further consideration. She was never uncertain. There was much to think about, and questions nagged at Veronica throughout dinner, although it scarcely mattered. She could have had a bag over her head for all the difference it made. While she was not ignored, at any given moment there were at least two different conversations in progress around her.

Sebastian sat at the head of the table to her left, Miranda to her right, and Bianca directly across from her. Hugh was next to Bianca and beside Diana, with Adrian at the far end, flanked by Evelyn and Diana's husband, James. There was scarcely a moment of silence throughout the meal, with family gossip mixed with discussions that touched on everything from politics to the weather. In spite of Veronica's feelings of discomfort, it was a fascinating group to observe. There was affection here, of course, not overtly expressed but rather as an undercurrent. Something they all expected and accepted as their due. It was also apparent that no one in this family kept their opinions to themselves, nor did they hesitate to intrude in the affairs of their siblings.

The meal drew to a close, and at the far end of the table, Adrian stood to address the group. "First, I should like to thank my brother for so graciously welcoming us into his new home. Despite the fact that we took it upon ourselves to surprise him."

"Christmas is always full of surprises," Diana said firmly. "And, given the sorts of surprises we have had in the past, I would think this is one of the best." She cast her younger brother a chastising look. "It has been too long since you were with us for Christmas. And if it took us coming to you to remedy that, so be it."

Sebastian stared at his older sister and smiled. "It's not

the worst surprise I've ever had." He paused. "Thank you all for coming."

Adrian nodded. "In spite of the fact that Miranda warned me that no one wanted a fuss made, I think anytime there is a wedding in this family, it should be noted."

Was Miranda marrying again? Veronica smiled at the younger woman, who looked vaguely horrified.

"And, as the head of the family, it falls to me to do so. I would ask that we all lift our glasses." Adrian raised his glass. "And welcome the newest member of the family." Adrian's gaze met hers. "Veronica, I realize intruding on newlyweds is perhaps not the best introduction and you must think us lacking in manners, but when we heard Sebastian had married—"

Veronica's smile froze on her face.

"—on the heels of his purchasing this house and was, apparently, at last settling down, well, you can see why—"

"You're not doing a good job of this." Diana heaved a long-suffering sigh and turned toward Veronica. "Veronica, we cannot tell you how happy we are that you have rescued Sebastian from the wasteland of eternal bachelorhood." She raised her glass. "Welcome, my dear. And may this be the beginning of many more Christmases together."

Cries of "hear, hear" and "best wishes" echoed around the table.

At once, everything became clear. This family had treated her as one of them because they thought she was! Her gaze slid around the table. The look of horror still lingered on Miranda's face, while Bianca appeared to be holding her breath. It was obvious from the conversation with Bianca on their trek to the village that both sisters were aware of the truth of the situation. Evelyn studied her curiously. As for Sebastian, the man looked very much as if he had just eaten something unexpectedly awful and wasn't at all sure what the consequences might be.

"Thank you all." Veronica summoned up her brightest smile and downed her wine, wishing for something stronger.

"You are a lucky man, Sebastian." James chuckled, then glanced at his wife. "Not as lucky as I am, but lucky nonetheless."

Diana nodded, and the rest of the family laughed.

Sebastian's gaze met hers, and her heart caught. "Yes, I am," he said.

She stared at him for a moment, then drew a deep breath. She might not be the true mistress of the house, in more ways than one, but now was not the time to shatter that particular illusion. She had no intention of confronting Sebastian in front of his family. Until she spoke privately with him, she was not going to announce to these people, whose opinion he valued, that either they had made an assumption he had let stand or he had lied to them. She would not embarrass him. Nor would she embarrass herself. And she was nothing if not an accomplished hostess. She rose to her feet, the men immediately following suit.

"Ladies, I suggest we adjourn to the other room and allow the men to indulge in their brandy and port without us."

"And cigars, I hope," Hugh said with a grin.

Ah, well, in for a penny, as they say. Veronica fixed him with a firm look. "Not in this room, I'm afraid. However, there is a billiards room you might prefer."

"We'll be quite content right here, sans cigars," Adrian said firmly. "Tonight at least."

Veronica smiled, then addressed the other women. "I shall join you in a few minutes. I should speak to Cook about tomorrow."

Diana winced. "I'm afraid my cook would be in a bit of a dither if I presented her with a houseful of unexpected guests." She and her sisters filed out of the room. "But then she tends to be rather inflexible and even at the best of times . . ."

"Not too long, now, gentlemen." Veronica smiled in her best hostess manner and met Sebastian's gaze. "Given the enthusiastic nature of tonight's dinner conversation, I'm sure there is much more we all wish to talk about."

The men echoed their agreement. Veronica nodded and pushed through the swinging door to the corridor that led to the kitchen. She leaned back against the wall and caught her breath.

They thought she and Sebastian were married? Where could they have come up with such an idea? Bianca and Miranda certainly knew they weren't married. Surely Sebastian didn't tell them they were, although he did not seem to be in any hurry to correct the wrong impression.

And why should he? She sighed, straightened, and started down the corridor. Bianca had made a point of telling Veronica how Sebastian had always felt like something of a disappointment to the family. How now, with the purchase of a house and staying in England, he was trying to prove himself worthy of being a member of a family where he'd never quite fit. How on earth could he tell them the truth? How could she?

She wasn't sure if she was angry or merely annoyed or even a bit amused. Now that the shock of discovering herself married had faded, it seemed best to wait until she spoke with Sebastian and heard whatever feeble explanation he had to offer before doing anything at all. Yet another awkward situation one was not adequately prepared for in finishing school.

However, right now she squared her shoulders. She had a houseful of guests for Christmas and an untried staff. Regardless of whether she was Lady Smithson or the new Lady Hadley-Attwater, she was an accomplished hostess with any number of successful house parties to her credit. Why, people vied to receive one of her invitations. She was not about to let a little thing like confusion over her marital state destroy that reputation.

Indeed, Sebastian was right. This would be a splendid Christmas. A Christmas to remember.

God help them all.

Chapter 15

"**I** must say, I am surprised." Hugh swirled the brandy in his glass.

Sebastian smiled absently, fully intending to follow Veronica at the first opportunity. He couldn't imagine what she was thinking. She must be furious.

"Surprised?" James chuckled. "*Shocked* seems a more accurate word."

Certainly she didn't seem angry, but she was too well bred and entirely too clever to make a scene in front of his family. As for his brothers, what would they think of this deception? This mistake? This fiasco?

"Why?" Adrian asked. "Didn't you suspect someday Sebastian would come home to stay?"

"Yes, I suppose." Hugh sighed. "But it did seem that he was having rather a good time of it. I would be hard-pressed to give it up."

How was he going to tell them the truth, and more to the point, when? A deception of this magnitude would surely shatter any possibility of them approving his inheritance. Lying about a wife and having a mistress share his house for Christmas were not the type of things that would impress his brothers with how much he had changed.

James and Adrian traded glances.

"Regrets, Hugh?" James sipped his brandy.

"That my younger brother has traveled the world in search of adventure, while I am in a profession that requires that I wear a wig?" Hugh scoffed. "None at all."

The other men laughed.

"We all choose our own paths, and I have been content with mine. As for Sebastian . . ." He aimed a firm look at his younger brother.

Sebastian's attention jerked back to the conversation at the table. "Me?"

"I am deeply disappointed in you." Hugh studied Sebastian over the rim of his glass.

"Disappointed?" Adrian's brow rose. "Surely not in his choice of wife?"

Hugh shook his head. "Not at all. She's entirely too good for him."

"She's amazing," Sebastian said abruptly. "She's as intelligent as any man I know and more so than any number I could name." The words continued of their own accord. "She's fearless. She's not afraid to give her opinions, no matter how awkward that might be for her. She says exactly what she thinks, but I have yet to see her be unkind to anyone."

His brothers stared.

"She's extremely loyal to her family, and they are an odd lot."

"She will fit in well," James murmured.

"She's quite sensible and rational and yet . . ." The look in her eye at the thought of making love at the Explorers Club flashed through his mind. "She's not." He shook his head. "She's strong and independent but there's . . ." *A faint hint of vulnerability that I don't think even she is aware of. She needs me and I need her.* He drew a deep breath. "We suit one another, in more ways than I can name."

"And she is lovely," James said, "which isn't at all important but appreciated nonetheless."

"Most appreciated." Sebastian nodded. And tonight, in a fashionable French gown, of a blue color that made her dark eyes glow, she was nothing short of remarkable. There were moments during dinner when he forgot she wasn't really his wife, wasn't really *his* at all.

"You have always liked women with red hair." Hugh raised his glass.

"You have always liked *all* women." Adrian studied his brother. "Are you willing to give that up?"

"This is the woman I want to be with for the rest of my days. The only woman." A firm note sounded in his voice. "I want to draw my last breath with her hand in mine."

For a moment, silence hung in the room.

"She certainly is a good influence on you," Adrian said at last.

"I was right the first time," Hugh said. "She is entirely too good for you."

"It's nice to know the high regard in which my family holds me," Sebastian said wryly.

"We hold you in extremely high regard." Adrian sipped his brandy.

Sebastian aimed a suspicious look at Hugh. "Then the disappointment?"

"I thought I could count on you, but thanks to you, I am the only unmarried man left in the family." Hugh blew a long breath.

James snorted back a laugh.

"Now that you're married, Mother will redouble her efforts to get me wed." Hugh sighed in a mournful manner. "I am next on her list."

Sebastian shook his head. "Her list?"

"Mother has a list." Adrian grinned. "Of who should be married next. There's a specific order."

James chuckled. "The list is infamous."

Sebastian's gaze slid from one man to the next. "Why haven't I heard about this list?"

Adrian sipped his drink. "It's not a secret. Mother is more than willing to talk about it. There are things you are going to miss if you aren't here. The details of life, as it were."

"There's a hierarchy to the list," Hugh said. "Females at the top in order of age, then the men from oldest to youngest. Oh, and never married takes precedence over previously married."

"So I was—"

"At the very top of her list." Adrian chuckled. "But you haven't been here, so you haven't felt the full force of her—"

"Powers." James shuddered. "Diana calls them powers."

Sebastian stared. "Magical powers?"

"Who knows?" James said darkly.

Sebastian scoffed. "You don't believe that."

Hugh and Adrian glanced at each other.

"So Portia is also at the top of her list?"

"Which is why she chose to flee the country," Adrian said.

"I always knew Portia was more intelligent than she lets on," James said with a knowing nod.

"And why Mother went with her," Adrian continued.

"She's not about to let a little thing like distance deter her. I suspect she sees Italy as fertile hunting grounds."

"However, Mother's departure left us free to come here," Hugh added.

"I'm so glad it was convenient." A dry note sounded in Sebastian's voice.

"We're glad we could come." Adrian's gaze met his. "It's been too long, little brother. We've missed having you with us."

The oddest lump lodged in Sebastian's throat. "Yes, well, it has been a long time."

"But you're home now. Settled for good, it appears." Hugh cast him an affectionate smile. "With a house and a wife. Why, you're very nearly a responsible English gentleman." He grinned. "Who would have imagined such a thing?"

"Yes, about that . . ." Sebastian cleared his throat. "I should tell you—"

A crash sounded from behind the servants' door. Sebastian ignored it. "What I was about to say—"

Another crash reverberated in the air.

James glanced at the door. "That sounds like a problem."

"Perhaps your cook isn't pleased with your new wife's plans." Hugh chuckled.

Adrian scoffed. "I'm sure Veronica is more than capable of handling whatever the problem might be."

"More than capable." Sebastian drew a deep breath. "Now, as I was saying—"

A third crash rang from behind the door. Sebastian jumped to his feet. "If you will excuse me, perhaps I should—"

"Handling the staff is the domain of a wife." A warning

sounded in Hugh's voice. "She will not appreciate your interference."

"Still, as you bought the house and hired the staff before you so much as met her, it might not be a bad idea to at least make your presence known," Adrian said thoughtfully. "If I recall correctly, it's awkward for a lady to abruptly find herself the mistress of a house used to running without one."

"Yes, of course, awkward," Sebastian said under his breath. He pushed open the door to the kitchen corridor, stepped through, and let it swing closed behind him. Veronica stood a few steps away, holding a large serving tray out in front of her, obviously preparing to drop it. Again.

"What are you doing?" He snatched the tray from her hands.

She raised a brow. "Attracting your attention."

"You needn't demolish the house to do so."

Her eyes narrowed slightly. "I was not demolishing the house. I simply dropped a tray."

"Three times." He set the tray on the serving counter that ran the length of the hall.

"It would have been four if that was what was needed to distract you."

"Distract me? From—" He frowned. "Were you eavesdropping?"

"Do you mean, was I standing with my ear pressed against the door?"

"Well, no, I didn't—"

"Of course I was. Goodness, Sebastian." She crossed her arms over her chest. "You didn't think I would abandon you, did you?"

He drew his brows together. "I thought you were going to speak to the cook?"

"I did." She nodded. "It only took a moment. She has things well in hand and is rather pleased to have a houseful of guests. In fact, she intends to bake gingerbread for the children." She cast him an admiring look. "You have already earned her loyalty, you know."

"Because I have filled the house or because I am paying her well?"

She shrugged. "Among other things."

"That's good to know." He eyed her cautiously. "What did you hear that prompted you to drop the tray?"

"You were about to confess all to your brothers, were you not?"

"Yes."

"Don't you think you should have talked to me first?"

"I did, but when the opportunity presented itself—"

"You told them we were married." She studied him closely.

"I most certainly did not," he said indignantly, then winced. "Miranda and Bianca told them."

"Oh?"

"I told them not to say anything," he said quickly.

"Obviously, I am asking the wrong question." Her eyes narrowed. "Why did your younger sisters think we were married?"

How to explain this to put himself in the best possible light? He thought for a moment. There really wasn't any way to make this sound better. He drew a deep breath. "They saw us at the theater and came to see me the next day. I told them we would be married by Christmas."

"Then that was before you asked me?"

"I never imagined you'd say no." He tried and failed to hide the indignation in his voice. "I had fully intended to be married by Christmas."

She arched a brow. "My apologies for mucking up your plans."

"Apology accepted," he said in a lofty manner.

"Obviously when they arrived—"

"Uninvited."

"—you told them the truth."

"It seemed best," he muttered.

"On occasion, the truth does seem to be best."

"You're not angry?"

"Apparently not." She considered him thoughtfully. "Whose idea was it not to let the rest of your family know the truth? And, as well, not to let me know what they thought?"

"Not mine." He shook his head vehemently. "It was their idea. Well, Bianca's, really. But I said it was wrong."

"And yet?"

He shrugged helplessly.

"Not merely wrong, dear man, but not especially clever. It took all of what? The length of dinner? For me to discover I was married." She shook her head. "You should have told me what you and your sisters were up to."

He blew a long breath. "Or not have deceived everyone in the first place."

"That, too, might have been wise. But, as I don't have brothers and sisters, I don't know what it's like to want them to think well of me. And having a mistress here, when they were expecting a wife, might have been distressing."

He snorted.

"I can see where Bianca's scheme would be most appealing. However, it's long been my observation that telling the truth initially is much easier than having to confess to a lie."

He scoffed. "Do you think so?"

"This is not the time for sarcasm, Sebastian," she said firmly. "And while honesty does have its place . . ." She waved a dismissive hand. "What's done is done."

"What do you mean?"

"I mean, you can't tell them the truth now."

He stared in confusion. "I can't?"

"Absolutely not."

"Why not?"

"Because it would upset everyone and ruin Christmas in the process." She moved closer and rested her hand on his arm. "That is not how you want to spend your first Christmas back with your family."

He stared down into her brown eyes. "What are you saying?"

"I'm saying there's no need to tell them we aren't married until after Christmas. Your family is delighted to have you again in their midst. Perhaps the best gift you can give them is a practically perfect Christmas. In your new house. With your"—she rolled her gaze at the ceiling—"new wife."

Surprise widened his eyes. "You?"

"Unless you have another fraudulent new wife on the premises."

He tried and failed to hide a smile. "No, just the one."

"Excellent answer, Sebastian." She blew a long breath. "And, given as you still have a look of stunned confusion on your face, I am further saying, for purposes of clarification, I am willing to go along with this deception until after Christmas."

"This is not what I expected."

"Good." She smiled up at him. "I do so hate to be expected."

Without thinking, he pulled her into his arms in a gesture easy and natural and right. This was where the blasted woman belonged. How long would it take her to realize that? "Why are you doing this?"

"Oh dear, that is a difficult question."

Although, she didn't pull away.

Veronica thought for a moment. "If you had asked me to pretend to be your wife before we came, I would have been most indignant and refused. Even if I had known upon my arrival that this would happen, I would not have gone along with it."

"I had no idea this would happen when you arrived," he said quickly.

"I know, which is a point in your favor." She paused. "It's been somewhat chaotic all day with arrivals and greetings and all, but amusing as well. Your family has been most welcoming and friendly. They strike me as very nice people." She slid her arms around his neck. "The opinion of your family is obviously important to you. Therefore it is important to me."

His gaze meshed with hers. "Is it?"

"It is." Her brow furrowed. "You sound surprised."

"No, just pleased." He stared down at her. "And that's why you're going along with this?"

"Well . . ." She sighed. "You are a rather nice sort."

"Is that all?" His gaze searched hers.

"And I do like the way you write."

"I see." She was still in his arms, her body pressed against his, warm and soft and irresistible. He lowered his head and ran his lips along the curve of her neck. "Anything else?"

"Oh . . ." She moaned softly. "You're somewhat famous, I suppose."

"You don't care about fame," he murmured against her skin.

"No . . ." Her eyes closed and her head fell back. "You can be quite pleasant and gracious. . . ."

"My brother thinks you are too good for me." She tasted of heat and desire too long denied and promises yet to come.

"I might have heard something like that," she murmured.

"He's right, you know." He trailed light kisses to the base of her throat.

"Yes, well . . ." She gasped. "Possibly."

He pressed her back against the wall. His lips moved lower to caress the curve of her breast revealed by her bodice. "This dress is entirely too low for a wife."

Her hands clutched at his lapels and his shoulders. "I'm not a wife."

"Then it's too high for a mistress." Her scent of flowers and spice enveloped him, claimed him. "Will your door be locked again tonight?"

"You noticed?" Her words were barely more than a breath.

"I did indeed." He kept one arm around her waist; his other hand inched her skirt up.

"We shall see." She sagged against the wall. "I haven't decided yet."

"What can I do to persuade you?" His fingers found the smooth silk of her stocking-covered leg.

She shivered. "I thought you had rules against seducing the woman you wished to marry."

"As far as everyone is concerned, I am married. And a man should always seduce the woman he is married to." He drew his hand up her leg until he found bare flesh. "Frequently and with a great deal of enthusiasm."

"You do realize the kitchen is just steps away and a servant might pop through the door at any moment." Her breathing was labored; her chest rose and fell against his lips. She was every bit as aroused as he was. "It wouldn't do at all for them to catch Sir Sebastian kissing Lady Hadley-Attwater. They would be scandalized."

"Ah yes, we wouldn't want to embarrass the servants."

"They are difficult to replace." She could barely gasp out the words.

"Still, it's my understanding that it is permissible for a man to kiss his mistress in his own house."

"You can't have it both ways." She drew a deep breath, then another. "And that, my dear man, is called having your cake and eating it, too." She kissed him quickly, the barest whisper of her lips across his, brushed away his hand, and pushed out of his arms. "You said it yourself. Until after Christmas, you don't have a mistress." She straightened her skirt, smoothed her hair, and smiled in an altogether wicked manner. "You have a wife."

Veronica's hand rested on the key to the door between her room and Sebastian's. As much as she didn't want to lock the door between their rooms, the whole idea of making Sebastian want what he couldn't have was working nicely. Why, the man had practically seduced her in the kitchen corridor tonight. And she had come very close to letting him. Which, of course, was what she had wanted from the start. And, dear Lord, she did want him. But something had changed. Something too vague and elusive for her to put her finger on, but something nonetheless. She sighed, turned the key in the lock, then started for her bed. No.

She turned on her heel, yanked the key from the lock, tossed it in the bottom drawer of the dresser, then covered it with clothes. Not that hiding the key would remove temptation—she knew where it was, after all. Still, searching for it in the dead of night, when dreams of him overtook her common sense, would prove difficult, if not impossible. Dreams that left her with a longing to be in his arms, and a sweet, awful aching need only he could ease. If the blasted man had cooperated in the beginning, this wouldn't even be an issue. She would, no doubt, be in his embrace right this very moment, having a delightful time. Now, it seemed wise not to leap into his bed too quickly.

What had happened to her? She extinguished the lamp and collapsed onto the bed, her mind struggling to find answers to questions she still didn't quite grasp.

She had wanted to be Sebastian's mistress because she didn't want marriage and all that came along with it. She wanted to keep her independence; she wanted to maintain control of her finances and her life. That was all well and good in theory. But Portia was right. There was much she hadn't considered.

She hadn't considered that this evening, in the company of his sisters after dinner and later, when the gentlemen had rejoined them, she would not mind being Lady Hadley-Attwater. Indeed, she might possibly have enjoyed it.

Nor had she considered what it would be like to be in the midst of a group of people who cared for one another without question or condition and didn't hesitate to tell you what they thought was best. Oh, her father and aunt and grandmother cared for her. But her aunt and grandmother were great believers in independence, in choosing one's own path. She couldn't recall them ever offering advice on matters of a personal nature. Certainly they had strong opinions on very nearly everything, but when it came to what Veronica should do with her life, they encouraged—no, expected—her to make her own decisions. Nor could she remember ever asking for their help. As for her father, he was quiet and pleasant and lived quite happily in his books and his collections of whatever had happened to strike his fancy at the moment. He, too, had let her make her own choices.

She hadn't considered that living a life of independence meant that she would be alone. Bianca's words still rang in her head. Independence paled somewhat when coupled with alone. And if she was independent, wouldn't Sebastian be independent as well? If she was not to be trapped with one man for the rest of her days, as Bianca had said, wouldn't he be just as free to leave as she? She had thought all along about *her* freedom and *her* independence, but didn't the pendulum swing both ways? She hadn't considered the possibility of his choosing to leave her. Of her living her life without him.

And she hadn't considered the man himself. If she were to make a list of those qualities she wanted in a man, he had them all. He was amusing and kind and clever. Arrogant and, at the same time, not entirely sure of himself. And he was not the least bit perfect, which might well be the most endearing trait of all.

And he loved her. He'd said all those things about her to his brothers. He wanted to die with his hand in hers. Her throat tightened.

She hadn't considered the possibility of falling in love with him. She hadn't wanted love. Hadn't thought she'd know it again, and yet here it was. Confusing and uncertain and a warm comfort around her heart.

She rolled over and curled around her pillow. Damnation. She hadn't known what to do since the moment she met him. And, blast it all, she did hate it when Portia was right: She hadn't given this mistress idea due consideration.

No matter how many times she punched her pillow or covered her head with her blanket, she couldn't block out the questions lingering in her mind.

This was their first Christmas together. Was she willing to accept that it could be their last?

Chapter 16

"I never thought I'd enjoy things like this," Evelyn said thoughtfully.

"They do seem to have a fondness for trudging along in the out of doors." Veronica pushed her hands deeper into her fur muff. "In the cold."

"I didn't mean that." Evelyn laughed.

She and Veronica trailed behind Miranda, Bianca, and Diana. Diana's two nannies walked off to one side. In the distance, Sebastian and his brothers traversed the grounds, vanishing and reemerging over the rise of the rolling, snow-covered hills or the small stands of trees. The children bounded along beside them like eager puppies, gathering boughs of evergreen and holly and long, trailing vines of ivy. They filled the huge baskets their father and uncles carried, so later all could be used to decorate the house.

Shouts and laughter, from children and adults alike, drifted back through the crisp December air.

It had been late morning by the time everyone had arisen for the day. They turned to Veronica, as hostess, for direction as to the day's activities. While she was well versed on ways to pass the time for guests at a house party, this was a family Christmas gathering complete with children. Somehow, croquet or lawn tennis or archery did not seem appropriate. Besides, it was bloody cold. Bianca came to her rescue and pointed out that nothing had yet been collected with which to decorate the house. And an hour later, here they were, tramping through the cold.

"I meant all this excitement about Christmas," Evelyn continued. "The preparation and anticipation."

Veronica raised a brow. "You didn't do this as a girl?"

"No," she said simply, then paused as if debating whether or not to say more. "I have no family to speak of. My parents died when I was very young, and I was left the ward of a distant relative, now deceased. I spent most of my girlhood in boarding schools."

"I see," Veronica murmured.

"It wasn't at all unpleasant. One doesn't miss what one has never had." Evelyn slanted her a smile. "The schools were in France and Switzerland. There are worse places to be."

"Yes, I suppose." Veronica chuckled. "I have always liked Switzerland. My husband"—she caught herself—"my first husband and I spent our Christmases there. It was quite lovely."

"It is lovely, but it's not like this." Evelyn scanned the scene spread out before them. The men and children had disappeared over a low rise. "This looks like an illustration from a Christmas story or a card." She shook her head in a wry manner. "And I sound like the overly sentimental greeting."

"Not at all." Veronica looked around. "I was thinking much the same thing myself."

"This is my third Christmas with the family. It makes them all children again, even Adrian, who is the least childlike man I know. I thought he was quite proper and even a bit stuffy when I married him. I should have seen him at Christmas."

"Would it have made a difference?"

"Oh my, yes. I would have married him even sooner, although that probably wasn't possible." She laughed. "I suspect that's why they like all this festivity. It brings them back to the carefree days of their youth. Before any of them had known loss or heartache or disappointment." Evelyn slanted a glance at Veronica. "I hadn't expected this, either, you know."

"What?"

"This family, these people." She shook her head. "Aside from his proper nature, I had thought Adrian was a solitary sort. At least that's the impression I had before we married. Now I find myself part of this large group of people who are connected in a way unfamiliar to me. I had always been rather used to being, oh, independent." She thought for a moment. "Certainly, they have their disagreements, often at the top of their lungs, but there isn't one of them who wouldn't do whatever was necessary to help another. Sometimes when that help is neither expected nor wanted."

Veronica laughed.

Evelyn smiled. "They do have a tendency to interfere."

In front of them, Diana and Miranda laughed at something Bianca said.

"Yes, I have noticed that," Veronica said wryly.

"You couldn't miss it, as we have all showed up uninvited for Christmas." Evelyn chuckled. "You do have my apologies for that."

"There is nothing to apologize for." Veronica shrugged.

"I suspect such things are to be expected when one is part of a family like this." *Even if only for just this Christmas.* The oddest pang stabbed her at the thought.

The children, their father and uncles appeared at the top of a rise and headed toward the rest of the gathering. Laughter and high spirits filled the air and grew louder with each step.

"They care for one another, although I imagine affection is to be expected in a family. But they like each other as well, which I suspect is rather rare." Evelyn studied the approaching group with a smile. "Look at them all. It never fails to amuse me. The largest of those children—"

"The men?"

Evelyn nodded. "They have the most fun of all."

"So it appears." Veronica chuckled and considered the other woman. She appeared to be about Veronica's age. "You don't have children?"

"Not yet." She sighed. "Possibly not at all, although I would like children. I would hate to see all this end." She glanced at Veronica. "I assume you want children."

"I do." Even as she said the words, she realized the truth of them. When she had turned down Sebastian's proposal, children had been mentioned. But it hadn't so much as crossed her mind then that, regardless of her views on propriety, she would never bring a child into this world out of wedlock. Apparently, she was not as free spirited as she thought. Yet another one of those things she hadn't considered. Sebastian waved, and without thinking, she waved back. It was the most natural thing in the world.

"We found it," Sebastian called.

Veronica bent her head toward Evelyn. "Dare I ask what they found?"

"You'll see." She grinned. "They have all sorts of traditions. This is one."

Diana called to Evelyn, and she hurried to catch up with the oldest sister. Miranda dropped back to take her place.

"I wanted to thank you," Miranda said quietly.

"No thanks are necessary," Veronica said with a smile. "Although a warning would have been nice."

"I know." Miranda winced. "I am sorry we thrust you into this situation."

"It isn't what I expected." Veronica chuckled. "But it will definitely be a memorable Christmas."

"Having a mistress here, well . . ." She shuddered. "It would be difficult to explain. It's important to him, Sebastian, that is, that his brothers not think of him as irresponsible and flighty and undependable. He's trying to prove that he has changed, grown up, if you will."

Veronica raised a brow. "And does he need to do that? I should think his considerable accomplishments would prove that."

"One would think." Miranda chose her words with care. "In truth, I'm not certain if he's trying to prove something to his brothers as much as to himself."

"I haven't noticed any lack of confidence about him." Veronica tried and failed to hide a defensive note in her voice. "Indeed, in many aspects he is most arrogant."

Surprise widened Miranda's eyes. "Well, yes, I suppose. . . ." She sighed. "I could be entirely wrong. We haven't seen much of him in recent years, you know."

"I know." Veronica laid her hand on the younger woman's arm. "And thank you."

"For embroiling you in a family dilemma?"

"No, darling." She squeezed her arm and smiled. "For including me."

Miranda stared at her for a moment, then returned her

smile. Veronica had the oddest sensation that she had just passed a test or been approved.

The two groups merged, the ladies chattering almost as much as the children. Sebastian's gaze met hers and he grinned. His face was ruddy with the cold; his blue eyes sparkled with amusement.

"We located the tree the groundskeeper had selected, and the children have approved it. It won't be cut until tomorrow, of course." Sebastian leaned close and spoke low into her ear. "I have a groundskeeper, you know."

"Imagine that." She bit back a grin.

Emma tugged at Veronica's skirts. "It's a tradition, Aunt Ronica."

She smiled down at the little girl. "What is, dear?"

"We get to approve the tree," the six-year-old said solemnly.

"The youngest in the family always gets to approve the tree." At age ten, Peter was the oldest. "Mother says it's been that way for centuries, since she was a girl."

"Not that it has been centuries since she was a girl," Diana said under her breath.

"It has to be just right." William, the second oldest, crossed his arms over his chest. He was a year younger than Peter. "Because it's a *Christmas* tree."

"For *Christmas*," Richard, the youngest boy, repeated, as if he wasn't entirely sure she understood the significance of the tree. He mimicked his older brother's stance. "So it's important."

"Now that we have all agreed on the importance of the proper tree . . ." Diana signaled to one of the nannies. "I suspect the winner of a race back to the house will be able to claim a special treat from your uncle's cook."

The boys exchanged looks and grins, then took off toward the house.

"Mummy." Emma glared up at her mother. "It's not fair. The boys are bigger and faster than I am. I never win."

Diana smiled. "Someday, darling, boys will be falling all over themselves to let you win. Now, go on." A smiling nanny came and took the little girl's hand. "I am certain the cook will have something special for you, too."

"We could all use something a little special." Sebastian set down his basket, then slid his arm around Veronica's waist and pulled her close. "Have I told you that you look even more beautiful in the cold?" He grinned down at her.

"Sebastian." She gasped and tried to pull away. "Stop it this instant. Goodness, in front of your family. What are you thinking?"

"I'm thinking you are the best thing that has ever come into my life." His voice was low and for her ears alone. "And don't forget, we are newly wed. We should act like it."

"Regardless . . ." She pushed against him with far less enthusiasm.

"I'm further thinking you are the very thing I have always wanted for Christmas."

"Sebastian!"

"Something special . . ."

She laughed in spite of herself. "Your family . . ."

"My family thoroughly approves of tradition." Without releasing her, he bent and grabbed a bunch of greenery from his basket. Mistletoe.

Her gaze shifted from the mistletoe to his eyes, and she surrendered. "Oh well, as it is tradition . . ." She wrapped her arm around his neck and pulled his face down to hers.

His lips met hers, and everything around them faded

away. He kissed her hard, for a moment or forever. And nothing existed save the feel of his lips on hers, his arm around her, the warmth of his body next to hers.

A throat cleared and Sebastian raised his head. He grinned down at her and released her. Heat washed up her face, and she wondered that she could still stand.

"Sebastian," Adrian said in a voice well used to command. His brow furrowed and he held out his hand. "The mistletoe, if you please."

Hugh frowned. "Adrian, you don't—"

"Now," Adrian snapped. At once the group stilled. Sebastian handed him the mistletoe. "You needn't all look at me in that manner," he said in a gruff tone. "I simply wished to kiss my wife as you did." He smiled at Evelyn. "It was most inspiring."

Sebastian's mouth dropped open.

"Adrian." Evelyn gasped in mock horror. "In front of everyone?" The twinkle in her eye belied her words.

"Well, it is Christmas." He dangled the mistletoe over his head. Evelyn laughed and stepped close to him. She placed her palm on his cheek, gazed into his eyes, and kissed him. Veronica resisted the impulse to sigh. Now, that was love.

She glanced at Sebastian and her heart fluttered. As did his.

"Well?" Bianca addressed Diana. "Don't you want mistletoe?"

"Don't be absurd." Diana sniffed and started toward the house. "We know what comes of mistletoe. We have children."

James grinned, grabbed the greenery from Adrian's hand, winked at Sebastian, and started after his wife.

Adrian laughed, took Evelyn's hand, and headed after them. Sebastian took Veronica's hand and followed suit.

If she hadn't glanced back, she would have missed Bianca and Hugh and Miranda watching their brother and sister and their respective spouses with varying degrees of wistfulness or sorrow or regret in their eyes. Regret for decisions made out of pride or anger perhaps. Sorrow for what had been lost or wistfulness for what might have been. Veronica's gaze caught Hugh's, and he shrugged in an offhand manner, as if those sorts of emotions weren't significant. But then, displays of emotion that personal wouldn't be entirely proper.

Tomorrow was Christmas Eve, and they would all decorate the house together. The tree would be set up in Sebastian's great hall, and again they would share in the decoration. Veronica couldn't remember the last time she had looked forward to Christmas, but this year, well, this year was different. This year she was with a family that wasn't nearly as proper as she'd been told. And a man who was somewhat more proper than one would have thought. It was all so confusing.

Sebastian had kissed her like it was his right. Like she was his. And, Lord help her, she'd kissed him back, in front of his family, like he was truly hers.

Sebastian sat at his desk in the library and looked over the papers his estate manager had left for him. *His estate manager.* He grinned. Once again all was going well in his world.

Veronica hadn't been angry with him, although he still wasn't sure why. The woman he loved was pretending to be his wife, which was not as good as her really being his wife but wasn't bad nonetheless. Everyone in the family seemed to be enjoying themselves. And Christmas was only a day away. Yes, indeed, all was going extremely well.

"Sir," Stokes said from the open door. "You have a visitor. An American." He sniffed. "A Mr. Sinclair."

"Sinclair is here?"

"Yes, sir."

"How odd." What on earth would Sinclair be doing here? "Show him in."

"Yes, sir." Stokes turned, then turned back. "And might I say, on behalf of the staff, you have our heartiest congratulations."

"I do?" Sebastian said cautiously.

"Apparently, there was some confusion upon your arrival. We did not realize that Lady Smithson, or rather Lady Hadley-Attwater, was your wife." A slight hint of reproach shone in his eyes.

"Yes, well." Sebastian tried not to squirm. Yet another deceit he would have to confess to, although this one could really be called a mistake and certainly not intentional. He brightened at the thought. "Nothing to worry about, Stokes. Misunderstandings happen all the time."

"Yes, sir." Stokes nodded and left the room. Sebastian had the distinct impression the butler knew exactly what was going on in the house.

Sinclair strolled into the library. "Greetings and felicitations of the season, old man. Quite an impressive little place you have."

Sebastian eyed his friend. "What are you doing here?"

"I came to warn you, and at no little inconvenience, I might add."

"Warn me about what?"

"First, your sisters came and demanded to know exactly where your new house was located." He sank into a chair and shook his head. "The older one, the fair-haired one, is . . . Well, to call her annoying is being kind. What a demanding bit of baggage she is."

Sebastian chuckled. "Bianca does have a way about her."

Sinclair lowered his voice as if to guard against eavesdroppers. "She's frightening is what she is. She threatened me with dismemberment if I didn't give her your location. And from the look in her eye, I'd wager she would do it, too."

"If you're here to warn me about their arrival, you are too late."

"I considered warning you about them, but I decided a man who doesn't tell his closest friend that he's married doesn't deserve warning." He shook his head. "How could you not tell me?"

"Keep your voice down." Sebastian jumped to his feet, strode to the door, and shut it quickly. "I'm not married."

"What do you mean, you're not married? Your sisters said—"

"I mean, I asked her, and as you know, she said no. You suggested I accept her offer to be my mistress, at least for now, and I did so." He strode back to his chair and sat down. "Unfortunately, my younger sisters jumped to the conclusion that we had married. They told my brothers and older sister, all of whom took it upon themselves to join us for Christmas." He blew a long breath. "And only Miranda and Bianca know Veronica is not my wife."

"And Lady Smithson is?"

"Acting as my wife." Sebastian nodded. "Just until after Christmas."

"Then you'll tell your family?"

"I'll have to."

"After Christmas but before your birthday? Or afterward?"

"Bloody hell." Sebastian groaned. "I hadn't thought of that. It very nearly slipped my mind. I haven't mentioned it to Veronica, either, and I probably should."

The American stared in obvious disbelief, then snorted back a laugh. "Good God, man, what were you thinking?"

"Apparently I wasn't." Sebastian shrugged. "But it seems to be going well. . . ."

Sinclair laughed. "Not for long."

"What do you mean?" Sebastian narrowed his eyes. "You said you came to warn me. Warn me about what?"

"There is nothing I like better than a good farce." Sinclair grinned. "And, as I have no particular plans for Christmas, I shall stay and see how it ends. Indeed, I wouldn't miss this for all the adventure in the world."

"You aren't invited," Sebastian said sharply, then rolled his eyes at the ceiling. "Yes, of course, you're more than welcome to stay." He paused. "Warn me about what?"

"Your brothers and sisters are the least of your problems." The American chuckled.

"Warn me about what?"

The door to the library flew open.

"I'm not sure if I should be furious with you or quite, quite delighted."

Sebastian smiled weakly and got to his feet. "Good day, Mother."

Chapter 17

"**I** have decided to be pleased." Helena Hadley-Attwater, the dowager Countess of Waterston, swept across the room and presented her cheek for her son to kiss. "You are a fortunate man."

Sebastian dutifully kissed her. "Am I, Mother? For what?"

"Why, that I have decided to forgive you for marrying without so much as a word to me. And marrying a woman I have yet to meet, although from everything I know, she is more than appropriate for you. Indeed, she is an excellent match."

Behind her, Sinclair was on his feet. He choked back a laugh.

"Ah, Mr. Sinclair." She turned toward the American.

"Lady Waterston," Sinclair said with a knowing grin. "How delightful to see you again."

"Did you think you would beat me here, young man?"

"I don't wish to sound impertinent, Lady Waterston, but I believe I did." Laughter lurked in his eyes.

"Only by a few minutes or so." She waved off his comment. "And, as we did have a stop or two to make, why, I would say we arrived at very nearly the same time." Her eyes narrowed slightly. "Don't you agree?"

"Absolutely." Sinclair nodded. "Indeed, if one subtracts the time your stops took—"

"As I would consider most fair." She nodded.

"—then one could say that you arrived before I did."

"You are a clever sort." She beamed. "You're not married, are you, Mr. Sinclair?"

Sinclair cast a startled look at his friend. Sebastian shrugged. "No."

"Betrothed?"

"No," Sinclair said slowly. Sebastian wondered if he still wished to stay for Christmas.

"How sad for you." She hooked her arm through Sinclair's and escorted him to the door. "I do hope you're joining us for Christmas."

"Us?" Sebastian said cautiously.

"Of course, dear." She pinned her son with a firm look. "You didn't think I would go to Italy and miss my youngest son's first Christmas with his new wife in his new house?"

"I hadn't thought—"

"I daresay there's a great deal you hadn't thought about." She turned her gaze toward his friend. "Mr. Sinclair, you will stay, won't you?"

Sinclair had the distinct look of a man caught in a trap of his own making. Good. "Well, I haven't really—"

"Of course he will, Mother," Sebastian said smoothly and with far more satisfaction than one friend should have for another's plight. "He was just saying how pleased he is to be here."

"Excellent." She favored Sinclair with a satisfied smile.

"Then we shall have time to have a nice, long talk." She opened the door. "I should like to know all about your family. You're American, aren't you?"

"Well, yes, but—"

"How lovely." She nudged him out the door. "I look forward to our chat." She shut the door behind him.

"And who do you have in mind for my poor, unsuspecting friend?"

"No one, as of yet."

"I thought Portia was at the top of your list?"

She raised a brow. "You know about my list?"

"Everyone knows about your list."

"It's an excellent list and serves a most beneficial purpose."

"No doubt."

"However, Mr. Sinclair would never do for Portia." Mother crossed the room and settled into the chair Sinclair had vacated. "He is American, and Portia would never allow herself to become involved with anyone who did not conform to her ideas of a perfect match." She shook her head. "No, Portia is not the right woman for him. And Miranda has only been a widow for less than two years. She is not at all ready for a new husband, although at some point, an adventurous type might suit her nicely. It's almost a pity Bianca is not a widow, although I would not wish that annoying husband of hers ill."

"No?"

"No, dear." She sniffed. "That would be wrong."

"Aside from that tiny detail," Sebastian said, "Mr. Sinclair is not overly fond of Bianca. He thinks she's frightening."

"Nonsense." Mother scoffed. "I daresay Mr. Sinclair isn't afraid of anything. Regardless, Bianca doesn't like him, either. Precisely what would make it so much fun for the rest of us, and her as well, although she would deny it. It scarcely matters, anyway, as she is not currently free to be on my list. And Bianca is not why I am here." Her eyes narrowed. "I should tell you I do not appreciate finding out that my youngest son has wed through a chance encounter in Paris with an acquaintance of my daughter's mother-in-law."

He stared. "A what?"

She sighed. "Portia and I were on our way to Italy, and we had planned on spending a few days in Paris. I have always liked Paris, and it does seem the sort of city one doesn't simply go through but should stop and enjoy."

"And?"

"And." Her brows drew together. "And as I am telling this story, I shall tell it in my own time. Impatience, Sebastian, is not a virtue."

"Very well, Mother." He crossed his arms over his chest, propped a hip on his desk, and studied her. "Go on."

"It scarcely matters now. Suffice it to say, I heard of your marriage . . . Oh, what would it be?" She thought for a moment. "At least fourth hand. Why, I have had more direct knowledge of political scandals than I had of my own son's marriage."

"I am sorry," he said with genuine remorse. He was indeed sorry. And the list of precisely what he was sorry for grew with every passing day. "I fully intended to tell you, but, well, it was all quite unexpected." Which was very nearly the truth. His spirits brightened. Indeed, he did intend to tell his mother when he married, and almost everything that had happened from the moment he'd met Veronica was unexpected.

"Well, what's done is done, I suppose." Mother studied

him. "I cannot tell you how pleased I am. Indeed, we are all pleased. While I have never met Lady Smithson, I do know of her. And of course, I am acquainted with her family."

"You are?"

"Oh my, yes. I have known Charlotte Bramhall and her brother, Viscount Bramhall, for years, although I was better acquainted with his wife, Lady Smithson's—"

"Veronica."

"Yes, of course, Veronica. I knew her mother. Lovely woman. As was Miss Bramhall. But, of course, we all were then. Now, if we're lucky, we're considered to have held up well. Or worse, we are described as handsome women, which seems to mean while we were considered beautiful once, now we simply have character. And if we have had the fortitude to have survived our husbands, our titles are coupled with the word *dowager,* which is a dreadful, dreadful word and, to me, has always conjured up images of farm animals that have outlived their usefulness. Growing older is not at all pleasant for a woman, although it is somewhat better than moldering in a grave, I suppose." She shuddered. "Now, what was I saying?"

He bit back a smile. "You were talking about—"

"Ah, yes," she continued. "Why, I recall being present at her engagement ball."

He drew his brows together. "Veronica's mother's?"

"Oh no, I'm speaking of Miss Bramhall's engagement ball. To . . . Oh, what was his name? Ah yes, it was Tolliver."

Sebastian stared. "Hugo Tolliver?"

"*Sir* Hugo Tolliver now, if I'm not mistaken. They were the perfect couple, or so people said at the time." His mother smiled at the memory. "She was lovely and spirited. He was a dashing explorer, always off wandering the world." She cast her son a pointed look. "Very much like you."

"How interesting." There was nothing his mother liked more than gossip, even long-ago gossip, although she would adamantly deny it. Still, as long as she was talking about the past, the present might be avoided. "Please, go on."

"There's nothing more to say." She shrugged. "One minute they were planning to marry, and the next they weren't. There was some gossip, of course, as to what passed between them, but I did not know either of them well enough to know the truth of it. Veronica would know, I suspect. Or you could ask Miss Bramhall herself, although that might be somewhat presumptuous of you. It was a very long time ago."

"The shrew and the old fool," he said under his breath. "Who would have imagined?"

"As I said, it was considered a perfect match. Do let me know if you find out the truth of it. I have always been curious as to what happened. In the meantime, I am quite looking forward to meeting your wife." She nodded. "And of course, her family is interested in meeting you."

"I have met Miss Bramhall," he said uneasily. "As for the rest of her family, I'm sure that time will come."

"I do believe family should be together at Christmas, you know. And apparently, the fates have conspired to ensure that we will be. Most of us, anyway," she added. "I was only going to Italy with Portia in the first place because Diana and her family had other plans. Adrian and Evelyn have always been a world unto themselves but would include Hugh and Bianca and Miranda for Christmas. In spite of what you have said, you could not be counted on to even stay in the country, let alone join us for Christmas, and Portia could not be dissuaded. Of all of you, it seemed she needed me, even if she would not admit it. Besides, I thought it might be time for something different." She met his gaze firmly. "Even those of us past the first blush of youth, we who are *handsome,* are not immune to the occasional desire for adventure, albeit as minimal as changing location for Christmas.

"However, when I heard Diana's plans had changed because you had at last married, well, I had to turn around and come back to England." She shook her head. "It was fate telling me I was shirking my motherly responsibilities by abandoning my family at Christmas."

"I imagine Portia wasn't especially pleased."

"I don't know what's gotten into her." She heaved a long-suffering sigh. "She refused to come with me. She said she had planned to spend Christmas in Italy and Italy was where she intended to be. Besides that . . ." She narrowed her eyes. "Portia refused to believe you were married. She said there must be some mistake and she was not going to change her plans because of an obvious misunderstanding. Why on earth would she think such a thing?"

"I have no idea." He shook his head in as innocent a manner as he could muster. No doubt Portia knew of Veronica's desire to be a mistress rather than a wife. "Portia is a good friend of Veronica's. Perhaps, as it has all happened so quickly . . ."

"Perhaps." She considered him thoughtfully, and he resisted the urge to squirm.

Blast it all, he wasn't a child caught doing something he shouldn't. He ignored the thought that he was involved in a deception that had taken on a life of its own. Still, he was a grown man, a man who had made a mark in the world, with his own house and an estate manager. "Well, we shall miss her, as I intend for this to be a splendid Christmas for all of us."

After Christmas was another matter, but it did no good to dwell on it now. Best to take this one day at a time, or rather, one unexpected guest at a time.

A thought struck him, and he drew his brows together. "If Portia isn't with you, then who—"

A knock sounded at the library door.

"You told Sinclair, '*We* had a stop or two—'"

The door opened. Stokes's protest could be heard over a vaguely familiar female voice.

He stared at his mother in horror.

"You should send for your wife, dear. I can't wait to meet her." His mother leaned toward him in a confidential manner. "I have a lovely surprise for her. I do so love surprises at Christmas." She cast him a satisfied smile. "And you are absolutely right. It's going to be a splendid Christmas."

He'd sent for her? Sebastian had *sent* for her? Like a . . . a *wife?* It was all Veronica could do to keep from hurrying toward the library, but she would not give him the satisfaction of thinking, for so much as a single second, that she was at his beck and call. Ha! It was difficult to keep a sedate pace as the sooner she saw him, the sooner she could tell him in no uncertain terms that she would not be fetched! Besides, she couldn't help being curious. The footman who had been told by Stokes, who had been told by Sebastian, to *fetch her* was most confused as to why she was being summoned. Admittedly, confusion was to be expected. None of the servants here were used to having as many unexpected guests, or any, as had arrived thus far.

Her step slowed. Admittedly, Sebastian was not the type of man who sent for his wife like Petruchio in *The Taming of the Shrew*. Sebastian was the type of man willing to accept a woman's advice and accept as well that she might be better versed on some matters than he. Still, marriage changed a man. Good Lord, what was she thinking? Sebastian wasn't married. Nor was she.

Stokes stood outside the closed library doors, as if guarding the entry. Even as well trained as he was, he couldn't hide the relief that showed on his face at her approach. The moment she saw the servant's face, she realized she had jumped to irrational conclusions. Perhaps Sebastian had sent for her because he needed her. She couldn't recall ever having been needed before. Charles had loved her, but he hadn't needed her. The oddest warmth spread through her at the thought.

"The plot thickens, my lady," Stokes said under his breath, then opened the doors. What on earth did the butler mean by that? She stepped into the library and froze.

In a distant part of her mind that could still appreciate the inherent humor in the farce that held her captive, she noted the tableau looked as if it had indeed been staged for maximum effect. Her grandmother and a lady of about Aunt Lotte's age were seated in the chairs near the desk. Lotte stood nearby. Her father perused the bookshelves, as, of course, he would. Sebastian stood as well, a stunned look in his eyes, as if he couldn't quite believe the trap he found himself caught in. If she had been sitting in a theater, the scene onstage would have been most amusing and she would have wondered what in the world could possibly happen next. As it was, for perhaps the first time in her life, words failed her.

"You should have told us." Aunt Lotte hurried forward and kissed her cheek. "I had no idea you were so much as considering marriage."

"It came as quite a surprise." Her father cast her a wry glance. "But then you have never done the expected."

She managed a weak smile, wondering if she looked as shocked as her *husband.* She tried to wrest a measure of composure, then crossed the room to her father and kissed his cheek. "Good day, Father."

"Is it?" Amusement shone in his eyes. He lowered his voice. "I had my doubts."

"As do I," she said under her breath, then turned to the others. She forced a pleasant note to her voice. "What are you doing here?"

"Plum pudding," her grandmother announced, as if it was obvious. "That's why we are here. Plum pudding."

Apparently, Grandmother was having one of her *special* moments.

"Plum pudding?" Veronica said cautiously.

"Plum pudding." Grandmother nodded. "You will be having plum pudding, won't you? I do so love plum pudding." She turned an annoyed eye on the lady sitting in the other chair. "You said there would be plum pudding."

"And I'm sure there will be, Lady Bramhall." The lady smiled and patted Veronica's grandmother's arm.

"Goodness, Mother." Lotte huffed. "We have not come for plum pudding." She turned a firm eye on her niece. "Although it is expected."

Veronica stared.

"For Christmas dinner?" Lotte said.

"Plum pudding," Veronica repeated. "For Christmas dinner."

Lotte frowned. "Have you taken leave of your senses?"

"If I am lucky," Veronica murmured.

Lotte studied her. "We have come for Christmas, of course."

"They've come for Christmas, Veronica," Sebastian said with a forced smile and an edge of panic in his voice. "Christmas."

"Why?" she said without thinking.

"When Lady Waterston told us that you had married her son and that her entire family was joining you at your new home in the country, we decided your family should be here as well." A chastising note sounded in her aunt's voice. "You should have invited us."

"We didn't invite anyone," Sebastian said quickly, as if that was an important point. "Everyone just . . . appeared."

"For the plum pudding." Grandmother nodded.

"For you." Her father's gaze met hers. "It seemed to us if you were going to be surrounded by your new family, it might be nice to have your old family around you as well."

Her heart caught. "Thank you, Father."

Her father cast her an affectionate smile, and at once she was a little girl again. Her father, grandmother, and aunt were indeed an odd lot, but they were hers. And even if she didn't realize she might have need of them, they realized it in their own unique way.

Sebastian cleared his throat. "Veronica, I should like to introduce you to my mother. Helena, Lady Waterston."

"Your mother?" The same edge of panic she had heard in Sebastian's voice now shaded hers. "How delightful."

"The delight, my dear girl, is mine." Lady Waterston rose from her chair and moved to Veronica. She took her hands and kissed her on both cheeks. "Evelyn calls me

Helena, and I would be pleased if you would do the same. I had very nearly given up on Sebastian staying in one place, let alone finding the right woman." She smiled and squeezed Veronica's hands. "I cannot tell you how happy this has made me."

Guilt surged through Veronica, and it was all she could do not to confess everything.

"Mother decided not to go to Italy, after all," Sebastian said. "So she could join us for Christmas. Isn't that wonderful?"

"Wonderful." If Sebastian's mother hadn't gone to Italy . . . "Then Portia is with you?"

"I'm afraid not." Helena sighed. "When we heard that you and Sebastian had wed, well, I am afraid Portia simply didn't believe it."

Veronica's stomach twisted. "How very odd. Did she say why?"

"Oh, she spouted some nonsense about how neither you nor Sebastian wished to marry." Helena rolled her gaze toward the ceiling. "Utterly absurd, of course, as you obviously are married."

"Obviously." Veronica paused. "Then you went to my family—"

"Helena and I used to be friends," Aunt Lotte said.

"Goodness, Lotte, I would hope we still are." Helena smiled at the other woman. "Admittedly, we have taken different paths through the years." She turned to the others. "Lotte champions causes. I have championed my children. Although they scarcely need me these days."

"Nonsense, Mother," Sebastian said without the least bit of conviction.

"Regardless, I, for one, am looking forward to spending Christmas with old friends and new additions and a family who, at the very least, will pretend to need me."

Helena smiled at Veronica. "Now, if you don't mind, I should like to be shown to my room. It's been a very long day thus far."

Lotte nodded. "For all of us."

Veronica started for the door. "I should speak to Mrs. Bigelow about your accommodations."

"No need." Her grandmother rose to her feet. "We informed your staff upon our arrival that we would be staying for the plum pudding."

"They seem very efficient." Lotte nodded approvingly.

"One does hope so," Veronica murmured. It would be one less thing for her to worry about.

"And I suspect you would like to have a word with your husband," Helena said.

"Oh, more than one." Veronica laughed an odd sort of strangled laugh.

"Well done, Sebastian," Helena said to her son, then hooked her arm through Lotte's. "You and I have a great deal of catching up to do."

"It has been a long time. Why, I remember . . ."

The ladies filed out, Grandmother pausing to speak to Veronica in a low voice. "Do make sure your cook understands the importance of brandy in a plum pudding. There can never be too much, but if there's not enough . . ." She shook her head. "It's scarcely festive if there is not enough brandy, and it is Christmas, after all."

"It is indeed." Veronica managed a weak smile.

"I should like to have a closer look at your library later, if you don't mind," her father said to Sebastian. "You have quite an extensive collection here."

"Please do, sir. Consider it as you would your own."

"Excellent." Father cast her an encouraging smile and followed the ladies out of the room. Stokes closed the door behind him.

She stared at her *husband*. "What are we going to do?"

"Right now I am going to follow your grandmother's advice." He strode across the room to where a decanter of brandy sat on a side table, poured a glass, and downed nearly half of it in one swallow.

"That is not going to help," she snapped, crossed the room, took his glass and finished the brandy, then returned the glass. The potent liquor burned her throat, but it was well worth it.

"It's not going to hurt," he muttered and refilled his glass.

"Now, tell me." She drew a deep breath. "How did your mother get the happy news? I thought she was safely out of the country."

"She was." He took a sip. "She met someone who knows Diana's mother-in-law in Paris—"

"In Paris?" Her voice rose. "Paris?"

"Yes, Paris," he said sharply.

She stared at him with growing horror. "Do you realize what this means?"

"Any number of things occur to me, but what are you thinking?"

"If your mother heard about this in Paris, can you imagine what is being said in London?"

He stared at her for a moment, then poured her a glass of brandy and handed it to her.

She took a long swallow. It didn't help. "Everyone we know, everyone who admires the well-known Sir Sebastian Hadley-Attwater will think we're married. Married!"

"Well, yes, but—"

"But we're not!" She shook her head. "Good Lord, Sebastian, when people discover we're not married . . . Can you imagine the scandal?"

"I thought you weren't concerned with scandal?"

"I wasn't when it was someone else's scandal! When it was"—she searched for the right word—"*theoretical* scandal! I have no problem with scandal when it is an amusing topic of conversation. But this is different." She drained her glass and set it down. Inebriation had a huge amount of appeal at the moment. "This is our scandal, and we are up to our noses in it!"

"You should have thought of that before you decided to become a mistress instead of a wife."

"Admittedly, it was a flaw in my plan!" She glared. "Not that I have truly become a mistress yet, have I?"

"You locked your door!" Indignation rang in his words.

"And one doesn't seduce the woman one intends to marry!" she mimicked.

"Admittedly, that might have been a flaw in *my* plan!"

She stared. "This is the most absurd argument I have ever had!"

"Appropriate, then, as this is the most absurd situation I have ever found myself in!"

"And whose fault is that?"

"Mine!" He ran his hand through his hair. "I should never have assumed you would marry me simply because I asked."

She huffed. "I would never marry you simply because you asked."

"Then why would you marry me?"

"Because I can no longer imagine my life without you!"

"You can't?" He stared.

"Apparently not." She crossed her arms over her chest. "But it doesn't change anything."

He grinned. "It changes everything."

"It simply . . ." She thought for a moment. "It changes

the discussion, that's all. Broadens it, if you will. And it's not a discussion we should be having now." She turned on her heel and paced. "Now, we need to think of a way out of this mess."

"We could marry."

"Unless we are going to wed secretly and in the next hour or so, that is not a solution." She paced. "We should be able to think of something. We are both intelligent people, although I am starting to question your intelligence somewhat."

He laughed.

She stopped in midstep and stared at him. "This is not funny."

"No, of course not." He struggled to suppress a grin.

"What do you find so amusing?"

"Nothing, absolutely nothing." He set his glass down, stepped close, and swept her into his arms.

"What are you doing?" She glared at him.

He grinned. "You're smitten with me."

"Nonsense." She sniffed. "You are the most annoying man I have ever met."

"Nonetheless, you are head over heels." He kissed the curve of her neck.

She shivered and tried to push out of his arms. "Stop that at once. This is not the time."

"It's always the time," his lips murmured against her neck.

"You are as arrogant as you are annoying."

"You're mad for me."

"I am furious with you." Good Lord, what was he doing? "It's your arrogance that got us into this."

"I know, and I feel a great deal of remorse."

"I'm not sensing your remorse at the moment."

"Then you're not paying attention." His lips trailed along the line of her jaw. "I am deeply, deeply sorry."

"Oh . . ." She moaned in spite of her best intentions. "I didn't like lying to your mother."

He raised his head and frowned. "You do realize bringing up a man's mother at a time like this is not conducive to . . ."

She raised a brow. "To what?"

"To everything." He blew a disgruntled breath and released her. "And you didn't lie to her."

"She thinks we're married."

"Yes, but you never said we were married. Therefore you didn't lie."

"I didn't say we weren't."

"Which still isn't a lie."

She shook her head. "I have been known to tell an occasional mistruth when necessary. Indeed, I have been rather creative on occasion, but I've never lied to a mother. I don't have a mother, but it seems to me one doesn't lie to one's mother. Or, in this case, one's fraudulent husband's mother."

"Ha." He shrugged. "One lies to one's mother all the time. There are some things it's better if mothers don't know. Do you think my mother would rest easier if she'd known exactly what my plans were before I undertook any particular expedition?"

"Probably not."

"Definitely not." He nodded. "Why, lying to one's mother could be considered doing one's best to protect her."

She stared. "You have a clever way of twisting the world to your own advantage, Sebastian."

"It's a gift." He flashed her a wicked grin, then

sobered. "As I see it, we have two options. We can confess all, but as you pointed out, that would ruin Christmas for everyone."

"Or?"

"We can bravely carry on."

She widened her eyes. "I can't lie to my family."

"You lied to my family. And"—he paused to emphasize his words—"to my mother."

"For her own good, according to you. Nonetheless . . ." She shook her head. "I cannot lie to my family."

He studied her for a long moment. "Do what you think is best."

She stared. "Aren't you going to try to dissuade me?"

"No." He chose his words with care. "I would never ask you to do anything that makes you uneasy. Although, as I recall, it was your idea to go along with this deception."

"Yes, I suppose but—"

He held up his hand to quiet her. "That is neither here nor there at the moment. I trust you, Veronica. I trust your intelligence and your judgment. Whether or not you tell your family the truth is your decision. I shall deal with the repercussions, whatever they may be. But know this." He reached for her again, and she let him pull her close. He gazed into her eyes. "No matter what happens next, it makes no difference to me."

She stared up at him. "It doesn't?"

"No. You are the only thing that matters."

"And you trust me?"

"With my future." He nodded. "With my life."

"Oh." For the second time today she had no idea what to say. "Oh."

He grinned. "Have I rendered you speechless?"

"No." She sighed. "Perhaps."

"Do you know why?"

"I have no idea."

"Because . . ." He kissed the tip of her nose. "You are mad for me."

She gazed up at him and sighed. "Or just mad."

Chapter 18

"I thought I'd find you here." Veronica closed the door of the library behind her and smiled at her father.

"This is a most impressive collection." Father stood near the shelves behind the desk, paging through a book. "I understand it came along with the house."

Veronica nodded. "Sebastian hasn't yet had the chance to thoroughly assess exactly what's here."

"From what I've seen thus far, he's in for quite a treat. Your husband is a lucky man."

Veronica winced.

She'd never imagined that deception would settle like a heavy weight around her heart. But settle it had.

Dinner, however, would have made any hostess proud. The company was congenial; the conversation spirited. Much of it centered around Christmas and decorating the house and the tree tomorrow. Even her family joined in and had a pleasant time. She wasn't certain if it was due to the festive nature of the season or if Sebastian's family always enjoyed one another's company or a combination of both, but there was an easiness about the gathering and a warmth that included her relations that she had not anticipated. She and Sebastian were the only ones not completely enjoying themselves, although he did make a good show of it. And why not? He had become all that was expected of him, at least for the moment.

But every time her marriage was mentioned, her stomach clenched. She hadn't had a chance to speak to anyone in her family, and she still wasn't sure if confession was wise. But wise or not, she had decided she couldn't get through Christmas with unease and guilt threatening to consume her.

In addition, she'd never imagined she'd be at all bothered by the specter of scandal, but there it was, hovering over her like Marley's ghost. That, too, made her stomach twist.

She drew a deep breath. "There is something I wish to discuss with you."

"First." He snapped the book closed. "I owe you an apology, Veronica."

"You do?" She drew her brows together. "Whatever for?"

"Being here, in this house, with this family . . ." He shook his head. "It made me realize how I failed you."

"I have no idea what you're talking about."

"No, I suppose not." He replaced the book on the shelf. "It struck me tonight at dinner with Sir Sebastian's family, now your family, of course—"

"About that—"

"Allow me to finish." He met her gaze directly. "This is not an easy thing to confess."

"Confession is often awkward," she said under her breath. "But I'm afraid I don't understand."

"It's not something I did but rather something I never did." He nodded at the brandy. "May I?"

"Yes, of course."

He moved to the decanter and filled a glass. She'd never noticed before, but he was a handsome man, or perhaps distinguished was a better term. Taller than she, graying around the temples, kind eyes. Sad eyes. She'd never noticed that, either. But then he was her father; he was simply there.

"Would you care for some?"

"No, thank you." She'd had enough brandy for one day.

He swirled the brandy in his glass. "When your mother died, I felt as though I had died as well."

"Father, you don't have to—"

"No, I do." He blew a long breath. "I turned your upbringing over to Lotte and my mother. It wasn't a deliberate thing. They were competent and I was not. You were only five. I simply had no interest in anything."

Her heart twisted. "Father."

"When you married Charles, I thought it was a mistake. He was so much older than you, nearly my age. But I had never advised you before. I felt I had no right to do so then. And you did seem happy."

She swallowed past the lump in her throat. "I was."

"Tonight I realized how much of a failure I had been as a father. All that talk of Christmas." He paused. "Did you know your mother and I met at a Christmas ball?"

She shook her head.

"That first Christmas after she died, I couldn't bear it. She loved Christmas." He smiled a sad sort of smile. "I could never bring myself to celebrate Christmas the way she did. The way she would have wanted us to. In that, I failed her as well."

"Father—"

"So, whenever possible, I preferred to be out of the country for Christmas. Those years that we remained in England, well, my mother and sister understood and made little fuss about the day. Now I see how wrong I was."

"I don't think—"

"Christmas is a time to celebrate family, those we love. To give thanks and to share and be with one another." He shook his head. "I denied you that. I only thought of myself, and what I had lost at Christmas. I should have remarried, given you brothers and sisters—"

"Father, you needn't—"

"At the very least I should have cherished what I had." He met her gaze. "I should have cherished you."

Her throat tightened. "I've always known you loved me."

"Oh, I was never unkind." A wry smile curved his lips. "I will say that for my behavior."

She chose her words with care. "I have always wondered if you would have preferred a son."

"I suppose I would have liked a son. But in addition to, not in place of." He shook his head. "But I did you a grave disservice, my dear girl. I don't know if I can forgive myself. I didn't realize there was anything to forgive until tonight, but I hope that you might see your way clear . . ."

"As I didn't know you were doing me a disservice, there's nothing really to forgive." She smiled. "You never said the words, but I have always felt that you would be there if I needed you. You are my father, and I shall always love you."

He winced. "Obligatory love."

"Not at all," she said staunchly.

"Perhaps you will allow me to . . ." He paused. "I shall try to be a better father, not that a grown woman needs a father, I suppose."

"I shall always need my father."

"And perhaps we could become friends as well." He smiled. "You've turned out quite nicely, you know. The credit for that goes to my sister and mother. I have no right to be, but I am proud of you."

She studied him for a moment. "Why did you tell me this?"

"As I said, it struck me tonight, seeing you with your new family." He shrugged. "Christmas is a time of beginnings. I should like to begin anew with you. I should like to be a . . . a better part of your life than I have been up to now. If you will allow me that privilege."

"I would like that."

"You fit in with them. I saw that tonight. I saw all that you had missed. They're exceptional people, I think, your new family and your husband."

"He's not my husband," she blurted.

He narrowed his eyes. "What?"

"It's a misunderstanding, if you will. One that has gotten completely out of hand."

"Then perhaps you should explain it to me."

"Well . . ." She thought for a moment. "It's quite simple, really. Sebastian wishes to marry me, but I would rather be his mistress than his wife—"

"You what?"

"I wish to make my own decisions, keep my independence—"

"Good Lord." Father groaned. "This is my fault. I should have anticipated this. It's the inevitable result of your grandmother and aunt's influence."

"A moment ago you were giving them credit."

"And now I am blaming them!"

"It scarcely matters, Father. Not really. I am who I am."

"Strong and independent?"

"I hope so." She sighed. "There is nothing wrong with being strong and independent. Even for a woman."

"No, there isn't. If I had been stronger . . ." He shook his head. "As you said, it scarcely matters. What's done is done. Now, about this misunderstanding."

"Sebastian's family arrived, unexpectedly, I might add—"

"As did we."

"Yes, and they thought we were wed. So we have pretended to be married." She sighed again. "Sebastian has always felt like something of a disappointment to his family. He sees himself as the black sheep. It seemed to me that it really wouldn't hurt anyone to allow them all to have a pleasant Christmas. Not to ruin it for everyone with an insignificant thing like the truth."

"I see." He studied her. "So you aren't his wife?"

"No."

"But you are his mistress?"

"That's not entirely accurate, either." She grimaced. "And that part is rather complicated."

"Apparently." He took a long drink. "As your father, I should probably thrash him thoroughly for besmirching your honor."

"Nonsense. He hasn't besmirched anything yet."

"Now I am completely confused." He raised a brow. "You are not sharing this man's bed?"

"Father!" She gasped.

"Not the sort of thing a father asks a daughter?"

"I wouldn't think so. I am a grown woman, after all, a widow."

"Yes, well, when one's daughter says she wishes to be a mistress but is not exactly a mistress, these are the questions that come to mind." He studied her. "Why did you tell me this?"

She met his gaze directly. "I didn't want to lie to you. I never have before."

"Will you be telling Lotte and my mother as well?"

She nodded. "Aunt Lotte at least. I'm not sure if telling Grandmother is wise."

"Perhaps not. One never knows what she might say at any given time. She blames it on age, but she's always been that way. Well, then, if you don't want me to thrash him, what do you want me to do?"

She stared at him. "I don't know. I hadn't thought that far. Indeed, I seem to be plagued of late with not thinking things through."

He thought for a moment. "It seems to me, your initial agreement to carry on with this charade, while ill advised, was well intended. You're doing this for him."

She nodded.

"How very interesting," he murmured. "Why?"

"Because his family's opinion is important to him."

"And therefore you are willing to help him."

"Of course."

"You love him, then?"

"Well . . ." She raised her chin. "Yes, I believe I do."

"I see."

She sighed. "Then perhaps you could explain it to me. I have been nothing but confused since the moment I met him."

He chuckled. "I know I have no right to do so, and I have never done so before, but might I offer you a piece of advice?"

"Please do."

"Love, my dear girl, is rare and fragile and not to be treated lightly. One must weigh the sacrifice against the gain. Let me ask you this. Do you wish to spend the rest of your life with him?"

She blew a long breath. "Yes."

"Then any sacrifice is worth it, isn't it?" His eyes softened. "Do you really think a man worthy of your love would wish you to be anything you aren't? If Sir Sebastian returns your love, and given the way he looked at you tonight, I suspect he does, he loves you for your strength and independence and all those other sterling and not so sterling qualities of yours that make you uniquely you. Although . . ." He smiled. "You do look very much like your mother."

"That's the loveliest thing you have ever said to me." She sniffed back an unexpected tear.

"I should have said it years ago. It was entirely too long in coming." He sipped his brandy. "I shall keep your secret as long as you wish. I won't say anything to Sir Sebastian's family. I don't especially approve, but I do understand. One does what one must for those we love."

"Even if one would prefer not to?"

"Especially if one would prefer not to."

"Even so . . ." She shook her head. "I . . ." She met his gaze. "I'm, well . . . I don't know—"

"Afraid?"

She nodded. "Somewhat."

"As well you should be, dear girl. Love is the most terrifying thing in the world. Second only to losing it."

"I don't want to lose him." She drew her brows together. "What shall I do?"

"I can't tell you that. However, as I am giving you the benefit of my years of wisdom in one dose, as it were, allow me to give you one more piece of advice." He paused for a long moment. "One can't count on anything in this world except love. Life hands us all sorts of surprises, good and bad. And life can be entirely too short. Now then." A brisk note sounded in his voice. "Shall we call for your aunt, or would you prefer to speak to her alone?"

"Would you stay?"

"If you wish."

"I would like nothing better. Although . . ." She cast him a wry smile. "I think I would like that brandy now."

"And?"

"They are still in there, sir," Stokes said. "And they have just sent for Lady Hadley-Attwater's aunt."

"Very well." Sebastian nodded. "Let me know when they've concluded their talk."

"If you have need of me, sir—"

"I will call for you. Thank you, Stokes." Sebastian resumed pacing the width of the drawing room.

He shouldn't be at all nervous. He had meant it when he had told Veronica he trusted her to do what she thought was best. While he was indeed ready to deal with the repercussions of the truth, he much preferred to avoid it as long as possible. Regardless of what his family's response was, whether or not it impacted his inheritance or their opinion of him, despite her family's reaction, she was the only thing that mattered.

Still, he did hate feeling helpless.

"Your butler said you were in here pacing." Sinclair strode into the room.

"I seem to be doing a lot of that of late."

Sinclair shook his head in a mournful manner. "This is what comes of not having a well-thought-out plan."

"I had a plan," he snapped. "Let her think she had won. Agree to have her as my mistress, at least through Christmas. Bring her to the country and convince her, seduce her, if you will, into marriage."

"And that has worked out how?"

"Not bloody well. We were invaded by my family and then her family, as you might have noticed." He shook his head. "I am now trapped in a farce of my own making."

"Well, it is entirely your fault."

"For more reasons than I can list." He narrowed his eyes. "But what precisely do you mean?"

"This whole nonsense about not seducing the woman you intend to marry." Sinclair snorted. "It's absurd."

"It seemed the proper way to go about this," Sebastian said in a lofty manner.

"But it's not your nature. You have been with how many women?"

"I don't know." He shrugged. "A few."

"Quite a few that I know of," Sinclair said. "I say forget about that nonsense and seduce her. Seduce her now. Then convince her to marry you, if marriage is what you still want."

"Of course it's what I still want." He paused. "She's locked the door between our rooms."

"She's what?"

"You heard me. She's locked the door between our rooms."

Sinclair stared for a moment, then laughed. "That's the oldest female trick in the world. Deny a man what he wants and a woman can get exactly what she wants."

"I no longer know what she wants." He heaved a frustrated sigh. "But at this very moment she's confessing all to her family."

"Ouch." Sinclair winced. "Do you think her father will shoot you?"

"More likely her aunt."

"Then you have nothing to lose. I say seduce her, seduce her tonight. Break the door down if you have to. Tell her all those things you said to me about her. You will love her more tomorrow than today and how you want to die with her hand in yours—which is an excellent line, by the way, that I fully intend to borrow when the time comes."

Sebastian stared. "Feel free."

"And so on and so forth." Sinclair leveled him a firm look. "She loves you, old man. Why on earth would she continue this deception otherwise?"

"She hasn't said it, but then neither have I."

"That's another problem. Tell her, for God's sakes." Sinclair heaved a resigned sigh. "And you used to be so accomplished with women."

"My mind has been muddled since the moment I met her." Resolve surged through Sebastian. "You're right. I'll declare myself, seduce her, and eventually, she will marry me."

Sinclair grinned. "That's the Sir Sebastian I know. Now, in the meantime, your brothers are in the billiards room, smoking your cigars and drinking all of your best liquor. I suggest we join them. A little male companion-ship is exactly what you need before doing battle with the female of the species."

"Agreed." Sebastian nodded, and the two men headed for the billiards room.

It wasn't much of a plan, it probably wasn't even a good plan, but nothing else had worked.

Sinclair was right. Sebastian had been trying to be a proper sort and follow silly rules when that wasn't his na-ture at all. He wanted her in his bed for the rest of her life. And he wanted her there as his wife. And, damnation, he would have her.

Chapter 19

"I never thought I would say such a thing." Lotte stared at her niece. "But, Veronica Smithson, you are a fool."

Veronica widened her eyes. "Why? Because I wish to keep control over my own life?"

"Because you don't understand what you risk," Lotte said firmly.

Her aunt as well as her grandmother had joined them in the library. Grandmother had promptly fallen asleep in a nearby chair.

"You and this man love each other. It was obvious to everyone at that table tonight, if not to you." Lotte glanced at her brother. "Aren't you going to say anything?"

"I have already had my say." He raised his glass. "And you are doing an admirable job."

"I have always treasured my independence and my freedom," Veronica said. "I didn't see why I should have to give that up."

"There is such a thing as compromise, my dear. Sir Sebastian does not strike me as the type of man who would demand complete acquiescence to his every whim." Lotte shook her head. "Men like that are rare and should be snatched up at once."

"Marriage has been known to change a man," Veronica said staunchly.

Lotte snorted. "Not that much. This man has fallen in love with the woman you are now. That is the woman he wants, not some insipid, sniveling creature."

"I can't believe you, of all people, are encouraging marriage." She drew her brows together. "You have always been completely independent and done exactly as you wished."

"And I live in a house that is not my own with my brother and my mother," Lotte snapped.

"You've always seemed quite content with your causes and your charitable work and your travel."

"And I go to bed every night alone! And I shall be alone until I breathe my last." Lotte paused for a long moment. "The worst things in the world, Veronica, are being alone and regret. And knowing you have no one to blame but yourself. There isn't a day that goes by that I don't regret my past decisions. That I don't wonder what might have been if I had not been so afraid of breaking that I was unwilling to bend. Do not use me as an example. I let stubbornness and pride ruin my chances for happiness."

Veronica stared. "I had no idea."

"Of course you didn't. My regret is private. I have never spoken of it to you or anyone."

"I had my suspicions," her father said under his breath.

"And you, dear brother, would indeed recognize regret, but at least yours is not of your own making." She huffed.

"You were unfortunate. I was a fool." She turned to her niece. "Have you ever wondered why I am so adamant about getting women in the Explorers Club?"

"Because women shouldn't be denied membership based simply on their gender," Veronica said firmly.

"That's the official reason, of course, but . . ." She drew a deep breath. "It gives me the opportunity to argue with Hugo. There is nothing in my life that is more fun than debating with that man. It fairly makes my blood rush through my veins."

Veronica gasped. "Are you still in love with him?"

Lotte scoffed. "I detest the very ground beneath his feet."

"My, we are a sorry lot," Grandmother said with a wry chuckle.

Lotte raised a brow. "You haven't been asleep at all, have you?"

"I have been asleep in much the same manner as I have my *special* moments. One hears so much of interest when one is thought to be daft or asleep." She fixed Veronica with a firm eye. "Although I am quite serious about plum pudding. I shall be thoroughly disappointed if it is not as expected." She sighed. "It's the only thing about Christmas that I enjoy anymore. Which I blame on my children as well as on myself. You . . ." She turned toward her son. "You should have put your grief behind you a long time ago."

"I thought I had," Father said simply.

"Perhaps." Grandmother nodded. "But by then you were trapped in a certain manner of living, and it was easier to continue on rather than change. Dear boy, I know how difficult it is. Your father has been gone for thirty years now, and I still expect to turn around and see him or hear his voice or feel the touch of his hand. But you had a daughter that you sadly neglected. As for you . . ." She addressed her daughter. "You lost the love of your life because you were too stubborn to accept that what he wanted was every bit as important as what you wanted."

"I know that." Lotte glared at her mother. "I've had a quarter of a century to realize that."

"Perhaps . . . ," Veronica said cautiously, "it's not too late?"

"You are obviously more romantic than one would think. It is entirely too late, as I have spent a great deal of effort deliberately annoying him through the years. Besides . . ." Lotte shrugged as if it didn't matter. "He despises me."

"And yet, he has never married," Grandmother said thoughtfully.

"Nor have I, which isn't the least bit significant," Lotte said sharply. "And this discussion is not about me, or at least it shouldn't be."

"Ah, yes." Grandmother turned a firm eye on Veronica. "A mistress? For goodness' sakes, Veronica, you are smarter than that. Whatever were you thinking?"

"I have already admitted that I did not think this through as thoroughly as one might have hoped."

"It appears you didn't think it through at all," Grandmother said in a reproving manner. "We did not raise you to become a mistress. What on earth made you think of such a thing?"

"It seemed like a good idea at the time," Veronica said. "I would retain my independence, control of my finances, of my life and still have . . . well . . ." She squared her shoulders. "I was tired of not having a man in my life."

"But you didn't expect to fall in love with him, did you?" Grandmother studied her. "And you have."

Veronica sighed. "So it would appear."

"I never dreamed . . ." Grandmother shook her head. "It was to be expected, I suppose. Being raised by a bitter spinster—"

"I am not bitter." Lotte glared.

"—and a domineering old woman." Grandmother looked around the group. "What? No one is going to protest that?"

"You haven't always been old," Father said with a smile.

"Humph." Grandmother huffed, then met Veronica's gaze. "My apologies, my dear. Much of this is our fault."

"No, Grandmother, it's not," Veronica said firmly. "It's not your fault, nor Lotte's nor Father's. You taught me to be independent, which also means being responsible for my own decisions, right and wrong. And in this instance . . ." She shook her head. "You're right. I didn't expect to love him. And I know Sebastian well enough now to see that he would never want me to be anyone less than who I am."

"Might I point out as well that you have an excellent solicitor who can make certain there are legal arrangements that allow you to maintain control of your fortune," Father said. "If you decide to marry him."

Veronica blew a long breath. "I believe I already have."

"Excellent." Grandmother nodded. "Now, what do you wish us to do?"

"To do?" Veronica drew her brows together. "What do you mean?"

"About the fact that his family thinks you are already married." Lotte rolled her gaze toward the ceiling. "That's even harder to believe than that nonsense about being a mistress."

"It wasn't planned," Veronica said.

"One would hope not." Grandmother nodded. "If it had been planned, one would think it would go better."

"Although it does seem to be going rather well," Father murmured. "I don't believe anyone suspects you're not married. And as you have not been with him in a carnal sense—"

"Father!" She groaned.

Lotte stared. "You haven't?"

"Whatever is wrong with the man," Grandmother said under her breath.

"Not being with him in a *carnal sense* was not part of the plan, either! Indeed, it's always been part of my plan." Veronica sighed. "He doesn't think it's"—she winced at the word—"*proper* to seduce the woman one intends to marry."

"A man with his reputation?" Lotte stared. "Whoever would have imagined?"

"That's the most . . . honorable thing I have ever heard. He is indeed a unique man." Grandmother pinned her with a firm look. "Marry him, Veronica. Marry him at once."

"Not that it's necessary or that you need it," Father began, "but you have my approval."

"And mine as well," Grandmother added.

"You're right. I don't need it." Veronica's gaze skimmed over the group. They were not the Hadley-Attwaters, who had an effortless ease with one another and marked Christmas with enthusiasm and joy and family. Indeed, this family of hers was eccentric and unusual, but she loved them dearly and she'd never doubted they loved her as well. "But I am most pleased to have it. As for this deception, I do apologize for making you conspirators. But, as the opinion of his family is important to Sebastian, I would prefer he be the one to tell them the truth."

"So you want us to continue this farce?" Lotte asked.

Veronica nodded. "We don't want to ruin Christmas, and this revelation might well do just that."

She glanced at her father and he nodded.

"I see." Grandmother thought for a moment, then grinned. "What fun this will be. It's been years since I've been part of a secret of this magnitude. Very well, then, none of us will say a word. Unless of course . . ." Her brow furrowed, but there was a twinkle in her eye. "The plum pudding does not live up to expectations. Then his family will be the least of your problems."

Pounding sounded at her door, jerking Veronica out of a fairly sound sleep. Indeed, this was the best she'd slept since her arrival. The pounding continued without pause. She flung off her covers, raced to the door, and yanked it open.

Sebastian stood there with his fist raised, about to pound again.

"What has gotten into you?" She glared. "Do you know what time it is? Do you want to wake the entire house?"

"It's a very big house." He grinned. "Did you know I have a house?"

She stared. "Yes, I did."

"It's very responsible of me," he said in a confidential manner. "I have become very responsible. And respectable."

"What do you want?" What on earth was the matter with him?

"I want you to unlock your door." He crossed his arms over his chest. "A wife doesn't lock her door."

"I'm not your wife."

"Oh." He paused. "Well, then, a mistress doesn't lock her door."

"My door wasn't locked."

He stared for a moment, then grinned. "Excellent."

"Good Lord, Sebastian." She waved her hand in front of her face. "You smell like cigars and . . ." She leaned forward and sniffed. "Whisky?"

"Very good Scottish whisky."

"And apparently quite a lot of it." She studied him for a moment. "You're inebriated, aren't you?"

"Inebriated?" Indignation rang in his voice. "I most certainly am not." He leaned close and lowered his voice. "I am drunk."

"Yes, you are." She stifled a smile. "What do you want?"

"You." He pulled his shirt off over his head and tossed it aside. "I want you."

"I'm flattered," she said wryly.

"As well you should be." He grabbed her hand and started toward his bed, fairly dragging her behind him. "I am quite a catch, you know."

"Are you?"

"Yes, I am. Women fall all over themselves for me." He reached the bed and stopped. He released her hand, turned toward her, and frowned. "You did not fall all over me."

She laughed. "Nonsense, Sebastian. Of course I did. I attempted to seduce you, remember?"

"One does not seduce the woman one intends to marry," he said in a lofty manner, then sighed and shook his head mournfully. "That was a mistake."

"Was it?"

"A man should always seduce the woman he intends to marry." He sank down on the bed and crooked his finger at her. "Come here and allow me to seduce you."

She laughed. "I have no intention of being seduced by a drunken sot."

"I am not a sot." He frowned. "What is a sot?"

"I suspect it is someone who drinks entirely too much."

"Oh. Well then . . ." He grinned. "I am a sot."

"At the moment at least."

"Did you know that my brothers thought they could drink more than me?" He scoffed. "They were wrong."

"And are they in the same state you are?"

He furrowed his brow and thought for a moment, then nodded. "Worse."

"I doubt that."

"Better?"

She shook her head. "Tomorrow should be interesting if you're all in this state."

"Veronica." He grabbed her hand and tried to pull her onto the bed. "I need you."

"You need sleep."

"Yes, I do." He fell back on the bed. "But I need you. Have I told you that?"

"Not really."

"Well, I do." He struggled to sit back up. "Have I told you that I love you?"

"Now is not the best time."

"More today than yesterday," he announced with a grand gesture. "And I shall love you more tomorrow than today."

"That's very nice, darling, but when we look back at the first time you told me you loved me, I should like you to remember it."

"Excellent idea." He collapsed back on the bed and patted the spot beside him. "Let me seduce you."

She laughed. "Not tonight."

"I should have seduced you when I had the chance."

"You will have the chance again, I assure you." She studied him for a moment, then shook her head. "You can't sleep with your boots on."

He sat up. "I have slept with my boots on before." He sighed and fell back. "It's not very comfortable."

"If you scoot back, I shall help you take them off."

"Would you?" He propped himself up on his elbows. "That's very wifely of you."

"Don't become accustomed to it. But now and again, when you need my assistance, I shall be there."

"Marry me?"

"Very well."

"Very well?" He narrowed his eyes. "What do you mean by 'very well'?"

"I mean, very well, I shall marry you."

"Really?"

"Really."

"Why?"

"Because I love you, too."

"More tomorrow than today?"

"Definitely more than tonight."

He nodded at the bed beside him and grinned. "Let me seduce you."

She laughed.

"You could seduce me," he said hopefully.

"I suspect anyone could seduce you at the moment."

He shook his head slowly. "I don't wish to be seduced by anyone. Just you. I have given all that up."

"That's good to know." She grabbed his foot, and he fell back. "I shall hold you to that."

"See that you do." He heaved a heartfelt sigh. "They're a very imposing lot."

"Who is, darling?" She tugged off his boot.

"My family. Most imposing. It's the hyphen, I think."

"What?"

"If we were Hadleys or Attwaters, we wouldn't be as imposing. But Hadley hyphen Attwater . . ." He gasped. "Is your father going to shoot me?"

She drew her brows together. "Why would my father want to shoot you?"

"For . . ." He paused, allegedly to think. "For ruining you."

She laughed. "I am nearly thirty years of age and a widow. You couldn't ruin me. And even if you could, you have yet to come close to ruining me."

"I know." He heaved a mournful sigh, then brightened. "I could ruin you now."

"I doubt that." She smiled and grabbed his other foot. "While you are surprisingly amusing in this state, I would prefer that you not make inebriation a habit."

"Never?"

"Preferably."

"You have my word." He lowered his voice confidentially. "May I tell you a secret?"

"Please do."

"I do not drink to excess." He nodded smugly. "I know how to hold my liquor."

"Yes, I can see that." She tried not to laugh. "And an excellent job you do, too."

"Thank you." His brow furrowed. "Do you think I'm worthy?"

"Worthy of what?" She pulled off his remaining boot.

"You. My family. Everything." He sighed. "I have tried to be. At least lately."

She stared down at him. What was he talking about? "You," she said firmly, "are Sir Sebastian Hadley-Attwater. Knighted by the queen, who obviously thought you most worthy, adored by your readers, as well as all those women who fall all over themselves for you."

He grinned. "I'm quite a catch."

"And I have caught you." She dropped his foot and pushed his legs onto the bed.

"I am a lucky man."

"Yes, you are."

"And you are a lucky woman."

Even in this state he was charming and irresistible. At least to her heart. "Yes, I am."

"I have an estate manager, you know."

"Yes, darling, I know."

"And a groundskeeper."

"Yes, dear."

"And a house and a wife."

Now was not the time to disagree with him. "You do have a house."

"I have changed."

"Have you?"

"I am responsible now. I am respectable. Almost boring."

She laughed. "I doubt that you can ever be boring."

"I would hate to be boring." He frowned. "And proper. I would hate to be proper. Will you tell me if I ever become dull and staid and stuffy and boring?"

"You have my word." She leaned over and kissed his forehead. At once, he wrapped his arms around her and tried to pull her down onto the bed. It was a measure of his intoxication that she easily pulled free. "Go to sleep and we shall discuss all of this in the morning."

He studied her. "Do you love me because I'm a black sheep or in spite of it?"

"Both."

"Oh, well then . . . that's good. I am no longer a black sheep, you know." He rolled over and muttered. "I am worthy."

A moment later he was unconscious.

Charles had once told her that even the best of men, every now and then, needed to overindulge when life was awkward or difficult or uncertain. Or when one's friends gathered. Or, in Sebastian's case, in the company of his brothers. And as long as that overindulgence was in food or drink and not women, it could certainly be forgiven. And Charles had been speaking from experience.

She'd never imagined a drunken sot could be even the tiniest bit appealing, but this was different. This drunken sot was hers. And like it or not, she was his. He needed her, and while she'd never expected it, she needed him.

He looked like a small boy lying there, dreaming of sugar plums, no doubt. Peaceful and, if one didn't know better, innocent. She wondered if their children would look like him and warmed at the thought of *their children*. Sebastian scratched himself, and the illusion was shattered.

Not that it mattered. Some illusions were meant to be shattered. The face he presented to the world—confident and somewhat arrogant—was not who he truly was. Her own ideas of independence were little more than illusion as well. Shattered by the reality of understanding that freedom meant living her life alone, living without him.

Lotte had mentioned sacrifice measured against gain.

But perhaps there really was no sacrifice at all given all she had to gain. He'd said he trusted her, and she trusted him as well. Trusted that he loved her for who and what she was. Trusted that he would not try to make her into something she wasn't. And trusted him with her heart.

Trust might well be the greatest gift they could give one another. At Christmas and forever.

Chapter 20

Sebastian drew a deep breath, tried to ignore the pounding in his head, and slipped into the dining room as discreetly as possible. The last thing he wanted was to draw attention to himself and his less than stellar state this morning.

Adrian, James, and Hugh sat at one end of the long table, looking no better than he felt. Sinclair was nowhere to be seen, probably still in bed. He wasn't sure exactly why, but somehow he was certain the American was to blame for last night. At least in part.

It was obviously not mere coincidence that the ladies were at the opposite end of the table, as far away from the gentlemen as possible. Sebastian would have wagered that was by unspoken mutual agreement, as the men could scarcely utter words of more than one syllable today while the ladies were discussing where to begin the decoration of the house, exactly which room the tree should be placed in, and any number of other details that needed attending to on this last day before Christmas. On any given morning, the volume of chatter and level of enthusiasm might be mildly annoying to gentlemen trying to enjoy their breakfast. Today they were painful.

He nodded a silent greeting to his family and caught Veronica's gaze. She looked appropriately sympathetic, although there was a spark of amusement in her eyes. She met him at the sideboard, handed him a plate, and began to fill her own from the platters of hearty fare Cook had laid out.

"Cook has risen admirably to the occasion. Indeed, all the staff is managing quite well given they are all new and unused to guests." She nodded approvingly. "Don't you agree?"

He murmured his agreement.

She tilted her head closer and spoke in a soft voice, for his ears alone. "And how are we this morning, husband dear?"

He winced. "Fine, thank you. And do be so good as to lower your voice."

"Darling, if I lowered my voice any more, I'd be writing."

"Was I, well, um . . ." Sebastian searched for the right word. There wasn't one.

"Intoxicated? Inebriated? Drunk?" she said pleasantly.

"No, I do know that much." He shook his head and grimaced at the movement. "But much of last night is, well, cloudy."

She gasped in mock surprise. "Imagine that."

"Are you angry?" He held his breath.

"Because you and your brothers overindulged?" She raised a brow. "Do you make a habit of it?"

"No," he said with as much indignation as he could manage.

"Well, then, I daresay you are suffering far more severe consequences than I could possibly inflict." She glanced at the other men. "You and your cohorts are all quite pale and a bit green." She shook her head. "It would be cruel of me to berate you. Rather like taking on an unarmed opponent. It wouldn't be any fun at all."

"Your restraint is appreciated." He wasn't at all used to having to explain his behavior to anyone. It was not easy, especially as he wasn't entirely clear what exactly he needed to explain. Or what, perhaps, required apology on his part. "I was just wondering if I said or did . . ."

"Oh, you said a great deal." She selected a slice of bacon. "Doesn't this all look delicious? Have you tried the eggs?"

He shuddered.

She cast him a sympathetic smile. "Is it very bad?"

"No," he muttered. "Not if one ignores the pounding in one's head or the queasiness in one's stomach."

"I'm sure food will help." Veronica scooped a heaping serving of deviled kidneys onto his plate.

On any other morning he quite liked kidneys. Today . . .

"You don't remember what you said?"

"Bits and pieces." He shook his head carefully and glanced at her. "Perhaps you could assist with those empty spaces."

"I would be happy to help. Let me think." Her brow furrowed. "You did wish to seduce me."

He groaned. "And?"

"And you also offered to allow me to seduce you."

"Good God." He stared at her. "Did you? Did we?"

"Goodness, Sebastian." She sniffed. "If you can't remember something like that . . ." She stepped farther down the sideboard and considered the smoked haddock.

"Veronica." He stepped closer. "Of course I would remember." He scoffed. "And as I don't, I would say there was no seduction," he added with far more confidence than he felt.

She leaned closer. "If you don't keep your voice down, darling, you'll draw the attention of your family. Your brothers might not notice, but I would not try to slip anything past Bianca or your mother." She looked at the ladies and chuckled. "Or my grandmother, for that matter."

"Quite right." His brow furrowed. "I remember . . ." He stared at her. "You took my boots off. Like . . . like a wife."

"Indeed I did. I also told you not to expect such behavior in the future." She nodded. "However, it was the highlight of the evening."

"Not for me." He took a piece of toast and glanced at her. "What, exactly, did I say?"

"You mentioned how women fell all over themselves for you."

He winced. "I didn't."

"Oh, but you did. You also talked about how responsible and respectable and worthy you'd become."

"Worthy?" he said uneasily.

"My, yes. You went on and on about it." She nodded soberly. "And in an effort to continue your newfound worthiness, you promised to give up spirits in any form for the rest of your days."

"I did what?"

"You gave your word not to let so much as a drop of liquor touch your lips. No whisky, no brandy, no port—"

He stared.

"—no wine, no champagne."

"Not even with dinner?"

"No, you were quite adamant about that. 'Veronica,' you said, 'I shall be a teetotaler from this point forward.'"

"I didn't."

"And then you demanded I abstain as well." She shook her head. "I don't mind saying I do like the occasional glass of brandy or wine with dinner, and champagne, well, I am quite fond of champagne."

"I can't believe—"

"However, you did agree that you could have an occasional glass of sherry when there were ladies present."

"Sherry?" He stared in horror. "I certainly don't remember. . . ."

He would be far more likely to give up spirits on a morning like this rather than an evening like last night. When one was imbibing more than was wise, one rarely considered the inevitable consequences. Indeed, he did recall having had a smashing good time. He and his brothers and his friend had played billiards and cards and told stories that couldn't possibly have more than a grain of truth in them. And then he'd returned to his room, determined to entice Veronica into his bed. He'd pulled her into his room, collapsed on his bed, and she'd helped him with his boots. . . . "I never promised to give up spirits."

She bit back a smile. "Perhaps *my* memory is faulty in that respect."

He narrowed his eyes. "You said it wouldn't be any fun to take on an unarmed opponent."

"I was wrong." She choked back a laugh.

"I'm glad you're finding this all so amusing."

"It's even more amusing this morning than it was last night. And you were most amusing last night."

"That's something, I suppose. Still, it's not at all nice of you to make me think I made promises. . . ." He stared with abrupt realization. "You said you'd marry me."

"Did I?"

"You did." He stared at her. "Did you mean it?"

She drew her brows together and considered the question.

"Veronica?"

"Why, yes, I believe I did."

At once he felt much, much better. Regardless, every single time he'd thought everything was going well, something had happened to shatter that particular illusion. But try as he might, he couldn't think of anything that would muck this up now.

"When?"

"If I recall correctly, there was no discussion of when. It didn't seem the right time. You were really in no condition to . . . Oh, what is the right word? Ah yes, *stand,* let alone decide when to wed."

"Nonetheless, now that you have agreed, I see no need to wait."

Of course, it had nearly slipped his mind. He'd never told her about his birthday and his inheritance. Odd how something that had once been so important to him now paled in comparison. She was the only thing he wanted. They would have the rest of their lives together. Still, he should mention his birthday to her. But not now. After all, there was plenty of time. "Unless you have changed your mind."

"Now that I have seen you at your very best, you mean?"

"I suppose."

"No, I have not changed my mind. I want to marry you, Sebastian. I shall love you more tomorrow than today, you know."

He stared at her for a moment, then grinned. "It's an excellent line."

"It is if you mean it."

He met her gaze firmly. "I've never meant anything more."

She smiled slowly. "Then, there is one more thing about last night that you should remember."

"Oh?"

She leaned closer and whispered into his ear. "My door was not locked."

Veronica had no idea preparing for Christmas could be so exhausting. And so much fun. Bianca had taken her aside to explain that, while servants could manage all this on their own and were certainly expected to do so in other households, it was something of a family tradition to help in the decoration.

Early in the afternoon the men had recovered enough to assist the ladies and the staff. Evelyn was right: Everyone in this family was behaving no better than the children among them and having at least as much fun. And Sebastian was wrong. Regardless of their hyphen, they weren't the least bit imposing. At least not today. Laughter rang through the halls of the house. Children's voices clashed and blended with those of the adults. There was more than a little use of the mistletoe. Her father and the rest of her family had joined in with surprising enthusiasm.

By midday, the house had been swathed in swags and garlands. Doors had been decked with wreaths of holly and boughs of evergreens. Banisters had been festooned with ribbons and ivy and pinecones. Every nook, every niche, very nearly every piece of furniture that did not move hosted a crown of greenery or a wreath of berries. It was nothing short of magic. In spite of her age and general rundown state, Lady Greyville looked every inch the grand dame she once was and was always meant to be. And would be again.

At one end of the grand hall, the tree that had been cut and brought to the house earlier in the day was being set up with the help of Sebastian and the other gentlemen. Said help consisting more of unneeded advice than anything else. The groundskeeper and his men were more than able to erect the tree on their own. Most of the ladies were unpacking the boxes of ornaments that very nearly everyone had brought along. At the other end of the hall, a table had been set up for Diana's children and their nannies. They now strung berries and crafted small dolls and animals out of twigs and bits of fabric for the tree, their faces intense with concentration. Having observed the endlessly energetic children today, Veronica doubted that distraction would last long.

She surveyed the scene with satisfaction. It was well worth the tiny little cuts on her hands from handling the greenery. Next year she would wear some kind of gloves. Next year? She smiled to herself at the thought. She still had no idea how they were going to explain this year, but at the moment it scarcely mattered. At some point today it had dawned on her that once she and Sebastian were truly married, they would have two houses in the country and a house in town between them. It might be best to sell her country house to Harrison. It had been Charles's, after all, and Harrison had expressed an interest in acquiring it. She would put the money to good use. This house of Sebastian's needed a great deal of refurbishing. It would be great fun to bring it back to its former glory and fill it with parties and friends, children and family.

"It's coming along quite nicely," Helena said beside her.

Veronica glanced at Sebastian's mother and smiled. "It is, isn't it?"

"This has always been my favorite time of year." Helena looked around, satisfaction on her face. "There is nothing better than having one's family together at Christmas." She sighed. "I do wish Portia was here, but I suppose that can't be helped." She paused. "Letting one's children go is as important as keeping them near, although substantially more difficult."

"Even Portia?"

"Because she's my niece and not my daughter?"

Veronica nodded.

"One would think it would make a difference, but it never has. Portia has been with us since she was a baby. She was my sister's child and is all that I have left of her. Portia is as dear to me as if I had given birth to her myself." She thought for a moment. "Perhaps even more so, although I would never tell the others. One doesn't play favorites with one's children." She nodded. "You'll learn that, my dear, with your own children."

"I look forward to it."

"There is nothing that can compare to having children in the house, especially at Christmas. And nothing that makes adults forget their age quite like Christmas. Even me."

Veronica laughed. "You're right. It is lovely to have the house filled with children. Of all ages. I'm afraid, though, you have caught us unprepared."

"Nonsense. Everything is going splendidly."

"I do hope so. But as I didn't expect you, any of you, I have no gifts for anyone." It wasn't until Mrs. Bigelow's sister had delivered the pennant for Sebastian a few hours ago that Veronica had realized she didn't have gifts for anyone else. "I brought ornaments for Sebastian for Christmas and I have another gift for him, but I didn't know everyone else would be here."

"Oh dear, that is awkward." Helena frowned.

"I was thinking, perhaps, after Christmas—"

Helena laughed. "My apologies, but I couldn't resist. The children will be showered with so many presents, they won't notice. As for the rest of us . . ." Her gaze strayed to Sebastian. He and his brothers were directing the men attempting to put up the tree as to the proper angle, amid much debate and discussion. It didn't look particularly complicated to Veronica, but apparently it was a matter of some concern. "You have already given us the greatest gift we could have asked for."

"I have?"

Helena nodded. "Even though my youngest son bought this house and said he intended to stay in England, I had my doubts. But now . . ."

"Now?"

"But now he is here for Christmas and, of course, his birthday. . . ."

"His birthday?"

Helena nodded. "Two days after Christmas. You didn't know?"

"He hasn't said a word."

"It is a significant birthday, but I suspect, in the midst of everything, it has probably slipped his mind. It scarcely matters." Helena met her gaze. "Now he has you. You've made him want to stay. We can have no greater gift than that. Together, you will fill this house with love and laughter and children." Helena's gaze wandered toward her own children. "Indeed, my dear, you already have filled this house, however unexpectedly, and I shall be forever grateful."

Veronica ignored a twinge of guilt. After all, they fully intended to marry as soon as possible. She chose her words with care. "I don't imagine he will give up his travels altogether."

"Of course not." Helena shook her head. "Only a fool would think otherwise, and only a mother would hope. Regardless, he now has you to come back to."

"I would rather go with him."

Helena laughed. "Why am I not surprised?" She sobered. "But that, too, is a gift. Do you know about my list?"

Veronica shook her head.

"It's silly, really, at least my children think it is. I have a list of who in my family should be the next to be married. And that is who I focus my efforts on."

"I see." Veronica grinned. "I gather, from what Portia has said, she heads your list?"

"Currently." Helena nodded. "Although Sebastian has been at the top for years. However, it's decidedly difficult to find the right match for a man who is never around."

"I had the distinct impression from Portia that you are not alone in your matchmaking efforts."

"My daughters do what they can to assist me." Helena chuckled. "As they have all been the beneficiaries of my efforts at some point, they think it's wise to help." She cast the younger woman a wicked smile. "It keeps me from active interference in their lives. My children fear that the moment they are all settled and married, I shall turn my attention to correcting whatever problems I might see in their households."

Veronica grinned.

"And I will, you know." Again Helena's gaze turned toward her children. "I only want them to be happy. I do know that one doesn't need to be married to be happy, but I know, as well, that being alone is a dreadful thing. I would not wish that on my greatest enemy."

"Are you lonely?" Veronica said without thinking.

"My, you are direct." Helena smiled. "On occasion, I suppose I am. I do have plans, though, once I have them all seen to."

Veronica's brow rose. "Do you?"

"I do indeed." Helena grinned. "They involve being independent and doing precisely as I please. I never have, you know."

"I see."

"It sounds rather selfish, I suppose, but when much of your life is behind you rather than ahead, I think you have earned the right to be a bit selfish." She studied Veronica for a moment. "I'm not sure what I envy more. The fact that you have known such independence or the fact that you are no longer alone."

"It's a trade, isn't it?" Veronica said thoughtfully. "One simply has to decide what one wants more. What is more important." She shook her head. "Independence has a very high price."

"As does love." Helena smiled. "But well worth it, don't you think?"

Veronica nodded. "Yes, I do."

"As for my plans, they are quite specific. No doubt you would think them silly. Perhaps one day, when the spirit moves me, I shall confide them to you, but not yet. Have you ever had a secret, Veronica?"

"A secret?" Veronica stared at the older woman. "I suppose, probably, at one time or another. I daresay we all have secrets on occasion. Why do you ask?"

Helena's gaze turned back toward her children. "They

all have secrets of some sort or another. Some I suspect. Others I shall probably never know. My plans are my secret. Perhaps not my greatest or my most important, but the only thing I've never shared with anyone. Precisely why no one should go through life alone. One needs someone one can trust implicitly with that which is most important to them." She smiled. "And that, Veronica dear, is one of the greatest gifts of all."

Chapter 21

Aknock sounded at the door between her room and
Sebastian's. At last. Veronica had wondered if Sebastian and the other male members of the family would talk
well into Christmas morning.

The entire family had joined in putting decorations on
the tree. The children hung their garlands and toys on the
lower branches. Candies and gingerbread men Cook had
fashioned for them were also hung, although it did seem
there were far fewer on the tree than had been provided.
Veronica noted not all the telltale gingerbread crumbs
were on the youngest members of the family. The ornaments she and Sebastian's sisters had provided were hung
and candles carefully placed among the branches, accompanied by wry joking about a past Christmas fire.

The Yule log, which had caused nearly as much discussion between Sebastian and his brothers as the tree, had
been lit in the massive great hall fireplace and would stay
burning through Twelfth Night. The Hadley-Attwaters
were full of traditions to which Veronica's own family had

never paid any mind, yet her father, aunt, and grand-mother had refused to be left out. The proceedings were accompanied by the singing of Christmas songs, those silly or sentimental or sweet. Diana's children had insisted on leaving mincemeat and brandy for Father Christmas and a carrot for his reindeer before they were put to bed.

All in all, the day had been quite wonderful. Veronica smiled, kept her gaze on the book in her hands, and adopted a noncommittal tone. "Come in."

She heard him come through the door and pause. "Is that one of my books?"

"The second, I think."

"I thought you had read them all."

"I have." She turned a page. "They are worth reading again. And, as you were not here . . ."

"Oh." He drew a deep breath. "Veronica, there is something we need to discuss. Something I should tell you."

"Secrets?" She glanced up at him.

"No, not at all."

"Pity. I do love secrets." Her gaze returned to her book, and she tried not to grin.

"This is not a secret."

"Is it important?"

He thought for a moment. "Not really. Of some interest, I would think, but not especially important."

"I suspect there are all sorts of things you should tell me and quite a few I should tell you as well. Although I imagine mine are much more interesting and far more important."

"I see." He paused. "For example?"

"It wouldn't be at all fun for me to tell you. I'd rather you find out as we go along. Think of it as an endless adventure." She turned another page. "It should take, oh, twenty or thirty years, I should think."

For a long moment he didn't say a word. "For a minute, I thought you were going to tell me you had changed your mind about marrying me."

"Goodness, Sebastian, I was not the one whose judgment was impaired last night. I said I'd marry you, and I have every intention of doing so." She shrugged. "This, then, is your first discovery. Once I have decided upon a course of action, I rarely change my mind." She closed the book and smiled at him.

He chuckled. "Ah, but you changed your mind about becoming a mistress."

"About becoming *a* mistress, not about becoming *your* mistress." She rose to her feet. "There's a difference."

He eyed her suspiciously. "What do you mean?"

"Well, while I thought the idea of being a mistress in general was rather brilliant, it wasn't until I met you that I truly decided." She moved toward him.

He narrowed his gaze. "You're saying you only wanted to be *my* mistress?"

"So it appears." She grinned. "It's a brilliant idea."

"I still don't understand."

"I know. It's most endearing." She gazed up at him. "I don't see any reason why I can't be both your mistress and your wife." She slid her arms around his neck. "Do you?"

He paused, then wrapped his arms around her waist. "Why, no." He bent his head to nibble the curve of her neck. "In fact, you're right. It is a brilliant idea."

She shivered. Good Lord, when he did that . . . "I suspected you might agree. However . . ." She pulled out of his arms. "As I am not your wife yet and have never, in truth, been your mistress . . ."

"But . . ." He stared. "It's Christmas Eve."

"I know that, darling, but it has occurred to me that the only thing that might save us from complete, utter, devastating scandal is the fact that we have not shared a bed."

His eyes widened in disbelief.

"We have not really done anything that, oh, can't be undone. We have not yet made love." She cast him a pleasant smile.

"Well, no, but . . . it is Christmas Eve," he said hopefully.

"Indeed it is." She nodded. "And tomorrow is Christmas Day, and sometime after that, we shall tell your family that we aren't married, and soon after, we shall likely be wed."

He studied her for a long moment. "Then, you and I, we are not, that is, tonight . . ."

"All things considered, it would be best."

"Did I mention it's Christmas Eve?"

"More than once." Oh, this was fun.

"Still . . ." He chose his words with care. "Given that it is Christmas Eve, and we are going to be married . . ."

"But we're not married yet." She shook her head. "And you did say it was not proper to seduce the woman you intended to marry."

"I did say that." He considered her thoughtfully. "As you are already dressed for bed—"

"And you have already discarded your coat and are scarcely properly attired—"

"It's probably most improper for me even to be here."

She heaved an overly dramatic sigh. "I would think so."

His gaze traveled over her, over the French lace and silk dressing gown that revealed no more than a hint of the provocative sheer nightgown underneath. "That is . . . most becoming."

"Do you think so?"

"Only a dead man would fail to be . . ." He cleared his throat. "Moved by it."

"And you are certainly not dead."

"It's the sort of thing a mistress would wear."

"Really?" She glanced down. In the right light, he could probably see right through it. "I thought it might be the sort of thing a wife would wear."

"One can only hope. But you are now my . . ." He thought for a moment. "Betrothed?"

She flashed him a brilliant smile. "Indeed I am."

"Then I should give you a chaste kiss good night and retire to my bed," he said smoothly.

"It would be best," she murmured, ignoring a vague twinge of disappointment. Apparently, two could play at this game.

He took her hand and raised it to his lips, his gaze locked with hers. Her breath caught. "I should say good night."

"Yes, well, probably . . ."

"It seems only proper," his lips murmured against her hand. "And I have tried my best to behave properly with you."

"I have noticed."

He turned her hand over and kissed her palm. "In hindsight, it might have been a mistake."

"Oh?" She swallowed hard.

"But, it seemed to me, when something is as important as finding the woman with whom you intend to spend the rest of your days, one should probably follow the rules of propriety." His lips moved to her wrist.

"Why?" she asked without thinking.

"I'm not sure. Apparently, there's more of the proper Hadley-Attwater in me than I suspected." He brushed aside the lace of her sleeve and trailed light kisses along her arm to the inside of her elbow.

"Sebastian . . ." Who would have imagined that particular spot would be quite so sensitive? She scarcely noticed his free hand untying the belt of her dressing gown.

"Although I have never been fond of rules." He pushed the gown off her arm, then bent to kiss her shoulder. Her breath caught, and she was only vaguely aware of the silk and lace confection drifting to the floor.

"I had heard that about you."

He wrapped one arm around her waist and pulled her closer. A tiny voice in the back of her head, sounding suspiciously like Portia's, demanded she wait, as they would be married soon. Veronica ignored it.

His other hand slid over her silk-covered hip, and he leaned in to cover her mouth with his. She opened her mouth to his, and he tasted of brandy and promises and desire. And forever. Her breath mingled with his, and his tongue dueled with hers, teasing and tempting. Need shivered through her. He pulled away and kissed that spot where her neck met her shoulder. She wasn't sure how he knew, but that particular spot, and the way his lips caressed her, fairly melted her bones.

She moaned softly. "When you do that . . ."

"Yes?"

She abandoned herself to the sensation of his lips on her skin. "You're very good at this."

She felt his smile against her neck.

"You've had a lot of practice."

He raised his head and gazed into her eyes. "And that's all it was, Veronica, practice. For this. For you."

Her heart caught. "It doesn't matter to me, you know. Anything before we met. It's not the least bit important."

"Good, because it doesn't matter to me, either." He

smiled into her eyes. "Nothing in my life mattered before the moment we met. My life began with you."

She swallowed hard, tried and failed to adopt a light tone. "My, that is polished."

"Only because it's true." Again his lips met hers. Passion surged between them, strong and overwhelming and irresistible.

His hand on her hip gathered the silk of her nightgown until his fingers touched the bare flesh beneath it. She shivered and tugged his shirt free from his trousers. He shifted to allow room to pull her gown up over her head and toss it aside. She pushed his shirt up until he pulled it over his head and let it drop. She rained kisses on the base of his throat; her hands roamed over the hard muscles of his chest. His fingers explored the curves and valleys of her derriere and skimmed over her hips and the small of her back. She pressed her hips against his, the hard evidence of his arousal pressing into her through the fabric of his trousers. His hands caressed her, his fingers tracing the seam of her bottom. She slid her hand between them to fumble with his buttons, frantic with desire. Dear Lord, she wanted this man.

She popped open his buttons and slid her hand into his trousers. Her fingers found his hard, swollen cock straining against the confining fabric. He sucked in a sharp breath. His chest rose and fell faster against her. Her hand curled around his cock and stroked him, and he moaned.

"Oh God, Veronica."

He shoved his trousers down his hips, let them fall to the floor, and kicked them aside. She caressed his cock and his ballocks, trailing her tongue and her lips down his chest. She slowly sank to her knees and gazed up at him.

He stared down at her, his eyes glazed with desire. She cupped his ballocks with one hand and wrapped the other around his cock, pulling back the foreskin. Still staring up at him, she flicked her tongue over the tip of his cock. He gasped, his hands clenching at his sides. She wanted to give him pleasure. Wanted him to ache to take her. Wanted him mindless with desire, with wanting her. Charles had taught her well. And, God help her, she had enjoyed it all. A mistress at heart.

She circled the head of his cock slowly with her tongue. He shuddered, and she sucked him slowly into her mouth until he filled her. She pulled away, raking her teeth lightly over the length of him. He groaned. Moisture pooled between her legs, and she throbbed with need. She sucked at the head of his cock, squeezing gently and caressing his ballocks. He rocked his hips slightly toward her, driving himself into her mouth, as if he were trying to restrain himself but couldn't.

She drew back, and he pulled her to her feet. He slid his hand down her hip and lifted her leg to wrap around his. His mouth took hers. Claimed hers. Plundered hers. His cock slipped between her legs and rubbed against her wet, slick center of desire. She moaned into his mouth.

He shuddered and pulled away, then scooped her into his arms and strode into his room to deposit her on his bed. She propped herself up on one elbow and stared at him. She'd only ever seen one other naked man. Charles had been a handsome man, but Sebastian was . . . finely chiseled. Sculpted. Like a marble statue. Or a god. Broad shoulders, tapered hips, long muscled legs. All that coupled with the scar above his eyebrow and the desire darkening his blue eyes and . . . She was his for the taking.

He slid onto the bed beside her and took her in his arms. Her breasts pressed to his chest. His legs tangled around hers. His mouth, his hands were everywhere at once. He cupped her breasts and teased her nipples with his tongue, sucked and nipped with teeth and mouth. She writhed beneath his touch. Everywhere he explored, every inch of her, was alive with sensation, intense and overwhelming. He slid lower, trailing kisses between her breasts and over her stomach. She moaned and arched up to meet his mouth, his touch.

He moved to kneel between her legs and feathered kisses over the inside of her thighs. He parted her with his fingers, and his thumb rubbed over her. She cried out and her body jerked and she raised her hips. He held her open, bent low, and blew over that sensitive, throbbing point of pleasure. He lowered his head and flicked it with his tongue, and she wondered if one could die of unbridled bliss. And didn't care. He licked and suckled, and exquisite pleasure washed through her, over her. Her hands twisted the bedclothes, and her hips rocked against his mouth in a mindless aching need for more.

"Sebastian . . . dear Lord . . . please . . ."

He shifted and positioned himself between her legs, then slid into her until he filled her, possessed her. Her muscles tightened around him. He withdrew slowly, allowing her to feel every inch of him, then slid into her again. She hooked her legs around his and urged him on, urged him deeper. His movements grew rhythmic, faster. She rolled her hips against him, meeting his thrusts with her own.

Faster and harder, he pushed into her. Tension, exquisite and demanding, built within her. And she wanted, she needed, more. She clutched at him and moaned and rocked harder against him. And lost herself in the feeling of pleasure, of being one with him, connected body and soul. Until he thrust hard and groaned and shuddered within her. Her muscles tightened around his cock, and her body exploded in release. Waves of sheer bliss washed through her, and she arched upward and called his name. And wondered at how very good and how very right and how very consuming it was. She was his and he was hers and would be forever. And in a corner of her mind not completely incoherent, she thanked Charles for teaching her to revel in the relations between men and women, and thanked the heavens for once again bringing her love and joy and Sebastian.

They collapsed in each other's arms, and for a long moment they lay exhausted, struggling to breathe, their hearts beating together as one.

At last she raised her head. "What happened to not seducing the woman you intend to marry?"

"I have already admitted that was a flaw in my plan. And a man should be willing to admit when he is wrong." He cast her a tired but altogether too satisfied grin. "I was wrong."

She snuggled against him. "There is something irresistible about a man who acknowledges his mistakes."

"Which reminds me." He paused. "Now is probably a good time to tell you—"

"A confession? Oh, good." She kissed his neck. "Almost as much fun as secrets."

"It's not a secret, nor a confession." He sighed. "My birthday is two days after Christmas."

"My, that is a revelation." She chuckled softly. "But I already know that."

"You do?"

"Your mother told me."

"Oh." He blew a relieved breath. "And you're not at all bothered by it?"

"Not in the least." She shook her head. "I was born in April. Do you mind?"

"No."

"Very well then."

He grinned. "Do you know why I want to marry you?"

"Yes." She frowned. "No. Why?"

"Aside from the fact that I love you."

She smiled. "I knew that, too."

"I want your face, your smile, to be the first thing I see in the morning and the last thing I see at night."

"I look dreadful in the morning." A warning sounded in her voice.

He chuckled. "I thought you liked mornings."

"Oh, I do." She shrugged. "They don't like me."

"There is something else. . . ." He untangled himself from her, rolled over, opened the drawer in the stand beside his bed, and pulled out a small, ribbon-tied, velvet-wrapped packet. "This is for you."

"For Christmas or to celebrate Christmas Eve?" She grinned wickedly.

He laughed. "Both."

She hefted it in her hand. "It's heavy." It was also padded, no doubt with tissue, which made it impossible to discern a shape. "May I open it now?"

"Absolutely not." He plucked it from her hand and put it on the stand.

She sighed. "You're just teasing, then?"

"I am." He kissed the tip of her nose. "It's great fun."

"Is this another of your family traditions?"

He nodded. "Father Christmas fills the stockings of the children overnight. In the morning we shall all attend church in the village." He met her gaze. "I am not particularly a churchgoing sort, but it is Christmas."

"And allowances should be made for Christmas."

He nodded. "Dinner will be early afternoon."

She bit back a grin. "I have still heard no mention of presents. When do we open our gifts?"

"After dinner," he said firmly.

She sighed. "Your family has a great number of traditions."

"Indeed we do, and we shall abide by them all."

"You've never seemed the type of man to follow traditions."

"It's Christmas," he said firmly.

She laughed. "And I don't get my present until after dinner?"

He shook his head. "It would be wrong."

She hooked her leg over his and nuzzled the side of his neck. "We would hate to do anything wrong."

"I would say we do a great deal right." He shifted and pulled her to lay on top of him. "I should tell you one more thing."

She sat upright, her legs straddling him. Already she could feel his arousal growing once again behind her. The man was apparently insatiable. Good. "Yes?"

He grinned. "I had no intention of spending Christmas Eve alone."

"What a surprise." She gazed into his eyes and smiled in a slow and wicked manner. "Neither did I."

Chapter 22

Sebastian was right. He gazed around the table with the sort of satisfaction only a man who knew he was right could feel. It was indeed a splendid Christmas.

His family was gathered under his roof. The woman he loved was by his side. Even her family was here, as well as his closest friend. Spirits were high; there was much laughter and joking and reminiscences about Christmases past. The meal itself was excellent, although the plum pudding had yet to be served. That was yet another source of his satisfaction. He had done a damn fine job of hiring servants. He ignored the fact that they had all been highly recommended by Stokes and Mrs. Bigelow. And every time his gaze met Veronica's, she smiled a secret sort of smile and his heart beat faster.

It was Christmas, and at this table were nearly all the people he held dear in the world. Life had never been as good as it was at this moment, and he knew, with the sort of certainty one could only feel when all was right, that this was just the beginning.

"The children are planning a play," Bianca announced. His niece and nephews were dining in the kitchen under the watchful eye of their nannies and, no doubt, being fed all sorts of things by Cook and Mrs. Bigelow they shouldn't be fed but were permissible on Christmas nonetheless.

"How lovely." His mother beamed. All was right with her world today, too.

"And what a surprise," Evelyn said with a smile.

Veronica glanced at her. "Another tradition?"

Evelyn chuckled. "One of many."

Sebastian leaned toward Veronica. "We always have a play put on for Christmas."

"You don't know what you have missed, Sebastian." A chastising note sounded in Miranda's voice. "Diana's children do almost as good a job as we did."

"Runs in the blood, no doubt." Miss Bramhall nodded.

"Usually it's just the children," Miranda continued. "Although several of us have been pressed into service through the years. It depends on what play is being presented."

"Do you remember the year Portia and Bianca and Miranda dressed as the three wise men for the play?" Adrian grinned. "And offered their own versions of what their gifts should be?"

His mother sniffed. "My favorite pearls, my good French perfume—"

"And Father's best brandy." Hugh laughed.

"It would have been brilliant if Miranda hadn't spilled the brandy." Diana frowned. "Or was it the perfume?"

Miranda winced. "Both."

Laughter washed around the table.

Diana aimed a pointed look at Bianca. "How is it you know about the play and I do not?"

"They want to surprise you." Bianca smirked.

"Wonderful," James murmured.

"Besides," Bianca said in a lofty manner, "I am the favorite aunt—"

"Today," Evelyn said under her breath, and Veronica choked back a laugh.

"—and I have a starring role. Miranda is also in it, and Mr. Sinclair has been pressed into service as well. The children are quite taken with his manner of speech." She rolled her gaze toward the ceiling.

Sebastian met his friend's gaze. The American shrugged helplessly.

"So good of you to help, Mr. Sinclair." Mother favored Sinclair with an affectionate smile. "You have my thanks."

"It is I who should thank you, all of you," Sinclair said in a gracious manner. "I am not a sentimental sort about Christmas, but being here, well, it reminds me of what I am missing with my own family in America. And how neglectful I have been with my mother's relations in England."

"Do think of us as your family this year." Mother patted his hand. "And perhaps you can travel to your mother's family tomorrow."

"Excellent idea, Lady Waterston." He nodded. "I will indeed, after I fulfill my theatrical obligations." He glanced around the table. "The play?"

"Well, I, for one, can't wait for the play." Sebastian chuckled, then paused. "I know I have missed a great deal—"

"Twelve Christmases." His mother nodded.

"Four births," Diana said with a sigh.

"Six weddings," Miranda added.

"Five deaths," Hugh murmured.

"And a partridge in a pear tree." Bianca huffed. "Now is not the time—"

"My apologies, but I must disagree, my dear," Lord Bramhall said. "It is a lesson I have only recently learned, but it is not necessary to abandon the delight of Christmas in the recognition of those we have lost. Indeed, there may well be no better time of year than this to acknowledge those who touched our lives and left us the better for it. Who would want us to remember them not with the sorrow of death but the joy of life. And who would want us to live our lives to the fullest.

"Therefore, in this family of numerous traditions, let me offer one more that I would hope would become a new tradition as we gather for this Christmas and those yet to come." He rose to his feet, and the other men joined him. "Allow me to propose a toast with affection and gratitude and love. To those who live in our hearts all year through but especially at Christmas." He raised his glass. "To my dear wife, who gave me the greatest gift of all"—he cast a fond smile at his daughter, whose eyes looked suspiciously bright—"and who loved every moment of Christmas."

"To my beloved husband." His mother raised her glass. "Whose stubbornness I see in every one of my children. He would have been proud to have sat at this table."

"To Richard," Adrian said. "Who never sang a Christmas carol in the correct tune."

"He was dreadful," Diana said with a smile.

Veronica lifted her glass. "To Charles, a very good man."

"To my late husband, John," Miranda said softly.

"To Jane, my wife." Hugh smiled.

"And to my dear, departed husband, wherever he may be," Lady Bramhall said firmly. "A man who never admitted when he was wrong, always insisted on the last word, and who loved a good plum pudding." She aimed a pointed look at Veronica. "Need I say more?"

The men retook their seats among smiles and chuckles and renewed comments of "I remember when . . ." and "Do you recall the Christmas . . ." Sebastian met Lord Bramhall's gaze and raised his glass slightly toward the older man. Veronica's father smiled and nodded. Sebastian breathed a sigh of relief. He hadn't been sure what Veronica's father's reaction would be to the revelation of their marital state. He vaguely remembered Veronica saying that her father didn't intend to shoot him. And the older man had been quite cordial and friendly yesterday and today. Obviously, Veronica had told him they did intend to marry. Still, one never knew with a woman's father.

"So is the play after dinner?" Sebastian asked.

"It was a matter of some debate," Bianca said. "The children thought tomorrow would be a better day as it is Boxing Day, and they agreed it would be best not to distract from Christmas."

"They mean presents," James said in an aside to Hugh, who was seated beside him.

"I'm rather fond of presents myself," Hugh murmured.

"Then it was suggested they perform the play in honor of their uncle Sebastian's birthday, and they thought it was a smashing idea." Bianca shrugged. "So you may all look forward to Sebastian's birthday celebration including the annual Christmas performance of the Hadley-Attwater Players."

"It will certainly add to the festivities," Miranda said.

"Appropriate enough as it is a most momentous birthday," Adrian added.

"My youngest son will be thirty-three." Mother grimaced and turned toward Miss Bramhall. "Do you realize how old that makes us?"

Miss Bramhall winced. "I would prefer to avoid such realizations, thank you."

"And do you have family traditions about birthdays as well as Christmas?" Veronica glanced around the table.

"Well." Miranda's brow furrowed. "When we were children, whosever birthday it was, was given a crown to wear all day. They were allowed to select their favorite foods for meals, and the rest of us were all supposed to be very nice to him or her."

"Which lasted until one of Bianca's birthdays in which she declared herself queen and did not rule wisely." Hugh shook his head. "Power went to her head."

"And I was overthrown rather rudely. Someone pushed me in the pond." Bianca's eyes narrowed. Her gaze slid from one sibling to the next. "I still have my suspicions about that."

"You needn't," Diana said blithely. "It was one of our rare cooperative efforts."

"Nonetheless, I am expecting a crown." Sebastian grinned. "And while I intend to rule firmly, it will be with great wisdom and kindness."

"You should be kind." Diana sniffed. "You finally get your inheritance, after all."

"Inheritance?" Veronica said.

"It's one of those foolish family things." Bianca shrugged. "Scarcely worth mentioning."

"It's annoying is what it is." Diana sniffed. "Father, in his infinite wisdom, decreed each of his younger sons— not the oldest, as he was the heir to the title—would come into his inheritance on his thirty-third birthday, but only if his older brothers approved. Deemed them worthy or some such nonsense."

"Worthy?" Veronica said. "What do you mean?"

"Diana, I think that's enough," Sebastian said quickly. "Veronica doesn't want to hear about—"

"Nonsense. This is about you as you are the last brother to reach this particular milestone, and I'm sure Veronica wants to know all about the man she married." Diana smiled at Veronica.

"Of course I do." Veronica's gaze slid to his. "I want to know everything."

"It's archaic, but apparently it goes back generations." Diana continued, "Richard had to approve Adrian's receiving of his inheritance. Richard and Adrian had to approve Hugh, and now it's Adrian and Hugh's turn to approve Sebastian."

"Forgive me, I'm not sure I understand." Veronica shook her head. "What do you mean by 'approve'?"

"Oh, you know." Diana shrugged. "The usual kinds of things. Is he a responsible sort? Has he truly grown up? I don't believe there's a specific list of requirements—"

Adrian scoffed. "Of course not."

"And I would think," Diana continued, "as Sebastian seems to have changed so very much this year, what with his settling down with a house and a wife, there would be no question as to his worthiness."

"Is a wife, then, a requirement?" Veronica said slowly.

"No." Sebastian shook his head. "Not at all."

"I was not married when I received my inheritance," Hugh said. "But then again I never traveled the world in search of adventure."

Adrian chuckled. "No one has ever thought you were anything less than proper."

"Dull, you mean." Hugh sighed. "It's my lot to bear."

There was the oddest look in Veronica's eyes. Sebastian's stomach clenched. "But if Sebastian was not married . . ."

"It scarcely matters, as he is." Diana shrugged.

Veronica's gaze met his. "I see."

"No," he said quickly. "You don't."

"It certainly explains a great deal." Veronica rose to her feet. "If you will excuse me for a moment, I believe I need a breath of fresh air." She pushed back her chair and left the room.

"Sebastian." Bianca's eyes were wide with realization. "She didn't know about the inheritance?"

"Apparently not." He got to his feet and followed Veronica. She knew about his birthday, and he had assumed she knew as well about the significance of it.

She'd barely gone a few feet past the door when he caught up to her. "Veronica, let me explain."

"No explanation is necessary." She stared at him, hurt and anger in her eyes. "It's all perfectly clear."

He shook his head. "It's not what you think."

"Isn't it?" Her hands clenched by her sides, but her tone was cool, calm, lethal. "I had thought it was odd that a man of your reputation would be so eager for marriage. Indeed, your reputation was one of the reasons I chose you."

He narrowed his eyes. "What do you mean, you chose me?"

"I mean, I selected you." She shrugged. "You were well suited, if one wished to be a mistress."

He chose his words with care. "You said you hadn't decided to be a mistress until you met me."

"As you were the perfect choice. A man of adventure, uninterested in permanence of any sort." She snorted. "Yet another flaw in my plan."

"So any man would have suited you? What about Sinclair? Would he have done as well?"

"If I had met him first, perhaps," she snapped. "Does he wish to be married?"

"No!"

"Does he stand to gain an inheritance if he is married?"

"No," he said sharply. "And neither do I."

"Ha! First you bought this house. Then all you needed was a wife to occupy it."

"I did not buy this house with a wife in mind."

"Obviously! But you did buy it with an eye toward showing your family how much you've changed. How responsible and proper you've become. How the black sheep was now one of the herd!"

"No!"

She raised a skeptical brow.

"Very well." He huffed. "I suppose some of that was a factor in buying the house. But it was the right time to do so."

"Right before your birthday." She cast him a scathing look. "Excellent timing."

He drew his brows together. "Is it so hard to believe that, when one reaches a certain age, one wishes to live one's life differently?"

"When the one in question is you—yes!" She shook her head. "I trusted you. I thought you were honest and honorable."

"I am." He glared at her. "I have never lied to you. I have never misled you."

"You didn't tell me about your quest for . . . for *worthiness!* And the part I was to play in it. You didn't tell me about your inheritance."

"It slipped my mind," he said without thinking, then winced. As true as it was, it was not a good answer. "Once I met you, you were all I could think about. All that mattered."

"You said you would love me more tomorrow than today. That you wanted to die with your hand in mine."

"And I meant every word."

"I should have known." She shook her head. "Your words were entirely too polished."

"They were from my heart." Indignation rang in his voice.

"You admitted they were excellent *lines*."

"Which makes them no less meaningful," he said firmly.

"Which makes them worthless." Her eyes narrowed. "How many other women have you said those things to?"

"None," he said staunchly. "I love you."

"And have you said that to other women as well?"

"I don't know." He ran his hand through his hair. "I don't recall, but I never meant it before."

"And now you mean it?"

"Yes! Which is why I want to marry you."

"So it is nothing more than happy coincidence that you find a woman you wish to marry right before your brothers are to judge whether or not you are worthy to receive your inheritance?"

"Coincidences do happen, you know."

She scoffed. "Not like this."

"I love you, Veronica, and you love me."

"Yet another flaw in my plan!" she snapped, then drew a deep breath. "You say marrying me has nothing to do with proving yourself worthy of your inheritance."

He nodded. "Which is the absolute truth."

"Then tell me this." She studied him carefully. "Did the thought ever cross your mind that a wife would be the final element to prove to your family that you were no longer a disappointment?"

He hesitated.

"I see."

"No, you don't." He shook his head. "I admit, the thought had occurred to me. But that was before I met you."

Her eyes widened in outrage. "So anyone would have suited you?"

"No, of course not, you are twisting my words."

"It seems to me you do a very good job of that on your own." She turned and started toward the stairs.

"Where are you going?"

She turned back. "I am going to my room, where I intend to throw the few things I cannot live without into a bag. Then I am returning to London. I shall send for the rest of my belongings. If you would be so good as to call for my carriage and tell my family we are leaving at once."

He stared. "But it's Christmas."

"I am well aware of that."

"But this is our first Christmas."

"And apparently our last." She drew a deep breath. "I have been confused since the moment I met you, Sebastian. I haven't known what to do next. I have made any number of silly decisions and, admittedly, more than one mistake. I haven't been at all myself. My plans never go awry. And I certainly did not intend to fall in love." She shook her head. "I was very lucky in my first marriage. Charles accepted me for exactly who I was, independent and outspoken and rather flawed. I never thought I would find that again."

"But you have. I love your flaws."

"And you have been trying to be someone you weren't.

Rather proper and following other people's rules and forging a life that has never been a good fit for you."

He stepped toward her. "But it is now. A fit, that is. This." He spread his arms in a wide gesture. "You. A home, a wife, a family. I've changed, grown, if you will. I want all this. I want you."

"No. You want what you think you should have." She shook her head. "And I want more than to be a means to an end." She turned and climbed quickly up the stairs.

He stared after her for a long moment. He had assumed his mother had told her about the inheritance. Regardless, he should have told her and told her, as well, the conditions for acquiring it. He should have known what her reaction would be when she found out. What an idiot he was. However unintentionally, he had hurt her. His stomach twisted. He had to do something. He refused to live without her. Footsteps sounded behind him and he turned.

Veronica's father, aunt, and grandmother stood in the doorway of the dining room.

"We heard it all." Miss Bramhall sniffed and brushed past him. "And to think I gave you credit for honesty."

"I am most disappointed, young man." Lady Bramhall cast him a hard look. "Disappointment that has nothing to do with plum pudding, mind you, although I will remember this." She leaned closer and lowered her voice. "I know my granddaughter, better than she does herself. She is not one to change her mind. However, she is not a fool. I suggest you give her a few days to consider the situation."

He stared at her. "Is there hope, then?"

"It's Christmas, my boy. There is always hope." She nodded and continued after her daughter.

"She's right, you know." Lord Bramhall's gaze met

Sebastian's. "Veronica is not a fool. But she is a woman in love, and they can be fragile and delicate creatures."

"Apparently," Sebastian muttered.

"I have read your books. You are not the sort of man to give up easily, nor are you lacking in courage in the face of adversity." Lord Bramhall's voice was firm. "I hope, for the sake of my daughter's happiness, in all the ways that you claim to have changed, that has not."

"I shall do my best."

"Humph." Lord Bramhall cast him a doubtful look, then proceeded after the rest of his family.

At least Sebastian had two allies in Veronica's family. Now, to face his own. He turned and stepped back into the dining room.

Silence greeted him, along with nine pairs of eyes, accusing or sympathetic, depending on their owner.

"Well?" He crossed his arms over his chest and braced himself. "Go on. Say it."

They all decided to do so in unison.

"What were you thinking?"

"Why didn't you tell her about the inheritance?"

"How could you?"

"You're not married?"

"Obviously, I wasn't thinking," he said to Miranda, then turned to Bianca. "I don't know why I didn't tell her. It didn't seem important, and then the longer I didn't mention it, the harder it was to say anything." He looked at Diana. "How could I? I don't know. I'm not entirely sure what I did."

Diana snorted.

He ignored her and addressed his mother. "And yes, Mother, we are not now married. I wanted marriage. She did not. I had finally convinced her. Now she thinks it's only because of that blasted inheritance."

"My God, you are an idiot." Hugh stared.

"We need to talk, Sebastian," Adrian added.

"Then you shall have to convince her otherwise." A firm note sounded in his mother's voice.

"You're not shocked." He stared at his mother. "That we aren't married?"

"I did wonder why she wasn't wearing a ring," Evelyn murmured.

"I am stunned beyond words. Nonetheless . . ." His mother pinned him with a hard look. "You love that woman and she loves you."

"Shouldn't you go after her?" James said.

"Not today. Besides . . ." He blew a resigned breath. "She isn't entirely wrong, and I need to come up with a way to make this right. Until then . . ." He narrowed his eyes, his gaze shifting from one member of his family to another. "I would appreciate no further discussion of this for now, as difficult as that may be. I know each and every one of you has advice or a possible solution. I don't want to hear it, not today. Consider it a gift. It is still Christmas, after all, and I believe there are presents to open."

Adrian studied him thoughtfully. "As you wish."

A few minutes later a much more subdued group gathered around the Christmas tree. Still, with the addition of the children, and the opening of a few gifts, spirits were at least partially restored. For that Sebastian was grateful. He would hate to have ruined Christmas for everyone. Although there was no longer any satisfaction in knowing he was right about one more thing.

This was indeed a Christmas to remember.

Chapter 23

"Are you going to open that, or are you going to stare at it until next Christmas?" Annoyance rang in Grandmother's voice.

"What are you doing here?" Veronica glanced up and frowned at the older ladies. "How long have you been standing there?"

"Long enough." Grandmother and Aunt Lotte swept into Veronica's parlor like missionaries determined to save lost souls. Veronica braced herself. She was in no mood for either advice or persuasion.

"You look quite pathetic, my dear." Grandmother settled on the sofa beside her. "Your eyes are puffy and your nose is red."

Veronica narrowed her eyes. "You do realize you are much more charming when you are pretending to be *special*."

Lotte choked back a laugh and sat down on Veronica's other side.

"Even I cannot be special all the time." Grandmother

gestured in a blithe manner. "The question isn't, 'Why are we here,' but, 'What are you doing?' Or not doing, as the case may be."

"You scarcely said a word all the way back to London yesterday." Sympathy sounded in Lotte's voice. "We are quite concerned."

"There didn't seem to be a great deal to say."

Although there did seem to be a great deal to weep about. And weep she had, periodically through the night, with anger and pain and loss—which was most distressing as she was not the type of woman to weep profusely, if at all. Still, by morning she had begun to wonder if perhaps she hadn't been a little hasty in judging Sebastian. Now, a full day after they'd left Greyville Hall, she wasn't at all sure her actions were right or justified or completely mad. If she did indeed trust him, did this error in judgment on his part negate that? Was she throwing away something remarkable that she never thought she'd find again because of a foolish mistake on his part? She'd never thought he was perfect. Why was she expecting him to be perfect now? Veronica had always prided herself on being reasonable and rational. Qualities that had apparently deserted her. She didn't know if she should blame that on the season or the man. Probably a bit of both. She did so hate feeling like a fool.

Her gaze strayed back to the package on the tea table she'd positioned in front of the sofa. Placed there precisely for the purpose of staring at the small, velvet-wrapped gift. She'd done so all day and grappled with questions she didn't know how to answer. That was not the least bit rational, either. "And there's no need for concern."

"What is that?" Lotte nodded at the package.

"Obviously, it's a gift from Sebastian, dear," Grandmother said in a sage manner.

Veronica cast her a sharp glance. "Why would you think that?"

"Goodness, Veronica." Grandmother heaved a long-suffering sigh. "We left before anyone else exchanged presents, and you haven't opened it. Therefore it's obvious that it's from Sebastian." She raised a brow. "You took it with you?"

"It was intended for me." Veronica shrugged.

"Good for you." Lotte patted her arm. "As well you should."

"I went into his room to leave his gift, as I had no need for it, and saw where he had left this. . . ." On the table by the side of his bed, right after . . . "It was intended for me," she said again.

"And you were right to take it." Lotte nodded firmly. "Why, it's the very least you deserve. After all, that man lied to you."

"He never lied to me," Veronica said sharply.

"Misled you then."

"I wouldn't say . . ." She shook her head. "He didn't mislead me."

"Of course he didn't," Grandmother said. "He simply failed to tell you something he should have, even if he didn't think it significant."

"He was trying to lure her into marriage so that he might inherit a fortune." Lotte sniffed.

"Perhaps. Although given the way he looked at her, I suspect he was trying to lure her into marriage because he loves her." Grandmother shrugged. "Although I could be wrong."

"Men are not to be trusted," Lotte said firmly.

"Absolutely not." Grandmother nodded.

"I did trust him," Veronica said, staring at the gift. "The more I was around him, the more I trusted him. The more I liked him. The more I thought . . . He is a good man," she added under her breath.

"Ha," Lotte scoffed.

"Good men are not easy to find." An overly casual note sounded in Grandmother's voice. "It does seem a shame to discard one."

"Good?" Lotte stared at her mother. "Even ignoring his failure to tell her his true reasons for wanting marriage, he let his family believe they were married. He might not have lied to her, but he certainly did to everyone else."

"That's as much my fault as it is his," Veronica said quickly. It was only fair to acknowledge her part in all this. "I can scarcely blame the man for wanting his family to think well of him."

Lotte rolled her gaze toward the ceiling. "To gain a fortune."

"No, it's not that." Veronica shook her head. "In spite of his success, Sebastian has always felt that he was a disappointment to his family. He simply wants to be . . . part of them."

"Even so," Lotte began.

Veronica drew her brows together. "You said he was rare and should be snapped up at once."

"That was when I thought he was rare, not like every other man." Lotte glared. "That was before he broke your heart!"

Grandmother considered her. "Has he broken your heart, my dear?"

"Yes." Veronica sighed. "Oh, I don't know. On one hand,

I do feel that he was using marriage as a way to get what he wanted—"

"An inheritance." Lotte nodded.

"Acceptance," Grandmother murmured.

"On the other . . ." Veronica rose to her feet and paced. "It's not the type of man he is."

"You couldn't love him otherwise." Grandmother smiled.

"I have never been so confused."

"Love will do that." Grandmother nodded.

"I have been confused since the moment I met him. Not at all my usual self." Veronica stopped and glanced at the other women. "Haven't you noticed?"

"Around the eyes, perhaps," Grandmother murmured.

Lotte grimaced. "And that mistress nonsense was not your best idea."

"It's an interesting thing about men," Grandmother said thoughtfully. "It's been my observation that no matter how intelligent they may be, they can do things that are completely stupid."

"If he had told me in the beginning . . ."

"You wouldn't have given it a second thought. Indeed, it might have become something of a joke between you."

Veronica met the older woman's gaze. "Do you really think so?"

"It's entirely possible. Unfortunately, we shall never know." Grandmother shook her head. "The problem with something like this is that its significance grows the longer it remains unknown. As if it were something to hide."

"I thought he loved me."

"And does he?"

Veronica stared at her grandmother.

"It scarcely matters at the moment, I suppose," Grandmother continued. "What's done is done."

"Veronica." Lotte studied her closely. "Have you been too hasty? Have you made a mistake?"

"Another one, you mean?"

"If you believe you have . . ." Lotte chose her words with care. "Do not wait too long to admit it. Pride is no comfort when one is alone."

"Veronica is not you, Lotte. She is willing to admit when she is wrong. She is not afraid that in bending, she will break. And as for you . . ." Grandmother pinned Veronica with a firm look. "The only thing sadder than missing plum pudding at Christmas is unopened gifts. Christmas is now behind us, so do sit down and open this present. I, for one, am dying to know what it is."

"Very well." Veronica retook her seat between her grandmother and her aunt and reached for the package, noting an odd tremble in her hand. This was absurd. She did not cry, and she certainly never trembled. She drew a deep breath and grabbed the package.

She pulled off the ribbon and unwrapped the velvet cloth. A folded note lay upon a tissue-wrapped packet, far heavier than it looked. She set the note aside and pulled off the tissue. Her heart caught.

"For goodness' sakes." Lotte scoffed. "It's nothing but an old compass."

"I doubt that," Grandmother said softly.

Veronica turned it over in her hand. It felt as warm as it had when he had handed it to her in the park. As if it had just come out of his pocket.

How could he have given this to her? He'd had it since he was a boy. It had accompanied him on all his adventures. This was the one thing he valued most in the world.

"Read the note, dear." Grandmother's voice sounded as if from a far distance.

Veronica blinked hard and opened the note.

My Dear Veronica,

While I have always believed the glory was in the quest, I find now that I was wrong. In Ambitu, Gloria *no longer suits me. I have found the true glory is in the end, in the prize, in the one who claims my heart. It seems only right, then, that I entrust my most prized possession to her whom I prize above all else in life. My quest ends with you, and together a new life awaits.*

And it is indeed glorious.

> *Yours,*
> *Sebastian*

"What rubbish." Lotte sniffed back a tear.

"It's not rubbish at all. It's nonsense. Utter nonsense." Veronica wasn't sure if she was laughing or crying. "He's very good at utter nonsense and infernal nonsense and splendid nonsense and . . ." She sniffed. "And, dear Lord, I love him."

"Just because the man gives you a silly trinket—"

"This doesn't make me love him. This means he loves me."

"That was my observation." Grandmother nodded toward her daughter. "And I'm very astute."

"Even so, Veronica—"

"Either I trust him, Lotte, trust that he loves me, that he did not intend to hurt me or keep anything of significance from me, or I don't. It cannot be halfhearted." She paused for a long moment. Forgiving him would be easy compared to forgiving herself if she lost him. "I have to believe in him." She drew a deep breath. "And I do."

Lotte and Grandmother traded glances.

Veronica's eyes widened with realization. "I have to go

back. I ruined Christmas. I should hate to ruin his birthday as well."

"It's entirely too late to leave today. We shall go the first thing in the morning," Grandmother said firmly.

Veronica shook her head. "I should go now."

"Absolutely not." Grandmother adopted her best no-nonsense voice. "First, you need to determine exactly what you are going to say. Then you need to ponder precisely how much groveling you expect from him. And you need a good night's rest." She shuddered. "You look dreadful."

"But I do feel better than I look." Veronica smiled.

"You would have to." Grandmother met her gaze directly. "You are certain of this? That you wish to forgive him?"

"I have never been more certain of anything."

"I suppose one must make sacrifices to get what one truly wants." Lotte shook her head and sighed. "You will allow him, then, to make you the means to his own ends?"

Grandmother smiled. "But a happy ending nonetheless."

"No, Lotte, dear." Veronica summoned a determined smile. "He shall be the means to mine."

"You do realize you look like an idiot?" Sinclair eyed his friend with barely concealed amusement.

"As I feel like one, it's appropriate." Sebastian slumped back farther in his chair and swirled the brandy in his glass.

"You could probably take the crown off now."

"I like the crown," Sebastian said under his breath. "It's still my birthday, and I'm keeping the crown."

"I suppose it suits you, at least today." Sinclair sipped

his brandy. "You haven't told me how outstanding I was in the play." He thought for a moment. "Perhaps I shall go on the stage."

"The applause was entirely for the children. As for you . . ." Sebastian snorted. "I will say, your performance was adequate given that most of your fellow actors were much shorter and younger. But I would not count on even minimal success on the professional stage, unless you consider success a barrage of rotten fruit thrown at you."

"You're not particularly pleasant to be around today, you know."

"I hadn't noticed," he muttered.

He and Sinclair sat at the far end of the hall, in comfortable, if well-worn, chairs facing the fireplace and the burning Yule log. The hall had become the center of the Christmas festivities. The rest of the family was at the other end of the room, near the tree, although the children had already dispersed after being soundly praised for their theatrical accomplishment. Sebastian had rallied from his melancholy state to put up a good face for the duration of the play and the children's sake. Why should everyone be as miserable as he was?

His mother and siblings had honored his request to keep their opinions, as well as any advice as to how to proceed with Veronica, to themselves thus far. He knew that wouldn't last. Indeed, he was shocked that they had left him alone for the most part yesterday. Patience was not a virtue Hadley-Attwaters embraced willingly. He had spent a good portion of the day staring at the pennant Veronica had left for him. It was amusing and whimsical and touching. And perfect. Most of the evening and well into the night, he'd been in the company of his brothers and Sinclair, partaking of whisky and brandy and whatever else had been available. Even in his gloom, he appreciated that the others had steadfastly avoided all mention of women in general and Veronica in particular. It was good to be with men who understood that a man didn't like to have his mistakes thrown in his face. Especially when he didn't know how to fix them. Adrian had broached the subject of his inheritance once or twice but had ceased when Sebastian made it clear that that, too, was a subject he did not wish to discuss.

"So . . . ," Sinclair said in a casual manner. "Have you made any decisions? Come up with any sort of plan? Formed a coherent thought?"

Sebastian cast his friend a withering look.

Sinclair chuckled. "I thought as much." He nodded at the other end of the hall. "If I'm not mistaken, you have another hour at best before they descend on you. I've heard the talk among them, and you're lucky they have let you go this long."

"I know." Sebastian drew a deep breath. "I'm going to London tomorrow."

"To win back the fair Veronica?"

Sebastian nodded.

"Excellent." The American studied him. "How?"

"I don't see that I have any choice, nor do I wish one, I suppose." Sebastian paused for a long moment. He hadn't actually lied to her, nor had he told her the complete truth. Or rather, everything. "I have to be completely honest with her."

"I thought you had."

"I thought so, too, but I was wrong. Apparently, a lie of omission is as bad as an outright lie." He shook his head. "The oddest thing about all this is that I had nearly forgotten about my birthday and the inheritance. All I wanted was her, as my wife. In my life forever."

Sinclair cast him a wry smile. "Tell her, not me."

"I shall."

Sinclair chose his words with care. "What if it's not enough?"

"I do not intend to give up. I am counting on the fact that she loves me enough to forgive me. If I'm wrong about that, too . . ." Sebastian shrugged. "I don't know. But first . . ." He shuddered and got to his feet. "I shall have to deal with them."

He started toward his family. Better to let them have their say and get it over with. They weren't going to tell him anything he didn't already know. Once again, he was a disappointment. But for the first time, he didn't care.

He had very nearly reached the circle of chairs and sofas facing the Christmas tree where the family had gathered when Bianca caught sight of him and nodded to the others. Almost as one they turned expectant eyes toward him.

"I suppose you are all wondering—"

"Sir Sebastian," Stokes called behind him. Sebastian turned. The butler hurried toward him. "Sir, you have guests."

"Guests?" He grimaced. "The last thing we need at the moment is more guests."

"But it's Lady . . ." Stokes paused in confusion. "Lady . . . um . . ."

"It suits you, you know," a familiar voice said from the entry to the hall.

His heart caught. "What suits me?"

Veronica strolled toward him, her family a few steps behind.

"The crown, of course." She shrugged. "It's not as fashionable as one of my hats, but it does make a statement."

"I like it," he said cautiously.

"So do I." She considered him for a moment. "Although it's a bit shabby. You do need a new one."

"Perhaps next year."

He was well aware that a dozen or so pairs of curious eyes were fixed on them, but he didn't care. The rest of the world faded away. He stepped toward her, and he lowered his voice. "Will there be a next year?"

"Oh, I do hope so." The faintest tremor sounded in her voice.

His gaze met hers. "I never lied to you."

"I know."

"But I should have told you about the significance of the birthday."

"I know that as well."

"I admit, in that I was wrong."

"Yes, you were."

He stared at her for a long moment. "Why are you here?"

"Goodness, Sebastian." A faint, tentative smile curved her lips, as if her heart was thudding as hard as his. "It is your birthday, and I have come to wish you many happy returns of the day."

"Is that all?"

"No." She drew a calming breath. "I believe you asked me to marry you."

He nodded.

"And I agreed."

"Yes, you did."

"Then you cannot get rid of me that easily," she said staunchly. "You asked to marry me, and I am here to hold you to that promise. I am not the type of woman to ignore a promise of that nature simply because a man has what is hopefully a momentary lapse in judgment. Although I do expect him to be more intelligent in the future."

"I see." He thought for a moment. "I assume you expect me, as well, to spend the rest of my life making amends for my mistakes."

She scoffed. "Without question."

"Very well then." He shook his head. "But that's not why you came back."

She arched a brow. "It isn't?"

"No." He pulled her into his arms and gazed into her eyes. "You said it yourself. You cannot imagine your life without me."

"Well, yes, that is a consideration." She shrugged as best she could in his arms.

"You're smitten with me." He smiled slowly. "Head over heels, mad for me."

"I am probably mad." She slipped her arms around his neck. "And you, Sir Sebastian Hadley-Attwater, you want to die with your hand in mine."

"More than anything I've ever wanted. But not . . . ," his lips murmured against hers, "for a very long time." He pressed his lips to hers, and she returned his kiss with the kind of love he had no doubt would indeed endure until they had both breathed their last. And perhaps beyond.

A throat cleared somewhere behind him.

Veronica drew away and smiled up at him. "I had nearly forgotten that we are not alone."

"Pity." He grinned down at her, then sobered. "I would give up the inheritance if it would prove to you that you are all I want."

"Nonsense. It would be absurd to give up a fortune."

He drew his brows together. "Veronica, it's not a fortune."

"Amounts scarcely matter. We certainly aren't lacking for money, but this is something your father wanted you to—"

"Forgive me for interrupting," Bianca said in a loud voice. "But none of us can hear a word you're saying."

"More's the pity," her grandmother said.

Evelyn chimed in. "Although we are fairly confident all has turned out well."

Sebastian kissed Veronica again, hard and quick, and released her. She adjusted her hat and surveyed the gathering with a cool demeanor that belied the way the feathers in her hat quivered. Damnation, he loved that.

"Then, as that is settled, and no one is more pleased than I, and as it is Sebastian's birthday"—Adrian cast his brother an affectionate smile—"there are a few things that need to be said."

"Indeed there are." Indignation flashed in Veronica's eyes. "And I intend to say them."

Behind Sebastian, her father chuckled.

Adrian stared. "Very well, then, go on."

"I realize it's some sort of tradition, but how dare you, any of you, presume to judge whether Sebastian is worthy of an inheritance or of being part of this family or anything else?" Veronica glared at the assembly of Hadley-Attwaters. Sinclair wisely stepped away from the others, no doubt to avoid any misdirected fury.

"Sebastian is a man of courage and intelligence and, for the most part, honesty. He's certainly not perfect—"

Someone, Sebastian wasn't sure who, choked back a laugh.

"—but then few of us are. I wouldn't want a man who was perfect. I would certainly not fare well in comparison. And yes, he can be most annoying, and he is certainly one of the most arrogant—"

Sebastian leaned toward her and lowered his voice. "Are you defending me?"

"Yes, darling, I am," she said firmly.

"Interesting way to go about it," Diana murmured.

"But it's those very flaws that make him so endearing." She crossed her arms over her chest and glared, looking for all the world like an irate governess chastising naughty children. "The man has been knighted. He has traveled the world. He has faced all sorts of adventures that would have had most men shaking in their boots, and he has written about his exploits so that others, whose lives are not nearly so exciting, may experience adventure through his eyes. He has represented his family, and indeed this country, with courage and fortitude and intelligence and honor and . . . and . . ."

"Humor?" Sinclair suggested.

"Yes." Veronica nodded. "Thank you. He can be most amusing. He makes me laugh even as I want to smack him."

Sebastian stared at her. "My God, I am a catch."

"Thank you, dear, for proving my point." She turned back toward his family, narrowed her eyes, and continued. "For any of you to think, for so much as a moment, that he is not worthy of receiving an inheritance left to him by his father is absurd. You should be proud of him."

Hugh stared. "We are proud of him."

"Nonsense." She sniffed. "You think he's a disappointment."

Adrian's gaze slid from Veronica to Sebastian. "Is that what you think?"

"Well, yes. I have always thought that. However . . ." He drew a deep breath. "It appears it no longer matters. Not that I don't love you all but . . ." He smiled at his soon-to-be wife. "This is a remarkable woman. And if I am worthy enough for her, that's all I need. Or want."

Hugh rolled his gaze heavenward. "I said it before and I shall say it again. You are an idiot."

"Sebastian." Adrian pinned him with a hard look. "This is exactly what I've been trying to talk to you about since Christmas. We have always intended for you to have what Father left to you. There was never a question about that."

"We were shocked that you thought otherwise." Hugh shook his head. "The very idea that you would need a house and a wife and whatever else to make us think you were worthy to receive what Father wanted you to have is absurd."

Sebastian stared at his brothers. "But I—"

"Some of this may be our fault." Adrian continued, "Obviously, we have not let our pride in your accomplishments show."

"Although, might I point out, you were never around," Diana said. "It's difficult to let someone know your true feelings when they're never present."

"I know when you went off on your first expedition, Father was not pleased." Adrian shook his head slowly. "But he was proud of you. He said you had the courage to follow your dreams. He didn't agree with you, but then what father wishes to see his son go off to places where his life is in frequent jeopardy? Where he might never be heard from again? Where his family might never know what has become of him?"

"That's never been my favorite part," Mother murmured.

"We are all proud of you. Of what you have done and who you are. Of the man you've become." Hugh directed his attention to Veronica. "We could have given that speech ourselves, Veronica. Perhaps we don't find him quite as endearing as you do, but that's for the best."

"Although that portion about finding him amusing and wanting to smack him at the same time does sound familiar." Miranda smiled.

Sebastian shook his head in disbelief. "This is not . . . that is . . ." His gaze slid from one smiling face to the next.

Veronica nudged him. "A man should admit when he is wrong, remember?"

"Well, yes . . ." Sebastian grinned. "This is an excellent birthday, after all."

"And you get your inheritance as well." Veronica nodded with satisfaction.

"About that," he said to her. "This is another one of those misunderstandings we seem to be so good at. It's not a fortune."

"Well, however much it is."

"It's not money, Veronica."

"It's not?" She stared at him in confusion. "What is it, then?"

"It's a watch," Sebastian said simply.

Veronica's brow furrowed. "A watch?"

"Father had three possessions he valued above all others," Adrian began. "Three things that were always on his person. A signet ring, which went to me. Gold cuff buttons—"

Hugh raised his hand. "Those are mine."

"—and his pocket watch. All are engraved with the family crest," Adrian added.

"You did all of this, buying a house, changing your life, not to mention pretending to be married, for a watch?" Disbelief rang in Sinclair's voice. "A watch?"

"For *my father's* watch," Sebastian said firmly. "But no, I did all this because it was time for me to do so. Not the pretending to be married. That was a misunderstanding grown out of control. Admittedly, I was hoping to show my brothers that I am a different man than I once was, but only because I am. The watch is nothing more than a symbol."

Veronica smiled up at him. "I rather like that, you know. That it wasn't money."

"I have money." He shrugged. "What I didn't have, what I *thought* I didn't have, was the respect of my family." He chuckled. "In that, too, apparently, I was wrong."

"I know." Her eyes sparkled with amusement. "It's most endearing."

"As for pretending to be married, I know I should apologize for that to all of you, but I can't honestly say I regret it." His gaze met hers. "It did allow me to have the woman I love as my wife for Christmas, even if it wasn't entirely real."

She smiled into his eyes. "Wasn't it?"

He leaned close to her, his words for her ears alone. "It has been from the moment we met."

And disregarding his family and her family and anyone else who might be observing, he pulled her back into his arms and kissed her for a long moment. A kiss that promised she would be his mistress, and his wife, for next Christmas and all the Christmases to come.

And each and every one would be a Christmas to remember.

A blazing fire, an English country house . . . and the ultimate game of charades. In this charming holiday novel from #1 New York Times bestselling author Victoria Alexander, a beautiful widow finds her plan for a Christmas proposal going perfectly awry . . .

Camille, Lady Lydingham, knows precisely what she wants for Christmas—an official engagement to a handsome, dashing prince. Her very proper suitor expects a proper English family and the perfect Dickensian Christmas, which leaves the lovely widow with a slight problem. The last thing Camille wants is for the prince to meet her unconventional relatives. But with the aid of a troupe of actors, Camille intends to pull off a Christmas deception of massive proportions.

At least until Grayson Elliot shows up. A dozen years ago, he declared his love on the day before her marriage to another man, then vanished from her life. Now he's back, gate-crashing Camille's already chaotic house party, playing absolute havoc with her scheme—and with her heart. Because for Grayson, losing Camille once was quite bad enough. Losing her twice? Unthinkable. And he'll find a way to show her they belong together—for this season, and every Christmas yet to come . . .

**Please turn the page for an exciting sneak peek of
Victoria Alexander's
WHAT HAPPENS AT CHRISTMAS,
now on sale!**

December 1886

"And you believe this is a good idea," Beryl, Lady Dunwell, said to her sister. Her expression failed to reveal whether her words were in the guise of a question or a comment which was, as always most annoying. More so as her sister's face was the mirror image of her own and one should never be in doubt as to what one's own twin was thinking

"No, in truth I don't believe it's a good idea. Wearing the appropriate cloak for the weather is a good idea. Insisting on references before hiring a new servant is a good idea. Having an equal number of ladies and gentlemen at a dinner party is a good idea. This. . ." Camille, Lady Lydingham, leaned forward slightly and met her sister's gaze with a firmness which belied any niggling doubts in the back of her mind. "Is a brilliant idea."

"I suspect the brilliance of it is dependent upon whether or not it goes awry." Beryl studied her sister over the rim of her teacup.

In recent months, the twins had made it a habit to meet

at least every other week at the Ladies Tearoom at Fenwick and Sons, Booksellers. It had become quite the place for ladies of society to gather. Even now, there was scarcely an empty table to be had. Camille wasn't sure why it had become so popular; the room itself was not unlike the other rooms in the bookseller's establishment, lined with shelves and filled with books in what appeared to be a random order. The tea and cakes were excellent but excellent did not always go hand in hand with fashionable in society. Regardless, the sisters were nothing if not fashionable and if this was the place to be, this was indeed where they would be.

"And it does seem to me there are any number of things that could go awry," Beryl continued. "Horribly, horribly awry."

"Nonsense." Camille waved off her sister's warning. "I have given this a great deal of thought and it is a practically perfect plan."

"It's the practically that should give you pause," Beryl said in a wry tone.

"No plan can be completely perfect, although . . ." Camille thought for a moment. "I daresay this is as close to perfect as possible. Mother and Delilah are spending Christmas in Paris with her friend, Countess Something-or-other, and will not return to England until well after the new year. Uncle Basil is on safari in Africa and, as you well know, when he goes off like this, he will not be back for months. Which serves me quite well as I need a proper English family, having a proper English Christmas in a proper English country house." Camille heaved a long-suffering sigh. "And while we might well appear proper from a safe distance, close at hand there is very little truly proper about our family."

"Millworth Manor is rather proper," Beryl murmured.

"Thank goodness for that." Camille nodded. "And this year, that proper country house will be filled with a proper family for Christmas." She narrowed her eyes. "There shall be no dallying between Mother and whatever potential lover has thought the spirit of the season would ease his way into her bed. There shall be no lecherous uncle pursuing any unsuspecting females who have caught his eye. There shall be none of Mother's usual stray foreign exiles bemoaning the olden days in whatever country they're from. Nor will there be aspiring poets, flamboyant artists and absolutely no creative sorts of any type hoping to curry favor and patronage from Mother or any of us."

Beryl raised a brow. "You make it sound like a circus."

"There's very little difference between Mother's house and a circus, especially at Christmas, although a circus is probably less chaotic." Camille heaved a heartfelt sigh. "If Father were still with us—"

"Well, he isn't," Beryl said sharply. "He's been gone for twenty years now and even at Christmas, there is nothing to be gained by wishing for what one can't possibly have." She drew a deep breath. "However, I suppose, as you are going to a great deal of trouble and expense no doubt—"

"Good Lord, yes." Camille shook her head. "I had no idea the price of hiring a troupe of actors would be so dear."

"Well, you are replacing an entire household. Let's see." Beryl thought for a moment. "There's one to play the role of the well-meaning, ambitious, somewhat flighty mother, another for the aging rogue who doesn't quite understand he is neither as charming nor as dashing as he once was, one for the role of the always indignant, somewhat superior, younger sister—" Beryl fixed her sister with a firm look. "Delilah would never go along with this, you know."

"Then it is fortunate she is in Paris with Mother." It never failed to amaze either Camille or Beryl that their younger sister had a distinct lack of imagination and an overdeveloped sense of propriety. Where did she get it? "And don't forget, aside from the primary players, there's the supporting cast." Camille ticked the roles off on her fingers. "I needed a butler, of course, as well as a house-keeper, a cook, and an assortment of maids and footmen. I am bringing my lady's maid, however."

"What did you do with Mother's servants?" Beryl stared. "What have you done with Clement?"

"You needn't look at me as if I've done away with him and buried him in the garden." Camille rolled her gaze to-ward the ceiling. "As even Mother is rarely at the manor for Christmas, in recent years, Clement has spent Christ-mas with his niece in Wales, I believe. It's silly to have a butler on the premises if there is no one there. I sent the rest off on holiday, paid of course."

"Of course," Beryl murmured.

"Yet another expense. However, I have been assured most of the troupe is better at keeping a house than they are on stage which is fortunate as I do expect them to do so." Camille lowered her voice in a confidential manner. "From what I understand, most of the players have been in service fairly recently. So that part of it should work out nicely."

"Oh, well, as long as they can tend to the house . . ."

"They are not the least bit famous, as actors that is, which, on one hand is convenient and on the other, some-thing of a concern." Camille drummed her fingers ab-sently on the table. "I do need them to be believable but I should hate to have any of them recognized, so their lack of theatrical success is a benefit."

Beryl stared as if she couldn't quite believe her ears. "It is so hard to get good help."

"Indeed it is. However, as they are not in particular demand, they are more than willing to take on this . . . production, as it were. And as costly as they are, they would have charged so much more if they were well known." Camille smiled smugly.

"It's fortunate you can afford them."

"Thank goodness Harold left me with a tidy fortune."

Harold, Viscount Lydingham, had been substantially older than Camille when they had wed. But then, older men with wealth and position were precisely the type of gentlemen their mother had trained her three daughters to wed. And Beryl, Camille, and Delilah had obediently done so. Their reward was to be widowed and financially independent at an age young enough to enjoy life and pursue love should they be so inclined.

Still, Harold had been a very nice man. Camille considered herself fortunate to have found him and they had been, for the most part, happy or at least content. His demands on her had been minimal through the eight years of their marriage. She had proven herself an excellent wife and, indeed, she had been quite fond of him. Why, she hadn't even considered dallying with another man for a full two years after his death out of respect. Even now, four years after his passing, she still rather missed Harold.

"And you're doing it all to impress a man—"

"Not merely a man. A prince," Camille said in a lofty manner. Yes, both of her sisters had married well and Beryl's second husband might well be prime minister someday but neither of her sisters had ever come close to genuine royalty. "Prince Nikolai Pruzinsky of the ruling family of the Kingdom of . . . of . . . Oh, I can't remember where but it's one of those tiny countries that litter central Europe."

"But you barely know this man."

"Marriage will solve that."

"Still, this scheme of yours seems rather excessive."

"Perhaps it is but it's well worth the trouble and the expense. He has an immense fortune and his own castle, besides which he is quite handsome and dashing and, well, he's a prince. Which means I shall be a princess. He is everything I have ever wanted and he is this close—" Camille held up her hand and pinched her forefinger and thumb to within an inch of each other—"to proposing. He hasn't actually said the words yet but he has dropped more than a few hints. I'm confident all he needs now is to be assured that our family is worthy of being elevated to royalty."

"Which you shall prove by presenting him with a proper English family and a proper English Christmas?"

"Exactly." Camille nodded.

Beryl refilled her cup from the pot on their table and Camille knew, the way one twin nearly always knew what the other was thinking, her sister was choosing her words with care. "It seems to me that, should you indeed marry him, at some point in time he shall have to meet Mother and Delilah and Uncle Basil. The real ones that is. Perhaps at the wedding. Have you considered that?"

"Admittedly, I have not worked it all out but I will." She waved off her sister's comment. "First and foremost is Christmas, which involves a great deal of planning. You may not have noticed, but Christmas is bearing down upon us with the inevitability of a . . . a . . ."

"A boulder rolling downhill ready to obliterate all in its path?" Beryl asked with an overly sweet smile.

"I wouldn't put it quite that way, but yes."

"And after Christmas? What then?"

"Admittedly, I don't really know. Yet, but I will. The rest will fall into place," Camille said with a confidence she didn't entirely feel. "I shall cross those awkward roads when they present themselves. I can't be expected to know every minor detail as of yet but I am certain I shall come up with something brilliant."

"As brilliant as hiring actors to play the part of your family for Christmas?"

Camille clenched her teeth. Beryl had an annoying habit of being entirely too sensible on occasion. "Even more brilliant I should think."

"You'll need it. Your current brilliant idea is the most ridiculous thing I have ever heard. It can't possibly succeed."

"Goodness, Beryl, at this time of year in particular one should have a little faith."

Beryl stared in obvious disbelief. "Faith?"

"Yes, faith," Camille said firmly. "Before the wedding, I suspect, I will confess all. He is already smitten with me and by then, I have every confidence he will forgive this tiny farce on my part—"

Beryl choked on her tea. "Tiny?"

"Relatively tiny." Camille nodded. "He will probably find it most amusing. He is easily amused. And it's not as if I am misrepresenting who I am or who we are. Not really. Our family lineage is exactly as I have said; it's just the individual personalities that can be a bit . . . unorthodox. Mother and Uncle Basil, that is. In truth, I am simply trying to protect the poor man and give him the traditional English Christmas that he expects and deserves. In many ways it is my Christmas gift to him. And I am confident we shall have a good laugh about all this. Eventually."

"You do realize you're quite mad."

"Or quite clever." Camille tapped her temple with her forefinger. "Like a fox."

"An insane fox perhaps. You haven't thought this through, Camille. This is another one of your impulsive adventures."

"Nonsense. I gave up impulsive adventures at least a year ago."

"After the Brighton incident?"

"Yes, well, probably. It's of no significance now." She waved off the comment. "I have given this a great deal of thought." Indeed, she'd had so much to accomplish she hadn't thought of anything else.

"I can't believe you are going to all this trouble." Beryl narrowed her eyes and considered her sister. "It's not for his money. Harold left you with more than you can possibly spend in a lifetime, certainly more than enough to buy your own castle should you wish to do so. Is it for his title?"

"I have always thought Princess Camille has a lovely sound to it."

"Even so, I can't . . ." Beryl's eyes widened. "Are you in love with him?"

"There is nothing about the man not to love," Camille said in a cautious manner. Still, she'd only been in love once and that was when she was very young and quite foolish and hadn't quite realized she'd been in love until it was too late. She'd been extraordinarily fond of Harold and had loved him after a fashion but she'd never been in love with him. She wasn't at all sure there was much use for true love in a practical world although admittedly, it would be nice. "I suspect he may well be in love with me."

"That wasn't my question."

"We've never married for love in this family," Camille said staunchly. It wasn't entirely true. She had long suspected Mother had married for love, which was no doubt why she had raised her daughters to marry for other reasons. In this respect alone, Mother was a very practical woman.

"But do you—"

"Not at the moment. But I fully expect to," she added quickly. "Indeed, I am quite confident in no time at all I shall love him with my whole heart and soul. There is nothing about him not to love."

"You said that."

"It bears repeating."

"Yes, well, an immense fortune and a royal title does make it easier to love." Beryl cast her sister a pleasant smile.

Camille wasn't fooled for a moment. The smile might well be pleasant but the sarcasm was unmistakable.

"You're scarcely one to talk. You married your first husband, Charles, for precisely the same reasons I married Harold."

"I was quite fond of Charles," Beryl said firmly.

"Yes, but you weren't in love with him. Nor were you in love with Lionel when you married him."

"No." Beryl drew the word out slowly. "But . . ."

Camille stared. "Good Lord, Beryl, don't tell me you're in love with your husband."

"I might be."

"Nonsense, no one is in love with their own husband." Camille scoffed. "It simply isn't done. You certainly didn't marry him for love."

"No, I married him because his ambitions matched my own. Now however. . ." Beryl paused then drew a deep breath. "In recent months, since very nearly the start of the year, Lionel and I agreed to forgo our various amorous pursuits and restrict our attentions to one another."

Camille stared. Her sister and brother-in-law's extra-marital escapades were very nearly legendary. "And?"

"And it's turning out far better than I would have imagined." She shrugged. "As it happens I might indeed be in love with my husband." A bemused smile curved her sister's lips, as if she couldn't quite believe her own words. She looked, well, content, even happy. Camille wasn't sure she had seen a look like that on her sister's face before. But then she was fairly certain Beryl had never been in love before. The oddest twinge of jealousy stabbed Camille. She ignored it. If her twin was happy, she was happy for her.

"That's . . . wonderful."

Beryl's eyes narrowed in suspicion. "Do you mean that?"

"Of course I do. You know I wouldn't say it otherwise." Camille nodded. "Lord and Lady Dunwell have always had a certain reputation for dalliances and lovers and that sort of thing. It's simply unexpected, that's all."

"No one expected it less than I," Beryl said under her breath.

"What will the gossips do without you?"

Beryl laughed. "They shall have to make do."

"I am happy for you."

"Then you should consider following in my footsteps."

"What? Marrying a man who might run the country one day?"

"No." Beryl's blue-eyed gaze met her sister's. It was, as always, like looking in a mirror. "Fall in love."

Camille drew her brows together. "It's not at all like you to go on and on about love. I always thought you considered it rather silly."

"That's before I was in love," Beryl said simply, then paused. "You were in love once, if I recall."

"That was a very long time ago," Camille said quickly. It was not something she wished to be reminded of. She had turned her back on love then, although she'd really had no choice. And if, through the years, there had been a moment or two of regret, a chance thought as to what might have been, it was pointless. She had put him completely out of her head and her heart. She had never asked after him and her sister was wise enough never to bring up his name. Such was the way of life, after all. One did hate to be reminded of mistakes one might have made. There was nothing to be done about it and it was best left in the past where it belonged.

"Don't you want to know that again?"

"I scarcely knew it at all but I shall," Camille said firmly. "I fully intend to fall in love." She picked up the teapot and refilled her cup, taking the time to sort her words.

Why she wished to marry Nikolai wasn't at all easy to explain without sounding quite mercenary and extremely shallow. And while she certainly had a few mercenary moments and was, on occasion, a bit shallow, she did not think herself to be mercenary and shallow all in all. It wasn't the prince's fortune; she had more than enough money. It wasn't even his title, although Princess Camille did have a lovely ring to it. It was, perhaps, the adventure of it. Of being swept away by a handsome prince to a foreign land and there to live happily the rest of her days. Adventure that she scarcely knew existed. Adventure that appealed to something deep inside her. Beryl was entirely too levelheaded to understand but then she had always been the more sensible of the twins. It was the stuff fairy stories were made of, and what woman wouldn't want that? And want it Camille did.

"It isn't as if I set out to catch a prince. I didn't even know he was a prince when we first met. He is traveling incognito, which he much prefers to do when he is in a foreign country. He says it's much easier to get to know the people of a country when he is not beleaguered by all the trappings of his royal position. When he is not treated as royalty but rather as an ordinary person."

"What an. . . enlightened philosophy for a prince."

"He is most enlightened and very modern. He takes his responsibilities quite seriously and says he wishes to be a prince for the people. It's quite admirable even if I don't understand it entirely, but then he is foreign and therefore his minor eccentricities can be forgiven. Why, he even prefers that I don't address him by title, your highness and that sort of thing. He says, until he ascends to the throne, he prefers, when traveling abroad, simply to be known by one of his lesser titles, Count Pruzinsky. In most respects though, he is extremely proper. Why, he hasn't even kissed me. Although he has requested, begged really, that I call him by his given name. Not proper of course but so wonderfully intimate."

"Not what one would expect in a prince."

"I find it most charming. There is nothing at all like being in the confidence of royalty, you know."

"I don't but I shall take your word for it." Beryl considered her curiously. "And how did you meet this unusual prince?"

"We crossed paths quite by accident. I was leaving a ball and he was just arriving. I stumbled on a pebble and he caught me." She smiled at the memory. "It was quite romantic and, well, fate."

"I see."

"I like him a great deal."

Beryl nodded. "You wouldn't marry him otherwise."

"He might well be my last opportunity to marry and fall in love."

"You might consider falling in love first and then marrying the man in question."

"Odd advice coming from you. And how long shall I wait for that to happen, sister dear?" Camille wrinkled her nose. "We have, after all, passed our thirtieth year and who knows how many more opportunities for. . ."

"Happiness?" Beryl offered.

"Exactly." Camille nodded firmly. "This may be my last chance. I have no doubt he will make me very happy and I intend to be an excellent wife."

"And princess."

"I shall make a very good princess." Camille grinned. "We shall have little princes and princesses and grow old together. And we shall be very, very happy."

Beryl smiled. "Then you should let nothing stand in your way."

"I don't intend to." She drew a deep breath. "But I will need your assistance."

Beryl raised a brow. "Oh?"

"It certainly wouldn't be Christmas without my sister, my twin sister—"

Beryl's eyes narrowed.

"So. . ." The words came out in a rush. "I do hope yo
and Lionel will join us for Christmas in the country."

"Us?"

Camille nodded.

"As in you, the prince, and a troupe of actors pretend
ing to be family?"

Camille sighed. "It sounds rather absurd when you sa
it that way."

"There's no way to say it that it doesn't sound absurd.

"You must understand, it's not simply that we are no
especially traditional but Nikolai seems to have some sor
of odd passion for an English Christmas. Yet another ec
centricity but then foreigners can be so very . . ."

"Foreign?" Beryl offered.

"Exactly." Camille nodded. "He has read all of Mr
Dickens's Christmas works. Oh, *The Cricket on the Heart*
and *The Chimes* and, of course, *A Christmas Carol*. And
want to give him a traditional English Christmas with a
proper sort of English family. It's what he longs for." Sh
forced a wistful note to her voice. "It seems so very little
really."

"As well as convince him he would not be marrying
into a family of questionable propriety."

"Oh well, yes, that too." Camille waved off the com
ment.

Beryl thought for a moment. "This is not the sort o
thing Lionel would favor."

"But surely for a man who wishes to be prime ministe
it cannot but be helpful to know a foreign head of state."

"You do have a point there," Beryl said under he
breath.

Camille stifled a satisfied smile. "And you can make
him see how important it is to me. Besides, it's been year

ince either of us spent Christmas at the country house. It vill be like it was when we were children. We shall decoate and have a Yule log and sing carols and it shall be quite, quite wonderful." A pleading note sounded in her voice. "Oh please, Beryl, do this for me. I promise never o ask you to do anything involving actors for Christmas ver again."

"Oh well, as long as you promise, how could I possibly ay no? Besides, darling sister. . ." Beryl's eyes twinkled vith amusement. "I wouldn't miss this Christmas for anyhing in the world."